The Fallen Angel

Also by Tracy Borman

Fiction
The King's Witch
The Devil's Slave

Nonfiction
Henry VIII and the Men Who Made Him
The Private Lives of the Tudors:
Uncovering the Secrets of Britain's Greatest Dynasty
Thomas Cromwell:
The Untold Story of Henry VIII's Most Faithful
Servant
Witches: A Tale of Sorcery, Scandal and Seduction
Queen of the Conqueror:
The Life of Matilda, Wife of William I
Elizabeth's Women:
Friends, Rivals, and Foes Who Shaped the Virgin Queen

Tracy Borman

The Fallen Angel

Atlantic Monthly Press
New York

First published in Great Britain in 2020 by Hodder & Stoughton
An Hachette UK company

Typeset in Sabon MT by Hewer Text UK Ltd, Edinburgh

Published simultaneously in Canada
Printed in Canada

First Grove Atlantic hardcover edition: November 2020

Library of Congress Cataloging-in-Publication data is available for this title.

ISBN 978-0-8021-5761-4
eISBN 978-0-8021-5763-8

Atlantic Monthly Press
an imprint of Grove Atlantic
154 West 14th Street
New York, NY 10011
Distributed by Publishers Group West

groveatlantic.com

20 21 22 23 24 10 9 8 7 6 5 4 3 2 1

In affectionate memory of my uncle David Reeson
'Keep your powder dry'

PART 1

1614

CHAPTER I

4 August

The warm breeze whipped about her as she spurred the horse into a gallop. To either side, the heads of wheat drooped heavily in the scorched fields, but she kept her eyes fixed on the rise of the hill.

'Frances!'

She heard her husband's voice above the thundering hoofs, pulled on the reins and her horse slowed to a trot. The searing heat seemed to close in around her and the strands of hair that had escaped from her braid clung to her temples.

'I had not expected you to be so eager to see His Majesty.' Thomas smiled.

Frances gave a rueful grin. The undulating fields stretched out for miles, their golden hue interspersed with the dark lines of hedgerows and, in the distance, a thick mass of woodland. As she gazed towards the horizon, she made out a series of delicate spires and a glimmer of light reflecting off windows.

Apethorpe.

It had taken them two days to get there and would have been longer still if Thomas had not agreed that they could travel the last fifteen miles on horseback. Frances had been desperate to escape the suffocating confines of the carriage, which had rumbled and jolted along the cracked track that led north from Tyringham

Hall. That was why she had urged her husband to let them ride: God knew she had no desire to reach their destination more quickly.

More than a year had passed since she had last set eyes upon the King. It had been one of the happiest times of her life, cosseted at Tyringham Hall with Thomas and their young son. With a pang, Frances thought of John, his arms outstretched and his eyes imploring as his nursemaid prised him from his mother's embrace. *I will return soon, my sweeting.* Now, looking towards Sir Anthony Mildmay's sprawling estate, her skin prickled with foreboding.

Thomas reached for her hand. His lips felt warm as he pressed them to her fingers. Frances stroked his cheek, his beard tickling her palm. She had been averse to the idea of his growing it, but she had to admit it suited him.

'Must we stay for the full two weeks?' she asked.

Thomas shrugged. 'If His Majesty finds the hunting grounds to his taste. He tires more easily these days, though.'

'I wonder he hunts at all, given how it pains him.' She turned towards the woods. 'I could harvest plenty of willow bark there, and Sir Anthony will have marjoram and rosemary in his herb garden. I could mix a salve that would reduce the swelling in his joints.' She cast a sly glance at her husband and saw his mouth twitch.

'You should not tease me, Frances,' he chided. 'The King may have been content to let you live in peace since his daughter left for the Rhine, but he is still eager to hunt down witches as well as stags.'

Frances experienced the familiar pang at the mention of her former mistress. Princess Elizabeth – or Electress Consort Palatine of the Rhine, as she must now think of her – had left for her new husband's domain shortly after their wedding the previous February. Elizabeth had married Frederick out of misguided loyalty to her late brother, Prince Henry. He had swept aside her doubts about the young count's suitability, caring little for his sister's happiness in his pursuit of a Protestant alliance. Frances suspected that she would never have gone through with it but for Henry's sudden death. Her marriage was a penance for trying to defy him. It pained Frances to think that Elizabeth had made such a sacrifice for one so unworthy.

Though the princess had begged Frances to go with her to the Rhine, promising to find positions for her husband and son George, she had declined. Elizabeth had assumed that her favourite attendant had not wished to risk such a long journey when the birth of her child was imminent, but there had been other reasons, too. Frances had known she could never relinquish Longford Castle, her beloved childhood home – not after everything she had almost lost for its sake. Neither could she leave her mother so far behind. Helena was settled at Longford now, having promised to care for it until her grandson came of age: George had stayed with her for much of the past year, delighting in his position as heir. Her mother's last letter had told of how her grandson had presided over his first tenants' meeting, conducting himself with an authority well beyond his eight years. Sir Richard Weston, Longford's faithful chamberlain, would have ensured the business was dealt with, but she was as proud of George as his indulgent grandmother was.

Longford had not been the only place that had stopped her leaving England. Tyringham Hall had seemed almost a prison to her during the early years of her marriage. Then she had been so consumed by grief for George's father that it had blinded her to the love Thomas bore her. He had married her for Tom's sake, having assured his friend that he would take care of her if the Powder Treason failed. Frances had only narrowly escaped implication in it: the whole court had known of her friendship with Tom Wintour. Thomas had made great sacrifices on her behalf, yet she had repaid him with coldness, determined that theirs would be a marriage in name only. She had defied him, too, breaking her promise not to involve herself in the Catholic conspiracies that had swirled about James's throne in the aftermath of the

Powder Treason. It still frightened her to think how close she had come to losing everything.

'Shall we walk the rest of the way?'

Lost in thought, Frances had hardly noticed that they had reached the end of the long path that swept down to the hall. She nodded. Watching her husband dismount, she noticed him wince as his right shoulder pressed against the horse's flank. 'You will not accompany the King on every hunt, will you?' she asked, her brow furrowed. Though it had been three years since the riding accident that had almost claimed his life, she worried every time he set out for the hunt. She wished that the King would bestow the mastership of the buckhounds upon one of his younger favourites.

'I had hoped my senses would return by now,' Thomas said, rubbing the back of his head. The deep wound she had stitched was hidden, but she could still feel its smooth edges when she ran her fingers through his hair. He placed his hands on her waist and pulled her towards him, kissing her deeply. 'But the madness still has me in its grip,' he murmured, his lips brushing her neck, 'for I love you more than ever.'

Desire pooled in her stomach. His eyes closed as she coiled the hair at his nape around her fingers, pulling him closer for another kiss, her lips parting. She could feel his arousal as she pressed her hips to his, trailing her fingers down his spine.

The whinnying of her horse startled them and they sprang apart, breathless.

'It is well that we have Hartshorn to remind us of our manners,' Thomas said, patting the horse's neck. 'Though who will safeguard our respectability when we are in the privacy of our chambers, I am at a loss to say.'

Frances planted a kiss on her husband's cheek. 'I hope we will soon be alone again,' she whispered.

Taking Hartshorn's reins, she led him slowly forward, Thomas and his horse at her side. As they neared the hall, the hedges that lined the path grew thicker. Frances breathed in the sharp tang of yew, relishing the shade it offered. A movement ahead caught her eye and she paused as a young groom hurried towards them.

'Sir Thomas, my lady,' the boy said, with a quick, awkward bow. 'Please, allow me.' He took the reins from them and led the horses towards the stables.

Frances saw another figure approaching from the gatehouse. He was tall and slim, and walked with an easy grace that belied his years. It took her a moment to recognise Sir Anthony Mildmay. It had been many years since she had seen the handsome courtier who had been a great favourite with the old Queen. His absence from court since James's accession suggested that his hopes for further advancement had been disappointed.

'Sir Anthony,' Thomas said, with a bow, as his wife curtsied.

'Welcome to Apethorpe. And Lady Frances,' he said, bending to kiss her hand. 'What a pleasure it is to see you after all these years.'

Frances could not but admire his gallantry. She doubted he had any recollection of the shy young girl who had accompanied her mother to court in the later years of Elizabeth's reign.

'Tell me, how does the marchioness fare? I see you have inherited her beauty.'

Frances smiled. 'My mother is in excellent health, thank you, Sir Anthony.'

'How is His Majesty enjoying Northamptonshire?' Thomas asked, diverting their host's attention from his wife.

Frances sensed the older man's hesitation, but his smile never wavered.

'Very well – though he will welcome you. His buckhounds have grown quite unruly of late.'

Thomas grinned. 'We shall soon tire them out on the hunt. I hear the woodlands of your estate are unsurpassed in these parts.'

Sir Anthony inclined his head in acknowledgement.

'I am sure the King will find even greater diversion with your arrival – and that of some other attendants,' he replied. 'Sir John Graham has secured a place for a new protégé. Let us hope he does not serve the King ill at this evening's banquet or it will put him out of humour.'

Frances exchanged a glance with her husband and saw her surprise mirrored in his face. Sir John guarded his position in the privy chamber jealously and was not known to encourage potential rivals.

'Well now,' Sir Anthony said briskly, 'I must not keep you from your chambers. You will be tired after your journey.' He motioned to the page, who was standing a few paces behind him, then bowed his farewell.

Frances looked out across the neatly appointed privy gardens that stretched across the expanse of the south front. The heady scents from the orangery that lay below came to her on the breeze. She looked forward to tasting some of its bounty. Sir Anthony was famed for the delicacies that were served at his banquets – they had certainly won favour with the old Queen.

'Will you not come to bed, Frances?' Thomas whispered, as he nuzzled the back of her neck.

Still gazing out of the window, she felt him begin to unlace her gown, his fingers working slowly at first, then with growing impatience. When at last her stays hung loose, he eased them from her shoulders and untied her heavy skirts, which rustled to the floor. Savouring the touch of his hands as they snaked from her back around to her belly, she drew in a breath as they moved downwards, caressing the inside of her thighs through the soft linen of her shift.

She turned to face him, kissing him hungrily as her fingers worked at the laces of his hose. When he had pulled off his doublet, she lifted his shirt over his head and ran her hands along the contours of his chest, relishing the warmth of his skin against her fingertips. He bent to kiss her again, but she led him towards the large mahogany chest that lay at the end of the bed and pushed him down onto it.

Taking a step away from him, she slowly, deliberately, drew up her shift, gradually revealing her nakedness. Seeing his eyes fill with longing as they roved over her body stoked her own desire. Unable to withhold any longer, she moved to sit astride him. Slowly, she began to move, her hips pressing against Thomas's until they matched her rhythm. A bead of sweat trickled down her back as she felt the delicious, rising tension deep inside her, crying out as the waves of pleasure pulsated through her. The muscles of her husband's back grew taut, then he gave a deep shudder and sank down against her, his damp forehead pressing into her neck.

They remained like that for several minutes, caressing each other's cooling skin as their breathing slowed.

'I think the King was right all along, Frances,' Thomas said, his eyes glinting. 'You must be a witch. How else can you have such power over me?'

She kissed his forehead, which tasted salty. 'Then you shall be forever cursed, husband,' she said.

CHAPTER 2

4 August

'Come, my love,' Thomas urged. 'We are late enough already.'

Frances looped her arm through his and together they weaved their way through the clusters of guests in the hall. Even though the windows had been flung open, the air was already stifling. Not for the first time, Frances regretted the fashion for tightly laced dresses in brocade silk and other heavy fabrics. Already, she longed for the hour when she and her husband could retire to their chamber and divest themselves of their finery. But Sir Anthony was renowned for his hospitality: the feasting and entertainment would continue long into the night.

The minstrels struck up a lively flourish and the courtiers fanned out on either side of the room in preparation for the dance. Frances was thankful they had started with a sedate pavane, for the heat was sapping her energy.

They had performed only a few steps when the music came to an abrupt halt and everyone turned at the rapping of a staff on the flagstones. As it echoed into silence, Frances heard the slow shuffle of footsteps.

'His Majesty the King!'

There was a rustle of skirts as the assembled company made a deep obeisance. Frances was aware of holding her breath and had to remind herself that she had no reason to feel uneasy. Her husband had become one of the King's most regular companions since she had last been in his presence. But her apprehension came of years spent under his suspicious gaze, the threat of arrest for witchcraft or treason always present. She thought back to her ordeal in the Tower and shuddered. Time had not lessened the terror. It was as if she were being tortured anew whenever she allowed her thoughts to stray to that terrible night, the witch-pricker's blade piercing her flesh as the King looked on, impervious to her screams.

Now there was a scraping of chairs and a heavy sigh as James sat down. Frances was shocked to see the change in him. His hair was almost entirely white, which made his jowly face appear all the ruddier. Only his thin beard and moustache showed the red hair that had been his most distinguishing feature. As he reached for his glass she saw that his knuckles were swollen and his fingers misshapen, like the gnarled old branches of an oak tree. He took a long swig, then set the vessel roughly on the table.

'Play on!' he shouted.

The musicians took up their instruments at once and the murmur of chatter in the hall soon grew louder. A line of guests eager to be presented to the King had already formed in front of the dais. Frances glanced at her husband, who smiled his reassurance. It seemed an age until they, too, were standing before James – though Frances wished it had been longer. She swept a deep curtsy.

'Ah, Sir Thomas!' James cried, with genuine warmth. 'Y'are back at last and I am glad of it. My hounds have grown restless wi'out ye.'

'Forgive my having stayed at Tyringham for longer than I planned, Your Majesty.' Frances kept her gaze downcast as her husband spoke. 'I had much business to attend to there.'

James gave a derisive snort.

'I have nae doubt. Are two bairns not enough for ye, Lady Frances?'

She raised her eyes to his and gave a tight smile.

'I'll wager there'll soon be another in that small belly of yours – if there isn't already,' he persisted, oblivious to the discomfort of those around him. 'I await news that my daughter has been brought abed again too. She was barely out of her wedding gown before her belly was swelling with the first.'

Frances hid her disgust that he should speak so of the princess.

'I hear Prince Henry is thriving, Your Grace,' Thomas cut in.

Frances had thrilled at the news that her former mistress had been safely delivered of a son at the beginning of the year. She hoped the count would be kind to her, given that she had fulfilled her duty as a royal wife so soon. Perhaps their marriage was happier than Frances had dared hope it would be when she had bade the princess farewell. She still remembered the young woman's tear-stained face as she had clung to her.

James grunted. 'So my ambassador tells me. Let's hope he dunnae choke out his breath like his namesake.'

A shocked hush descended. It was known to all that the King had despised his late son and heir, but he had refrained from speaking ill of him since his demise – in public, at least.

There was a small cough. Glancing along the dais, Frances saw Robert Carr. She wondered that she had not noticed him before. He was never more than a few feet away from his master. Even his marriage to Lady Frances Howard at the end of the previous year had not interrupted the frequency – or, it was rumoured, the intimacy – of his attendance upon the King. His recent promotion to Earl of Somerset was testament to that.

'Sir Anthony is desirous to know whether you are ready for the banquet to be served, Your Grace,' he said, in the simpering tone she remembered.

'Aye, tell him to get on wi' it,' James barked, with a dismissive wave.

Frances was grateful to take her place at one of the long tables that lined the walls. Soon, the attendants began to file in from the far end of the hall, laden with platters of sweetmeats, candied fruits and marchpane.

'Lady Mildmay is famed for her confectionery,' a gentleman opposite remarked, his eyes roving over the exquisitely crafted dishes that were being laid in front of them.

Frances glanced at the dais. Grace Mildmay was sitting next to her husband, Sir Anthony. She was about the same age as Helena, Frances judged, but her figure was much fuller. Her pale blue eyes were kind and intelligent, and she had a gentleness about her that made Frances warm to her at once. She hoped they might have the opportunity to become friends.

Just then, her attention was drawn to the arrival of another server, who had thrown open the door with such force that it thudded against the fireplace. Frances had never seen the young man before, and judging from the curious stares of her fellow diners, he was a newcomer at court. He was exceptionally tall and slender, with skin as delicate as porcelain. His dark blue eyes flitted about the room, and Frances saw the flicker of a smile on his lips as he looked towards the dais. She followed his gaze but James was too distracted by the array of sweet delicacies before him to notice. Next to him, Somerset was staring in the attendant's direction with a mixture of surprise and consternation. Clearly, he had been unaware of his appointment. Frances knew that the King lived in daily fear of assassins and that every new arrival in his service had to be carefully scrutinised by his closest advisers before they were permitted to attend him. Perhaps this one had slipped through the net.

She sipped some spiced wine and raised her eyes again to the young man, who was slowly moving down the hall, a gilded flagon in one hand and an embroidered napkin in the other. The position of royal cupbearer was as highly sought as the other roles that involved attendance upon the King. Frances was wondering who his patron was when she recalled her conversation with Sir Anthony earlier that day. Sir John Graham must have some game in play.

'Have you tried the apricots? I have never tasted sweeter.' Thomas was offering the platter to her. She smiled her thanks and tried to focus on slicing the delicate flesh of the fruit. 'Do you suppose that is Sir John's new protégé?' she whispered, as the cupbearer passed directly in front of where they were sitting.

Thomas's eyes narrowed but he gave a slight shake of his head. 'For a moment I thought I knew him, but I must have been mistaken.' He glanced around the room. 'I have not noticed any other newcomers, so I suppose this must be Sir John's man.'

A loud clatter reverberated around the hall. Everyone turned to see the young man staring aghast at the dark red stain splattered on his white shirt. The flagon lay at his feet, the rest of its contents spreading over the marble tiles. Behind him, Frances noticed one of the other attendants smirking. She recognised him as the man who usually served the King his wine.

'God's wounds! You churl!' the newcomer shouted, his face now even paler and his chest heaving with suppressed rage. The other man's smile grew broader as he stared back at him.

The King was gazing at them both, open-mouthed. Somerset stood abruptly and was about to intervene when the young man strutted from the hall, slamming the door behind him.

A deathly hush descended. Somerset seemed unsure whether to go after him or stay and attend his sovereign.

'Well, clean up the mess, man!' he shouted at last, then gestured to the minstrels to resume their playing.

After a long pause, the guests resumed feasting, the hum of conversation more muted than before. Frances darted a glance towards the smirking man, who was soaking up the spilled wine with a napkin. He had just finished when the door at the far end of the hall was flung open again and the tall young man was back. He had changed his shirt and appeared as composed as when he had first entered. All eyes turned to him as he walked slowly down the centre of the hall. The man who had caused him to spill the wine was now standing bolt upright, his eyes fixed upon his adversary.

'Thank you for taking care of the flagon for me, Carlton,' the young man purred, his voice as smooth as silk, then wrested it from the attendant's grasp.

Before the other man could reply, he swung back the vessel and brought it crashing against the side of his face. There was a sickening crack and Carlton slumped to the floor, his jaw broken. For a moment, nobody stirred. Then the King's guards rushed forward to seize the young man, while Somerset ran about the hall barking instructions to whoever would listen. Thomas grasped Frances's hand as they watched in dismay. Among the press of bodies, she could see a pool of blood where the spilled wine had been and heard the low keening of the man as he clutched the side of his face. At least he was still breathing, she thought.

'Peace!'

The King's voice rang out across the hall. His chair scraped loudly across the tiles as he rose to his feet, then limped down from the dais. Everyone seemed to be holding their breath as he walked slowly towards the young man.

'I have not seen you in my service before,' he remarked. 'What is your name?'

The man made as if to bow, but the guards on either side of him had his arms pinioned so tightly behind his back that he could not move.

'George Villiers, Your Majesty,' he said. He did not lower his eyes as convention dictated, but stared directly at his sovereign.

James held his gaze. Frances recognised the intensity of that look. She had seen it many times before, when the King had been entranced by a new masque or the grisly spectacle of the hunt in which he so delighted. Now, he seemed as likely to kiss the man as strike him.

'Who brought ye here?'

Someone cleared their throat. A moment later, Sir John Graham stepped forward. Frances had not noticed him among the company – he had probably been keeping a discreet distance. His face was flushed and there was fear in his eyes as he addressed his sovereign. 'Forgive me, Your Majesty. I was given full assurance of the young man's credentials, or I would never have agreed to his appointment in your service.'

Frances saw his eyes flick to Somerset. *So that was why he had accepted Villiers's suit.* Sir John's rivalry with him had dominated the privy chamber for years. Although Sir John was too advanced in years to enjoy the same favour with James as his beloved 'Rabbie,' he evidently hoped to divert their master's attention with a younger, more beguiling, alternative.

'You should have consulted me, Sir John,' Somerset snapped. 'All those who aspire to serve His Grace must gain my approval first. I would never have allowed such a man as this,' he cast a disdainful look at Villiers, 'to come into His Grace's presence.'

'Hush, Rabbie', the King interrupted. Frances caught the scowl that crossed his favourite's brow before he recovered his usual composure. 'Well now,' James continued, taking a step closer to his captive. 'What shall I do wi' thee?'

Villiers's eyes glinted as he stared back at the King.

James nodded to the guards to release their hold, then reached forward and took the young man's right hand in his. There was an audible intake of breath around the room.

'Do you know the penalty for striking a man in the King's presence?' he murmured, stroking his thumb across the attendant's delicate fingers. 'It is to have your hand smitten off.'

Behind the King, Frances saw Somerset give a satisfied smile. Villiers's expression did not change.

James gazed down at the man's wrist, as if imagining the blade slicing through it. 'But I would not be a merciful king if I punished a novice in this way.' Frances stared at him. He had shown no such mercy to witches or Catholics – or any other of his subjects who displeased him, she reflected bitterly. 'Besides,' he added, lifting the young man's hand so that his lips almost touched it, 'I could not destroy something so beautiful.'

Frances saw Villiers's eyes darken with something like desire – or triumph, perhaps.

'And so I am minded to pardon you—'

'Your Grace,' Somerset interrupted, stepping forward. 'This man has shown himself to be violent and unruly. Surely you cannot risk—'

The King held up a hand to silence him. 'You would have me jump at my own shadow, Rabbie,' he said, without taking his eyes off Villiers. 'Such passion as this young man has shown must not be suppressed but, rather . . . channelled in another direction.'

Somerset's face flushed with anger but he pressed his lips together, defeated.

'Now, George' – the King said the name slowly, as if savouring its taste – 'you may kiss my hand and I will release yours.'

The young man lowered his head to James's outstretched hand and held it there, his lips so close that the King must have felt his breath. Frances noticed James's fingers tremble as he gazed down at the attendant's mass of dark hair. Very slowly, Villiers brushed his lips against his master's skin, letting them linger. At last, he straightened, his heavy-lidded eyes meeting James's again. Then he swept an elegant bow and walked slowly from the hall, the King staring after him.

CHAPTER 3

16 August

Frances bent to rub the velvety sage leaf between her fingers, releasing its aromatic scent. It was the first time she had allowed herself to visit Sir Anthony's famed herb garden, even though they had been there for almost two weeks. Her years at court had taught her caution, as well as restraint. She must not appear over-hasty to explore such a place, lest she arouse suspicion that she was gathering ingredients for her potions. It was a long time since she had been accused of witchcraft but she knew that the stain would never be erased.

'You are admiring my plants, I see.'

She turned sharply at the soft voice and curtsied as Lady Mildmay drew level with her.

'Forgive me. I did not mean to startle you,' the older woman continued. 'Please,' she gestured for Frances to follow, 'I do not often have the chance to show off my garden so I would be delighted if you would indulge me.'

'With pleasure, Lady Grace,' Frances replied. 'It is one of the finest I have seen.'

Her companion smiled at the compliment. 'I have been fortunate to have more time than most wives to tend it. Sir Anthony and I wished to fill this house with children, but God has seen fit to bless us with only our dear Mary. She is of an age with you, I think.'

'I am sorry not to have made her acquaintance,' Frances remarked. 'Does she live far from here?'

'Too far!' Lady Grace replied, with feeling. 'Her husband's estates lie in the north-west, many days' journey from here. I have seldom seen her since her marriage, though she is a faithful correspondent. She loves to tell me of the herbs and plants she has cultivated in Westmorland, despite the chill winds that blow from the hills thereabouts.'

'She must be as skilled as her mother,' Frances observed, as she admired the neatly kept beds, each one bordered by fragrant myrtle hedges.

'I hear you are skilled in such matters yourself, Lady Frances.'

The remark was lightly made, but Frances experienced the familiar surge of fear.

'I knew your mother,' Lady Grace continued, sensing her hesitation. 'We served in the old Queen's chamber together for a time. I still remember her arriving at court. As pretty as a peach, and with such modesty that she was bound to win favour with our mistress. You are very much like her, I think.'

'I wish that were true,' Frances said, with feeling. 'I miss her dreadfully – my son George, too. He is under my mother's guardianship at Longford until he comes of age and inherits the estate. I hope to visit them again soon.'

'It is a beautiful castle,' Lady Grace observed. 'I was raised in Wiltshire, too, and visited Longford when it was newly built. Your mother and father were almost as proud of it as they were of their young brood. Such a large family! How do your brothers and sisters fare?'

Though she had six siblings still living, it was Edward whom Frances thought of first. She had heard little of him since her departure from court the previous year. After Prince Henry's death, it had soon become clear that Edward could not hope for the same favour from the new heir, Charles, so he had given up the court without troubling to take his leave of her. Theo had written some weeks later that he had loaned their brother some money for a voyage to Italy. Frances had often thought of him since, jostling for favour among the rapacious courts of Florence or Rome. She hoped he would find enough to keep him there.

'Very well, I think,' Frances replied, 'though I rarely see them now.' She decided to change the subject. 'I fear that I will soon need to loosen my stays. It is little wonder that your confectionery is celebrated throughout the kingdom.'

The older woman chuckled. 'I have long since despaired of my figure,' she said, patting her generous hips. 'But I use sugar in my remedies, too. It can be most effective.'

'Oh?' Frances knew that they should not speak of such things but she was intrigued.

'Indeed,' Lady Grace replied, warming to her theme, 'and many other things besides – seeds, roots, nuts, spices . . . as well as the herbs here, of course. One of my balms contains over a hundred ingredients,' she added proudly. 'I write down all of my recipes, with notes for their application. I should be glad to show them to you. It is rare that anyone takes such an interest. My husband calls me his wise woman.'

Frances stopped walking and stared at her companion. 'Are you not afraid? Such practices have been deemed witchcraft since King James took the throne.'

Lady Grace smiled. 'His Majesty enjoys our hospitality too much to cut it off at its source,' she remarked wryly. 'He is so fond of my confectionery that I am obliged to send him regular supplies whenever he is away from Apethorpe.'

Frances bit back a scornful remark at the King's hypocrisy. After a pause, they resumed their stroll through the garden.

'I hope the King has had good hunting today,' Lady Grace said. 'It will put him in a favourable humour for this evening's feast.'

'They will soon return,' Frances replied. She had noticed the lengthening shadows. 'I have a mind to walk in the parkland before this evening – to sharpen my appetite,' she added, with a grin.

'Of course, my dear,' her hostess replied. 'You will forgive me if I do not accompany you, but I must attend to the kitchens.'

Frances walked towards the gate on the north side of the herb garden, shielding her eyes against the sun as she decided which path to take. On the rise of the hill that lay to the east of the hall, she could see the outline of a hunting lodge. It was too small to be the one she had heard Sir Anthony speak of having commissioned the previous year, so she hoped it was no longer in use. Solitude was a rare luxury at court gatherings. There would be fine views of the estate from there, too, and she could rest in its shade before returning to her chamber to make shift for the feast.

Frances quickened her pace as she went up the hillside. By the time she reached the small circular clearing that lay in front of the lodge, she was obliged to rest for a few moments. The views were as spectacular as she had envisaged. The hall seemed to shimmer in the late-afternoon light, and she was struck by the symmetry of the gardens that surrounded it. The air was cooler there, and Frances closed her eyes as a breeze blew across the exposed skin of her face and neck.

Turning towards the lodge, she noticed that the door was ajar. She pushed it open and walked inside. It took a moment for her eyes to adjust to the gloom of the small entrance hall, which had no windows. It was deliciously cool inside and she breathed in the comforting smell of damp stone. A noise from the floor above made her start. She waited, straining her ears to listen, but all was quiet.

She made her way up the spiral stairs, gripping the iron rail that ran along the cold stone wall. With every step she took, she feared a rat would scurry out from the shadows, but her soft leather soles disturbed only the years of dust that had formed on the steps.

As she reached the top, she heard another sound – like a faint moan. Her heart began to thrum in her chest. It was easy to imagine an ancient tower such as this being haunted by some restless ghost. Then she chided herself. It was probably nothing more than the breeze rushing down the chimney into the fireplace.

Once her breathing had slowed, she edged towards the light that showed around the door on the left of the landing. She opened it and stood on the threshold, blinking against the brightness that streamed in through the window. Her breath caught in her throat and she stared, at first unable to comprehend the scene that was being played out in front of her.

The King was lying on the heavy oak table that stretched the length of the room. He was wearing only a linen shirt, his doublet and breeches discarded on the floor. His legs dangled over one end of the table, and a man was kneeling between them, his head rising and falling in a steady rhythm as he stroked James's thighs.

Frances felt as if the air had been knocked out of her lungs. She stood stock still, struggling to breathe. The King gave another moan and the man raised his head to smile at him, exposing the shock of his arousal, before lowering his mouth once more.

As if suddenly released from an enchantment, Frances backed hurriedly out of the room, willing her feet to make no sound on the dusty floorboards. Back on the landing, her heart was pounding so hard in her chest that she feared it could be heard. But, after a long moment, the King cried out. As she padded quickly down the stairs, the sound of the other man's silken laughter echoed around the walls.

George Villiers.

CHAPTER 4

21 August

'Ha!' James exclaimed, as the dice clattered to a halt. 'I have it again. Surrender your fortune, Somerset.'

Frances peered over Lady Grace's shoulder and saw Somerset give a resigned grin, pushing the remainder of his coins towards the King. His mouth dropped as Villiers stepped forward and refilled his master's glass. The young man paused for just a moment too long after performing this task, the flagon suspended in his slender fingers. Frances saw James's eyes rest upon them and he inhaled deeply, as if trying to catch his lover's scent. She knew that her husband had seen it too. He had been shocked, but not surprised, when she had told him what she had witnessed in the hunting lodge a few days before. 'We must keep our counsel,' he had urged.

Frances knew he was right. The secret would be out soon enough anyway. The King was doing little to disguise his growing infatuation.

'That will be all, Villiers.'

Somerset's voice, sharp as flint, sliced through the heavy silence. Still his rival did not move. Only when the King gave a reluctant nod did he bow and step back into the shadows.

'Come, Thomas,' James said. 'It is just you and I now.'

Frances took a sip of claret and forced her attention back to her companion. 'You will be glad to have your house to yourselves again,' she said quietly. 'My husband tells me that the King plans to depart for Nottingham before the week is out.'

Lady Grace smiled. 'We are greatly honoured by his visits, of course.' She continued in a low voice: 'Though they do place a burden on our estate – and those of our neighbours. Sir Anthony has been obliged to offer recompense for the damage wreaked upon their crops by His Grace's incessant hunting.'

Frances shot a quick look in the King's direction, but he was too intent upon his game to heed their conversation. She knew it was the same wherever James stayed – Thomas had often spoken of it. He had tried to persuade his master to lay out his own funds as a means of securing goodwill, but to no avail. This king had ever been careless of his subjects' welfare, she reflected.

'I would be glad if the Queen would accompany her husband sometimes,' the older woman went on, 'but it seems she prefers to remain in London.'

It was true. For most of the years that Frances had served at court, Anne had lived in a separate household at Greenwich. She had claimed the air was more beneficial to her health than that of Whitehall or St James's, but her recent move to Denmark House on the Strand exposed this as a lie. It was hardly a secret that she could not bear her husband's company – or he hers.

'The King was ever best when furthest from the Queen,' she whispered.

'You have the luck of the devil, Thomas!'

Both women turned to the King, who was staring in mock-horror at Frances's husband.

'If you did not keep my hounds in such good order, I would have you whipped,' he added, with a grin, as he handed Thomas a large pile of coins.

'Another game, Your Grace?'

'And let you further deplete my treasury? No, Tom, we will have no more sport this evening. Besides,' he added, casting a glance over his shoulder, 'I am tired after the day's hunting so will seek my bed.'

The other men around the table rose as the King prepared to depart. Somerset was at his side, as if fearful that Villiers would forget his position and offer to accompany their master. As he reached the door, James turned and addressed Thomas again. 'I have a mind to visit my hounds tomorrow morning, before we set out for the hunt. Bring some of the venison from tonight's supper. Oswyn will enjoy feasting on that.'

Thomas bowed his assent. The affection that James lavished on his buckhounds – Oswyn in particular – had always surprised Frances. Thomas would often tell her of the latest gift he had bestowed upon them, from bejewelled gold collars to the choicest morsels from the royal kitchens. They were better served than even his closest attendants.

Frances watched as the King shuffled out of the room, Somerset half a pace behind. Thomas held out his hand for her to accompany him. She was glad to retire. Though it was still early, she felt unusually tired.

'Goodnight, Sir Anthony, Lady Grace,' Thomas said, as he and Frances made their obeisance.

Villiers was still standing by the door. He made the slightest of bows as they passed, his eyes glittering in the gloom.

The sun was already high by the time Frances awoke the next morning. She twisted towards her husband's side of the bed but knew he would have risen early for the hunt and to accompany his master on the visit to the hounds that preceded it. It would be many hours yet before they returned. Perhaps she would go for a ride herself today, she mused, as she summoned the will to lift her head from the soft down pillow. She had not yet explored all of the parkland – her excursion to the hunting lodge had deterred her from venturing further than the formal gardens surrounding the house. But she would be returning to Tyringham Hall in two days' time, as soon as the King and his entourage left for

Nottingham, so she should make the most of the opportunity. The thought of being parted from Thomas again made her heart contract. Now, more than ever, she longed to be with him – their son, too.

Raising herself onto her elbows, she experienced a wave of nausea and hurried to the ewer. When at last the retching had subsided, she sank onto the bed, exhausted. She had been right, then. She had only missed one of her courses, so it was early for the sickness to begin. Perhaps this child would prove even lustier than John, who had wriggled and kicked inside her belly for many weeks before the birth. Gingerly, she edged herself back into bed, fearful in case this small movement sparked a fresh onslaught.

Frances did not know how long she had been sleeping when she was awoken by the sound of the door latch lifting. Rubbing the sleep from her eyes, she peered at her husband. Her smile of welcome faded as she saw his agitation.

'Is the hunt over already?' she ventured.

He did not answer but came to sit next to her on the bed.

'Oswyn is dead,' he said, without preamble.

Frances sat upright. 'The King's favourite hound?'

Thomas nodded miserably, then put his head into his hands.

'We had only ridden out as far as Fotheringhay when I noticed he was lagging behind the rest of the pack, though he always outstrips them with ease. By the time I had dismounted, he had collapsed. It was then that he began to vomit. Soon, he was coughing up blood. I tried to calm him, but he was panting so fast and his eyes were wild with terror.' Frances reached out to touch his arm, and he raised grief-stricken eyes to hers. 'The poor beast died in torment, and there was nothing I could do to help.'

Frances knew he loved the hounds as much as his master did. 'It was not your fault, Thomas,' she said gently, taking both of his hands in hers.

'The King turned back as soon as he realised Oswyn was missing,' he continued. 'I will never forget the look on his face when he saw him lying dead in my arms. It was as if his own son had been taken from him.'

Frances mused that Prince Henry's death had caused the King a good deal less grief than the loss of one of his cherished hounds. 'What do you think was the cause?' she asked.

Thomas shook his head. 'I cannot think. He was in good spirits when the King and I visited the stables this morning. I took him the venison, as requested.'

'Perhaps it was too rich for him to stomach?' Frances suggested.

'He has had it many times before.'

She fell silent. They had eaten the same meat last night. Even if it had turned bad so quickly, it would not have caused such violent symptoms: the hound would have had a brief bout of sickness and recovered. As she held her husband's gaze, she saw that he knew it too.

Oswyn had been poisoned.

CHAPTER 5

23 August

'You are sure that you are well enough for the journey?'

Frances smiled at her husband's concern. He had asked her the same question a dozen times since they had awoken that morning. 'Quite sure,' she replied firmly. 'Travelling by carriage has always made me nauseous, so I will hardly notice the difference.' She kissed him. 'I have more cause to worry about *you*,' she said, reaching up to touch his cheek. He held her hand there for a moment before pressing his lips to the palm. 'I wish you could come home with me. Are you sure you cannot petition the King for a few weeks' leave? You could attend him again when he returns to court next month.'

Thomas gave a heavy sigh and drew her into his arms, holding her tightly. 'You know that is my dearest wish,' he murmured into her hair. 'But I cannot ask it of His Grace so soon after—' He stopped abruptly.

Frances felt a jolt of anxiety for him. The King had been in a dark mood since Oswyn's death and the atmosphere at Apethorpe was strained. Even the Mildmays' lavish hospitality had failed to raise his spirits, and he had eschewed the feasting and entertainments, retreating to his private apartments with just a few favoured attendants. Thomas had not been among them.

George Villiers had, though. Frances did not know why she was so disturbed by it. He was merely the latest in a long line of young men to bask in the King's fleeting favour. Somerset had far more cause to feel uneasy than she did. But she had seen how Villiers eyed those he regarded as rivals – her husband among them. She had her suspicions, too, that it was he who had poisoned the King's favourite buckhound. What better way to sever James's trust in the man who cared for them? She had not yet voiced her fears to Thomas – her years at court had taught her that matters were not always as they first appeared. She wished that she might go with her husband now so that she could continue to observe the new favourite at close range. At the same time, she could not but feel relieved to be escaping James and his entourage.

'Promise you will write as soon as you reach Tyringham,' Thomas urged. 'And give our boy his father's blessing – and this kiss.'

Frances nodded, unable to speak. The pain of their parting did not lessen; if anything, it grew worse each time.

'Sir Thomas!'

Somerset's voice rang out across the courtyard. He had already mounted his horse and was waiting, his face set in a now familiar scowl, for the master of the buckhounds to take his place in the procession.

Thomas pressed his lips to hers once more, then walked briskly away. He climbed onto his horse, his mouth set in a grim line. A few moments later, Somerset gave the signal and the King's carriage rumbled over the cobbles and out onto the gravelled path, the long cavalcade following close behind. She remained standing until her husband had disappeared from view, then went slowly towards her own carriage.

'God keep him safe,' she whispered, as the coachman cracked his whip and she lurched forward.

1615

CHAPTER 6

2 September

Frances breathed the scent of Michaelmas daisies that was carried on the warm breeze. Looking into the small copse, she could see their delicate purple petals nestled among the tangled stems and ferns. She remembered her father telling her that the tiny flower symbolised a farewell. As if sensing her sadness, her infant son began to snuffle and writhe in her arms. She bent to kiss the downy hair on his head, inhaling deeply. She wished to commit the sweet, milky smell of him to her memory, as much as his light blue eyes and wispy red hair.

Robert was five months old now. He had been born on Easter Day. 'That child shall never know want, or care, or harm,' the elderly midwife had pronounced, as she had placed the mewling baby at her breast. Frances knew the old saying about Easter babies was mere superstition – such as those who claimed that a baby born when the moon was rising would be a girl, or that a firstborn child would be protected from witchcraft. But gazing down at him now, she hoped it would prove true.

Thomas had arrived two days after the birth, exhausting several horses in his eagerness to meet his new son. It would have cost him dear to leave the court during the Easter festivities. He had struggled to regain the King's favour since their return from last year's summer progress. Though it was hardly Thomas's fault, the death of James's favourite hound lay like a canker between them.

Villiers had been quick to take advantage, as he had any other opportunity to discredit those close to the King. The precious few days that Thomas had spent at Tyringham with his wife and newborn son had been marred by the news that James had appointed Villiers a gentleman of the bedchamber, as well as bestowing on him a knighthood and an annual pension of a thousand pounds. Frances had no doubt that more promotions would follow. James was always generous to his favourites.

Somerset had had even more reason than her husband to feel aggrieved. His own title must have lost much of its lustre when he heard of Villiers's rise. Thomas had written many times of how the rising antipathy between the two men now dominated the court. Somerset had succeeded in blocking his rival's appointment to the bedchamber for several months, but there was nothing he could do to stem the tide of the King's infatuation. Frances thought back to that day in the hunting lodge. James would want his new favourite close at hand, day and night.

Thomas had returned once more since Robert's birth. Frances had been dismayed to see how haggard and careworn he had looked. At first, he had not wanted to speak of court matters, assuring her that his only desire was to spend time with her and their sons. But she had seen how the worries with which he was oppressed had followed him from Whitehall. He had been as loving towards her as he always was, and his delight in Robert and John had been undiminished. But he had often fallen silent, and she knew that he had slept only fitfully.

On the night before his departure he had unburdened himself. 'Villiers will stop at nothing to destroy those he has marked as rivals, Frances,' he had told her. 'He means to have the King entirely to himself, and then he will rule the court.'

And the kingdom, Frances had thought. She knew that her husband was among those upon whom Villiers had set his sights;

she knew, too, that he had gathered a powerful faction about him. The Earls of Pembroke, Montgomery and Bedford would have ransomed their own mothers to get Somerset out of the way, little seeing that the viper with whom he was replaced would likely turn and bite them.

With all her heart, she wished that her husband might resign his post and return to Tyringham Hall so that they could raise their growing family and live out their days in peace. But she knew that James would never allow it. He spent nearly all of his time hunting now, so his master of the buckhounds was more essential to him than ever. Despite Oswyn's death, he knew Thomas was by far the most suited to the position. The hounds adored him even more than they did the King and would always do his bidding. James would no more wrest him from them than he would a suckling baby from its mother's breast.

She thought of the fierceness of Thomas's embrace as he had bade her farewell, his eyes dark with foreboding. Robert had grown fretful in his arms and even John had fallen silent, gazing up at his father with his little brow furrowed. That was two weeks ago now. She had been unable to settle to anything since, her thoughts too full of how her husband might be faring. He had written only once, and the letter had contained little news, apart from that of his safe arrival at Whitehall. How much else might he have said, if his desire to protect her from worry had not been so strong? It was that which had decided her. *She must go to him.*

'Hush, sweeting,' she soothed, as her little son began to cry.

The wet-nurse she had appointed was well respected in the area and had been recommended by a neighbour. Frances had already begun to bind her own breasts so that the milk would soon cease to flow. She knew that she had courted scandal by suckling the baby, as she had with John and George. Well-born ladies were not expected to do so, not least because it prevented their falling pregnant with another heir. But Frances had cared little for the idle gossip. People would soon find other matters to occupy their conversation at dinner.

She had not told Thomas that she would soon be joining him at court. She knew he would do everything he could to dissuade her, anxious to keep her away from the danger that surrounded him. But he needed her – of that she was certain. The thought strengthened her resolve as she gazed down at Robert. She prayed it would stay with her as she bade him and his brother farewell in the morning.

She had forgotten the noise. The endless clatter of hoofs on cobbles, the incessant cries of stallholders. The stench, too – so different from the fragrant woods that surrounded Tyringham Hall. It was a little over two years since she had last set foot in the city, but it felt like a lifetime.

As the carriage rumbled into the palace courtyard, she had to push away thoughts of her departure from Buckinghamshire two days earlier. But images of Robert's chubby arms held out as his wet-nurse tried to comfort him, and of John clinging to her skirts as she made to climb the steps of the carriage, flooded back. The jolt as it reached an abrupt halt brought her back to the present. Wiping away her tears as the coachman opened the door, she stepped down onto the cobbles.

Frances stared around her. The courtyard was the usual bustle of carriages arriving, wagons laden with provisions and servants hurrying to and fro. How happy she had been to leave this place, soon after Princess Elizabeth had embarked for the Palatine with her new husband. Thomas had been at her side, his hand resting protectively on her swollen belly. The memory quickened her steps now as she made her way to his apartment. She had heard the bells of St Martin's strike four as the Holbein Gate had come into view. Her husband would soon return to make ready for the evening.

Just before she reached the end of the passage that led from the state rooms to the first set of courtiers' lodgings, a noise made her pause. She listened. There it was again – a gasp, quickly suppressed. It came from a dark recess to her right. She waited another moment, glancing around her to make sure she was not being watched, then took a step towards it.

As she peered through the archway, she could see a faint glimmer of light at the far end of the recess. There must be another opening or a window just out of view. She knew she should continue on her way, ignore whatever clandestine tryst was taking place, but curiosity triumphed over discretion and she took another step forward. She heard the rustle of clothing and a man's breath, quick and sharp. Slowly, she peered around the corner.

A thin shaft of light illuminated the young woman's face, which was contorted with pain or pleasure – Frances could not tell which. Her skirts were raised around her waist and her legs were held apart by the man who stood between them, bucking against her like a rutting beast. Next to the girl was a groom Frances recognised from the King's household. He was naked and his eyes were alight with desire. She watched, transfixed, as the older man leaned over and kissed him deeply, his fingers stroking his arousal. As the light caught his face she drew in a sharp breath. *George Villiers*.

His thrusting was rougher now, more urgent. The woman closed her eyes as he gave a shudder and cried out. Frances drew back and pressed herself against the wall, trying desperately to slow her breathing. As she padded silently from the recess, she heard Villiers give a low chuckle.

'Now it is your turn, my young master.'

Frances ran the rest of the way to Thomas's lodgings. As she lifted the latch and stepped over the threshold, she breathed in its familiar scent, hoping it would calm her. Though it was a warm autumn day, the room felt cold and she noticed a thick layer of dust on the fireplace, which added to the air of neglect. Mrs Knyvett had grown less attentive in her duties without her master's wife to keep an eye on her, Frances thought. Well, she would soon set it to rights, she resolved, as she unfastened her cloak and crossed to the grate. As soon as she had coaxed the damp wood into flame, she would begin cleaning.

It was almost two hours before the rooms were arranged to Frances's satisfaction. Polishing away the dust, sweeping the floors and putting fresh linens on the bed had helped to distract her from the rising anxiety that Thomas still had not returned. She had just decided to go and enquire after him when she heard the scraping of the door latch.

'Frances!'

The surprise on his face was soon replaced by anxiety.

'What has happened? Is it Robert? John?'

She rushed to embrace him. 'All is well, my love,' she murmured into his chest. 'I came here for you – please, do not be angry. You would never have allowed it, but I could no longer abide to remain apart, knowing the dangers that surround you.'

'Oh, Frances . . .' He folded his arms around her, stooping to kiss her. 'I cannot deny that my heart rejoices you are here, even though I should wish you safely back at home.'

Gently, she led him to the fireplace. As he sank down into one of the chairs she had set there, she fetched him a goblet of wine. His hand clasped hers as he took it.

'How are my boys?' he asked, after taking a long sip. His face brightened at the thought of them, but Frances was concerned to see the pallor of his skin, the dark shadows under his eyes. She resolved to say nothing of what she had just witnessed in the cloister: no good could come of it. The King was more likely to punish whoever told him of it than believe his favourite to be capable of such debauchery.

'Thriving,' she replied, with a smile. 'Robert still cries lustily whenever he is hungry – which is often. John is learning to show more patience towards his little brother, though he rails at him for chewing his toys.'

Thomas chuckled. 'And what of George?'

Frances felt the familiar surge of pride at the thought of her eldest son. She had visited him at Longford two months earlier, arriving in time for his birthday. It was hard to believe he was nine already – although he had grown tall and slender since she had last seen him. 'His appetite has quite exhausted our supplies,' her mother had said, with a fond smile. George had the same restless energy as his late father and much resembled him. Tom would have been as proud as she was of the young man he had become.

'My mother's letter arrived last week. He is well, though as greatly spoiled by his grandmother as ever. He misses his papa.'

Thomas was the only father George had ever known – or would know, pray God. He had doted on the boy since the earliest days of their marriage. Frances still marvelled at the sacrifice Thomas had made in taking his dead friend's lover as his wife, their bastard child as his too. She would never tell George the truth. It carried too much heartache – danger as well. The son of a notorious traitor would hardly thrive in these times.

'I miss him too,' her husband replied. 'And I have missed you, Frances. Though it is only a little over two weeks since I left Buckinghamshire, I have yearned for you.' He took her hand, pressing his lips to it. She saw his expression turn grave. 'But I cannot let you stay. The court is even more dangerous now than it was at the time of the Powder Treason. There is endless sniping between the factions that gather about the throne, and their war of words will soon turn to bloodshed. Only yesterday, a servant of William Herbert challenged one of Somerset's men to a duel. The hostility between them spreads like a contagion throughout the court.'

'And the King does nothing to stop it?' Frances asked.

Thomas's mouth curled with derision. 'He encourages it. He seems to find it as diverting as the cockfighting that has become such a regular pastime here.'

A weak king will always encourage division among those around him, Sir Walter Raleigh had once observed. She knew he was right. 'What of Villiers?'

A muscle twitched in her husband's jaw. 'The King's appetite for him grows ever greater. He no longer troubles to hide what passes between them. They have shared a bed since our visit to Farnham last month.'

Frances tried to hide her dismay.

'Sir George had arranged for the progress to call at his mother's house at Gotley the week before. It soon became apparent from whom he inherited his character. Mary Villiers is every bit as ambitious and ruthless as her son, but clever, too. She dissembled so skilfully that, by the time we took our leave, the King declared her a perfect model of motherhood.'

'He has little enough to compare her with,' Frances observed drily. 'He hardly knew his own mother and did not trouble to observe his queen's efforts in that regard.'

Thomas smiled weakly. 'That may be true. But it seems that, in His Majesty's eyes, everyone associated with Villiers is as faultless as the wretch himself. He has even managed to advance his brothers, though they are strangers at court.'

'The King's obsessions burn brightly but are soon extinguished,' Frances reminded him. 'Many believed that Somerset was unassailable, yet he now clings to favour with his fingertips.'

Her husband fetched a deep sigh and rubbed his forehead. He looked utterly exhausted. Frances rose to her feet and held out her hand. 'Come to bed, my love,' she said gently. 'The King can spare you for one evening – he has company enough to divert him.'

Thomas seemed uncertain, but then his shoulders sagged with relief. 'You are right. And I must be up early tomorrow for the hunt.' He stood and drew her to him, kissing her deeply. 'But do not think to sleep just yet.'

CHAPTER 7

6 September

'Well played, Your Grace!'

The Earl of Pembroke's voice rang out across the bowling green. William Herbert was a small, stocky man with a high forehead and a dark, pointed beard. His small, beady eyes flitted from the King to his favourite, who was standing close by. Behind them, Somerset was a brooding presence.

Thomas stepped forward to take his turn. He looked more rested than he had when his wife had first arrived at court and had slept much better with her at his side. Although he still insisted that she must return to Tyringham at the earliest opportunity, he could not disguise how much comfort he drew from her presence. Frances watched as he drew the ball back with a steady arm, then released it so that it rolled, straight and true, down the centre of the green. There was a soft tap as it clipped the edge of the jack, followed by polite applause.

'Your husband is greatly skilled, Lady Frances,' observed her companion.

'I wonder that yours does not play, madam.'

The Countess of Somerset formed her pretty mouth into a smile and rested her hands lightly upon her swollen belly. 'He enjoys observing how the game will play out.'

Frances knew she was no longer talking of bowls. She decided it was safer to change the subject, given their proximity to Villiers and his friends. 'I must congratulate you. When do you expect your confinement to begin?'

The countess flinched at 'confinement', but she soon recovered herself. It was her first child – perhaps she was anxious. 'Next month, if my physician has it right,' she replied. 'My husband has ordered Sherborne to be made ready.'

Raleigh's beloved castle, Frances remembered. James had bestowed it upon his new favourite a few years earlier. She wondered if he would allow Somerset to retain it once he had been ousted from court, as seemed more likely with every day that passed. They lapsed into silence and Frances pretended to focus on the game. Villiers was taking his turn now. She saw James's eyes roving over his lithe body as he bent to pick up the ball. Without warning, he sent a blistering shot down the green. There was a loud crack as the balls were scattered in all directions.

'Bravo, Steenie!' the King cried, then strode forward to embrace the young man.

Frances had soon heard about the affectionate name James had bestowed upon Villiers. It was derived from St Stephen, who had the face of an angel. She and her companion watched as the King kissed his favourite on both cheeks, then whispered something in his ear. Sir George assumed a shocked expression, his long fingers pressed to his mouth, before they both collapsed with laughter.

'Our game is at an end,' the King declared. 'We will retire to our chambers for a time.'

The assembled company made their obeisance as he took Villiers's arm and began to walk slowly from the green. Frances waited, head bowed, for them to pass.

'Ah, Lady Frances, I heard ye had returned.'

Her scalp prickled at the King's voice. 'Yes, Your Grace – for a time at least.'

James eyed her closely. 'I hope you will not distract your husband from his duties, as wives are wont to do.' He shot a sideways glance at the countess. 'I mean to hunt as much as possible before the onset of winter.'

'My wife will soon return to Tyringham, Your Grace,' Thomas said.

'I wonder that you came at all, Lady Frances.' Villiers's voice was smooth as silk. She turned cold eyes to him. 'Your new son can be only a few months old and they are so vulnerable to sickness in their first year, are they not? I thank God that my own dear mother was more solicitous of my welfare.'

Frances saw her husband bristle and knew that Villiers was baiting him. 'I thank you for your concern, Sir George,' she said, before Thomas could respond, taking care to keep her voice light, 'particularly when there must be so many more pressing matters to occupy your thoughts.'

His smile became fixed as he stared down at her.

'Come, Steenie, I need my rest,' James grumbled impatiently.

It was as if a spell had been broken. At once, his favourite swept a deep bow, then proffered his arm for his master to lean upon. Frances gave a quick smile of reassurance to her husband as he passed, but she could see the anger still blazing in his eyes. Thomas had always been mild-mannered but Villiers had a knack of goading him, as he did his other rivals, finding out their weaknesses and scratching at them as he would a sore that had scabbed. As she watched his slender figure retreat from view, she resolved to find out what *his* weakness was.

A great company had assembled for the feast that evening. Frances was grateful that she was seated towards the back of the hall. Few others there felt the same, she knew. The tables closest to the dais were crowded with courtiers – her husband among them – but her own had several empty places. James was notoriously unwelcoming to the spouses of his close attendants. Thomas had taken it as an insult that his wife had not been assigned a place next to his, but Frances had soothed him with the assurance that she would be more comfortable at a distance from the King – and his favourite.

A fanfare of trumpets sounded as the King and his entourage entered the hall, Prince Charles among them. It was the first time Frances had seen James's younger son and heir since her arrival at court. He would turn fifteen next month. His limbs had grown straighter and he had lost the awkward gait his elder brother had delighted in mocking throughout their childhood. Though he would never be tall, and his delicate features gave him an air of fragility, he bore himself with a quiet dignity that formed a sharp – and welcome – contrast to his father.

'May I?'

Frances had been so focused upon the prince that she had not noticed the arrival of the finely dressed gentleman who stood before her now. There was something familiar about him, though she did not think they had ever met.

'Of course,' she said, gesturing for him to sit down.

He gave an elegant bow. 'Sir Francis Bacon, my lady.'

Frances could hardly believe that the greatest philosopher and scientist of the age was standing before her. She had read numerous of his books and had spent so many hours poring over *The Interpretation of Nature* that she felt as if the author was a close friend. Remembering her manners, she rose quickly from her seat and bobbed an awkward curtsy. 'It is an honour to meet you, Sir Francis,' she said warmly. 'I am a great admirer of your works.'

'Then you are clearly a lady of great discernment.' His dark eyes sparked with humour.

Frances stole another glance at her new companion. The engraving in the frontispiece of his *Essays* was a faithful likeness. His dark brown hair was thick and lustrous, and there were just a few flecks of grey in his beard. He was wearing a tall hat, which he removed with a flourish as he sat down. She judged that he must be in his fifties by now, though he appeared younger. He was much shorter than she had imagined and there was something delicate, almost feminine, in his looks.

'Forgive me,' she said, flustered, realising that she had forgotten to introduce herself. 'I am Lady Frances Tyringham.'

'Sir Thomas's wife?' he asked, glancing towards the front of the hall. 'Then he is even more blessed than I thought, for not only is he a favourite with His Majesty but he has the love of a beautiful and clever woman. If envy were not so great a sin, I should be entirely consumed by it.'

Frances smiled. 'You, too, enjoy His Majesty's favour, I think. Thomas told me of your appointment as attorney general. Such a position is only conferred upon a man whom the King trusts implicitly.'

'My years at Gray's Inn served me well,' her companion observed modestly.

She experienced a familiar pang at the name. Tom had been one of its brightest stars. She resisted the temptation to ask if Sir Francis had known him.

They turned at a peal of laughter from the dais. Villiers was leaning in towards his master, his mouth so close to the King's ear that it was almost touching. James's face was flushed – not entirely because of the wine, Frances thought. On his other side, Somerset was glowering at the dish in front of him.

'That young man will rule us all before the year is out,' Bacon mused. 'I know better than most that a sovereign's favour can be fickle, but I hear the King refuses him nothing. Now that he serves in the bedchamber, even greater promotions will follow.'

'It is not so very long ago that Somerset enjoyed the same intimacy with His Majesty,' Frances observed quietly. 'Fortune's wheel never stops turning at court, yet those who hanker for power seem to forget that.'

'Ah, but that is what makes the game so diverting, my lady,' Bacon replied. 'For just as the King bestows his favour on a fortunate few, so those men in turn bestow it on their associates. A skilful player must watch carefully before deciding where to place his bet.'

'Or not play at all,' Frances countered.

The older man studied her with interest, as if she were one of the rare species of exotic plant he had encountered in his research.

'I hope you and I will become better acquainted, Lady Frances,' he remarked. 'There are few in this place who share your candour – or your wisdom. I am sure to profit from both.'

Frances flushed at the compliment and inwardly chastised herself. She should know better than to be seduced by such flattery. Yet there was sincerity in Bacon's eyes as he smiled at her.

The moment was broken by the arrival of the first course of dishes. Sir Francis was assiduous in helping her to a number of them.

'You left court two years ago, I understand, just before I was called to office. I confess we have a mutual acquaintance,' he added, noting her surprise. 'I believe you knew my cousin, the Earl of Salisbury.'

It took Frances a moment to realise he was referring to William Cecil, who had inherited the title upon the death of his father, her old adversary. She was careful to assume a neutral expression.

'William Cecil, my lady,' Bacon offered, when she did not reply. 'You would have known him as Viscount Cranborne, of course.'

Frances gave a tight smile as she struggled to keep her expression neutral. An image of the young man when she had last seen him flitted before her. He had sought her out as she had walked in the privy gardens at Whitehall, the evening after Prince Henry's death had been announced, to congratulate her on carrying out their plan. In vain, she had protested that the prince had died of a natural sickness, not at her hands. The fear that he still believed her to be a murderess, a heroine of the Catholic cause, had haunted her ever since.

'I did not know you were cousins,' she observed at last, trying to keep her voice light.

Bacon took a sip of wine and helped himself to some trout. 'Second cousins. My mother's sister advanced our family's fortunes greatly when she married William's grandfather, Lord Burghley, though, of course, she did not know it then. Queen Elizabeth came to depend upon him utterly. She called him her "Spirit" '

'My mother respected him greatly, and always said that he placed the Queen's welfare above all else – his own included.'

'He was a most loyal servant,' Bacon agreed, 'more so, perhaps, than our present king has known.'

Frances did not reply. She knew her companion was referring to Burghley's son and successor, Robert Cecil, who had plagued her for so many years. He it was who had conspired to have her arrested for witchcraft, twisting her skills as a healer to further his own ends and convince the new King that he shared his obsession. The ordeal that had followed had intensified her hatred of James and his adviser, inspiring her to commit treason by supporting the Catholic plot to blow up Parliament. Only after his death had it been discovered that Cecil had secretly shared the same faith as those he had condemned.

'How does Lord Salisbury fare?' she asked, deciding to steer the conversation away from his father.

'Very well, I believe,' Bacon replied, toying with a piece of manchet loaf, 'though his duties as Lord Lieutenant of Hertfordshire are proving more burdensome than he expected. I fear it will be a long time before he is at leisure to return to court.'

Good. Frances had come to help her husband, not to be drawn back into the dangerous web of Catholic conspiracies. She glanced at Thomas, who was engaged in conversation with Lionel Cranfield, Earl of Middlesex, a wealthy merchant who yearned for a political career. Although her husband appeared to be listening attentively, she recognised the polite smile of interest and knew that he would be willing the evening to draw to a close.

At that moment, James stood abruptly, causing all of his courtiers to scramble to their feet.

'I propose a toast to Sir George,' he slurred, as he gestured towards his favourite, spilling wine from his glass. Frances saw Somerset swipe irritably at his doublet, the stain already showing on the pale grey satin. Further along the table, Prince Charles was watching his father with a mixture of dismay and embarrassment.

'To Steenie!'

The King's cry was echoed, half-heartedly, by the assembled throng.

'May he be long to reign over us,' Frances heard her companion whisper. She did not know if he was referring to the King or to his favourite.

CHAPTER 8

16 September

The cloister was damp and chill after the mellow sunshine that had warmed her in the privy garden. It was gloomy, too, and Frances slowed her pace so that her eyes could grow used to it. As she rounded the corner, she collided with a gentleman. He made an impatient noise as she stumbled against the wall and pulled her roughly to her feet. She looked up at him in surprise.

Somerset.

His face was deathly white and his eyes were filled with panic. Before she could address him, he pushed past her and strode purposefully in the direction of the King's apartments, a crumpled piece of paper in his hand. Frances watched his retreating back, then continued on her way. *Another spat with Villiers, no doubt.* But he had looked more afraid than angry.

At the far end of the passage, she could see a shaft of light from one of the apartments. As she drew closer, she caught muffled sobs. The door was ajar and she stood close to it, straining her ears for any other sound. She did not know who lived in the apartment, but its proximity to James's privy lodgings suggested it belonged to one of the higher-ranking members of his court. She hesitated. Decorum required her to continue past as if oblivious to the distress of the person within. Besides, she had no desire to

49

involve herself in Somerset's affairs if this related to them, as she was sure it must. But neither could she ignore the suffering of a fellow courtier.

Frances knocked lightly on the door. She heard a stifled sob, then silence. She waited for several moments, unsure whether to knock again. Then she heard the light tread of footsteps and the rustle of skirts from within. The door was pulled slowly back and Lady Somerset stood before her. Her chin was lifted high and her mouth was set in a firm line, but her beautiful eyes were swollen with tears.

'Forgive me, my lady,' Frances said, lowering her gaze so that the young woman could compose herself further. 'I did not mean to intrude upon your privacy, but I wanted to make sure that all was well.'

Lady Somerset remained silent for so long that Frances wondered if she would close the door on her. She glanced up and saw that her eyes had filled with tears again.

'I am quite well, thank you, Lady Tyringham,' she replied. 'It is just an imbalance of humours – caused by the child, no doubt.' She stroked her stomach distractedly.

Frances gave a sympathetic smile. 'You must be eager to set out for Sherborne.'

A shadow crossed the younger woman's face. 'My departure is in some doubt just now. I do not know—' She broke off, her voice cracking.

'Please, my lady,' Frances said, as she took her arm and steered her back into the apartment, closing the door behind her. Once the young woman was comfortably seated, she busied herself with plumping the cushion at her back and pouring her a glass of water. Then she took a seat opposite and waited.

'I am not used to such kindness,' Lady Somerset said quietly. On the few occasions they had talked in the past, Frances had never warmed to her. She was typical of so many other members of James's court, whose true thoughts and motives were concealed behind a veneer of charm and flattery. But it was clear that she was not dissembling now.

'You may have known my husband's former friend, Sir Thomas Overbury?'

The name was familiar to Frances. She remembered some gossip about the nature of their friendship, but that had been swiftly silenced by Somerset as he had risen in the King's favour. Not long after she had left court two years earlier, Thomas had told her that Overbury had been committed to the Tower, charged with contempt for refusing the King's offer of an embassy abroad. James had long been jealous of the intimacy that had existed between the two men. Overbury had died before the King could take any further action against him.

'I do not think I ever met him,' she replied.

'Then you are fortunate indeed, Lady Tyringham,' she retorted, her voice edged with bitterness. 'He was a dark-hearted villain, intent upon destroying anyone who threatened his hold over my husband.'

Including you, Frances thought, but kept her counsel. She had heard it said that Overbury had violently objected to Somerset's plan to marry the beautiful Lady Essex.

'He even defied the King, though he would have found Moscow a good deal more temperate than the Tower. Well, God saw fit to punish his defiance. You know that he died after only a few months of imprisonment?'

Frances nodded. She saw the other woman's hand tremble as she sipped the water.

'No doubt he choked on his own bile,' she went on. 'I confess that I rejoiced at the news, for I would no longer be plagued by him – and neither would my husband.' Her chest heaved as she struggled to control her emotion. 'But it seems that he is resolved to torment me from the grave.'

Her face was now deathly white and Frances saw the same fear in her eyes that she had in Somerset's. She wished she had ignored the impulse to help and continued walking back to her own chambers. She knew all too well that words could carry as much danger as deeds in this court.

'The King has received a letter from Sir Gervase Helwys containing such calumny that I hardly know how to respond.'

'The lieutenant of the Tower?' It had been with some satisfaction that Frances had heard of Sir William Wade's dismissal from that post. He must have expected to live out his days in his comfortable lodgings there: just reward for having hounded Tom and the other Powder Treason plotters to their deaths.

Lady Somerset nodded miserably. 'He alleges that Overbury was poisoned at my orders.'

Frances felt suddenly cold.

'My husband has denied it, of course, but he suspects me still,' she continued, twisting the russet silk of her skirt between her fingers. 'How could he believe that I, his own wife, would stoop to murder?' She clamped her hand over her mouth as if to suppress another onslaught of sobbing.

'Did Sir Gervase provide any proof, my lady?' she asked.

Her companion looked utterly wretched. 'He claims to have the written testimony of an apothecary from Yorkshire. Yorkshire!' she cried, her voice rising in agitation. 'I have no connection with that part of the kingdom and have never travelled further north than Oxford.'

Frances regarded the young woman closely. She seemed in earnest, and her panic-stricken eyes reminded Frances of a rabbit caught in a trap, the jagged spikes cutting ever deeper into its flesh as it struggled to free itself. 'How did His Majesty respond to the claims?' she asked.

Lady Somerset gave a heavy sigh and pressed her delicate white fingers to her brow. 'Robert says he has persuaded him that it is nothing but slander and the King seems inclined to let the matter rest. But already there is gossip. I wish I was far from here. I cannot bear to hear the lies that they will whisper against me – against my husband, too.'

'There is always gossip, my lady,' Frances soothed, 'most of it based upon half-truths and hearsay. The court will soon have fresh matter to occupy their conversations at dinner.' She hoped her smile conveyed greater certainty than she felt. Somerset's enemies would be quick to seize upon this – Villiers more than anyone.

The young woman's face hardened and she stood abruptly. 'I have detained you for too long, Lady Tyringham,' she said, her voice clipped.

Frances remained seated as she held the cold stare. Lady Somerset had taken a risk in confiding in her. Her own husband was one of the King's favourites and, for all that this young woman knew, he might twist the controversy to his advantage. 'You may rely upon my discretion, my lady,' Frances said, rising to her feet. 'I hope that the matter will soon be forgotten and you can journey to Sherborne as planned. The welfare of your child is of far greater importance than the fleeting scandals of this place.'

Her companion remained tight-lipped as Frances curtsied and walked slowly from the room. She had travelled only a few paces when the sound of the door slamming echoed along the cloister.

The King had decided to dine in private that evening with just a handful of favoured attendants. Frances knew she should count herself blessed to be among them – it was rare that the invitation extended to their wives – but the encounter with Lady Somerset had unnerved her and she found herself longing for the seclusion of the apartment.

So far, the conversation had been limited to the forthcoming hunting expedition, for which Frances was grateful. It had also enabled her husband to hold his master's attention for longer than usual when Villiers was present. She could not help feeling a stab of triumph at Sir George's obvious irritation. Lady Somerset was also present and looked radiant in a gown of azure blue satin, her creamy white bosom showing above the daringly low neckline. Her eyes had regained their former sparkle and she seemed the perfect model of composure as she listened with rapt attention to the chatter, even though Frances guessed that her nerves must be pulled as taut as her bodice.

'Tell me, Rob, what news of the Tower?'

The words were softly spoken but cut across the conversation like a rapier blade through silk. Frances darted a glance at Somerset, who bristled at his rival's familiarity. Next to her, his wife remained perfectly still and Frances sensed she was holding her breath.

'All is well, I believe, George,' he replied nonchalantly, then took a swig of wine. 'When shall we depart for Hertfordshire, Your Grace?' he continued, turning to the King. 'The weather seems set fair so we ought not delay.'

James opened his mouth to reply, but Villiers cut in. 'Oh?' he said, raising an eyebrow. 'Have you received no further reports of the Lady Arbella? I hear she lies mortally sick. I am surprised there are no rumours of foul play. You know how people like to gossip whenever there is news of sickness.'

'God grant the meddlesome woman soon chokes out her breath,' James muttered, reaching forward to spear a large piece of venison. 'She has done nothing but plague me since I took the throne of this Godforsaken kingdom.'

Frances's scalp prickled at the mention of the King's most notorious prisoner. Though she had been embroiled in the plot to put Arbella Stuart on the throne, she had never had any desire to further the arrogant woman's schemes.

'I am sure her miserable life will soon be at an end, Your Grace,' Sir George simpered. 'Perhaps you should ask Rob to speed Death's progress. He and his beautiful wife have more experience than most in such matters.'

'Damn you, Villiers!' Somerset cried, leaping to his feet. A goblet clattered to the floor, its contents spilling red on the white marble tiles. 'What do you mean by that?'

Sir George affected a look of surprise, but Frances saw his mouth twitch at the corners. 'Why, my dear Rob, how flushed you are! I do hope you have not caught a fever. You know that we must not put His Grace at risk of contagion.'

'Answer me, churl,' Somerset muttered, his voice dangerously low.

'Peace, my lords.' Thomas's voice echoed in the ensuing silence. He stood and placed a restraining hand on Somerset's arm, but was angrily shaken off. The King looked from one favourite to the other with a mixture of dismay and, Frances thought, anticipation.

After several tense moments, Sir George gave a shrug, then tore off a piece of bread, chewing it slowly and deliberately while his rival glared at him, waiting for a response. When he had finished the mouthful, he took a sip of wine. 'I meant only that you have both suffered the loss of those close to you – as have many others at this court,' he drawled as he set down his glass. 'I cannot imagine what insult you thought I was levying at you.'

The earl's jaw tightened as he scowled at his rival. His wife remained still and her eyes never left him. James leaned forward in his chair, no longer troubling to conceal his excitement. After a long moment, Somerset turned to his royal master and gave a stiff bow, then stalked from the room. Frances heard Lady Somerset exhale softly before she rose to her feet, curtsied and followed in her husband's wake.

CHAPTER 9

19 September

'Must you leave?' Frances murmured, as Thomas bent to kiss her.

It was still early and the light in the chamber was dim. She could hear the patter of rain against the casement window and the room felt colder than it had for the past few days.

Her husband sat on the edge of the bed and pulled on his riding boots. 'Believe me, I wish I did not have to ride out in this. The roads beyond the city will already be treacherous. It has been raining for hours.'

Frances stroked his back. 'You slept ill again?'

'It is my own fault – I indulged too much at last night's feast.'

She knew it was a lie. The dark shadows under his eyes told of the restless nights he had spent this week. It pained her to think that the comfort she had offered had proved so fleeting. What little she had seen of Sir George Villiers had convinced her that he was the cause of her husband's anxiety. Thomas spoke of him only seldom, but she could guess at the daily taunts and sideswipes he had to suffer at the favourite's hands. It must make his position intolerable, as it was for all others who were close to the King – Somerset in particular.

The hostility between the two men had deepened since that evening in the King's privy chamber. Thomas had told her how

Villiers had delighted in taunting his rival with hints about the controversy surrounding Overbury's death, without ever naming him directly. Everyone at court now knew of it. There were whispered conversations at dinner about apothecaries and poison, which stopped abruptly whenever Somerset entered the room. Frances suspected that Villiers had spread most of the gossip.

'How long will you be away?'

His shoulders sagged. 'I wish I knew. A week? Two, perhaps, if we have to wait until the weather improves.'

Frances moved closer and circled her arms around him, laying her head against his back. 'I shall miss you,' she whispered.

'And I you,' he replied, trailing his fingers over her warm skin. 'More than I can say.'

He made no move to go, and for a moment Frances hoped that he might stay with her in the quiet chamber, cocooned from the dangers of the world beyond. But he rose to his feet and slowly pulled on his cloak.

'Promise me you will stay out of mischief while I'm gone.' His smile did not quite reach his eyes as he leaned over to kiss her again.

She held his face in her hands. 'And you must promise to come home safe to me.'

After passing through the gatehouse, Frances stood at the entrance to the vast courtyard and gazed around her. She had passed Denmark House – or Somerset Place, as it had been then – many times when she had served the princess. It lay on the south side of the Strand, which was one of the busiest thoroughfares of the city, leading east to the Tower and west to Whitehall and St James's. The high wall that ran along the northernmost end of the courtyard meant that little of the mansion within could be glimpsed from the street. It had once belonged to Edward Seymour, Duke of Somerset, but upon his arrest for treason it had been forfeit to the Crown.

Frances had heard that Queen Anne had made a number of improvements to the house, but she had not expected it to be so grand – or so extensive. To either side of her, an elegant two-storey building stretched the length of the courtyard, and the low wall at the far end afforded a sweeping view of the river. In contrast to the cobbled courtyards of the other palaces, two huge, beautifully manicured lawns covered the quadrant. The one to Frances's right was lined with neatly trimmed yews – Anne's favourite. She hoped the Queen's health had improved enough for her to stroll among them when the weather was more clement.

The porter had directed her to the large door of a building on the western wall. It was higher than the rest and fronted by an elegant Palladian façade that contrasted with the Tudor style of the other apartments. Frances made her way towards it now.

She had been glad to receive the Queen's invitation earlier that day. Thomas's departure had left her bereft, as usual – but uneasy too. She hated to think of him so far away, with little except James's fickle favour to protect him from Villiers and his schemes. An audience with Anne not only provided some much-needed diversion, but also offered Frances the prospect of being able to do something to help her husband. Even though the Queen seldom attended her husband's court, she had always been well informed of everything that passed there. She was sure to know all about this loathsome new favourite. Frances was determined to find out everything she could. She remembered a remark that her old enemy Robert Cecil had once made: *It is often those details that seem of the smallest consequence that hold the greatest import.* The more knowledge she was able to gather about Villiers, the more likely she was to discover a weakness.

When she reached the door to Anne's apartments, the yeomen of the guard nodded her through. The presence chamber was deserted, but the sound of retreating footsteps indicated that an attendant had been sent to announce her arrival. The large windows flooded the room with light, even on a day such as this.

Frances admired the tasteful furnishings, which were far less extravagant than Anne's status demanded. The delicate scent of rose oil filled the chamber, rendering it much sweeter than those at Whitehall or St James's, where the air was made foetid by the constant crush of bodies.

Frances heard footsteps again – slower this time – and a few moments later Anne entered the chamber. As she rose from her curtsy, Frances was surprised to see that she was unattended. Anne had aged considerably since she had last seen her at the princess's wedding two and a half years before. Her hair had turned from light blond to white and her figure had grown even stouter. She leaned heavily on an ivory staff as she shuffled to the ornate chair underneath the canopy, then bade Frances to sit close by.

'How good it is to see you again, Lady Frances – and looking so well,' she said, reaching over to pat her hand. 'Marriage agrees with you.'

Frances smiled. 'I am blessed in my husband, Your Majesty – and for that, I shall ever be in your debt.'

She had been a good deal less grateful when she had first learned that Anne had prompted Thomas's proposal all those years ago. The Queen had confided to him that Frances had left court because she was carrying Tom Wintour's child. She would not have betrayed her confidence unless she had been sure that Thomas would come to her assistance. Frances knew that now, but at the time she had been furious. She would never have predicted that her prospective husband would become the love of her life.

Anne returned her smile. 'I am glad of it. You deserve such happiness, after all you have suffered.'

'And how does Your Grace fare?' Frances asked.

'Oh, my joints pain me more than ever,' the Queen replied, 'and I am tormented by an ulcer on my leg. I can quite see why old King Henry became such a tyrant in his later years,' she added, with a wry smile. 'But I take the waters at Greenwich often – Bath too, when I am strong enough for the journey – and my physicians have become my constant companions.'

Frances felt a wave of pity. Even though Anne was making light of it, she knew how much she must suffer. 'I would be glad to attend you myself, if you would permit me, Your Grace,' she offered.

'Thank you, my dear – though we would need to employ discretion, of course. Sir Thomas might be a favourite with the King, but my husband would not hesitate to have you arrested for witchcraft if he heard of it.'

Frances seized the opportunity. 'My husband has been eclipsed of late, Your Grace, as have others in the King's service.'

Anne gave a knowing smile and sank back in her chair. 'You mean his "angel", I suppose. I met Sir George a few months ago and understood at once why my husband is so enraptured. I have never seen such a pretty fellow. His delicate features and white skin must be the envy of all the ladies at court.'

Many times in the past Frances had wondered how the Queen had borne the humiliation of her husband's infidelities. He had done little to conceal them. Did the shame lessen with each bright-eyed young favourite he paraded in front of her? She doubted it, somehow.

'My ladies tell me that the King was heard to lament that he cannot make Villiers his wife,' Anne continued.

Frances failed to hide her dismay. 'I am sorry, Your Grace. How can you bear it?'

'I do not bear it, my dear,' she replied. 'I encourage it.'

Frances looked at her sharply.

'The King and I have not shared a bed since I fell pregnant with poor Sophia,' she went on. 'It was a difficult birth and left me with . . . well, no prospect of more children. So there was little point. Do not think to pity me,' she added, seeing Frances's expression. 'Daily I rejoice that my conjugal duties are at an end – in that respect, at least. And, given the pleasure I take in my own freedom, it would be churlish of me to begrudge my husband his.

Pray, would you pour me a glass of that cordial, my dear?' she asked, indicating the pewter flagon on the table by the window.

A sharp aroma filled Frances's nostrils as she did so. She recognised sage and marjoram, but there was something else too. Whatever it was, she hoped it would bring Anne relief. As she handed her the glass, she noticed that a sheen of perspiration had formed on her brow. *How greatly she must suffer.* Frances resolved to prepare a tincture for her that evening.

'Forgive me, Your Grace,' she said, when the Queen had recovered her composure, 'but you said you had encouraged this latest favourite. Surely that cannot be true. I was at Apethorpe last summer and witnessed their first meeting. From what I saw then and have heard since, Villiers needed no such assistance.'

Anne held her gaze. 'That is true – in part, at least. His looks were more than enough to recommend him. But my husband is not so easily manipulated as many believe. Often he takes his pleasure and rewards the giver only with fair words and promises. Somerset was clever enough to secure promotions, but most are not. If I had not intervened, Villiers would have remained a humble cupbearer.'

Frances stared. She had always respected Anne for her judgement and discretion. Had she, too, been deceived by Villiers's beguiling smile and easy charm?

'When I heard that Somerset had succeeded in frustrating his rival's ambitions for a place in the bedchamber, I invited Villiers to dine with me here,' the Queen continued. 'I knew that he lacked opportunity to spend time with the King alone – Somerset had made sure of that after their return from the progress. So I invited my husband, too. We made quite a merry party.' She chuckled, noting Frances's astonishment. 'I was a generous host and ensured the King's glass was always full of the Madeira wine of which he is so fond. It took only a mention or two of a bedchamber post that had lain vacant for some time to prompt him. By the time our feast was at an end, my husband had promised it to Villiers. I left them alone then, to seal the bargain.'

'But why?' Frances whispered. 'Sir George is ruthless and grasping, and will stop at nothing in his pursuit of power. He is a danger to all who serve your husband – perhaps even to the King himself.'

A flicker of a smile. 'He is all of those things, Lady Frances,' Anne replied quietly. 'But he is more, besides. Do not think that I have taken leave of my senses in placing this devil in our midst. In time, you will understand that he is our salvation.'

CHAPTER 10

25 September

At first Frances thought that she had imagined it. She waited, straining her ears for any sound. There it was again: a sharp tap. It seemed to come from the direction of the window. She pulled back the covers and, shivering against the cold, padded quietly over to it. Opening the shutters, she peered down into the courtyard. A young woman was staring up at her. Her face was obscured by the hood of her dark cloak, which was drawn tightly around her.

'Lady Frances?' Her whisper carried on the still night air.

Frances nodded, mute. *Was it Thomas? The boys?*

The woman spoke no more but beckoned urgently. Frances hesitated for just a moment, then turned and dressed hurriedly, her trembling fingers fumbling with the ties of her skirt. She was just about to open the door when a thought occurred to her. Moving quickly to the dresser, she drew out the small casket from under her neatly folded linens and, unlocking it, pulled out a selection of tiny phials. She knew it was dangerous to have brought them here, but her herbs and tinctures were part of her now. She could as well relinquish them as her own soul.

When she reached the courtyard, the young woman was still standing beneath her window. She turned at Frances's approach.

'Please, Lady Frances, you must come with me.' Seeing Frances's hesitation, she drew something out of her pocket and gave it to her. 'A trusted friend sent me.'

Frances glanced down at the gold signet ring in her hand. It was engraved with an elaborate R. She recognised it at once. *Raleigh*. He always wore it on the little finger of his right hand.

Not pausing to think any further, she followed the woman out of the courtyard, taking care to keep to the shadows even though the palace was deserted. She had no idea what time it was. With the King away on the hunt, there had been no feasting or entertainment that evening and she had retired early again.

They soon reached the water gate, where a boat was waiting for them. When they were seated, the oarsman pushed the vessel away from the landing stage and began to row eastwards.

'Where are we going?' Frances asked.

Her companion darted a glance at the oarsman. 'The Tower,' she replied, then gave Frances a look that made clear she must ask no more questions.

With the tide in their favour, progress was rapid. Frances tried to order her thoughts for whatever lay ahead. She reflected upon the last time she had seen Sir Walter. The sun had not yet risen on that cold October morning when she had visited him at the Tower. He had given her the mandrake root with which to prepare her deadly tincture for the prince. *God speed your endeavours, Lady Frances*. She could hear the words so clearly that it was as if he were sitting next to her now, whispering them in her ear. It still made her shudder to think of how close she had come to murdering the King's eldest son and heir. In the event, Prince Henry had breathed his last a few hours after she had left his chamber, the stoppered tincture full to the brim in her pocket. She had taken it as a sign that God was pleased with the more righteous path she had chosen.

Although she had felt betrayed when she had discovered the extent of Raleigh's involvement in William Cecil's plot, her anger had soon abated. She and Raleigh had shared many confidences during her visits to the Tower, and she had grown fond of him. He had been the King's prisoner for more than twelve years now. His lodgings were comfortable and he enjoyed greater liberties than most of the Tower's other residents, but Frances could not imagine being held captive for so long, not knowing whether the prospect of execution or pardon was more likely. She wondered if James would ever decide upon his fate, or if he hoped that God would make the decision for him.

They rounded the next bend in the river and the familiar outline of the Tower loomed into view, the mass of its central keep dwarfing the surrounding buildings. Frances felt another jolt of apprehension. She had a creeping suspicion, too, of whom she was here to attend. The boatman was drawing level with St Thomas's Tower now. As they passed under its sprawling archway, Frances could see the moonlight reflecting off the stone steps that led from the waterside, their edges worn smooth by the tread of hundreds of traitors who had passed that way. Tom's had been among them.

A yeoman stood sentry at the top of the steps. Frances saw the woman press some coins into his hand and he nodded them through. A single brazier lit the narrow walkway that led from the landing stage to the heart of the Tower. Once or twice, Frances stumbled on the cobbles as she followed the young woman under the archway of the Bloody Tower. She glanced upwards as if expecting to see Raleigh above. They mounted the steps to the green and her companion made for the small, squat tower next to the one in which Frances had been tortured as a suspected witch all those years before. With a jolt, she remembered that this was Arbella Stuart's lodging.

The King's cousin had been as much a thorn in his side as she had his predecessor's. Her royal blood had made her an irresistible prospect for disaffected subjects for at least twenty years. Frances remembered seeing her for the first time at the old Queen's court. Even then, she had been a proud, haughty young woman. Her arrogance had deepened in the years that followed, blinding her to the danger of hankering after the throne she saw as hers by right. She had been a prisoner for five years now, Frances calculated.

Her companion knocked softly on the outer door and it was opened. Frances followed her inside, mouthing a silent prayer. They climbed the stairs to the upper floor and entered Arbella's chamber. All was quiet within and briefly Frances thought it was deserted. But as her eyes slowly adjusted to the gloom, she saw a woman lying on the bed underneath a large canopy. She kept perfectly still as Frances moved towards her. The room smelt stale, as if no life had stirred within it for many years.

When she had drawn level with the head of the bed, Frances motioned for her companion to bring her the solitary candle that burned on the fireplace. Holding it close to the woman's face, Frances suppressed a gasp. Arbella was hardly recognisable from when she had last seen her. Her cheeks were sunken and the bones at the base of her neck showed through her wasted skin. Already she had the appearance of a cadaver. Although she could only be forty years old – five years older than Frances – there were just a few red hairs among the thin white strands that covered her skull.

Frances could not tell if she was still breathing so drew nearer. The stale aroma grew stronger as she brought her face close to Arbella's, trying to feel any warmth emanating from her dry lips, which were slightly apart. Nothing. Suddenly her eyes sprang open. Frances leaped back in shock and the candle fell from her grasp, plunging them into darkness.

'I will fetch another,' the attendant called, as she fumbled for the latch. Frances heard the door click shut and felt paralysed by terror. As she reached for the edge of the bed so that she might steady herself, an icy hand grasped her wrist.

'This king will perish,' Arbella's voice rasped, close to her ear. 'My husband is poised to strike.'

She broke off, gasping for breath. Frances held her own as she waited, heart thrumming.

'He has gathered a mighty army in Flanders and will sail across the Channel as soon as the King of Spain's fleet reaches Ostend.'

Frances's wrist throbbed as Arbella tightened her grip, the bony fingers pressing into her flesh. Desperately, she tried to calm her racing thoughts. She had heard such treasonous talk before. But for all his promises – real or imagined – the King of Spain had never stirred himself for invasion. Why should she believe that he was any more likely to do so now?

Arbella's short, grating breaths echoed in the darkness as Frances waited for her to continue. She could not have spoken a word in response, even if she had wished to.

'You must help him,' Arbella urged, then fell into a paroxysm of coughing.

Seymour?

At that moment, the young woman returned, a burning taper in her hand. Quickly, she moved to pick up the candle that lay at Frances's feet and lit it again. It seemed to glow much brighter now.

'Can you ease her suffering?' the attendant asked, as Frances kept her eyes fixed on the waxen skin of Arbella's face.

Frances knew that she was beyond all help; even the smallest drop of one of her tinctures would not slip down her swollen throat. Besides, it was safer to do nothing. She had no desire to be under suspicion of causing another death. She gave a slight shake of her head and heard a small sob escape the young woman's lips, before it was quickly suppressed.

Arbella's eyes opened again, and as she stared at Frances they blazed with the intensity she remembered so well. Despite all the danger in which the woman's schemes had placed her in the past, Frances could feel only pity for her now. She could see no obvious cause for her affliction: there was no fever, and she did not appear to be in pain from a tumour. Upon Frances's last visit to the Tower, Raleigh had told her that his fellow prisoner seemed likely to starve herself to death. At the time, Frances had thought it just another of Arbella's ploys to win attention, now that she could no longer be at the centre of plots against the King. But as she gazed at her skeletal form, she knew that Raleigh had been right.

'Raleigh.'

Frances jumped to hear Arbella whisper his name, as if she could read her thoughts.

'Help him,' she rasped, her breath rattling in her throat.

Frances watched as the woman's gaze became fixed and her chest fell still. Several moments passed, but all was silent.

'My lady?' the attendant whispered, moving slowly towards her mistress.

Frances rose to her feet and discreetly traced the sign of the cross over her chest. As she moved past the young woman, she saw that her eyes glistened with tears. She said nothing, but walked quietly from the room.

As soon as she was outside, she drew in a deep lungful of the cool morning air. The first tendrils of light were showing on the horizon and the faint shrill of birdsong echoed around the walls. With sudden resolve, Frances quickened her pace in the direction of Raleigh's apartment.

CHAPTER II

25 September

'Lady Frances,' Raleigh said, with genuine warmth, as he turned from the window to greet her. She knew that he would have seen her approaching, but he had always welcomed her as if she were the only person in the world he wished to see. She returned his smile and caught a glimmer of uncertainty in his eyes. *Did he fear she would rail against him for concealing the part he had played in William Cecil's plot?* If so, then he soon recovered himself. As she drew close to him, he took her hand and pressed it to his lips. 'It does my soul good to see you again.'

Frances gave a small smile, then reached in her pocket and drew out his signet ring. 'I believe this is yours.'

Raleigh looked contrite. 'Forgive me for disturbing your slumbers, my lady. I had heard that you had returned to court and could think of no one more suited to help that poor lady.' He turned and looked out across the green.

'I'm afraid I could do nothing, Sir Walter,' Frances replied quietly. 'She is with God now.'

A long breath escaped Raleigh's lips. 'Then I pray He grants her greater peace than she enjoyed in this world.'

'Arbella spoke of you,' Frances said. 'With her last breath, she urged me to help you.'

Raleigh turned back to her. 'Oh?' he remarked, raising an eyebrow. 'That was most kind of her but I have everything I require.'

Frances no longer had the patience for the hints and riddles that her companion had always indulged in. 'Are you involved in the plot she spoke of? She said her husband stands ready to invade as soon as the King of Spain joins forces with him.'

Raleigh's eyes widened and the smile faded from his lips. 'Come, let us sit by the fire. I will have my servant fetch some wine.'

'I cannot stay,' Frances said abruptly. 'I must return to Whitehall before my absence is noted.' It was not entirely a lie. Even though her formal duties there had ceased, she had often caught the curious stares of her fellow courtiers as she walked through the public rooms or took her place at dinner. No doubt the story of her arrest for witchcraft had been repeated – and embellished – by those who had been there to witness it. It made her yearn for the simple domesticity of her life at Tyringham Hall, with her precious children and woodlands for company.

'Then let us move from the window, at least.' Raleigh cupped her elbow and steered her towards the middle of the room. He picked up his pipe from the small table nearby and lit it with a taper he dipped into the embers of the fire. He sucked on it deeply, then blew out a long plume of smoke. Frances had loved the earthy smell ever since she had been a girl and had watched, mesmerised, as her father had prepared the tobacco, rubbing it between his fingers before pressing it down into his pipe. Five years had passed since his death but she missed him keenly. She knew she always would.

'I have petitioned His Majesty to release me from this place so that I might undertake an expedition in his name,' Sir Walter began. 'For several years now he has been obsessed with the idea of finding El Dorado.'

'The City of Gold?' Frances could not keep the scorn from her voice. She had heard many outlandish tales about the mythical kingdom from returning adventurers, eager to entice their patrons into funding a fresh voyage. Raleigh himself had undertaken one during the closing years of Elizabeth's reign, journeying to the furthermost edge of Africa with the promise of bountiful riches echoing in his ears. His fleet had returned laden with nothing more than some brightly coloured silks and caskets of exotic spices. Her mother had told of the Queen's fury. But it had not deterred Raleigh from launching another expedition the following year, with no more success.

'Surely you do not still believe that it exists,' Frances said, incredulous.

Sir Walter's mouth twitched. 'The beliefs of a humble subject are of no consequence next to those of a king. If His Grace desires it, then I shall set sail as soon as a fleet can be assembled.'

Frances regarded him closely. 'You plan to escape by this means?'

Raleigh clicked his tongue and affected a wounded expression. 'You think me so faithless a subject, my lady? No, I will be true to my word. King James is plagued by fear that his rival the King of Spain will reach the city first. I have therefore pledged to intercept Philip's fleet before it leaves the port at Cádiz.'

'Intercept . . . or join it, perhaps,' Frances wondered.

Raleigh did not answer at first, but his eyes glistened with triumph. 'Your mind is as sharp as ever, my dear,' he said eventually. 'The expedition to El Dorado will indeed be a joint venture between King Philip and me. The gold that we find there will enable us to assemble the mightiest fleet in history. King James's navy will be as child's boats fashioned from parchment. We will blow it away – thus,' he said, puffing out one of the candles on the fireplace.

'Nobody has yet succeeded in finding the City of Gold,' Frances pointed out. 'You yourself failed more than twenty years ago.'

Sir Walter's smile did not waver. 'Ah, but I discovered enough to convince me of its existence. I will not fail a third time. And with its riches, King Philip and I will set James's son Charles upon the throne.'

Frances thought of the pale-faced young man whom she had seen at the feast three weeks before. Though he was his father's heir, she could not imagine him ever growing in strength enough to wield power over the kingdom. But perhaps therein lay his appeal for Philip: the boy would be little more than a puppet, just as his elder sister Elizabeth would have been if the Powder Treason had succeeded. 'What has this to do with me?' she persisted, her voice edged with impatience.

'At present, the King's mistrust of me is proving stronger than his desire for riches. I require those who wield influence to speak on my behalf.'

Frances looked doubtful. 'You cannot think that I enjoy such influence. Even when I served his daughter, I was powerless to sway his opinions.'

Sir Walter sucked at his pipe. 'Ah, but the same is not true of your husband, I think.'

'I will not involve Thomas in this,' she snapped. 'I returned to court to help him, not plunge him into even greater danger.' She stopped, angry with herself for having said that much.

Raleigh's eyes searched hers, but he did not press her to explain. 'Any man would rejoice to have such a faithful wife,' he said, without a trace of irony. 'But Sir Thomas is not the only man who has the King's ear. I have heard much of young Villiers.'

Frances sniffed. 'You cannot hope for assistance from that quarter. Sir George serves only himself.'

Raleigh blew out another long plume of smoke. 'Then I must find a way to persuade him that he stands to gain from the expedition,' he mused, almost to himself. 'The dazzle of gold has blinded many a man to the darkness that lies at its core, Lady Frances.'

'I am so glad to see you,' Frances said as she buried her face in her husband's chest. She felt his lips against her scalp as he wound her hair around his fingers.

Thomas had been waiting for her when she had returned from her customary afternoon walk in the palace gardens. She had felt almost giddy with relief and joy to see him standing there, arms outstretched.

'I had not dared to hope it would be so soon,' he replied. 'We had only three days' hunting, once the rains had abated, and there was the promise of many more. But the King seemed suddenly anxious to return to London.'

'Was it the news of Arbella's death?' she asked, trailing her fingers idly down his back.

'I did not expect it to have reached the court so soon,' Thomas remarked. 'The King plans to announce it at this evening's feast.'

Frances drew away so that she could look at him as she spoke. She had thought of keeping it from him, but she knew from bitter experience how secrets gnawed at the intimacy between them. 'I only know of it because I was summoned to attend her.'

Thomas grew pale at her words. 'Frances, no!'

'Please,' she said, clasping his hands in hers. 'I did not know whom I was going to see. Her servant came here in the middle of the night and begged me to accompany her. You know that I cannot forsake the skills that God gave me.'

Her husband still looked aghast, but she continued before he could interrupt, telling him of Arbella's wasted limbs, of the words she had spoken before she died, of her visit to Raleigh. When at last she had finished, he remained silent for so long that she wished she had kept her counsel. But something in his expression told her that he did not share the shock she had experienced upon first hearing the revelations.

At length, he went to the table and poured two glasses of wine. He held one out to her, then sank onto a chair next to the fire. She moved to join him, trying to push down her mounting unease.

'I am glad that you chose to confide in me this time,' he began, 'but it brings shame on me too.' He sipped his wine. Frances brought her glass to her lips, though her throat felt too tight to swallow. 'I knew something of this voyage Raleigh is planning. I overheard the King speak of it to Villiers and made some discreet enquiries. It is many years since I was in Flanders, but I have acquaintances there still.'

Frances felt as if she was looking at a stranger. She knew that her husband had spent time in Flanders, quietly garnering support for Tom and his fellow plotters. But the pledge he had made her take on their marriage had been enough to convince her that he, too, would sever all contact with that part of his life.

'Do not think I have deceived you all these years,' he went on. 'It was the first time that I have revived such contact. What I learned was enough to make me think I had cause to doubt Raleigh's professed purpose in making this voyage – and you have confirmed it.'

'He surely has no hope of success,' Frances said. 'Even if the King could be persuaded to release him, there is little reason to suppose that the Spanish will stir themselves for an invasion – or that Seymour has gathered the army he boasts about.'

'I have proof of that, at least,' her husband replied. 'Arbella's husband has put his time in exile to profitable use, it seems.' He took another sip. 'And Philip has already amassed a huge fleet at Cádiz.'

Frances fell back in her chair. This was the moment for which all of England's Catholic subjects had been poised since the heretical King had taken the throne. Once she had counted herself among them. But that part of her had died with Prince Henry. Ever since she had been content to keep her faith only in her heart – as Thomas had urged her. She looked at him now. Although his brow was creased with concern, she saw that his eyes were alight with a fervour that made her blood run cold.

CHAPTER 12

3 October

It was an unseasonably warm day and the late summer flowers that had been wilting on their stems seemed to open their blooms to the sun. Frances inhaled their heady fragrance as she strolled alongside the neatly kept borders. She had been delighted at Sir Francis Bacon's invitation to join him on an excursion to St James's Park. They had seen each other often since their first meeting a month before. Her new friend had been so kind and attentive, showing such genuine interest in her thoughts and opinions, that her initial shyness had soon faded.

If Thomas was jealous, he did not show it. Frances knew he had no reason to be. Although Bacon clearly enjoyed the company of women – herself in particular – she had never once seen the flicker of desire in his eyes. Perhaps his passions lay elsewhere. Besides, her husband could hardly complain if she sought diversion. Even when he was not away on the hunt, his duties occupied him for most of the day because he needed to ensure that the buckhounds had sufficient exercise.

'*Myrtus communis*,' Bacon muttered, as he stooped to pluck one of the dark green stems. 'It will bring down a fever more quickly than anything else I have tried.'

And numb even the most severe pain, Frances thought, but merely nodded politely. Friendly though they had become, she knew better than to confide her knowledge of healing to so new an acquaintance.

'I will gather a few more sprigs now, to add to my collection,' he said, drawing out a pair of exquisite silver scissors from his pocket.

Frances experienced a jolt of envy. Bacon was respected as a man of science, and his interest in the natural world was therefore accepted and encouraged. If she spoke so openly of such matters, or was seen to be gathering herbs and plants with which to make remedies, she would be hanged as a witch.

'If you have every species of which you have written then it must be extensive indeed,' Frances observed, as her companion snipped at the myrtle.

Bacon gave a theatrical sigh. 'Alice quite despairs of it. She complains that York House is so full of my treasures there is no room for hers.'

Frances had known that Bacon was married, but the better acquainted they had become, the more it had surprised her.

'Cardinal Wolsey's former palace? There must be room enough for a whole woodland of species.' She had passed the mansion on her visit to the Queen two weeks before. It occupied a vast tract of land on the south side of the Strand and was second only to Denmark House in splendour.

Her companion chuckled. 'Ah, it is the same with plants as with books: one always needs space for more.'

Frances smiled. 'That is true. My husband has already extended the library at Tyringham twice since our marriage. Does your wife share your interests?'

His expression clouded. 'Sadly not, Lady Frances. She is much younger than I – we were betrothed when she was just eleven. Her time is spent counting her jewels and ordering new gowns. It is my own fault. I spoiled her during our courtship.'

'I do not think I have seen her at Whitehall,' Frances said.

Bacon shook his head. 'She prefers the company of her gems to that of the King and his courtiers.'

Frances resisted the temptation to say that in this, at least, she was in accord with her – though it was the company of her books she preferred, not her modest collection of jewels.

'You cannot have much leisure to pursue your studies, now that you are attorney general.' She moved the conversation away from his marriage.

'The burden of office does indeed weigh heavily upon my shoulders at present. I hope, in time, to use my proximity to the King to further the cause of scientific discovery.'

They exchanged a look.

'It will be akin to the labours of Hercules, I admit,' he added, rolling his eyes. Frances grinned. Her new friend's irreverence was one of the qualities she admired most in him. 'But perhaps the strength of his piety will bring him to understand their import-ance. "All knowledge appeareth to be a plant of God's own planting," the prophet Daniel tells us. It is beholden of all His people to help it spread and flourish.'

James never tired of reminding his subjects that he was God's representative on earth. He had justified all manner of acts on the basis that he was carrying out God's work, hunting down witches principal among them. She had wondered many times how God must view His servant's other activities. Surely even James was not so great a hypocrite as to suppose He smiled upon them.

They lapsed into silence as they continued their progress through the park. Looking at the trees on its western edge, Frances noticed that the leaves were already tinged with brown. The woods that surrounded Tyringham Hall were at their most beautiful in autumn, gold, red and rich brown. John had delighted in watching the leaves fall, scampering around the forest to catch them in his plump little fingers. She would miss him doing the same this year, would miss his infant brother's wonder at the spectacle. Pray God her husband's affairs here would soon grow more settled so that she could visit their sons before the onset of winter.

'Tell me, Lady Frances, what do you make of this matter with Somerset's former acquaintance?' her companion asked, distracting her from her melancholy thoughts.

'Sir Thomas Overbury?' she replied. It was safer not to confide what she knew of the matter. 'I hardly know. I was not at court when he died.'

'Hmm. It is a curious business. He was an objectionable sort of fellow and guarded his friendship with Somerset jealously. He despised Lady Somerset – the Countess of Essex, as she was then – on sight and did everything he could to obstruct their marriage. When I heard of his death in the Tower, I assumed he had choked on the gall of envy and spite. But perhaps it was something even more bitter.'

'Rumours of poison often accompany sudden deaths, particularly those of note,' Frances said dismissively. An image of Prince Henry flitted before her, his lips parted as she brought the deadly tincture to them.

'True enough,' Bacon conceded, 'but I wonder why there were no such rumours at the time. It is only now, two years later, that there is talk of foul play.'

'I am sure the court gossips will soon turn to other matters,' she replied, pretending to focus on a flock of wild geese that had just landed on the large expanse of water to their left.

'Perhaps.' A pause. 'But when such rumours emerge so suddenly, one must always consider whom they serve.'

Frances did not reply. She knew that he was referring to Sir George Villiers. Her suspicion that he had started the rumours had deepened into a firm conviction over the past few weeks. Thomas had also voiced it, though he had been careful to keep his counsel in the public court. He had no desire to sharpen Villiers's antipathy towards him.

They were nearing the gates at the eastern edge of the park now. Frances was in no hurry to return to Whitehall but knew that her companion would soon be required there. He motioned for her to pass through ahead of him. She had just walked out onto the street when the thundering of hoofs made her step back into the gateway. Bacon stood next to her, shielding his eyes as he gazed towards the carriage. She saw his expression harden as it drew level with them, but it passed so quickly that she caught only a fleeting glance of the white-haired man inside. As the carriage retreated from view, she could just make out an elaborate red and blue crest on the back. She struggled to think where she had seen it before.

'Do you know him?' she asked, turning back to her companion.

He nodded, tight-lipped. 'Yes – though I wish it were otherwise,' he muttered. 'Sir Edward Coke.'

Frances's blood ran cold. He had presided over the trial of the Powder Treason plotters. She could still hear his sonorous voice echoing around the lofty chamber of Westminster Hall, urging the severest penalty be visited upon them, *lest their contagion spread until the entire kingdom is in the grip of the devil and his minions*. How much greater a devil held the kingdom in thrall now.

'I wonder what business caused such haste,' her companion mused.

As she watched the dark outline of the carriage disappear from view, she felt a creeping sense of foreboding.

The apartment was almost in darkness by the time her husband returned later that day. The air had grown chill, too, and Frances had just stood to make up the fire when she heard the click of the latch. She exhaled slowly, relief washing over her. Irrational though it was, during the hours since her return from St James's Park, she had grown increasingly fearful that whatever had brought the lord chief justice to Whitehall might concern her husband. It made little sense, but in the febrile atmosphere of court it was all too easy to become gripped by the same paranoia that made the King see traitors everywhere.

Thomas smiled weakly at her as he pushed the door closed, then bent to kiss her.

'You are behind your usual time.' She tried to keep her tone light.

'Forgive me – I should have sent word,' he replied, crossing to the fireplace. 'The King called a conference with his attendants,' he explained, as he took some logs from the basket and placed them in the grate. When the flames had taken hold, he sat in front of it and Frances joined him.

'His Majesty has appointed Sir Edward Coke to investigate Overbury's death,' he said at length. 'He is concerned by all this talk of poison.'

'But surely that is nothing more than rumour and hearsay.'

Thomas nodded. 'That may be so, but the matter has excited enough attention to make the King anxious that justice is seen to be done.'

'No doubt he has been encouraged in this.'

'No doubt,' he agreed. 'But it seems that fresh intelligence has reached the King's ears, prompting him to look closely at the matter. Overbury's keeper, Richard Weston, has attested that his charge was murdered with a poisoned enema.'

Frances stared at her husband in dismay. No such claim had been made in the two years since Overbury's death. That it had been levelled now was surely a blatant slur on Somerset's relationship with his former confidant. Frances had heard of other sodomites being put to death by such means. If Villiers had bribed Weston to make the claim, then he was guilty of hypocrisy as well as slander.

'What did Somerset say to this?' she asked, after a long pause.

'I have never seen a man so enraged.' Thomas paled at the memory. 'He used such words against the King that I feared he would be taken straight to the Tower. He ranted against Villiers, too, accusing him of calumny and lies. Ralph Winwood and I were obliged to restrain him, lest he ran Villiers through with his sword.'

Pity he did not, Frances thought. It would have rid the court of that serpent.

'As soon as we released our grasp, he stormed out of the privy chamber, uttering curses against the King's lapdog, as he called him.'

'Where is he now?' she asked.

Thomas gave a shrug. 'With his wife in their apartment, I suppose. He begged leave to accompany her to Sherborne two days ago, but the King refused. Now it is obvious why.'

'So she must travel alone?' Frances asked, imagining the young woman being jolted along the rough tracks that lay between London and Wiltshire. She knew them all too well, having made numerous journeys from Whitehall to Longford. Somerset's estate lay forty miles further west so his wife faced a journey of some four or five days when at last she was given leave to depart.

Thomas looked at her, grave-faced. 'Lady Somerset is under suspicion too – perhaps even more so than her husband. Several of her associates have now been implicated in the scandal.'

Frances could not but feel pity for the young woman. Although she was certainly guilty of the sins of vanity and pride, she could not believe her capable of murder. 'She will be birthing that poor child here if Sir Edward's investigations are not swiftly concluded.'

'And if they are not concluded in her favour.'

Villiers must be congratulating himself at having come within tantalising reach of his rival's destruction. She wondered whom he would set his sights upon next.

CHAPTER 13

16 October

Frances held the letter close to her face and breathed in the achingly familiar scent of rose oil – her mother's favourite. She placed it back on her lap and began to read the elegant script.

You would rejoice to see how your son thrives here, Frances. He has grown so tall that he will soon outstrip me in inches, as well as energy. He loves Longford as if he has never known any other home. It would gladden your dear father's heart to know that he left our estate to one so worthy.

Frances had to look away. How she wished that he had lived to see his grandson mature into such an admirable young man.

I have appointed a private chaplain to attend us. He was a friend of the Reverend Samuels, so I know he can be trusted. George is glad that he no longer has to attend St Mary's. I was never able to stop his fidgeting during Pritchard's sermons.

Frances smiled as she read that part. She could hardly blame her son for not paying attention to the priest's moralising addresses. She had suffered many of them since his arrival in the parish soon after the old Queen's death. Eager to curry favour with the new King, he had made it his business to root out any remnants of the old religion that still lingered in those parts – as they did in many other parishes far distant from court. He had also proved as rapacious a witch hunter as the King himself.

I hope that my other grandsons are thriving and that Thomas's affairs prosper. He must be glad of your presence. Sending you every blessing, my daughter.

Frances read the note several more times, then kissed it and placed it carefully in the casket with the others. Although she always rejoiced to hear from her mother, it sharpened her longing to see her – George too. It would surely be many months yet before she was able to make the journey to Wiltshire. She hated living so far from her mother and sons, but tried to comfort herself with the knowledge that they were safest in the tranquillity of the country, well away from the perils of court.

It was almost two weeks since the lord chief justice had begun his enquiries and the brittle atmosphere within the King's privy chamber and throughout the court was almost palpable. Even the walls of the palace seemed to emit tension. Sir Edward Coke had summoned numerous courtiers and attendants for questioning – Thomas included. Her husband told her that he had been most thorough, demanding the details of any conversations he had had with Somerset or his wife, any visits to the Tower. She prayed that Coke would not extend his enquiries to her. Although her own visit there had had nothing to do with his investigation, she had no wish for her treatment of Lady Arbella to come to his ears – or her conversation with Lady Somerset, for that matter. A number of the Somersets' associates had been taken into the King's custody for far less.

Frances tried to shake the thought from her mind as she dipped the quill into the ink and began to write. She would not confide her fears to her mother: Helena already worried about her, now that she was back in the vipers' nest of court.

My dearest Mother

She set down the quill, suddenly too weary for the task of writing banalities and half-truths. The creak of a floorboard outside the apartment door made her start. She glanced at the clock. It was only just past three. Surely Thomas could not be back already. She waited for the click of the latch but everything was silent. Whoever it was could not have moved on because she would have heard their footsteps along the corridor. Suddenly uneasy, she moved quietly to the door and pressed her ear to it. Did she imagine the sound of steady breathing? That was ridiculous, she told herself. She had become as fearful as the King himself, seeing danger where none existed. She lifted the latch and opened the door.

Her breath caught in her throat. Standing before her, his sensuous lips curled into a smile, was George Villiers.

'Lady Frances,' he drawled, as he made a lazy bow, then leaned against the doorframe.

She stared at him, then forced a smile. 'Forgive me, Sir George, I am surprised to see you here.'

'But not disappointed?' he replied, with a wolfish grin.

Frances did not answer. Neither did she invite him into the apartment. Her instinctive fear of him was greater than her curiosity as to why he had come.

'I am afraid my husband is not here, Sir George,' she said, when he made no attempt to explain his presence.

'I should hope not.' His voice was laced with scorn. 'Those of us who serve His Majesty are obliged to dedicate many hours to the task. Why, my own duties often extend long into the night.'

His eyes glittered as she held his gaze.

'Then I would not wish to keep you from them,' she replied coolly. 'Are you here at His Majesty's request?'

'How eager you are to be rid of me, Lady Frances.' He clasped his hand to his breast as if wounded.

It was easy to see why he had so intoxicated the King. He was tall and lithe, and moved with an easy grace that drew all eyes to him. The skin of his face and long, delicate fingers was so white that Frances wondered if he used the same paste her mother had applied to the old Queen's skin every day. She peered closer, as if focusing on this trivial detail would distract her from the rising agitation his presence had provoked. *No, his beauty had been bestowed by Nature, not craft.* His artifice lay only in his words and deeds.

'You are blessed to have such a conscientious husband,' he continued, when it was clear that she was not going to respond. She saw his eyes flick behind her to the hall of their lodging. 'Our royal master values him highly – of that there is no doubt. A less favoured man might have found himself out in the cold after that accident at Apethorpe. His Grace did so love Oswyn. Poor beast.'

He affected a look of sorrow. Frances's scalp prickled as she stared at his downturned face.

'I am most fortunate indeed – as is the King,' she said carefully. 'Sir Thomas is as loyal a servant as he is a husband.'

'I am delighted to hear it, Lady Frances,' he purred. 'When you first arrived at Whitehall, I wondered if you had come to reassure yourself that he was not indulging in the many . . . delights that the court has to offer.'

She gave a humourless laugh. 'What a dim view you have of marriage, Sir George. It provides more joy and comfort than any passing diversion. I wonder that you have not sought it for yourself before now.'

He gave a heavy sigh. 'Ah, if only I could, Lady Frances. You make it sound so much more appealing than most other reports I have heard. I had begun to think that court marriages were made only for gain, not for love.' His mouth twitched with amusement. 'But sadly my duties here allow me no leisure to enter such a state myself, at present. The King requires me at his beck and call, day and night. Little wonder he calls me his wife!' He gave a high-pitched titter, but his eyes were watching Frances closely. She knew that he was trying to shock her into a reaction, so she was careful to keep her expression neutral.

'Well, I hope you may enjoy its consolations one day – when the King has moved on to a new favourite, perhaps.' She was gratified to see anger flare briefly in his eyes.

'You think His Grace's favour so lightly bestowed?'

She knew she must have a care. He would delight in twisting her words if he reported their conversation to the King, as he surely must. Why else would he have come here, if not to cause trouble for one of his rivals?

'Of course not,' she replied. 'No more so than any monarch.'

He shifted so that he was no longer leaning on the doorframe, then moved a step closer. 'I must heed your warning, Lady Frances,' he whispered, in a conspiratorial tone. 'Would that Somerset had done the same. He might have been better prepared for his fall from grace.'

Frances did not allow herself to look away, even though his face was now uncomfortably close to hers. 'I did not know that he had lost his position,' she said.

Villiers touched his index finger to his lips, as if to stop them betraying more confidences. 'You draw out my secrets as cleverly as a mother coaxes a toy from her baby's grasp,' he murmured. 'It is as if you have bewitched me.'

A long pause followed. Frances was only vaguely aware of holding her breath. She imagined the King recounting the details of her arrest to his favourite, proud of the part he had played in her interrogation. The thought sickened as much as terrified her. She had come here to help Thomas, not drag him into more danger.

Villiers straightened himself and glanced down at his pocket watch. 'Well, it has been such a pleasure, Lady Frances,' he said airily, 'but duty calls – as it always does. I do hope there will be another opportunity soon for us to become better acquainted.'

He bent to kiss her hand and she had to resist the urge to pull it away. His lips felt cool as they brushed her skin. She watched as he sauntered back along the corridor, towards the King's apartments.

The bedchamber was already flooded with light when Frances woke the next day. She had slept only fitfully, her mind turning endlessly over the conversation with Villiers. Thomas had been aghast when she had told him of his visit, as bemused as she about its cause. She had been hard-pressed to persuade him not to abandon his duties that day so that he could stay with her. He had eventually conceded that this would play into Villiers's hands. If the man's hints about Somerset had been true, then being absent from the King's service at such a time could be twisted into complicity with the disgraced favourite.

She flung back the covers and padded over to the window. It was a beautiful autumn day, the sun reflecting off the gilded weather vane above the gatehouse. She regretted having promised her husband that she would not venture out of their apartment, keeping the door locked against any visitors. The evening walk he had proposed seemed less of a consolation now that she had seen how fine the weather was. The sun would long have disappeared by the time she and Thomas stepped out into the privy gardens.

Resigned, she pushed open the window so that she might at least enjoy the fresh air during her confinement, then went to dress. As she tied the laces of her skirt, her eyes alighted on the slender book that lay on the table next to her bed. She could just make out the gold lettering imprinted on the rich blue binding: *The Wisdom of the Ancients*. She had been delighted when it had been delivered to her the previous morning by a young page wearing the livery of Gray's Inn. Bacon had spoken to her of it during their time in St James's Park, dismissing it as a collection of fables. It was a good deal more: that it had been dedicated to the late Earl of Salisbury was proof. Villiers's visit had left her too distracted to begin reading, but it would provide the perfect companion now.

She finished dressing, then took it to the hall and settled on the window seat. She had just opened it when there was a loud shout from the courtyard below.

'The King! I demand to see the King!'

Frances set down the book and knelt up on the seat so that she could peer out of the open casement. She felt as if her heart had stopped. Robert Carr, Earl of Somerset was being marched across the courtyard by two yeomen of the guard, each grasping an arm as he struggled to free himself.

'Unhand me, churls!' he yelled, thrashing like a fish caught on a hook.

Frances heard more rapid footsteps approaching. She craned her neck to see, then sprang back in horror as she saw Lady Somerset following in her husband's wake. She did not fight her guards but walked slowly and with dignity across the cobbles, her hands resting on her distended stomach. Frances fought the urge to look away, to press her hands against her ears and shut out the terrifying spectacle in the courtyard below. She watched the lady's skirts billow behind her as she made her steady progress, as if she were taking a leisurely morning stroll. *Surely the King would not confine a woman so close to her time in the Tower*. Even as she thought it, she knew with a creeping certainty that he would.

Another shout drew Frances's gaze back to Somerset.

'Villain!' he yelled, twisting around. His face was puce with rage. Frances followed his gaze. There, standing at the entrance to the courtyard, just below her window, was Sir George Villiers.

'This is your doing!' Somerset shrieked. 'I will see you hang for this!'

As the captive's frantic scuffling echoed into silence, Frances caught Villiers's low chuckle. He watched as his vanquished rival was dragged through the gateway that led to the river, his wife following quietly behind. Then, slowly, he raised his hand to his lips and blew a kiss towards their retreating shadows.

1616

CHAPTER 14

6 January

Frances stole a glance at her husband as Sir George Villiers mounted the steps to the dais. The King's eyes flashed as he watched him walk slowly to the throne. The jewels on Villiers's scarlet cloak glittered in the candlelight when he swept an elaborate bow. James rose unsteadily to his feet and looked up adoringly at the young man. He was a good deal shorter than Villiers, who towered over most others at court. An attendant stepped forward and handed his master a gold satin sash, from which was suspended a crest bearing the King's arms. Villiers sank to his knees and lowered his gaze.

'My most trusty and well-beloved servant, Sir George Villiers, I confer upon ye' the office of master of the horse.'

James bent to place the sash around the favourite's neck, his hand brushing against the skin that showed above Villiers's richly embroidered collar. 'Ye' are charged with the management of all ceremony attendant upon the office, as well as of the keeping of my stables, coach houses and kennels, and of the horses and hounds therein.'

Villiers had taken great delight in telling Thomas of his promotion two days before. It was one of the greatest prizes to be had at court, for as well as superintending all of the magnificent displays and pageantry associated with the King's public appearances and progresses, the master of the horse was also entitled to a place on the privy council. Thomas was not the only one to feel aggrieved at the young man's meteoric rise. But he had particular cause, for as master of the buckhounds he was now directly answerable to him. Frances knew as well as he that Villiers would delight in exercising his authority to the full. The prospect of his proving as fair a master as the Earl of Worcester, whose place he had usurped, seemed entirely distant.

The new master was rising to his feet now, his eyes triumphant as he turned to receive the obeisance of the assembled company. Frances gave her husband's hand a quick squeeze. As she rose from her curtsy, she saw Villiers staring at him with a look of faint amusement that made her blood run cold.

The banquet that followed was even more lavish than those staged in honour of visiting princes or ambassadors. Platters bearing exquisitely crafted sugarwork and intricate marchpane were carried aloft by the servers. As one drew closer, Frances noticed that the delicacies were all inspired by Villiers's new office: there were tiny stirrups, horseshoes and collars, the details picked out in bright dyes and gold leaf.

'I will take some air.' Thomas raised his voice to be heard above the growing cacophony. 'It is even more stifling in here than usual.'

'I will come with you,' she replied, but her husband shook his head.

'Please – stay and enjoy the banquet, my love. I shall be back soon.'

He had already started in the direction of the balcony at the opposite end of the hall before Frances could protest. She watched with a sinking heart as he weaved his way through the crowds.

'Have you tried the stirrups? They are quite delicious.'

Sir Francis Bacon was standing before her, his face lit with his usual good humour. She smiled. 'How are you, Sir Francis? I have hardly seen you these past few weeks.'

He spread his hands. 'I know, my dear – and I am sorry for it. But His Majesty has found much business to occupy my time.'

Bacon had told her that the King had appointed him to gather evidence for the Somersets' trial, which made her glad she had not confided what she knew of the matter. The couple had languished in the Tower since their arrest almost three months before. Lady Somerset had given birth to a daughter there in the early days of December. The King had shown no pity when informed that her labour pains had begun and had refused to have her moved to more comfortable lodgings. The child had been taken from her almost as soon as it had drawn breath. Frances's heart lurched with pity again as she thought of the young woman in that grim fortress, consumed by grief and terror.

'Is there a date for the trial yet?'

Bacon shook his head. 'Everything is made ready, but still the King has not given word.' He leaned towards her so that he would not be overheard. 'Another of Somerset's attendants was executed yesterday. That brings the tally to three. I fear there will be more before this business is concluded.'

Frances felt cold, despite the oppressive heat of the hall. She glanced towards the dais and saw James feeding his new master of the horse a sugared apricot. Their heads were so close together that Villiers's luscious brown locks brushed against the King's brow. It did not seem so very long ago that Somerset had enjoyed such intimacy. Now he looked set to be hanged at his master's orders.

The thunderous boom of a drum rang out across the hall, signalling the start of the dance. Frances almost dropped her glass, and her hand trembled as she clasped it more tightly. The crowds were forming two lines down the centre of the hall. Seizing the opportunity, Frances signalled to her companion to follow her to one of the window recesses, where they could talk at greater liberty. She judged that everyone else would be too intent upon the dance to heed their conversation.

'Have you found anything to support the accusations against Somerset?' Frances asked, when they were settled on the window seat.

'No,' he answered shortly, 'though the King would have me seize at even the most trivial of details and twist it into something darker.' A shadow flitted across his face and he hesitated before continuing. 'The same is not true of Lady Somerset, though.'

Frances took a sip of wine but struggled to swallow.

'It seems she used her influence to have Sir William Wade replaced as lieutenant of the Tower by Sir Gervase Helwys.' His dark eyes appraised her carefully.

'And you think Sir Gervase played a part in Overbury's death?' Frances asked.

'Perhaps – even if it was only to turn a blind eye to events.'

Lady Somerset's distress had seemed genuine when she had confided in her that day. Was she really such an arch dissembler? 'Is there other evidence?'

Bacon sighed. 'Trifles – an overheard conversation here, an apothecary's visit there. Not enough on their own, but when taken together . . .'

Frances knew too well how such details could be presented as conclusive proof. She herself had been arrested for far less.

'Coke is determined that they be made an example of, naturally,' he continued, with a sneer. 'Pity for him that his own enquiries did not turn up anything of use.'

'It must pain him that the King appointed you to succeed where he had failed,' she observed.

Bacon smiled. 'I cannot deny that it gave me some satisfaction – though my prospects of success are far from certain. And, to be plain, I would rather have nothing to do with the business.' He drank some wine and they turned to survey the throng. A volta was in full swing, and the hall was a riot of swirling silks and red-faced courtiers, all trying to keep pace with the music. The heat in the room was growing even more oppressive and Frances wished she had accompanied her husband outside. He was still nowhere to be seen.

'You do not care to dance, my dear?' her companion asked, when the musicians began the more sedate chords of the pavane.

'A lady of my age can be forgiven for preferring to observe,' she said, with a grin. Thomas never tired of telling her that she was at the height of her beauty, but at thirty-five she knew it would soon fade. Looking around at the other ladies now, their faces flushed from the dance and their eyes bright with excitement, they seemed so much younger than she. Most were, she admitted: her mother had introduced her to court when she was just fourteen. Had she ever been so fresh-faced, so hopeful? The court soon stripped young women of their innocence, turned naivety into cunning and ambition. She did not envy the nubile ladies their youth: the wisdom she had gained since first coming to this place – though hard-won – was a far greater prize.

'Here you are!' Thomas's voice, edged with irritation, interrupted her reverie. He nodded briefly to Bacon, who had stood to bow. 'I have been searching everywhere for you.'

'Forgive me, Sir Thomas – the fault was mine,' Bacon put in smoothly 'Your wife's company is far too diverting. I have detained her much longer than I ought.'

Thomas smiled tightly as the older man made another bow before bending to kiss Frances's hand. She watched as he made his way from the hall, then turned to her husband. 'Must you be so discourteous?'

Thomas looked momentarily ashamed. 'I was worried about you,' he said defensively. Studying his expression, Frances realised her assumption that he was not jealous of her friendship with Bacon might have been misplaced. His eyes flicked to the dais. 'Come – I have no stomach for tonight's revelries.' He held out his hand. Frances searched his face, hoping to see some of his usual good humour, but he was too agitated. She rose to follow.

The shock of the chill night air hit her as they stepped outside. But she was glad of it after the stifling heat of the hall and took a deep, cleansing breath. They walked on in silence, their footsteps echoing in the deserted courtyard. Frances's hand twitched to hold her husband's, but fell back to her side.

'I'm sorry,' he said quietly at last. 'I should not have taken out my ill humour on you – or Sir Francis. I must learn greater tolerance if I am to remain in this place.'

Frances felt the tension begin to abate and reached over to him. His hand felt warm as he clasped hers. 'You have much to bear,' she soothed, thinking of Villiers's smirk as he looked out from the dais, the emblem of his promotion glinting in the candlelight.

'I will have a good deal more yet,' he said grimly.

Frances brought his hand to her lips. 'We have borne much worse. The King's fancy will soon pass to another. And when it does, the best that Sir George can hope for will be to live out his days in peaceful retirement.'

They fell silent and Frances knew that her husband, too, was thinking of Somerset. She drew her cloak more tightly around her. They were close to their apartment now and she looked forward to the warmth of her husband's embrace as they lay cocooned in their bed. Those precious hours always acted as a balm to their troubles at court.

'I do hope you are not thinking of retiring already, Sir Thomas?'

She and her husband jumped at the silken voice as Villiers stepped out of the shadows. In the gloom of the corridor, she sensed, rather than saw, the smile that was playing about his lips.

Thomas moved in front of her and made a stiff bow. He did not return to her side but kept her hand tightly clasped in his. 'Sir George.'

The young man folded his arms and leaned against the wall. 'The King always speaks so highly of you. I have often heard him say that you are the most assiduous of all his servants for the care you show towards his beloved hounds.' A pause. 'I do hope he has not laboured under a misapprehension all these years.'

Her husband bristled, but when he replied his voice was calm. 'I have always sought to serve His Grace to the utmost of my ability – as my lord of Worcester would attest.'

Villiers chuckled. 'That preening old fool? I wonder he could find the stables, let alone ensure their efficient management.'

Thomas did not reply.

'Well, it is no matter. I mean to order things to my satisfaction. Hunting is the King's greatest solace – one of them anyway – so it is imperative that everything is made ready that we may depart as soon as His Grace gives the order. He was waiting a full fifteen minutes for his hounds when we set out for Hampton Court last week.'

Frances was glad that the darkness masked her dismay. It had been Villiers who had delayed their departure, insisting on changing his attire just as the King was about to mount his horse. Thomas had told her of it when he had returned that evening. She willed him to defend himself now but he remained silent.

'You may send word when you are done,' Villiers said, his tone suddenly brisk.

'Done?'

'Why, yes, preparing His Grace's buckhounds, of course. Surely you have not enjoyed so much of the King's hospitality this evening that you have forgotten your duties.'

Frances felt her husband's fingers twitch.

'A night's rest is the only preparation they require, Sir George,' he replied quietly. 'If I disturb them now, they will be tired and intractable by the time we depart for Ashridge.'

Villiers took a step closer but Thomas did not flinch. 'I am fully aware of that, Sir Thomas,' he snapped. 'But what of their accoutrements? The harnesses were still spattered with mud from the previous hunt when we rode out at Hampton Court. It is fortunate for you that the King did not notice them. Such slovenliness disgraces his honour.'

Frances bit down so hard on her lip that she tasted blood. How would her husband bear to serve this devil? His taunts had been infuriating enough before his promotion, but as Thomas's superior they would become utterly intolerable. Part of her wished that her husband would lash out at him. But she knew that that would be almost as deadly as striking the King himself.

She heard Thomas draw in a long breath. 'I will repair to the stables as soon as I have escorted my wife back to our chambers, Sir George.'

He made another stiff bow and strode down the corridor, gripping Frances's hand even more tightly than before. As they rounded the corner, she glanced back and saw Villiers still standing there, his eyes fixed upon them.

CHAPTER 15

20 February

Frances sat back on her haunches and waited for the sickness to pass. She knew that within minutes she would be ravenous again, though the thought of food made her stomach turn. She had been so preoccupied with worry for Thomas that she had hardly noticed the absence of her courses these past few weeks. It was only when the newly churned butter began to taste sour and she was beset by a craving for meat that she realised she was with child again. The knowledge had brought her less joy this time, for it meant she must leave Thomas as her confinement drew near, even though he needed her now more than ever.

Villiers had more than justified the dread she had felt upon first hearing of his appointment as master of the horse. She hardly saw her husband any more – indeed, she had been surprised to find herself with child. He would return to their apartment long after dusk, and some nights she had been unable to stay awake until she heard the click of the latch. It was barely light when he left for his duties each morning, and although she always rose with him, he spoke little and left untouched most of the breakfast she had prepared. It pained her to see him so pale and gaunt. Even the news that she was with child again had lifted his spirits only for a day or so. She supposed he had the same dread of her leaving as she had herself.

As she began to dress, she smoothed her linen shift over the swell in her belly. This child seemed to grow more quickly than the others. She hoped it might be a girl this time.

A knock disturbed her thoughts. She finished the lacing and pulled a shawl around her shoulders. When she opened the door, a page handed her a note, then scampered off on another errand. Frances recognised the hand at once and her heart leaped.

My dear Lady Frances,

You will think me quite a stranger – if, indeed, you have not forgotten me altogether. I beg your forgiveness for being so long out of your company. I have missed it greatly. The King's affairs are such that I am afforded little leisure, but I would be glad if you might accompany me on a short boat ride this afternoon. It promises to be a fine day and less cold than of late. I will wait for you by the water gate at two of the clock.

Your humble servant,

Fr. Bacon.

Frances brightened at once. She had barely seen her friend since the New Year celebrations. He had been absent from the few court gatherings that had been staged since, and she had begun to fear that her husband had been right. Thomas had not troubled to hide his disdain at how Bacon had fawned over Villiers when he had been summoned to attend the King in his privy chamber a few weeks before. She had been disappointed but not surprised. A seasoned courtier like him knew whom to flatter and whom to avoid. She doubted his admiration was sincere.

Frances finished dressing more carefully and took time over brushing her hair. The chestnut colour had deepened over time, just like her mother's. Helena's still had no trace of grey, though she was now a woman of sixty-seven. Frances hoped hers would be the same. She plaited it, then wound it around into a simple coif at the base of her neck. Although she now had far greater liberty for such vanities, she had little patience with them. Not for the first time, she found herself wishing she had some purpose at court, beyond supporting her husband. Her years spent in the princess's service had given her companionship, and she had taken pride in her duties. But there were few positions for ladies at court now that Elizabeth had left for the Palatine and her mother, the Queen, was a virtual exile.

She stood and crossed to the bookcase, taking down *The Interpretation of Nature*. If she could not be among her beloved flora at Tyringham, this was the next best thing. She had already marked several pages she wished to discuss with Bacon next time they met and was glad they would finally have the opportunity that afternoon. Settling on the window seat, she began to read.

'You look a little pale, my dear,' Sir Francis said, as he helped her into the boat. 'Are you well enough for our excursion?'

Frances smiled. 'The fresh air will soon bring the colour back to my cheeks. I have had too little of it lately.'

When her companion was seated opposite her, the boatman pushed the vessel away from the landing stage and rowed them upstream, towards Lambeth. Frances soon glimpsed the red-brick gatehouse of the archbishop's palace in the distance.

'I must beg your forgiveness again for being such a stranger to you these past few weeks. I wish it had been otherwise.'

'Please do not concern yourself, Sir Francis. I know that you have been much preoccupied with business lately.'

She saw him flick a glance at the boatman. 'We lawyers usually delight in being busy,' he said, with a grin, though his eyes were serious. 'But a man of my years needs his sleep. I hope matters will soon be resolved so that I might enjoy some.'

They lapsed into companionable silence as the boat headed slowly westwards. Frances turned her face to the sun, feeling its light seep into her skin and warm her bones. Such an unseasonably mild day made the spring seem within tantalising reach, but she knew that the brisk winds of March could soon bring back the chill of winter.

'Please make for that landing stage there,' Sir Francis instructed the boatman, then turned back to her. 'I thought we might take a stroll through the gardens of Chelsea, if that would please you?'

Frances gladly agreed. It had been many years since she had enjoyed the beauty and tranquillity of that village, which lay within easy reach of Westminster but felt like a world away. A few minutes later, they were strolling along the path that bordered the Thames. Frances looked across at the lush green lawns that swept down from the mansions lining the riverbank. Ahead, she could see the white marble gateposts that lay at the edge of Beaufort House. The gardens there were much more formal than those on either side of it and were laid out in a large quadrant with a circular lawn at the centre.

'Sir Thomas More liked things to be regular,' Bacon observed, following her gaze. 'Pity for him that he could not order his affairs with King Henry as easily as his gardens.'

Frances nodded. 'He must have longed to live out his days here, far from the dangers of court.'

They had drawn level with the gates now and paused to look towards the house. With its handsome gables, decorative carvings and honey-coloured bricks, it reminded Frances of Longford.

'The old earl keeps it well, though he spends most of his time in Lincolnshire,' Bacon remarked. 'Henry Clinton, Earl of Lincoln,' he explained, noting her confusion.

'His wife was a great favourite of the old Queen,' Frances remembered.

'Indeed – a great beauty, too,' her companion agreed warmly. 'Sadly not all those who found favour in the last reign enjoy the same in this one.' A pause. 'I believe you know Sir Walter.'

She looked at him sharply. *Raleigh?*

Many times in the past Frances had wondered at the intricate web of friendships and family ties at court. It seemed impossible to pull at one thread without becoming entangled in a myriad of others. Not for the first time, she found herself wishing she could escape the web altogether. But it was more than friendship that bound her to Raleigh. Together, they had plotted treason.

'A little,' she replied. 'Are you well acquainted with him?' She pretended to study a tiny bud she had plucked from the earl's neatly clipped hedge as they walked on.

'Indeed – more so than most of my fellow courtiers are aware. I would not wish to enlighten them.'

The silence that followed was so prolonged that she was sure he would say no more on the subject. During the many hours they had spent together, their conversations had tended towards nature, philosophy or other subjects upon which Bacon had written. To Frances, they had provided a welcome relief from the endless intrigues and gossip of court and she had assumed the same was true for her companion.

He stopped walking now and gently laid his hand on her arm. When she turned to face him, she saw that his expression was grave.

'Raleigh and I were not always so well acquainted as we are now,' he began in a low voice. 'Indeed, we were rivals for the late Queen's favour and could hardly bear to be in each other's company. But with the accession of King James, we found our interests became more . . . aligned.'

Frances's pulse quickened but she held his gaze steadily.

'You are wise to keep your counsel, Lady Frances,' he murmured. 'These are hazardous times for those of the Catholic faith. It is more than ten years since the Powder Treason, but the King still sees traitors everywhere – though he looks in the wrong places. Poor Somerset is no more capable of such devilry than my pretty young wife.'

Frances felt the chill she had experienced upon first learning that the Somersets had been indicted for murder three weeks before. 'Are they to be tried for treason, as well as murder?'

Bacon nodded grimly. 'It is rumoured that the earl was in league with Spain, that he put Overbury to death because his old friend knew he was plotting to destroy James and make himself king in his stead. Nonsense, of course,' he went on, noting Frances's astonishment, 'but the King loses all sense of reason in such matters. Sir George was able to whip up his fear as easily as a nursemaid might terrify her young charge into obedience with tales of goblins and sprites.'

Frances had long suspected Villiers was using the Overbury scandal to blacken the name of his rival, but could not have guessed that he would venture so far.

'The King has instructed me to look closely into the matter,' Bacon continued. 'I am applying all of my efforts, of course.'

'Have you discovered anything?' Frances whispered.

Her companion looked scornful. 'Of course not. Neither is there any prospect of finding any evidence that would be admissible in court. But that matters little. For as long as His Grace's attention is focused upon his former favourite, he will be blind to a threat that is at once more real and more deadly.'

Frances had to remind herself to breathe. She knew even before he spoke the words that he was referring to the plot Raleigh had hinted at.

'You have heard of Sir Walter's plans, I think?' His dark eyes never left hers as he waited for her to respond.

'To find El Dorado?'

His flicker of a smile showed that he was not fooled by her feigned innocence.

'As you wish, my dear,' he said quietly. 'I will speak the treason that your discretion keeps hidden. If the King agrees to Sir Walter's release, then he will assemble as large a fleet as he and his supporters can afford and set sail for Cádiz. The King of Spain will be waiting for him there. Their combined fleet will sail for Guiana, plunder the famed City of Gold, and return with riches enough to invade England. James will be ousted and his son Charles set upon the throne.'

It was exactly as Raleigh had told her – Thomas too. But despite his support for the scheme, her husband had been unable to

persuade his royal master to look favourably upon Raleigh's petition for release. Villiers had made sure that none of the King's
attendants was afforded more than the most fleeting of moments
alone with him. Clearly Raleigh's plans to secure the support of
Villiers himself had amounted to nothing.

'That is an ambitious plan,' she observed, 'and it rests entirely
upon the King's willingness to release a prisoner who has been
in his custody for thirteen long years. Surely even the dazzle of
gold is not enough to blind him to Sir Walter's alleged
treachery.'

Bacon took a small step closer. 'You think too highly of our
king, my dear,' he said slowly. 'He made friends with the woman
who had ordered his mother's head smitten off – and for less gain
than Raleigh now offers. Besides, Sir Walter has been an
exemplary prisoner, never railing against his confinement or
attempting to escape. That has made my task a great deal easier,
I can assure you.'

Frances regarded him closely. 'You have already petitioned him,
then?'

Her companion inclined his head. 'For many weeks now –
though gently, of course. A hint here, a mention there. Any more
and His Grace would have grown suspicious, even though his dear
Steenie' – his voice was laced with disdain – 'has facilitated my
access to the royal presence.'

'Villiers?' *She had been right: her friend had courted him for
political rather than personal reasons.*

'Do not look at me so, I beg you,' he countered. 'If it were not
to serve a greater purpose, I would strive to avoid that devil's
company even more than your good husband does. But a man as
vain and ambitious as he is easily won over with the promise of
riches. He spends far more than he could ever hope to gain at his
master's hands.'

'He is not aware of the real motive behind Raleigh's voyage?'
she asked, suddenly doubtful of everything – and everyone – she
had thought she knew.

'Of course not,' Sir Francis said earnestly. 'Even he would not be fool enough to bite the hand that feeds him – or strike it off altogether.'

'Why are you telling me all of this?' Frances asked. 'You have lived at court long enough to know it is as dangerous to speak of treason as to execute it.'

'Indeed it is,' he replied peaceably. 'And I would not have uttered a word of it had I not been assured that you already knew – and could be trusted. Sir Walter esteems you highly, for reasons he would not divulge.'

That at least was a blessing, Frances thought. Despite everything, she had always instinctively trusted Raleigh. Besides, he was as much at risk as she if their plot to poison Prince Henry ever came to light. She waited for her companion to continue.

'I have succeeded in persuading His Grace to look favourably upon Raleigh's proposal. But while he has agreed to his release – in theory, at least – he refuses to fund the expedition from his own coffers. Only when our friend is able to gather a fleet to match that of King Philip will he give the order for him to be freed. I have already pledged a large sum from mortgaging my estates. It is now beholden upon all faithful subjects to do likewise.'

Faithful to whom? Frances did not need to speak the words. Her mind ran on. Her father had provided a rich dowry for her marriage, and her husband's careful management of his estates had further swelled the resources at their disposal. With the income from his position at court, they would have enough eventually for Thomas to retire from James's service. They had spent many hours discussing it, each taking equal delight in the prospect of living out their days at Tyringham Hall, surrounded by their growing family. The idea of risking it all on a hazardous expedition that had little prospect of success was abhorrent. Thomas would surely never agree to it, even if she were minded to. But then she thought of the excitement in his eyes when they had spoken of Raleigh's scheme and she suddenly felt far from certain.

Frances shivered as a breeze blew in from the river. The sun was low on the horizon now and the air had grown chill. She began to walk back towards the landing stage. After a moment, her companion followed.

'I ask only that you think on the matter,' he said, taking her hand as he drew level with her.

Frances did not reply but kept her eyes fixed on the path ahead.

CHAPTER 16

19 March

By the time Frances and her husband arrived, the courtyard was crowded with people eager to catch a glimpse of the entourage. Word of Raleigh's release earlier that day had spread like wildfire. Thomas had known it was coming: he had overheard a conversation between the King and Sir George More, the new lieutenant of the Tower, two days earlier. He had woken Frances with the news when he had returned to their apartment that evening. She still felt the same mixture of anticipation and dread with which she had first received it.

Thomas had proved even more eager than she had feared to invest their fortune in the enterprise. *Our debt will be repaid in more ways than one*, he had told her. The King of Spain had promised to enrich all those who supported Raleigh as soon as their invasion had succeeded and James had been toppled from his throne. The small matter of who was to take his place was less certain. Although Philip had vowed to pledge his allegiance to the King's son and heir, Prince Charles, on condition that he reinstate the Catholic faith, Frances doubted he would hazard so much for so little personal gain. Thomas shared her scepticism but was of the view that even a foreign king was better than the heretic who now sat upon the throne. Frances suspected it was the desire to be rid of Villiers more than James that had driven her husband to hazard their fortune on the scheme.

A distant cheer could now be heard from the streets outside. At once, the excited chatter died and a hush descended upon the courtyard. All heads were turned towards the gatehouse where a large body of the King's yeomen stood in readiness to clear a path through the crowds. Frances glanced back towards the windows of the great hall. She knew the King would be seated there under the canopy of state, waiting to greet the man who had been his prisoner for almost as long as he had worn the Crown of England.

The clatter of hoofs echoed around the courtyard and Frances turned just in time to see Sir Walter emerge from underneath the gatehouse. How typical of him to make his entrance on horseback, rather than in the privacy of a carriage, she thought, with a smile. His white stallion was magnificently caparisoned in rich scarlet cloth edged with gold, and Raleigh was dressed in a satin doublet of black and white – the old Queen's favourite colours. His once ruddy complexion had grown pale from the long years of incarceration and his grey hair had receded, but as he drew closer Frances saw that his eyes glinted with triumph as he graciously acknowledged the adoration of the crowds. How their cheers must irk the King, she thought, with satisfaction.

The yeomen who walked in front of Raleigh's horse shouted for the crowds to make way. Thomas squeezed her hand as they stepped back. Raleigh was so close now that Frances could have reached out and touched his immaculately polished boots. He glanced down at her as he passed and flashed a smile of genuine warmth, then quickly looked away. She was grateful for his discretion.

Frances and her husband watched his retreating form. They did not surge after him, like most of the onlookers, and soon they were standing with just a few other stragglers. She breathed in a lungful of air, relieved to be free from the crush of bodies.

'God speed his endeavours,' Thomas said, in a low voice, his eyes still focused upon the archway through which Raleigh had disappeared.

'Amen,' Frances whispered.

Her husband turned to her. 'You don't still have doubts, my love? We have discussed this many times and I thought you were reconciled to what we have done.' She caught the edge of impatience in his voice.

'Of course,' she replied, casting a glance at a small group of courtiers as they ambled slowly past. 'But I worry for our sons – this child too,' she added, resting her hand lightly on her belly. 'We are risking their inheritance upon this scheme. If Raleigh should fail . . .'

Thomas moved closer and placed his hand over hers. 'We are doing this to safeguard their future, not to hazard it. If all faithful subjects sit on their hands while their king and his favourites steep themselves in wickedness, then by the time our boys become men, this kingdom will already be damned.'

Frances gave a tight smile. Not for the first time, she reflected on how much had changed in just a few short years. During the early days of their marriage, it had been Thomas who had urged her to keep their faith only in her heart, that to do otherwise would destroy everything they held dear. She had always known him to be such a peaceable man. The change in him had been wrought not by the King but by his rapacious favourite. Villiers seemed to have a knack of finding out men's weaknesses and exploiting them ruthlessly.

'Shall we?' Thomas said, holding out his hand. Frances took it and they followed the handful of courtiers who were still making their way towards the hall.

The smell of roasted meat hung about the kitchens as Frances crept silently through them. She had lit a taper from the dying embers of the great fire and relied upon its frail, flickering light to guide her to the small courtyard that lay beyond, next to the river. She was glad that Raleigh had not suggested meeting in her apartment. He had not been absent from court for so long that he had forgotten there were eyes and ears everywhere. As she lifted the latch of the outer door, she found herself wondering how many times he had used this place for his clandestine business.

The smell of tobacco smoke filled her nostrils as she stepped into the courtyard. In the gloom, she could just make out the intermittent glow of a pipe as it briefly illuminated Sir Walter's smiling mouth.

'Lady Frances,' he said softly, sweeping a deep bow. He held out his hand to guide her towards the bench he had been sitting on. 'I'll wager you never thought to converse with me here – and I a free man.' She heard the smile in his voice. 'I had almost given up hope myself, but our friend Bacon was most persuasive with His Majesty.'

'He is as skilled an orator as he is a philosopher,' she agreed. 'Is everything made ready for your voyage?'

Raleigh blew smoke. 'A few ships are assembled at Plymouth, but I will need many more yet. Even the King acknowledges that the fleet is too small for our purpose – though, of course, he does not know what purpose that is.'

'Will he grant funds himself?'

'Perhaps – if Bacon can persuade him. My word is as nothing to him, of course. He still eyes me with the same disdain he harboured before he made me his prisoner. He could hardly abide me in his presence.'

James had made painfully clear his distaste for the old adventurer at the reception held in his honour. Even Villiers had been unable to lift his royal master's spirits, and he had spent the entire feast glowering at his untouched plate and gulping even more wine than usual.

'I am deeply grateful to you and Sir Thomas, my lady,' Sir Walter continued. 'If every member of our faith proved as generous, I would sail to Spain with an even mightier fleet than the Armada.'

'My husband would gladly have laid out three times as much if he could,' she said quietly. Then: 'You are sure this enterprise will succeed? A great deal rests upon it, Sir Walter.'

'Not least my head.' He chuckled, then fell silent for a few moments. 'You have hazarded more for our faith than most, Lady Frances,' he continued, his voice now serious. 'I know that you have much to lose if I fail. But even if your fortune is destroyed, the reason you invested it will never be known. The King expects his subjects to be as greedy for gold as he is, so does not think to question why each of them risks such vast sums on the enterprise.'

'That is a blessing,' she said, and looked at her hands. Raleigh took them in his. Their warmth comforted her. 'Do you truly believe you are carrying out God's will, Sir Walter? That He wants our kingdom to be rid of the heretic who sits upon the throne, even though it will lead to war and bloodshed?'

There was a long silence.

'You doubt our faith, my lady?'

'No!' Frances cried, then held her breath as her voice echoed around the dark courtyard. Beside her, Raleigh waited. 'It is not our faith I doubt, but the means by which we express it. Is it not better for us to live peaceably than to murder the King and thousands of his subjects in the name of religion? That might satisfy the Catholics, but it would make enemies of many others. If your plan succeeds, then we will surely be plunged into civil war.'

She feared she had said too much. But the words had been swirling in her head for so many weeks now, depriving her of sleep until the small hours, that she could no longer bear to leave them unspoken.

'What you say is true, Lady Frances.' Raleigh's words were measured. 'Our old queen was of the same mind as you. She never wished to make windows into men's souls, but desired only that her subjects might live in peace with one another.'

Frances smiled. She had heard her mother say that many times. Would that the last of the Tudors still wore the crown.

'But such peace is only possible while someone of equal wisdom – of equal tolerance – rules us,' Sir Walter continued. 'King James will not rest until he has rooted out every last vestige of popery, as he calls it. It is no longer enough even outwardly to conform. He means to have our souls too.'

He drew on his pipe. Frances closed her eyes as she breathed in the earthy aroma. It brought back a memory of her father's library at Longford, so strong that she could almost believe herself there.

'I understand your fears, my lady,' he continued. 'You have a growing brood of sons and would not forfeit their lives for all the gold El Dorado could offer. My own son will accompany me on this voyage. Wat has grown into a fine boy,' he added fondly. 'Do you think I would risk his safety if I doubted the wisdom of our cause? I am an old man now and set my own life at a pin's fee. But his . . .' His voice trailed off and he grasped her hands more tightly. 'I promise that I will strive to my utmost to make this enterprise succeed, Lady Frances. All I ask is that you and the others who have supported it will keep faith while I am gone.'

'I will endeavour to do so, Sir Walter,' she replied. 'When will you depart for Plymouth?'

'A few days hence – if His Grace can bear to be parted from me,' he said, with a return of his old humour. 'God willing, when we meet again it will be to welcome our new king.'

Frances's smile did not reach her eyes. *But which king would that be?*

CHAPTER 17

23 May

'Their trial begins tomorrow, I've heard,' the gentleman opposite Frances said between mouthfuls.

'About time,' replied another. 'It's been so long since their arrest that I doubt they can remember the crimes for which they are to answer.'

His companion gave a snort of derision. 'I'm sure Sir Francis Bacon will be only too happy to remind them. He has been assiduous in his task, by all accounts.'

Frances helped herself to a piece of salmon and pretended not to listen. She knew her friend had indeed been assiduous, but not in the way these men believed. He had uncovered enough evidence – albeit circumstantial – to bring a case of murder against the Somersets, but had persuaded the King to show clemency. Villiers, of course, had striven for the opposite result but for once his royal master had proved resistant to his persuasion. It had sparked rumours of a rift between them, though Frances hardly dared give them credence.

'Well, I hope the lieutenant has made sure the axe is good and sharp,' the man next to her said.

Frances took a small sip of wine but her taste for it had still not returned, even though she could now stomach the other foods she had enjoyed before her pregnancy. The child was showing itself beneath the folds of her gown and she had been obliged to let out her stays again a few days before. If she had it right, she would be obliged to take her leave of court – of Thomas, too – before the summer was out. She wondered if Raleigh would have sailed by then. It was almost two months since he had departed for Plymouth and many more ships had joined his fleet, but still he claimed it was not yet ready to set sail. Little wonder the King was losing patience. Thomas had heard him mutter that he would have him brought back to the Tower if he had not raised anchor by Ascension Day, which had passed two weeks before.

A movement at the far end of the hall caught her eye. The yeomen were raising their halberds to let someone through. Frances glanced at the clock. Dinner was almost over so the new arrival would have to content themselves with the scraps that had not yet been devoured. It took her a moment to recognise the grey-haired gentleman who stepped into the hall. He stood uncertainly, scanning the long tables of courtiers as if looking for someone. *The Earl of Rutland.* It was barely four years since she had seen him, but he seemed to have become an old man. Just then, his gaze alighted on her and he smiled with such warmth that her heart swelled. He walked briskly to her table. She was only vaguely aware of the curious stares of her fellow diners as she stood to greet him.

'Lady Frances,' he said, after making his obeisance. 'I hoped to see you here. I had heard that you had returned to court.'

'I am very glad to see you again, my lord,' she replied warmly. 'Is the countess with you?'

She noticed his smile falter. 'Alas, no. Affairs at Belvoir required her presence. Our youngest son, Francis, is in poor health.'

'I am sorry to hear it,' she replied. His elder son, Henry, had died shortly after she had left court. How anxious he must be for his surviving male heir.

'My daughter has accompanied me, though,' he added, his face brightening a little. 'I do hope she might make your acquaintance. It is her first visit to court and she is anxious to be well received.'

Frances smiled. 'I would be delighted to meet her, my lord. I have few enough female companions so it would be a great pleasure. Forgive me,' she said, aware that he must be hungry after his journey. 'Will you join me?'

The earl shook his head. 'Thank you, but I have already eaten.' He seemed to hesitate. 'I would be glad of your company, though, if you have finished your meal. My bones ache from being cooped up in that carriage, so I have a mind to take a stroll by the river.'

'Gladly,' she replied, setting down her napkin and dipping a quick curtsy to the other occupants of her table, who had resumed their conversations and barely noticed her leave.

A few boats bobbed against the landing stage, but the river was quiet now, most people having either settled at court for the evening or returned to their homes. It was beautifully mild and there was not a breath of wind as they walked along the water's edge. It was Frances who broke the silence into which they had fallen.

'How old is your daughter now?'

'Katherine will be sixteen next month.' She could hear the affection in his voice at the mention of her name. 'Her poor mother did not live to see our precious girl grow beyond childhood.' Frances stole a glance at him and saw that his eyes were filled with sadness. 'She shared your name – and something of your looks too,' he continued. 'Her hair shone like burnished gold when the sun fell upon it. I was greatly blessed to have such a wife, even for a short time.'

'She was blessed too,' Frances remarked with sincerity. 'Was it long before you married Lady Cecily?'

The earl gave an audible sigh. 'Three years – though it would have been longer, had I not allowed myself to be persuaded. When Frances died, I vowed never to take another wife, for I knew that none would ever be so dear to me as she was. But my sister-in-law urged that I must do so for Katherine's sake – that a father could never supply the place of a mother, no matter how beloved he is.'

Frances said nothing. She knew Lady Cecily's character all too well and did not wish to appear disingenuous.

'Theirs has never been an easy relationship,' he went on. 'Katherine was such a loving, biddable child, yet the countess found nothing but fault in her. I hoped that when we had children of our own, it might soften her opinion, but it made it sharper. I would not have been without my boys, of course, and for that reason it is sinful of me to regret marrying her. But far from bringing my daughter comfort, it has blighted her life.'

Yours too, Frances thought, but did not say.

'What ails your young son?' she asked, deciding it was better to talk of other matters, even if they grieved him too.

'I wish I knew,' he said with feeling. 'He and Henry fell ill at the same time. The fever came on so suddenly. They had been playing happily in the morning, but by the evening they were both delirious. My wife summoned the best physician in the county, but he was at a loss to explain it. The boys' ranting frightened him, I think. He told us they had been bewitched.'

Frances saw her own scorn mirrored in his expression. 'How many other such claims have been made in order to conceal ignorance?'

'Incompetence too,' her companion agreed. 'I knew it was nonsense, of course, but word spread rapidly throughout the village, and soon people were casting about for someone to blame. It was not long before their malicious gaze alighted upon Mistress Flower and her daughters.'

Frances thought back to the woman whom she had met during her stay with Thomas at Belvoir Castle five years before. The earl had taken her to Joan's dwelling on the edge of Bottesford village so that she could supply Frances with salves for the wounds her husband had sustained from the riding accident. Frances remembered her small, bird-like frame and watchful dark eyes. Joan's younger daughter, Philippa, much resembled her, but the elder, Margaret, who also worked at the earl's castle, was a plump, fair-haired beauty. Little wonder the locals had whispered about the girls' parentage – especially since Joan was unmarried. She might have been a respectable widow for all they knew, but she had never troubled to enlighten them.

'Have they been accused?' Frances asked, fearing the answer. It took little more than gossip to bring a suspected witch to trial.

'Not yet,' he replied, 'though my wife is intent upon it. Many times, she has reminded me that to lift a curse the person who made it must be put to death.'

Frances shivered, though the shoreline was still bathed in warm evening sunshine. 'I wonder they have not already been taken to the assizes,' she remarked.

'I have ordered the countess to take no part in the matter – my tenants too. God knows I make few enough demands of her, and those I do she sets little store by. But even she would not venture so far as to act in this without my sanction.'

Frances wished she shared his conviction. 'It must have pained you to leave your estate at such a time.'

'In part, yes. My little boy looked so frail when I took my leave of him. He has lingered on like this since his brother died. Many times I have feared he would follow him to the grave, but still he clings to life, God save him.'

Frances had known scores of children carried off by a fever, but it was usually of short duration – as had been the case with the earl's elder son. That his younger brother was still labouring under the same sickness three years later was perplexing. She wished she might attend him so that she could judge his symptoms for herself. It would not surprise her if the ministrations of the various doctors and apothecaries who had seen him over the years had prolonged, rather than relieved, his malady.

'But I confess I was glad to receive the King's summons,' the earl continued, interrupting her thoughts. 'Lady Cecily's persecution of my daughter has increased since Henry's death. Worry for our surviving son has worn her nerves to shreds, and poor Katherine has suffered the consequences. It pains me to see how fearful she has grown,' he added. 'I hope the court might restore something of her former spirit. She was always such a happy child before . . .'

His voice trailed off into silence, and they continued their steady progress along the river.

'I will do everything I can to help your daughter, my lord,' she said. 'I hope you will soon arrange a time for us to meet. Tell me, does she ride?'

'Oh, yes,' the earl replied, with enthusiasm. 'She was in the saddle even before her feet could reach the stirrups. It has been her main source of pleasure ever since – though she has lacked the opportunity of late,' he added, his smile fading. 'Lady Cecily thinks it is bad for her complexion.'

Frances bit back a scornful remark. 'Then I shall be delighted to accompany her. There are many fine parks within reach of court, and the flowers and hedges are at their very best at this time of year. It will gladden her heart to see them.'

'You are every bit as kind as I remember, Lady Frances,' her companion said warmly. 'I have thought of you often since you and Sir Thomas stayed at Belvoir. I expect a young man such as he is quite recovered by now?'

Frances smiled. 'His shoulder pains him in the winter months, but otherwise he is in good health. He will be as pleased to see you again as I am. May I ask why the King has summoned you here?'

The earl gave a small cough, as if embarrassed. 'It was an honour as unexpected as it was unlooked for. I am to be appointed a Knight of the Garter, along with my former neighbour.'

Frances gazed at him in confusion.

'Sir George Villiers.' Frances's smile became fixed as he went on, 'His mother's estate borders mine. She is exceedingly proud of his rise to favour and we never lack for news of his latest advancements.' His voice held no trace of irony, but if what Frances had heard of Villiers's overbearing mother was true, her frequent visits could not have been anything other than irksome to so discerning a man as the earl.

'Then I offer you my congratulations, Lord Rutland,' she said. 'I can think of none so worthy.' He smiled his thanks as Frances hesitated. 'Does Sir George visit his mother often?'

The earl shook his head. 'Not so often as was his custom before he took up residence here,' he replied. 'But he visits whenever his royal master can spare him. I have never seen a man so devoted to his mother.'

'You know him well, then?' she asked, taking care to keep her voice light.

'In his youth, certainly. He loved to hunt in my parkland and often came to dine with us. My boys adored him – he was always a willing playmate. He was very kind to Katherine, too.'

Frances fell silent again. She wanted to ask more but the earl was a perceptive man and she was wary of exciting his suspicion. What was more, he had given no hint that he shared her antipathy towards his neighbour's son. She must be patient. With luck, there would be other opportunities. The more information she was able to glean about the royal favourite, the more chance she might discover something that would help her husband.

The sun was low in the sky now and Frances heard the distant chimes of a bell.

'We should return,' her companion said, echoing her thoughts.

With that, they turned their footsteps back along the riverbank, towards the setting sun.

CHAPTER 18

25 May

'Will you not be persuaded, Frances?' Her husband watched as she tethered the horse to the mounting block, his face a mask of concern.

She kissed him firmly by way of answer.

'If you should fall . . .' His voice trailed off.

'I am more likely to trip over the cobbles of the palace court-yards than to fall from this beauty,' Frances said, patting the mare's dark brown neck. 'Now, are you going to saddle her or must I do that myself?'

Thomas gave a resigned shrug and set to work.

'Lady Frances!' The Earl of Rutland was strolling into the stable-yard, a young woman at his side. She was much smaller than her father and walked half a pace behind him, her head bowed. Katherine had the same pale skin and long nose as the earl, but her hair was much lighter and her nose somewhat bulbous.

'It is a pleasure to make your acquaintance, Lady Katherine,' Frances said, curtsying to them both.

The girl's heavy-lidded eyes fluttered up and her small mouth lifted in a shy smile before she lowered her gaze again. Frances studied her. She lacked the fine features that society considered beautiful, but had a wide, honest face, with large eyebrows of the same dark blond as her hair, which was tightly curled along her forehead. Her fleshy neck and sloping shoulders gave her an air of softness – so different from the sharp, bird-like features of her stepmother.

'I am glad to see you greatly recovered, Sir Thomas,' the earl said. 'I expect His Majesty has found much to occupy you since you and I last met?'

Thomas smiled. 'Indeed, my lord – I am rarely idle,' he replied, as he tightened the girth on his wife's horse. 'But I know that Belvoir has allowed you no more leisure than I have here. I am sorry to hear your son still sickens.'

Frances saw Katherine's mouth tremble.

Thomas turned to the young woman. 'I will saddle a horse for you, my lady,' he said gently. 'Bracken is both fast and biddable – I think he will do very well for you.'

A blush appeared on Katherine's cheeks as she gave a quick smile, her gaze still fixed upon the ground.

'Kate can tame even the wildest of steeds,' the earl said proudly, giving his daughter's shoulder an affectionate squeeze. 'She is the finest horsewoman in the county and leaves her old father many leagues behind when we go out together.'

The young woman's blush deepened. 'You exaggerate, Papa.'

'I thought we might ride over to Greenwich,' Frances said. 'The palace boasts some of the best parkland in the country and the hawthorn will be in full bloom by now.' She did not add that it offered the additional advantage of being far from Westminster, where the Somersets' trial was being held. Bacon had predicted that the verdict would be swiftly delivered.

Her husband shot her a disapproving look – she knew that he did not wish her to ride so far – but he said nothing and strode off to fetch Lady Katherine's horse. He had just disappeared into the stables when the sound of brisk footsteps echoed around the yard. Frances stiffened as she saw Villiers approaching.

'My dear sir!' he cried, stepping forward to embrace the earl. Frances thought she saw the older man's shoulders tense as he returned the greeting. 'And Lady Katherine.' He swept an elaborate bow then stooped to kiss the young woman's hand. 'I swear you have grown even lovelier since I saw you last.'

Katherine was now a deep crimson as she jerked her hand awkwardly away. Frances could not tell if she was more pleased or alarmed by his attentions.

'Well now, my lord, I have looked for you every day since our honours were announced. It was remiss of you not to send word of your arrival – or that of your enchanting daughter. I would have welcomed you with a feast or a masque at the very least.'

'You are very kind, Sir George,' the earl replied, 'but I did not wish to trouble you.'

Villiers affected a serious expression. 'I cannot deny that the King has been greatly preoccupied of late – and therefore I, too,' he added pompously. 'This sorry business of Lord and Lady Somerset has shaken us all.'

'I had heard that their trial was under way,' Rutland remarked.

Villiers gave a heavy sigh. 'I am riding over to Westminster now. His Grace is most anxious for news of the proceedings.' He glanced around the yard. 'Where is Tyringham?' he muttered irritably.

At that moment, Thomas emerged from the stables with a fine dappled grey mare. He gave a tight bow to Villiers but did not quicken his pace.

'Fetch me my horse,' Villiers barked, as his master of the buckhounds drew level with them.

Frances was gratified when her husband did not immediately respond but took his time tethering the mare to the mounting block. She knew it was dangerous to antagonise the man but had no wish to see Thomas so demeaned.

'Be quick about it,' Villiers said, his voice rising with impatience. 'The King's business will brook no delay.'

Thomas gave a small nod, then walked steadily back to the stables.

Katherine's face had paled and her fingers were worrying at the seam of her dress.

'Please, let me help you, Lady Katherine,' Frances said gently, holding out her hand.

Katherine hesitated and looked up at her father, who smiled his reassurance. The young girl's hand felt cold and clammy as she placed it lightly on Frances's, but she mounted the horse with practised ease and leaned forward to pat its neck while she waited for her companion.

'We will be back before dinner, my lord,' Frances said, as she climbed onto her own saddle. Her husband was leading Villiers's horse from the stables. Their eyes met and she saw his apprehension, whether for her or his rival, she could not tell.

She tapped her heels into the horse's sides and its hoofs clattered on the cobblestones as she and Lady Katherine made their way out of the yard. They had just passed under the Holbein Gate when Villiers thundered past them. He pulled sharply on the reins and his horse reared. A less experienced horseman would have been thrown from the saddle but he appeared completely at ease, flashing them a smile as he leaned back, his head edging closer to the ground. Katherine was gazing at him open-mouthed and Frances, too, was unable to look away, though she despised his arrogant showmanship. After several moments, he loosened his grip on the reins and the horse lowered its front legs, whinnying as if with relief. Villiers doffed his hat to Katherine, then rode off at speed, his laughter echoing along the street.

Later, looking out beyond the parkland, the sunlight glinting off the river, a bead of sweat trickled between Frances's shoulder blades as she rested back on her elbows. It had been an exhilarating ride and her companion had proved as excellent a horsewoman as her proud father had boasted. Frances had been hard-pressed to keep pace with her as they had reached the open expanse of Greenwich Park.

'It is a fine view, is it not, Lady Katherine?' she said, still a little breathless.

'Kate – please,' her companion said shyly, then followed Frances's gaze. 'I did not think that anything could rival the park at Belvoir but this is beautiful. I hope we might come here again.'

'I would like that very much,' Frances replied. 'You are well acquainted with Sir George's family, I understand?'

The young woman drew in a breath. 'Yes – that is, their estate borders my father's. Lady Villiers visits Belvoir often. She and the coun— my lady mother have become close acquaintances. There was talk of her travelling to London with my father when she comes for her son's ennoblement,' she added, 'but my father thought she would not be comfortable in our carriage, with so little room.'

Frances suppressed a smile. From what she had heard of Villiers's mother, she did not wonder that the earl had persuaded her to make her own way to London. 'I will look forward to making her acquaintance . . . Her son clearly esteems you.'

Kate shifted uncomfortably and turned towards the palace, so that Frances could no longer see her face.

'It is my poor brother, Francis, who most interests him,' she replied. 'He visited him often during the early days of his sickness and has written many times to enquire after him since coming to court. My father is very grateful for his attentions, of course.'

Frances raised an eyebrow. She could not imagine Villiers had acted out of concern for the boy. 'How kind that he should take such trouble,' she observed, 'especially when the King allows him so little leisure.' She plucked a blackberry from the bush next to them. It was unripe and tasted a little sour, but the ride had sharpened her appetite. 'He is handsome, is he not?'

Her companion became very still, as if she was holding herself taut. 'Of course. But . . . ' It was barely a whisper. Frances waited. '. . . there is something about him that unnerves me. It is sinful of me to say so, for he has shown my family and me nothing but kindness. Yet I cannot shake off the feeling that he means us ill somehow.'

Frances sat upright and placed her hand lightly on her companion's arm. The young woman started as if scalded.

'You must not chastise yourself for being honest, Kate,' she said. 'I have long since learned to trust my instincts – more than the things I see and hear. Your caution will serve you well at court. I would that I had had as much of it when I first came here.'

Kate turned to face her now. 'I do not deserve your kindness, Frances,' she said. 'My lady mother is right. I am too much given to foolish fancies. At least I will not vex her while I am here. She has troubles enough to contend with.'

'I will pray for your brother's recovery,' Frances said. 'With God's blessing, by the time you return to Belvoir he will be out of all danger. But I hope that in the meantime you will permit me to keep you company as often as you desire it.'

'Oh, yes!' Kate brightened at once. 'I should like that very much. I feared I might lack for companions, as I do at home.'

Frances felt another pang of pity for her. She must have led a miserable existence since her father's marriage. 'We can ride out every afternoon, if you wish, and when the weather is less clement I have many books to keep you entertained.'

Kate's smile faded. 'Thank you.'

Frances wondered what she had said to upset her, but kept her counsel. She could not expect her new friend to confide in her so soon.

When they returned the stable-yard was deserted and light was already blazing in the great hall.

As soon as Kate had dismounted too, Frances took the reins of both horses and led them back to the stables, wondering why Thomas had not yet emerged. But there was only a young groom inside, busy raking out the hay. Pushing down her unease, she handed him the reins, then walked briskly back into the yard.

'I will escort you to your father's lodgings,' she said, taking Kate's arm.

The atmosphere was unusually subdued as they passed through the public rooms, just a few small clusters of courtiers talking in hushed tones. They turned curious stares towards her companion, so she quickened her pace, holding Kate's arm firmly so that she was obliged to do the same.

As soon as they reached the earl's apartment, Frances bade a swift adieu, saying she needed to make shift for dinner. She walked back through the palace towards her own chambers, her anxiety mounting with every step. Thomas never retired from his duties so early. When at last she lifted the latch on the door to their apartment, her husband rushed to greet her. Her relief at seeing him soon faded when she saw his expression.

'What has happened?' she asked.

He pulled her inside and closed the door. 'Somerset has been found guilty – his wife too,' he said, in a low voice, grasping her hands.

Frances's mouth dried. Bacon had been so sure they would be pardoned.

'Lady Somerset confessed to Overbury's murder before the verdict was given,' Thomas continued. 'Her husband maintained his innocence, despite pressure from the King to admit his crimes and receive clemency.'

'What will become of them?' Frances asked fearfully.

Her husband looked as stricken as she felt. 'They have been sentenced to hang.'

She sat down abruptly, like a puppet whose strings had been cut. An image of the poor wretch she had seen at Tyburn flitted before her, the young woman's eyes bulging and her tongue lolling from one side of her mouth. She swallowed bile as she stared up at her husband. He laid a hand on her shoulder but could offer no words of comfort.

'Will the King show them mercy?' Frances asked.

Thomas's mouth twisted into a grimace. 'There seems little prospect of that. He has already offered Villiers their estate at Sherborne.'

Frances slumped back in the chair. 'This is his doing, I am sure of it.'

Thomas sank down next to her, then raised bleak eyes to hers. 'He has the face of an angel and the heart of a devil.'

CHAPTER 19

7 June

'*Lonicera periclymenum*,' Bacon murmured, as he bent to breathe in the heady scent of woodbine, then gently rubbed the creamy white and yellow petals between his fingers. 'I have long preferred the Latin names. They are so much more poetic.'

Such remarks had earned him a reputation for pomposity. The same intellectual gifts that had been so lauded by the old Queen and her court were viewed with disdain by her successor – and, therefore, all those who sought his favour. Frances was glad that James had been prepared to overlook his natural aversion towards men of letters and appoint Bacon as his principal legal adviser. The Somersets' fate now rested in his hands.

'Efficacious in the treatment of mouth sores and defluxions of the throat,' he continued now.

'And a cure for maladies of the stomach, I believe,' Frances added. Enough trust existed between them for her to have confided her knowledge of such things.

Her companion chuckled. 'Little wonder it is grown here at the palace. The servers ought to hand it out at the end of each feast – it would save all manner of griping and groaning during the night . . . If I didn't know better, I would think you, too, had been indulging in an excess of rich fare.' He cast a sly glance at her stomach. 'Congratulations, my dear,' he added, with genuine warmth.

Frances opened her mouth to protest. Thomas had agreed to keep her condition a secret until it could no longer be concealed. She could not quite explain why she had willed it so. A desire to protect the growing child from the dangers of court? Or perhaps she wished to avoid the constant reminders that she would soon be obliged to leave her husband and return to Buckinghamshire. Whatever the reason, she could not feel the same joy in this child as she had in the others. It seemed to rest uneasily in her belly, like the restless spirits her old nurse Ellen had often spoken of.

'Forgive me, I should not have shown such presumption.'

Frances was suddenly aware that Bacon was watching her with concern. She gave a bright smile and reached out to squeeze his hand. 'You are truly a man of science, Sir Francis,' she replied, 'for you observe things that others fail to notice. But, pray, do not share your knowledge just yet. I have a foolish notion to keep it hidden for a while longer.'

Her companion nodded. 'Of course – though I think the young knave will soon show himself to the least observant of courtiers.'

Frances smiled. She had a fancy it was a girl this time.

They continued to stroll through the privy garden. It was a pleasantly warm day and the cloudless sky seemed to promise many more to come. Frances breathed in the scent of the roses that were in full bloom. Here, enclosed by the neatly clipped hedges on either side of the garden, she could almost believe herself a world away from the court. But even as she thought it, an image of Somerset and his wife, enclosed by the cold stone walls of the Tower, flitted before her. She shivered, despite the rising heat.

'I am indebted to you for meeting me, when you have so much pressing business to attend to,' she said.

Bacon inclined his head, but his expression was grave. 'I have endeavoured to make His Grace see the wisdom of clemency,' he replied, 'but as yet he shows little inclination towards it. There are other voices than mine and they ring more loudly in his ears.'

Villiers. Frances knew that his words had as good as tightened the noose around his rival's neck. 'You must keep up your persuasions, my lord,' she urged. 'Sir George might enjoy greater favour, but you have greater wit. The King must know how the people mutter against the conviction as founded only upon rumour and hearsay. The Somersets have gained more sympathy in the Tower than they ever did at court.'

Bacon opened his mouth to reply but closed it and swept a deep bow. In confusion, Frances turned her gaze towards the path ahead and froze. The subject of their whispered conversation was strolling towards them with his usual languor. At his side was an older woman, finely dressed in a gown of jet-black satin studded with pearls. As they drew closer, Frances saw that she had the same dark blue eyes as her son.

'Lady Mary,' Bacon said, stepping forward to kiss her hand. 'Permit me to introduce my companion, Lady Frances—'

'Tyringham,' the woman said sharply, pursing her thin lips as she eyed Frances closely. 'Your husband works for my son, I believe.'

Frances dropped a brief curtsy and assumed what she hoped was a polite expression. 'Sir Thomas is master of the King's buckhounds, my lady,' she replied, holding her gaze.

'Quite,' the older woman observed. 'Having the command of such men enables Sir George to attend to weightier matters,' she added, her expression softening as she turned to him.

'I trust your journey was comfortable?' Bacon asked.

'Not in the least,' the older woman snapped. 'The roads south of Leicester are quite shocking – those in London even worse. I wonder His Majesty has not ordered their repair.'

'I will speak to him about it, Mother,' Villiers told her. 'Though at present I fear he has more pressing matters to attend to.' He shot a look at Bacon.

'How long do you mean to stay at court?' Frances asked.

Lady Mary Villiers gave a sniff. 'I have no thought of returning to Brooksby Hall yet – why, I have only just arrived.' Her voice was laced with disdain. 'The Garter ceremony will take place next month, and I am sure that I will not lack for diversion here in the meantime.' The look she exchanged with her son made Frances feel uneasy. Even though she had only just met the woman, she suspected she was as black-hearted as he.

'Lady Katherine Manners will be delighted to keep you company whenever I am detained by the King's business,' Villiers remarked.

His mother's expression lightened at once. 'Dear Kate – such a sweet child, and so excessively fond of me. I promised the countess I would look out for her. She must be quite at a loss here at court.'

Frances experienced a jolt of apprehension on her young friend's behalf. During the two weeks since Kate's arrival, they had spent many hours together, riding out whenever the weather was fine or conversing over their needlework. Frances had soon understood the reason for her companion's reticence about books: the poor girl could barely read. That she had been denied the education her status demanded was entirely due to her stepmother – of that Frances had no doubt. It had made her determined to help her. Already, she had begun to read aloud to Kate from some of the books in her library to spark her interest and lessen her fear. Soon, she would encourage her to practise her letters.

'On the contrary,' she interjected now, 'Lady Katherine is greatly enjoying her time here and has not lacked for company.'

Lady Mary glared at her, but Frances's smile did not waver. The distant chiming of bells echoed across the garden.

'Forgive us, Sir Francis, my lady,' Villiers said, with an affectation of regret, 'but my lady mother and I are required to attend

His Grace at chapel.' He gave a stiff bow as his mother swept past them, skirts rustling. Frances slowly exhaled.

'A charming lady,' her companion observed wryly. 'It is easy to see from whom her son derives his manners.'

'Argh!' Frances cried, as she pricked her finger for the third time in as many minutes. She pushed away the embroidery as she sucked the blood. The shirt was a gift for George's birthday: he would be ten next month. She had been obliged to guess at the size, which had pained her. It did not seem so very long ago that she had chalked up his height on the stable wall at Tyringham, his back pressed against the bricks and head held as high as he could raise it. She closed her eyes until the familiar ache of longing had subsided, then carefully folded the linen back into the casket.

Glancing at the clock, she saw that it was almost two. She had arranged to call on Kate at half past, but she was sure her friend wouldn't mind if she was a little early. Besides, she was anxious not to be thwarted by Lady Mary Villiers again. Twice this week she had arrived at the Earl of Rutland's apartment only to find that his daughter had already been spirited away. The older woman showed the same disregard for prior engagements as she did for most other things – her precious son excepted. Kate had made no complaint, but Frances had seen enough to know that she found Lady Villiers just as irksome as she did herself.

The chapel bell was striking two as Frances reached the lodging. She knocked on the door and waited. Everything was silent within, and she began to fear that Lady Villiers had got there before her once more. She knocked again, louder this time, and was relieved to hear hurried steps on the other side of the door. A moment later, Kate appeared, clearly somewhat flustered.

'Forgive me – I am before my time,' Frances said, with a rueful smile. 'I can come back if—'

'No, please,' Kate said hurriedly, pulling her inside. 'I must attend to something for just a moment. Please – sit down,' she said, gesturing towards one of several ornate chairs that were arranged around the large mahogany table. The apartment was a good deal larger than Thomas's, and the light streamed in from the large bay windows overlooking the Thames. As she waited for her friend to return, Frances's gaze roamed over the rows of books that lined the walls on either side of the fireplace. It did not surprise her that the earl was so well-read, but she wondered why he had not made up for his daughter's woeful lack of education here, many miles from his wife's scrutiny.

Her thoughts were distracted by a familiar aroma emanating from Kate's chamber. *Incense.* That Rutland still clung to the old religion was well known throughout the court. The King himself was aware of it but his favour towards the earl had always been such that he had been prepared – for once – to turn a blind eye. But Rutland had always insisted his children had been raised in the reformed faith. Frances did not doubt that this was true of his sons – the countess would have made sure of that – but if the same neglect she had shown for her stepdaughter's education extended to her devotions, then it was possible Kate had grown to cherish the comforts of her father's faith. Perhaps it was her way of quietly rebelling against the countess's many cruelties.

Kate came back into the room, taking care to close the chamber door behind her. 'I'm sorry to take so long,' she said, still a little flustered. 'Where shall we go? Father says it will rain, but I see no sign of that. Greenwich, perhaps? Or Hyde Park?'

'Kate,' Frances said, reaching for her hand, 'you do know that you may confide anything to me?'

The girl paled as she fiddled with the cords of her cloak. 'Of course,' she muttered.

Frances waited but Kate showed no inclination to say more, so she decided to let the matter rest for now. Though she longed to talk of their shared faith, she must be patient. Such talk was heresy, after all, and theirs was a friendship as brief as it was affectionate.

'Here – let me help you,' Frances said, rising to her feet. As she deftly untangled the cords, she noticed the glimmer of a jewel beneath the young woman's cloak. Discreetly, she pulled back the fabric a little so that she could take a closer look. The large ruby was fashioned into a shell, with a diamond at its base. It was exquisite. 'A present from your father?' she asked, with a smile.

Kate flushed. 'Not my father, no—' She broke off and chewed her lower lip. Frances watched her with mounting unease. 'Sir George sent it yesterday, with a note – here,' she added, drawing a carefully folded parchment from her pocket.

Frances almost recoiled but forced herself to smile as she read its contents.

No jewel could outshine your beauty, but please accept this as a token of my esteem. I hope you might think of your poor servant whenever you look upon it.
GV

His initials were written with such a flourish that they took up more of the page than the message above. Even the gift boasted of the giver: the Villiers coat of arms included a red cross decorated with shells.

'Don't you like it?'

Frances became aware that the girl was watching her intently, her brow creased.

'It is very pretty,' she replied, taking care to keep her tone light. 'Sir George is certainly generous to his friends. He is forever giving out such tokens, I hear.'

It was not a lie. Thomas had told her how Villiers bribed his followers with gold and trinkets – though none as fine as this. She saw Kate's face fall and experienced a mixture of remorse and relief.

'Well now,' she continued brightly, 'I think you are right – the weather is set fair, so let us ride out to Greenwich, as you suggested.'

Kate's eyes sparkled, all talk of her errant suitor forgotten, for now at least.

CHAPTER 20

12 July

Frances glanced across the aisle to where her husband was seated with the other senior officials of the King's household. His jaw was tightly clenched and his lips were pressed into a thin line, but when their eyes met he flashed her a smile of such warmth that it melted her heart. She knew how much he had dreaded this day. Looking along the row of his grim-faced companions, she suspected he was not alone.

'Somerset's arms have not been taken down,' she heard someone whisper behind her. Scanning the brightly painted sculptures above the ornate pews where the knights would take their places, Frances saw the distinctive upturned V decorated with three black stars. It gave her cause to hope that the rumours were true and the King intended to pardon his disgraced favourite. She hoped to see Sir Francis Bacon soon so that he could confirm it.

'The King has granted him full liberty of the Tower,' remarked another. 'I hear he has been seen walking the ramparts, the Garter medallion around his neck.'

'Better that than a rope,' his companion sneered. The low murmur of laughter that followed was drowned by a sudden blare of trumpets. All heads were bowed as the King made his entrance into the hall, his heels clipping the ancient marble tiles. Stealing a glance at the procession, Frances was surprised to see the Queen following in her husband's wake. She was resplendent in a gown of silver taffeta with a high collar of stiff white lace. Her hair had been fashioned into an elaborate coif, which was studded with tiny pearls and diamonds. Behind her walked Prince Charles, pale and solemn as usual. He had grown even more slender these past few months, but had gained little in height. The Knights of the Garter came next, the long white plumes of their hats fluttering as they walked.

Looking beyond them, Frances could just make out Villiers and the Earl of Rutland walking side by side. The younger man was clearly revelling in the moment as he held his head high, occasionally touching his black velvet cap in acknowledgement of the cheers and smiles of his supporters. By contrast, the earl was staring straight ahead, his mouth set. Last of all came Lady Mary Villiers, straight-backed, face suffused with triumph, and next to her Kate, her head meekly bowed.

The ceremony that followed was interminable. Frances's skin prickled in the rising heat from the press of bodies and the hot July sun that streamed in through the stained-glass windows. She could see beads of sweat forming on the brows of the knights. How they must long to cast off their heavy velvet cloaks and caps, she mused. As Villiers knelt before his royal master, she wondered that he could appear as coolly indifferent to the searing heat as if his gown were made of ice.

She diverted her gaze towards the back of the dais, where the Queen was seated next to her son. Just then, Anne looked in her direction and her mouth lifted in the faintest smile of greeting. Frances slowly inclined her head in acknowledgement. The Queen's expression was as inscrutable as ever as she turned back to watch her husband confer the highest honour in the land upon his favourite. Did she inwardly recoil, as Frances did? Perhaps not, given that she had encouraged the King's obsession with him.

Unable to bear the sight of Villiers's triumph any longer, Frances cast her eyes downwards. The child had grown so quickly

this past month that there was no longer any hope of concealment. News of her pregnancy had spread rapidly throughout the
court but had been the subject of only the most fleeting interest.

Far more diverting was the continuing uncertainty of the
Somersets' fate, or the question of when Sir Walter Raleigh would
finally set sail for El Dorado. Frances was no less interested in that
than her fellow courtiers, given how much she and her husband
had staked upon the enterprise. But even though Raleigh had
assembled a considerable fleet and the winds had been favourable
for weeks, he had showed no inclination to embark. Frances had
begun to suspect he had some other game in hand – that their
fortune would be lost. She had confided her fears to Thomas, but
he had urged her to keep faith. His own seemed unshakeable.
Now, though, she saw in him the same air of desperation that had
hung over him ever since Villiers's rise to favour. She knew that his
faith in Raleigh's enterprise was grounded in the need to do something – anything – to rid himself of this devil.

'I present to you these knights of the most noble Order of the
Garter.'

The King's voice rang out in St George's Chapel. Everyone rose
to their feet and bowed towards the two men, who had turned to
face the crowds. Frances focused her attention on Rutland, who
bore himself with the same quiet dignity that distinguished him
from most of his peers – none more so than the one standing next
to him. Out of the corner of her eye, Frances could see Villiers,
proud as a peacock, relishing his moment of glory.

When the applause had died down, the King led the royal party
from the dais and they began their slow procession back down the
nave, closely followed by the knights. Frances caught the smile
Villiers flashed at Kate as she fell into step behind him.

After several long minutes had passed, Frances shuffled along
the pew to join the throng of guests making their way along the
aisle. The atmosphere in the chapel was now suffocating, and she
longed to fill her lungs with fresh air. She placed her hands
protectively over her belly as she was jostled along towards the

huge west door. Feeling faint, she focused her gaze upon the exquisite gilded ironwork, its curling leaves, flowers and tiny animals picked out against the deep crimson paint on the wood.

When she finally emerged onto the steps the sunlight was so bright that she was dazzled and had to pause, much to the annoyance of the courtiers who were almost treading on her heels in their eagerness to secure a good seat at the feast. She stepped aside to let them pass and, on a sudden impulse, slipped away in the opposite direction. Ahead of her was King Henry's Gateway. She hastened towards it, hoping that the guards who usually stood sentry there had been diverted to the great hall, where the feast would soon begin. The idea of taking her place among another stifling throng was unbearable. Thomas would soon look for her, but she must first gain the solitude she had craved ever since arriving at Windsor that morning. Soon, she was enveloped in the blissfully cool shade of the gatehouse. It appeared deserted, so she decided to rest there, her back pressed against the cold stone of the archway.

'You must have patience, Mother.'

Frances froze. She peered into the shadows but could see nothing.

'Our debts are mounting and you spend more than you receive at the King's hands.' A woman's voice, this time.

Frances felt a draught behind her and turned to see a narrow door. She had not noticed it before. It was slightly ajar. She held her breath and leaned closer.

'A Knight of the Garter must dress in robes befitting his rank.'

Frances could hear the smile in Villiers's voice.

'Money has always passed through your fingers like water, George. You could have the riches of Croesus and still find your pockets empty before you have bought all that you desire.'

'You fret too much, Mother. This marriage will make us one of the richest families in the kingdom.'

'Only if that boy should die – and you have not ruined your reputation in the meantime. I have heard people whisper that you prefer the King's bed to any other, and the earl will not want such a man for his precious daughter. She might be ill-favoured, but if the fragile thread that tethers her young brother to this life should snap' – Frances heard Lady Mary click her fingers – 'she will be the most sought-after bride in the kingdom. And you must make sure that you are her first choice.'

There was a long pause and Frances heard a faint rustle. When Villiers spoke again it was so softly that she was obliged to press her ear against the door. 'How can you doubt my ability to bewitch the fairer sex?'

The silence that followed was so prolonged that Frances wondered if they had become aware of her presence. She thought of running away, but the temptation to find out what was happening in that chamber proved too great. She took a breath, then quietly pushed the door open another inch so that she could peer inside.

What she saw made her clamp her hand over her mouth for fear of crying out. Lady Mary was seated on an ornate chair close to the window, the bright sunlight illuminating the flush that was creeping up her neck as her son trailed his lips over it. Her eyes were closed in ecstasy as his fingers stroked the plump flesh above her bodice before moving slowly down to her thighs.

'I will do as you have taught me, Mother,' he murmured, against her neck, as he lifted her skirts. Frances stood, transfixed and appalled, as his hand moved inside them. But when his mother gave a loud gasp, it was as if a spell had been broken, and Frances stole silently away. As soon as the gatehouse was out of view, she broke into a run, desperate to escape the depravity she had seen within.

'You are sure nothing ails you – or the child?'

Thomas was watching her closely. She knew she should have told him what she had seen the day before, but she hardly knew how to form the words. It sickened her every time she thought of it. She had slept little that night, the image of Villiers's hand sliding up his mother's thigh tormenting her until she wanted to scream out her revulsion.

'I told you, I – we – are quite well,' she said, a little too brightly. 'We will be better still for the ride back to Whitehall.' That, at least, was not a lie. It promised to be another fine day and the sun was already high in the sky.

'I will be with you by nightfall. The King is out of humour after last night's feast so will not wish to hunt for long.'

'Do you presume to know His Majesty's desires now, Tyringham?'

The sound of Villiers's silken voice made Frances's blood run cold. She kept her head bowed after a brief curtsy, unable to bear the sight of him.

'I have readied the hounds, sir,' her husband said quietly.

'Good. Now you may ready my horse – make haste, man. The King wishes me to ride out ahead of the party, to ensure the keeper of the Great Park is prepared for our arrival.'

Thomas glanced from his wife to his master. Frances gave a slight nod. He hesitated a moment longer, then walked briskly to the stables. Villiers waited until he had disappeared from view before turning to address her. 'I did not see you at the Garter feast, Lady Frances.'

'I felt a little unwell so retired early,' she replied, stroking her belly distractedly.

'I do not think I have congratulated you yet. When will it be born?'

Frances had been asked the question many times these past few weeks and had always been vague in her answer.

'I cannot be sure,' she repeated now, 'but it will be months yet before I leave court.'

'I rejoice to hear it,' he drawled, his mouth curling into a slow smile. 'I would find this place a good deal less diverting without you in it.' His long fingers stroked his chin. 'But I pity you, when the time does come for you to return to the country. I cannot imagine that a woman of your intellect, of your . . . *curiosity* will find enough to amuse her, so far from court.'

Frances stared at him, heart thudding. *Had he seen her yester-day?* Surely he had been too steeped in his perverted lust to have noticed her flee from the gatehouse. Seeing his eyes spark with fury, she suddenly felt far from sure.

At that moment, there was the clatter of hoofs and Frances exhaled quietly as she saw her husband approaching with Villiers's horse. 'I am sure I will find plenty to entertain me, Sir George,' she said pleasantly.

He looked at her for a moment longer, then went to the mounting block and leaped gracefully into the saddle.

'Will you not bid me adieu, Lady Frances?' he called.

She gave a tight smile.

'Come now,' he persisted, holding out his hand. 'Let us offer each other the mark of friendship.'

Frances's smile did not waver, though she inwardly recoiled at the thought of touching him. But to refuse would be an insult and, intense though her loathing was, she had no wish to make an even greater enemy of him. She made to step forward, but Thomas placed a restraining hand on her arm.

'Do not let him bait you, Frances,' he murmured, under his breath.

She closed her hand over his and gave it a squeeze to convey her reassurance, then walked slowly to Villiers. His smile broadened as she approached and he leaned towards her. 'I am glad to see that you are biddable after all, Lady Frances, but you must learn to be more so, if you and I are to be friends.'

His grip on her hand tightened as he lowered his lips to it. They felt cool on her skin, but she snatched away her hand as if they had burned it. He gave a low chuckle and turned his gaze to the road ahead, gently patting the horse's neck. Then, without warning, he jabbed his heels so sharply into its sides that it reared in fright. Before Frances could react, she fell backwards onto the cobbles, a crushing pain searing through her stomach. The last thing she was aware of was a hot, oozing wetness seeping between her legs. Then everything was darkness.

PART 2

1618

CHAPTER 21

28 June

Frances gazed down at the baby cradled in her arms. He was his father in miniature, with the same clear eyes and light brown hair. It had been an easy birth. *He entered this world as quietly as the old Queen left it*, her mother had said. Helena had insisted that she come to Longford for her confinement, where she could care for her. It had taken little to persuade her. The pull of her childhood home was as strong as ever, and she had rejoiced at the prospect of seeing George again – her mother, too. John and Robert had come with her, and it gladdened her heart to see how they worshipped their elder brother already. She wished she might stay long enough for William to know him too.

George would be twelve next month. His indulgent grandmother had not exaggerated: he had grown into as fine a young man as Helena had described in her many letters. He was as slender as a young colt and almost as tall as Frances, and had grown even more like Tom since the last time she had seen him. His initial shyness upon seeing her had soon dissipated, and Frances knew that she had her mother to thank for that. Helena had made sure that the boy had grown up to feel his mother's presence almost as if she had been at Longford every day of the past four years.

William's eyes began to close. Frances knew that she should put him into his cradle, but she could not bear to be parted from him quite yet. She felt the familiar ache as she thought of the other child she had cradled in her arms two years before. *Anne.* They had named her for the Queen. She could remember little of the birth – she had drifted, waking only when Thomas had laid the tiny form on her breast. Her daughter had been wrenched from her womb too soon – born sleeping, as her husband had said. But she had been perfect, her features as delicate as porcelain and downy red hair covering her scalp.

'You should rest, my dear.'

Her mother was standing on the threshold of the chamber. Frances wondered how long she had been there. 'I have done little else this past week,' she replied, quickly brushing away tears.

Helena walked over and bent to kiss her forehead. Frances breathed in the familiar scent of rose and chamomile. It was like a balm to her soul. She did not protest as her mother took the sleeping boy from her arms and laid him in the crib at the end of the bed, then came to sit next to her.

'What news did Thomas have?'

Frances glanced at the letter on the table.

'Very little,' she lied. 'His duties permit him scant leisure to write, as usual. The *marquess* makes sure of that.' She failed to keep the bitterness from her voice. The title had been bestowed upon Villiers at the beginning of the year. He had been formally admitted to the privy council the following month, so he now held sway in his royal master's public domain, as well as his private life. The only saving grace was that her friend Sir Francis Bacon had enjoyed similar good fortune. As well as becoming a privy councillor, the King had also seen fit to bestow upon him the lord keepership. She knew he had coveted his father's former position for many years, and for good reason: it carried considerable powers – more even than the new Marquess of Buckingham enjoyed. She hoped Lord Bacon would use it to his advantage.

Helena was gazing at her intently, as if waiting for the truth. She had always had an uncanny ability to tell when her daughter was keeping something from her. 'My servants carried talk from Salisbury that Raleigh has set sail for England. Perhaps they were mistaken.'

Frances drew a breath. She had hated to conceal their involvement in his scheme but had not wished to cause her mother as much anxiety as she felt herself. It was more than a year since Sir Walter had embarked for Cádiz, and with each passing month the prospect that the fortune she and Thomas had staked on his enterprise would be returned faded. Even her husband seemed to have lost faith and had begun to mortgage some of their estates to settle their mounting debts. What would her mother think of her if she knew how much they stood to lose? Most of the land surrounding Tyringham had now been leased, and Frances feared it would not be long before they were obliged to do the same with George's inheritance at Longford.

'No – Thomas did mention that,' she replied. 'But, then, Sir Walter has been away for so long and the court's attention is notoriously fickle, as you know from your years there.'

Her mother's gaze didn't waver. 'Well, there is a good deal less news to occupy the people in these parts, so they feast upon what little they receive,' she said. 'Sir Walter was always loyal at heart to the old Queen. I will pray for his safe return.'

'And I too.' Frances reached for her mother's hand. 'It does my soul good to see you, Mother.'

Helena smiled. 'I wish you could stay here longer – the boys as well. Longford will seem so empty when you are gone.'

Frances recognised the sadness in her mother's eyes. Time had dulled the pain of losing her beloved husband, but Frances knew that she still yearned for him. Theirs had been a love that few other noble marriages were blessed with. 'I miss Father too,' she said quietly, squeezing her mother's hand. 'You must be so lonely without him.'

'George provides me with all the entertainment I could desire,' Helena replied. 'He is such a credit to you, my dear. Your father would have been so proud of him – and our other grandsons. Just as proud as he was of you.'

The sound of rapid footsteps in the corridor beyond broke the silence, and a second later George burst into the room, closely followed by John, his cheeks flushed and his eyes alight with excitement.

'I caught you!' he cried, triumphant, flinging himself at his elder brother, who twirled him around, almost knocking a vase off the dresser.

'Careful, George!' Frances cried, but could not keep the smile from her voice.

'No, little brother,' her eldest son said, wagging his finger. 'The rules state that Mother's chamber is neutral territory.'

John looked up at him quizzically. 'What rules? And what's neu— that thing you said?'

Helena gave an indulgent chuckle. 'You should not tease your brother so, George. He is only five.'

Her younger grandson drew himself up to his full height. 'I will be six next year, so I'm almost a man,' he averred, jutting out his chin.

'Is that so? Then you must forgive an old woman, my dear. I had quite miscalculated,' Helena said gravely.

Frances saw George's lips twitch and struggled to maintain her own composure. Only when John giggled did they all collapse into laughter, stopping when a thin wail rose from the cradle. Helena was there before her daughter and scooped her infant grandson into her arms, rocking him until he quietened. Frances sank back against her pillows, her eyelids heavy. Catching the movement, her mother placed William back in his cradle and led her other two grandsons out of the room. Their voices faded as Frances surrendered herself to sleep.

CHAPTER 22

4 August

'It is a good likeness.'

Thomas stared down at the sketch and smiled. Helena had made it the day before her daughter's departure from Longford. She had already completed one for herself, telling Frances she needed something to remember William by. When the letter had arrived from Thomas with the unwelcome news that he would be unable to come to Tyringham for their return, Helena had made another copy to give to him. *He will meet his new son soon enough, my dear.* Her mother's words rang in her ears now. She wished she could believe them.

'He is very like you,' Frances continued, her voice filled with pride and longing. The pain of bidding her little boy and his brothers farewell had been unbearable. Many times on the journey to London, she had almost ordered the coachman to stop and turn back to Tyringham. But the thought of seeing Thomas again had stopped the words in her throat.

Her husband traced his finger around the plump outline of William's face. 'Forgive me,' he whispered, his shoulders heaving with silent grief. Frances was not sure if he was speaking to her or his absent son. At length, he set down the drawing and pulled his wife into a tight embrace. 'I was desperate to come to you, my love.' His breath was warm in her hair. 'I would have travelled to Longford as soon as your mother's letter arrived, telling me of the birth. But Buckingham would not hear of my being so long absent and made sure that the King was of the same mind,' he said bitterly. 'Yet he assured me I would be spared for the journey to Tyringham. When permission for that was withdrawn too, I almost resigned my position. Only the thought of what would ensue prevented me.'

'You were right,' Frances murmured. 'Courting the King's anger at such a time would have spelled danger for us all. We must be patient. God willing, Raleigh will soon return triumphant.'

She felt her husband's body sag, as if in defeat. He stepped away from her and went to pour them a drink. Frances noticed that his hand shook slightly as he took a sip.

'What has happened?' she asked, when they were both seated.

Thomas sighed and rubbed his brow. 'The expedition was dogged by ill luck from the beginning. Many took it for a bad omen that Raleigh's fleet was battered by storms almost as soon as it set sail from Plymouth, and I am inclined to agree with them. Soon after, Sir Walter fell prey to a fever so grievous that his life was despaired of. He is recovered now,' he said quickly, clearly noting his wife's stricken face, 'but there has been a fresh disaster.'

Frances took a small sip from her glass and waited. Her mouth still felt dry.

'Raleigh's fleet succeeded in joining with that of King Philip at Cádiz and they sailed for Guiana as planned. But when they reached the Spanish settlement of San Thomé, the garrison recognised Sir Walter's standard and began to fire upon his ships, assuming they had come for war. Before word could be sent to the commander of the town, a furious battle had ensued. A number of Raleigh's men were slaughtered – including his son.'

Frances's hand flew to her mouth and she stared at Thomas, horror-struck. Raleigh had spoken of young Walter with such pride and affection. He would be devastated by his loss.

'When Raleigh heard the news, he ordered that the city be razed to the ground. King Philip took it as a declaration of war and abandoned the expedition. He and his fleet have returned to Cádiz. He has written to James protesting that Raleigh has shattered the peace between our two countries and must be punished as a traitor. He says nothing of his own part in this, of course.'

Frances tried to swallow but her throat felt as if it was in a vice. 'Where is Raleigh now?' she whispered, fearing the answer.

'He continued along the coast of Guiana, intent upon finding El Dorado so that he could plunder its gold and fund an invasion of England without Spain's help. But his men were falling away, either through sickness or mutiny, soon leaving Raleigh virtually alone on board the *Destiny*. He was forced to abandon the expedition and turn his sails northwards again. The King received word that he has been spied off the coast of Ireland. It will not be long before he is arrested and brought back to London.'

'And the Tower,' Frances added. Thomas looked as wretched as she felt. 'Then we are ruined,' she said.

His face sank into his hands. 'I am sorry, Frances. This is all my doing. I have been so blinded by my hatred of that – that *creature*' – his voice was as bitter as bile – 'that I have failed to see how great was the risk I took to be rid of him.'

'It was more than that,' she replied softly. 'If he had succeeded, Raleigh would have rid us of this heretic king and restored the country to the Catholic fold.' Her words sounded insincere, even to her ears. She knew her husband had spoken the truth, that his desperation to be rid of Buckingham had lain at the root of this. They had sacrificed so much to that devil already, but Frances had a creeping suspicion that he would take more from them yet.

'How much have we lost?' she asked.

Thomas raised his eyes to hers. 'Everything we pledged for the voyage. The lands I have mortgaged too – I will not be able to buy them back now. We have only Tyringham Hall and the income from my position here at court.'

Frances bit back a scornful remark. She knew that her husband's salary, like most others here, did not reflect his status. Even the grandest of titles rarely brought riches. If it did, then Buckingham would not have cast a second glance at a woman such as Lady Katherine Manners.

'I will write to my mother,' she said. 'George does not come into his inheritance for a few years yet, but I will ask that we borrow a portion of it now. It will be repaid – with interest – long before he reaches maturity.'

'No, Frances,' Thomas replied firmly. 'It is enough that I have ruined my own estate – your fortune too – without hazarding Longford. I will find another way. The King himself might advance me the money. He has been in an excellent humour since our return from the hunt.'

Frances eyed him doubtfully but said nothing. She knew that he had only made the suggestion to allay her worry, that he had as little faith as she in his royal master's generosity.

'I will find a way,' he repeated.

'I am so glad to see you!' Kate Manners cried, embracing Frances warmly. 'I have missed you so much since you left. You are quite recovered?' she enquired anxiously, holding her at arm's-length. 'I know it is more than two years now since . . . since that terrible accident, but I was so afraid for you. I sent for word every day, but my father would not let me see you. He said it would distress me too much and that you needed to rest,' she rattled on, hardly pausing to draw breath. 'And when at last I heard that my prayers had been answered and you would live, you were already on your way to Buckinghamshire. I wasn't even able to say goodbye . . .' Her voice cracked.

The girl was as pure in heart as when Frances had last seen her, and she could not but rejoice at the fact. She had feared that in her own absence from court her friend would have been corrupted by its vices, especially with such a man as Buckingham to pay her attention. *Perhaps the marquess has found another focus for his acquisitive gaze.* Even as she thought it, she knew how unlikely it was. There were ladies of greater beauty at court, but none of greater riches than Lady Katherine.

'I am sorry,' Frances said. 'I tried to send word of my departure but it was all conducted with such haste. My husband was anxious for me to return to Tyringham as soon as I was able to travel.'

Kate clasped her hands. 'I know, and he was right to be so after all you had suffered here. He is a good man and loves you truly.' She bit her lip. 'I pray that I may be blessed with such a husband one day.'

'I am sure you have had many suitors here since I saw you last,' Frances replied, watching her closely.

'You have too high an opinion of me,' Kate said. 'I know I am not well favoured – the countess has often reminded me of that.'

Anger surged in Frances. 'It is your stepmother who is ill-favoured – in everything that matters. Your goodness and virtue far exceed hers.'

'Oh, I did not mean Countess Cecilia,' Kate responded, 'though she is of the same mind, certainly. No, it was the Countess of Buckingham I referred to.'

Frances stared, mute.

'The Marquess of Buckingham's mother,' Kate explained, seeing her confusion. 'She is very proud of the title that the King has bestowed upon her – rightly so, of course,' she added quickly.

Frances tried to hide her dismay. The title was as much a compliment to Buckingham as it was to his mother, who had clearly succeeded in ingratiating herself with the King during the time she had spent at court. Thomas had told her that Lady Mary had shown no inclination to return to her estates. What was worse, she and her son had succeeded in installing other members of the family in James's service. Buckingham's younger brother Christopher was now a gentleman of the bedchamber, and the King had entailed Buckingham's title on his elder brother John, should his favourite die without heirs. Frances suspected that James hoped he would.

'It is indeed a great honour for her,' she replied quietly. 'Her son the marquess showed you great courtesy when I was last at court,' she went on after a pause. 'Has that continued during my absence?'

The flush on her friend's cheeks told her it had, but she appeared more perturbed than pleased.

'Yes – even more so,' Kate replied quietly, her fingers working at a stray thread on the seam of her gown. 'I was flattered at first, of course – he could have his pick of the ladies at court. But there is still something about him that makes me uneasy.'

Frances tried to hide her satisfaction. She was glad that Kate was less naive than she had thought. Perhaps it would not be so difficult to save her from Buckingham's clutches after all.

'What is your father's opinion of him?' she asked.

Kate's frown deepened. 'He hardly speaks of him, but I have noticed he falls quiet whenever we meet, though the marquess takes great pains to win his good graces.'

Frances had no doubt of that. Buckingham was always at his most obsequious when he had something to gain. 'I thought your two families were well acquainted?' she ventured.

'As you know, our estates lie close to each other, but that is all. Father has never shown much interest in strengthening our connection, though my lady mother has encouraged him many times. She and the Countess of Buckingham are on very affection-ate terms.'

Frances fell silent, as if considering the matter. 'I have always known your father to be a man of discernment,' she observed carefully. 'If he harbours the same distrust as you for the marquess, then it must be for good reason. It seems your instincts may be right, so you are wise to behave with caution. I have long since learned that not everything at court is as it appears. Buckingham is high in the King's favour and has many men to do his bidding, but I do not trust him.'

Kate's eyes were wide with fright. Frances placed a hand on hers. 'There may be many dissemblers in this place, Kate, but you can be assured that I am not among them,' she said. 'I seek nothing from you but friendship.'

The young woman's eyes filled with tears as she grasped her hand tightly. 'I would trust you with my life, Frances.'

CHAPTER 23

16 August

The apartment had to be one of the finest in the palace. Rich tapestries lined the walls, their gold and silver threads shimmering in the light from the gilded sconces. Several chambers led off the main hall, and the large mullioned windows commanded extensive views of the river.

'You have done well, my lord,' Frances remarked to her host.

Bacon grinned. 'The gossips whispered that I lived like a king while the real one was parading around Scotland with his favourite last year, so I thought I should justify their claims.'

Frances had heard the rumours. Although her friend made light of them, Thomas had told her how vicious the sniping had been during James's absence. Bacon's promotion to the lord keepership had excited a great deal of envy.

'They were my father's lodgings,' he went on. 'I inherited them with his office. But I ordered their redecoration first – he and I had rather different taste.' His eyes glinted with humour. Though they had never spoken of it directly, they both knew he was referring to more than his taste in furnishings. Sir Nicholas Bacon had sired numerous children, both within and outside wedlock.

'I was delighted when I heard the news of your advancement,' she remarked with sincerity. 'Nobody deserves it more.'

'Or has waited longer.' His smile broadened. 'Well, it is all the sweeter for that.'

Frances took the glass he held out. She had been glad of the invitation to dine with him that evening. There had been little enough to celebrate since her return to court.

'To our absent friends,' Bacon said, raising his glass.

Frances's smile faded. 'One in particular.'

They both fell silent for a few moments. News of Raleigh's arrest had reached the court six days earlier. The lord high admiral had ordered his capture and he had been brought back first to Plymouth and then London.

'Would that he had escaped to France, as he had planned,' Bacon said quietly. 'But Lord Howard had instructed his men to watch him like a hawk. He knows Raleigh of old.'

'What will become of him?' Frances feared the answer.

Her friend shook his head. 'The King wants him dead.' His voice was flat, resigned. 'Raleigh has written a defence of his actions at San Thomé, insisting that Guiana was English territory and his aggression was therefore justified.'

'He is right, is he not?'

'Perhaps. King Philip has withdrawn his complaint – it seems he is not such a hypocrite, after all.' His knuckles showed white as he took a sip from his glass. 'But it makes little difference. Raleigh's real crime was in failing to bring back the gold he had promised. In James's eyes, he has always been a traitor and should have had his head struck off years ago.'

'But if the King of Spain is no longer demanding recompense for San Thomé, what grounds can there be to condemn him?'

'The original charge of treason was never revoked,' Bacon replied.

'But that was fifteen years ago!' Frances exclaimed. 'There are few people who can even remember what it was for. If James revived it now, he would appear ridiculous, as well as irresolute.'

'You are right and His Majesty knows it, which is why he has instructed his commissioners to interrogate every member of the crew, as well as Raleigh himself, of course. He means to find proof, however fragile, that Sir Walter was plotting to foment war between this country and Spain.'

Frances gave a derisive laugh. 'We should be grateful, I suppose. It would be worse for Raleigh if the King suspected his real motive was to ally with King Philip.' She paused, her expression grave. 'Our king is a master at deciding upon the crime before any evidence has been gathered to support it. I have experienced such justice at his hands. Can you do nothing to help?'

'God knows I have tried. But to the King's ear, my words are tainted. He has not forgotten how I argued for Raleigh's release so that he might undertake this voyage.'

'But as lord keeper your authority exceeds that of all his other advisers – even Buckingham,' she said weakly, knowing that the King paid little heed to the hierarchy of his council. In his eyes, the marquess would always be head and shoulders above the rest.

'In matters of state, yes,' Bacon replied. 'But I no longer have pre-eminence in the law. I was obliged to surrender the post of attorney general upon my recent promotion. My successor has no wish to endanger his position by speaking up for our beleaguered friend.'

Frances knew he was right. Sir Henry Yelverton had already courted James's disapproval on a number of occasions – not least for making an enemy of Buckingham. Little wonder that he wanted to avoid any further controversy.

'The people will protest against it,' she said. 'Sir Walter is as popular now as he was in the old Queen's time.'

He nodded. 'Which is why His Grace means to arrange this as a private matter.'

Frances sank down on one of the gilded chairs by the window. Tears of frustration pricked her eyes as she looked out over the Thames. The river was quieter now, and there were just a few small wherries tethered to the landing stage on the opposite bank. She thought of Raleigh, holed up in his apartments at the Tower. Had hope deserted him too? She prayed it had not, that his sharp mind was already turning over some fresh scheme to rid England of the heretic King. Even though he had lost her fortune – Thomas's too – she could bear him no ill will. God willing, he would meet his death with the same sanguinity that had sustained him throughout the long years of his imprisonment.

'Come, my dear,' Bacon laid a gentle hand on her shoulder, 'we should dine – though God knows I have little appetite for it.'

CHAPTER 24

12 September

Frances looked up at her husband and smiled. Despite everything that had happened these past few weeks, she was enjoying being in his arms as they followed the steps of the dance. His hand felt warm on the small of her back and she could smell his familiar scent among the heavy perfumes with which the ladies had drenched themselves.

'The count appears in good humour this evening.' Thomas glanced over her shoulder to where the Spanish ambassador was supping wine with the King and Buckingham.

Frances did not turn: she had seen enough of the marquess's fawning and simpering. The arrival of Diego Sarmiento de Acuña, Count de Gondomar, had caused a stir at court. Relations between England and Spain had been hostile for so long that even James's councillors had been of the opinion war was pending, especially after the disaster of Raleigh's expedition. But now all the talk was of peace and mutual accord. The ambassador had even been charged with opening negotiations for a marriage between Prince Charles and the Infanta Maria. Their new-found amity made Frances uneasy, particularly as Buckingham was going out of his way to encourage it. *What game was he playing now?*

'He seems to approve of the Madeira wine. It is fortunate that the King ordered such vast quantities,' she replied sardonically.

They had reached the end of the hall now and were obliged to change places as they began the slow procession back, keeping their steps in time with those of the other dancers. Frances's eyes were drawn back to the dais. She stared, astonished, as Queen Anne walked slowly onto it, accompanied by her son, Charles. She was much thinner than when Frances had last seen her and was leaning heavily on the prince's arm. Frances was as shocked by the change in her as by her sudden appearance at court. As she stared, she was jostled by the lady next to her, who gave an exasperated sigh. Quickly, Frances tried to fall back into step but stumbled over the skirts of another, who turned sharply and glared at her.

'Forgive us,' Thomas said, pulling Frances gently away. 'My wife is in need of a rest.' He steered her towards a quiet recess. 'What is it?' he asked.

Frances nodded towards the dais. She saw her husband's eyes widen briefly as he noticed Anne, who was now lowering herself onto the throne next to her husband's. It was placed there at every court gathering, but Frances had grown so accustomed to seeing it empty that she could hardly believe that the Queen was there now.

'You did not know she was coming either?' Frances murmured.

Thomas shook his head, still gazing at the dais. 'I had not thought to see her here again.'

The Queen was extending her hand to the ambassador now, while Buckingham looked on approvingly. Frances thought back to the conversation they had had at Denmark House. Anne had admitted she had encouraged the King's obsession with the young favourite, hinting that it was to serve a greater purpose than merely to satisfy her husband's lust. Ever since Frances had puzzled over what that purpose might be.

'Is it for Raleigh, I wonder?' Thomas mused. 'The Count de Gondomar has said his master expects the King to make recompense for San Thomé. Perhaps the Queen intends to soften his opinion.'

Frances hoped he was right: Sir Walter had little other chance of avoiding the fate that seemed more certain with each passing day. Bacon had confided at their last meeting that he had received instructions to prepare for a private hearing at Whitehall.

At that moment, the musicians struck up another tune and the courtiers formed themselves into two neat rows in preparation for the pavane. Frances saw Lady Kate Manners take her place among them, her eyes cast down but her face flushed with excitement. She loved to dance and would often beg to practise the steps with Frances when they were alone. Frances's smile vanished as she saw Buckingham weave his way through the assembled throng and come to a halt directly opposite Kate, pushing two gentlemen out of the way in his eagerness to be her partner. He made an ostentatious bow, one hand clasped to his chest as if in reverence, then stepped forward and pulled her towards him as the dance began.

Frances watched as the marquess swept her along. He moved with such impeccable elegance and precision that the rest of the dancers appeared awkward and graceless by comparison. Now and again, he cast a sly glance over his shoulder towards his royal master, whose eyes never left him, even though the ambassador was trying to engage him in conversation.

Unable to bear the sight of him any longer, Frances looked to the opposite side of the hall and was surprised to see Lord Rutland among the company.

'He does not approve of the dance, it seems,' Thomas observed, following her gaze. 'Or perhaps it is his daughter's partner who offends him?'

Frances did not reply. She had seen little of the earl in recent weeks, for he had been preoccupied by affairs at Belvoir Castle. She suspected he would have left to attend to them in person if it had not been for his fear that Buckingham would make the most of his absence. That he was intent upon marrying Lady Katherine was well known to everyone at court, the King included. Thomas had overheard a furious row between the two men, during which James had accused his lover of playing him false. Far from prompting Buckingham to employ greater discretion, this seemed to have encouraged him to flaunt his flirtation with the hapless Kate even more. Perhaps he knew that stoking the King's jealousy would intensify his obsession.

Frances glanced at the throne as James took a long draught from his goblet. She noticed the fleeting disdain on Gondomar's face as he watched a thin trail of red wine snaking down the King's chin. But he arranged his mouth into a smile as soon as James leaned forward to address him.

It was obvious they were talking about Buckingham, judging from the frequent looks they turned in his direction. The King's cheeks were flushed – with wine or rage, Frances could not tell. She watched as his favourite deftly twirled Kate towards the dais, drawing her even closer so that by the time they were within a few feet of the King their faces were almost touching. The dance was ending now, and as the other couples made their obeisance towards James, Buckingham kept his eyes fixed upon his partner. As the music faded into silence, he leaned forward and slowly pressed his lips against hers.

'How dare you, sir?'

There were murmurs of surprise as Lord Rutland pushed his way through the crowds. Kate had managed to pull away from the marquess and was standing, head bowed, colour rising to her face. Buckingham smirked at her father as he drew level with him.

'Your daughter is an excellent dancer, my lord,' he remarked languidly. 'She follows the steps perfectly.'

Rutland glowered at him. 'You dishonour her.' His voice was so low that Frances strained to hear. 'I should have you horsewhipped for this.'

The marquess opened his mouth to respond, but at that moment a loud scraping noise echoed across the room and everyone turned to see the King rising from his throne. 'Come, Steenie,' he commanded. 'You have had enough sport this evening.'

He did not wait for an answer before he staggered from the dais, the Count de Gondomar staring after him. An awkward silence followed. Frances could see tears pooling in Kate's eyes as she stared at the floor. She moved to help but Thomas laid a hand on her arm. He would not wish her to make even more of an enemy of Buckingham than he was already.

At that moment, a delicate cough sounded around the hall and Lord Bacon stepped from the shadows, the heels of his exquisite satin shoes clipping on the flagstones. 'My lord marquess.' He swept an ostentatious greeting. 'I have been admiring your dancing all evening. Why, you move with such grace that Apollo himself must be wringing his hands with envy.'

Frances held her breath as she saw Buckingham turn his gaze to her friend, eyes narrowed.

'And, if you will permit me to observe, your coat is the finest cut of any I have seen here at court – even in the old Queen's day. Is that Venetian silk?'

'Persian.' The younger man drew himself up to his full height.

His flattery has hit its mark, Frances realised, with a mixture of astonishment and admiration. She had not thought that even a man of Buckingham's vanity would be so easily distracted.

Bacon clicked his tongue, then reached out to touch the doublet, his eyelids fluttering closed as if in wonderment. 'You are the brightest jewel of this court, my lord,' he declared, hand on his chest, then raised his glass aloft. 'To the Marquess of Buckingham!' The words echoed into silence and Frances darted an anxious glance around the company.

'To the marquess.' The heavily accented voice came from the dais. Gondomar had risen to his feet and was holding his glass towards the assembled company. He gave a slight bow as his gaze fell upon Buckingham, then brought the wine to his lips.

The other dignitaries on the dais followed suit and, before long, the toast was repeated by everyone in the room, Frances and her husband included. For once, she was gratified to see how the King's favourite preened as he acknowledged the gesture. Then, without troubling to take his leave of Kate, he strutted slowly from the hall. Only when he was out of sight did Bacon turn to Frances and flash a brief conspiratorial smile.

CHAPTER 25

5 October

As the boat drew level with the landing stage, Frances reached into her pocket and clasped the note. Pressing some coins into the oarsman's palm, she climbed onto the platform and hastened towards the Byward Tower. The guards looked at her askance and lowered their halberds as she approached. This gate was usually reserved for the King and his family.

Frances held out the letter. The elder of the guards frowned but she saw his expression change as he recognised the seal. Anne had needed no persuasion to write it. She was as sympathetic towards Raleigh's plight as Frances was. Frances watched as he read it, then carefully refolded it.

'You must show this to the yeoman at the Bloody Tower,' he said, as he handed it back. 'I presume you know the way, my lady.'

Frances nodded and walked past them as calmly as she could. It was only a short distance to Raleigh's lodgings and she could see a light glowing from the upper window. She passed under the archway, the spikes of the portcullis above silhouetted against the grey sky. The huge edifice of the White Tower loomed into view on the left and she shuddered, quickening her pace.

As she neared the steps that led up to the Bloody Tower, Frances breathed in the faint scent of myrtle. Glancing down, she saw that Raleigh's garden was sadly neglected. The basil plants had long since withered and died, and the once neatly laid-out beds were now a mass of weeds. Only the hedge that encircled it still thrived, but it had grown unkempt. Bacon had told her that Raleigh had devoted many hours to the garden's cultivation. He was unlikely to be allowed such liberty again.

Feeling suddenly weary, she climbed the steps to his lodging. After she had shown the yeoman Queen Anne's letter, he nodded her through. When the door had closed behind her, she paused, inhaling the familiar aroma of tobacco and wood smoke. The apartment smelt damp, too, and was colder than she had remembered it. Neither was there any sign of the servants who had attended Raleigh throughout the long years of his incarceration. Everything was as still and silent as a tomb.

With mounting apprehension, Frances stepped quietly into the parlour. A meagre fire flickered in the grate, and on the table next to it was a plate of stale-looking bread and cheese. Neither had been touched. Turning, her breath caught in her throat as she saw Raleigh seated on the same high-backed chair she remembered from her many visits here. His eyes were closed and he was so still that she feared he might be dead. He seemed to have shrunk into himself. His once ruddy face was pale and wan, and his cheekbones showed beneath his waxen skin. Frances turned towards the window and brushed away a tear. He must not see her grief when he awoke.

'I am a pitiful sight, am I not?'

The softly rasping voice made her start. She looked back at him, tears now streaming down her cheeks. He held out his hand and she bent to kiss it. His fingers were icy cold.

'My brains are broken,' he said. ''Tis a torment to me that I still draw breath. I wish that God had stopped it long before now.'

Frances knelt at his feet, still clasping his hand in hers. 'You must not lose faith,' she whispered. 'The King may yet grant you a pardon – as he seems likely to do for Lord Somerset.'

Raleigh's mouth lifted into a faint smile. 'Ah, but my offences are far greater than his – and those of his pretty wife. He will not allow me to escape the axe a second time.' He closed his eyes again and leaned back in his chair. Frances had just begun to wonder if he had fallen asleep when he gripped her hand. 'I am sorrier than I can say, my dear.' His eyes misted as he looked at her. 'That I failed in my enterprise is torment enough to me, but knowing I have ruined the fortunes of you and many others in the attempt is more than I can bear.'

Frances pressed her lips to his fingers again. 'You must not plague yourself with such thoughts. We knew the risks as well as you did, but were driven by a desire to rid ourselves of this heretic king and the evil that surrounds him. You acted in God's name and it grieves me sorely that He did not smile upon your endeavours.'

Raleigh's mouth twisted. 'I can no longer see God's hand in any of this. For years, this country has been divided, each side claiming to know His will. And what has it brought us but misery and bloodshed?'

Frances felt a pang at hearing him speak the same thoughts that had plagued her these past few weeks. 'We can only keep faith in our hearts and pray that one day He might show us His purpose.'

'I think that day is closer for me than it is for you, my dear,' he replied, with a sad smile. 'Our friend Bacon tells me that my trial is imminent. That faithless wretch Yelverton has all the arrangements in place and waits only for the King to name a date. With the Spanish ambassador at court, it cannot be long now. James will not wish to appear irresolute in front of his new ally.'

Frances opened her mouth to reply, but fell silent.

'In my weakness, I even appealed to the King's beloved angel,' he continued. Frances struggled to hide her dismay. 'I deserve your censure. I should never have stooped so low and I despise myself for such cowardice. The *marquess'* – he placed a scornful emphasis upon the word – 'delighted in rejecting my suit and made sure that Gondomar heard of it. That man is the devil himself.'

'I know the truth of it all too well,' Frances replied. 'I pray that God may soon rid us of his presence.'

Raleigh squeezed her hand but said nothing. They knew her prayers were likely to go unanswered, and Frances had seen enough since her return to court two months before to convince her that Buckingham's hold over the King was stronger than ever.

'Bacon is hopeful that my sentence may be commuted to beheading,' he said, after a long pause. 'Though I should be thankful that I may be spared a traitor's death, terror still grips my heart. For many nights now, I have lain awake, imagining how it will be. Sometimes I think I can feel the blade against my neck. I cannot—' He broke off, his breath coming in rapid gasps and his eyes wide with fear. Frances reached out to him, and he clutched at her hand with trembling fingers. 'You must help me, Frances,' he whispered.

'I would do anything,' tears pricked her eyes again, 'but the King would never heed my word – or my husband's. He listens only to Buckingham, and his own foolish pride.'

'It is not your words I ask for,' Sir Walter replied softly, his gaze intensifying.

Frances held her breath.

'It was not so long ago that you prepared a . . . remedy for Prince Henry. Of course, God saw fit to claim him before you could administer it. But it would be a shame to waste it, would it not?'

She stared at him, aghast. 'The tincture was destroyed long ago,' she replied truthfully. An image flitted before her of Thomas pouring it into the fire. She could still remember the acrid stench that had filled their chamber.

'Ah, but the mandrake I supplied was enough to make several more of the same potency,' he persisted. 'I am sure that a woman with your skill would not have discarded such a jewel, knowing that the root has the power to heal as well as to kill.'

Frances tried to protest but the words died on her lips.

'I beg of you, please do this for me. I lack the courage for what I must face,' he urged, his eyes now wild with fright.

She longed to wrench her hand from him and run far from there. If she supplied Raleigh with the means to take his own life, he would surely be damned for all eternity. And if her part in it were discovered, she would be hanged as a witch – Buckingham would make sure of that. Her herbs had only ever been used for good. Although she had plotted to murder the prince with the tincture of mandrake, God had stayed her hand. Even though the King's son had worked to destroy her and those she held dear, to take a life was a sin.

An image came unbidden into her mind of a man lying on a pallet bed in a dungeon not far away. She tried to push it from her, but it seemed to grow so sharply into focus that it was no longer Raleigh's face before her but Tom's. He was smiling sadly at her as he replaced the stopper on the tiny glass phial. *I cannot let you forfeit your life for me.* She tried to swallow as his words sounded in her ears. She had begged him to let her save him from the horror that lay before him. Just a few drops of the tincture would have been enough to stop his breath, robbing the executioner's knife of its gruesome task of gouging out his entrails and performing all manner of tortures before his head was smitten off. She had replayed their whispered conversation so many times since that night, wishing she had had the strength to persuade him. But in her heart she knew there was nothing she could have said or done. Tom would never have allowed her to risk her own life by giving him a swifter, kinder death. He had loved her too much.

'Please.'

Sir Walter's voice brought her back to the present. He was staring intently at her, his eyes imploring. How could she deny him the same mercy she would have performed for Tom? She closed her eyes and uttered a silent prayer. Then, opening them, she gave the slightest of nods. Raleigh pressed his lips to her hand once more and sank back in his chair.

'Raleigh will appear before the privy council tomorrow.' Thomas's expression was grave.

Frances had waited for this moment for more than two weeks now, not wanting to deliver the potion to Raleigh until his fate was absolutely certain. There could be only one verdict and Bacon had warned that the King would want to see the sentence swiftly carried out.

'The lieutenant of the Tower has written to the King. He says that Sir Walter is too sick to travel to Westminster.'

Frances looked at her husband sharply. 'What ails him?'

'A fever, apparently. Sir Allen reports that he has not eaten for three days and has now fallen into a delirium.'

Frances considered this. Sir Allen Apsley had been appointed at Buckingham's behest the previous year. He was unlikely to do Raleigh a favour by exaggerating his condition.

'James will not hear of it,' her husband continued. 'He says it is all a ruse by Raleigh to escape his fate. Buckingham encourages him in this view, of course.'

Frances thought of her old friend suffering alone in that grim fortress. He had appeared frail enough when she had last seen him. If he was as sick as Apsley reported, her potion might not be needed after all. But she could not risk waiting, particularly as James was not minded to. She must go to the Tower tonight.

'The King will not want to be denied his prey,' Frances murmured, almost to herself.

Thomas nodded, grim-faced. 'He seems to take pleasure in the prospect of sending a sick old man to his death.'

Should she tell him? She had almost done so upon her return from the Tower, but fear of implicating him had prevented her. This was a burden she must carry alone. Besides, the task was now less fraught with danger. If Raleigh was known to be gravely ill, few would think to question it if God were to claim him before the King's justice could.

Frances moved to sit by her husband. 'We must keep faith that God will wreak his vengeance – in this world or the next.'

CHAPTER 26

21 October

As she turned under the archway and mounted the steps to the green, Frances tried to push away the thought that this once great adventurer, the hero of the old Queen and the scourge of her successor, would breathe his last in a matter of minutes. It seemed impossible, somehow. He had always been so full of life – of hope, too, despite living under the threat of execution for fifteen years.

When she reached the edge of Raleigh's garden, she looked up at the tower, its turrets silhouetted against the night sky. There was no sign of life within. Perhaps God had already taken him. She prayed that He had, though instinct told her he still drew breath.

Her pulse throbbed in her ears as she began to mount the steps. She saw that the yeoman was not at his post. He must have moved inside the lodging to shelter from the cold. She knocked lightly on the door and waited, her breath misting in the air. Everything was silent within. Slowly, she lifted the latch and pushed open the door, expecting to see the guard asleep. But the room was in darkness. She waited, straining her ears for any sound from the chamber beyond. *Nothing*. Summoning her courage, she took a step forward and reached for the handle. But just as her fingers closed over the cold iron ring, a hand gripped her wrist with such force that she cried out. There was an answering groan from Raleigh's chamber, then silence.

'Sir Walter does not usually receive visitors at this hour.'

The silken voice was so close to her ear that she could feel his breath. She felt like a rabbit caught in a snare and looked desperately about her, as if trying to find some means of escape. He took a step closer, his arm brushing against her back. Her breath was coming so quickly that she feared she might faint. Then he released his grip and there was a loud bang as he flung open the shutter. At once, the parlour was illuminated by the fragile light of the waning moon. Frances tried to turn but he pressed her against the door so that her head twisted painfully away from him.

'What is your business here, Lady Frances?'

There was no mistaking his voice this time. A moment later, he released his grip and she turned to see Buckingham standing before her. He eyed her with faint amusement, as if he had caught a child stealing a comfit from the palace kitchens.

'Where is the yeoman?' she demanded, hoping to distract him while she tried to order her thoughts.

The marquess waved his hand dismissively. 'I have relieved him of his duties for the evening. Some jewels are of such value that they should not be entrusted to others, as I advised His Majesty.'

'You are very assiduous, my lord,' she replied sardonically. 'Surely Sir Allen would have been happy to oblige.'

'I have no doubt of it. But the only means to be certain of an outcome is to perform the task oneself, is it not, my lady?'

His eyes glinted in the gloom. Frances held his gaze but did not answer.

'Now we have established why I am here, perhaps we could turn our attention to you.'

Frances thought quickly. 'I had heard that Sir Walter was ill and hoped to observe his symptoms so that I could seek a remedy from the court apothecary.'

Buckingham raised an eyebrow. 'Clearly I am not alone in my assiduity. Did you not think that the King might have assigned someone to attend to his prisoner?'

Frances gave a shrug. 'It hardly seemed likely, given that he will soon have him put to death.'

Buckingham eyed her. 'If you wished to observe Sir Walter's symptoms, then why did you not do so during daylight hours? It is very late for a lady of your status to be out alone.'

'I have been ill myself and was obliged to keep to my chambers all day,' Frances countered. 'But I felt better after some sleep so resolved to come at once, rather than wait until tomorrow when Sir Walter will no longer be able to receive visitors.'

Buckingham nodded slowly. She knew he suspected her, but was determined to give him no reason to detain her.

'May I see Sir Walter now?' she asked curtly. 'I do not wish to delay my return to Whitehall any longer.'

The young man wrought a heavy sigh. 'I wish that I could sanction it, but the King's orders were very clear. I am to admit no one to Raleigh's chamber tonight – not even his wife. She has made *such* a nuisance of herself today with her weeping and wailing. I wonder that she did not rouse the poor man from his bed.'

'But I seek only a few moments with him, my lord,' Frances persisted, her fingers closing over the tiny glass phial in her pocket.

Buckingham spread his hands. 'I wish I could oblige you. But I am sure you would not want me to defy a royal command. These are treacherous times, Lady Frances, and His Grace must be given no cause to doubt those who serve him. Your husband knows that all too well.'

Frances bit back a remark, determined not to let him provoke her into saying something she might regret.

'Then I will bid you goodnight,' she said, and curtsied. She stepped forward but he moved to block her path.

'The King can trust *you*, can he not, my lady?' he murmured. 'Only I have heard rumours that you were once a prisoner here – under suspicion of witchcraft, no less.'

Frances tasted bile but maintained her composure. She would not give him the satisfaction of seeing he had riled her. 'For a short time, yes. But I was soon acquitted. Perhaps Sir Walter will enjoy a similar outcome.'

Buckingham let out a bark of laughter. There was another groan from Raleigh's chamber. Frances glanced towards it, desperate to run inside and press the tincture into his hands. But instead she turned slowly back to face the marquess.

'Do not worry, my lady. I will take good care of him,' he said, with a slow smile.

Frances did not reply, but walked briskly towards the door. She had just lifted the latch when he spoke again.

'I will not trouble the King with news of your little . . . excursion,' he said softly. 'Not unless it becomes necessary, of course.'

Frances paused, her hand still on the latch. 'Goodnight, my lord,' she replied, then closed the door quietly behind her.

Frances glanced at the clock on the fireplace. A quarter past three. For almost an hour now her ears had strained for the shouts of the crowds gathered on the Strand.

'Lady Frances?'

She turned quickly back to Anne, her face flushing. 'Forgive me, Your Grace. I am but poor company today. What did you ask?'

The Queen gave a knowing smile. 'I am glad you came. The hours pass so slowly here some days, though I much prefer it to the ceaseless prattle of court.' She glanced towards the window. 'Sir Walter is a little behind his time, is he not?'

Frances nodded tightly but said nothing. He had been summoned to appear before the privy council that morning. If Buckingham had not prevented her from delivering the precious tincture to him last night, he would have been spared the humiliation of answering the charges against him – not to mention the long journey through the streets of London, which must have been an ordeal in his enfeebled state.

'You must not blame yourself, my dear,' Anne said kindly. 'You did everything you could to save him from this.'

'I cannot bear to think that he will go to his grave believing I had forsaken him,' Frances replied miserably. 'If it had not been for that devil—' She stopped short, remembering the conversation they had had about Buckingham more than three years earlier.

Anne smiled. 'You may speak freely here. I harbour no prejudice, so far removed from the heart of affairs.'

'But Your Grace once spoke in favour of Buckingham. I would not wish to cause offence.'

'I observed only that the young marquess may not be all that he seems,' Anne replied. 'That is very different from cherishing any affection for him.'

'And yet you said he could be our salvation,' Frances persisted. 'I have puzzled over your words ever since.'

With an effort, the Queen rose to her feet and limped slowly to the window. She stood there in silence for some time, leaning heavily upon the gilded frame as she gazed down on the street below.

'I would not say anything to place you in danger, Lady Frances,' she said at last. 'I ask only that you do not allow prejudice to blind you to what Buckingham is – to what he may be.'

Frances looked at her sharply. 'My opinion is based upon his treatment of me – of my husband too. I bear no man ill will unless he has deserved it.'

Anne held up her hand in a placatory gesture. 'I know what you have suffered at his hands, my dear. It is little wonder that you look upon him as a mortal enemy. But the same snake that has bitten you may sink its poison into one more deserving. My husband should have a care.'

Frances reeled at her words. That Buckingham was a threat to any who challenged his power, she could readily believe. That he posed a danger to the King himself seemed impossible. James was the source of all his authority, his riches. It would surely be madness to plot against him. He would stand to lose everything.

She opened her mouth to reply, but at that moment a loud cheer rose up from the Strand. The Queen turned back to the window at once, and Frances hastened to join her. In the distance, towards Westminster, she could just discern a cavalcade making its slow progress along the street. In the centre was a carriage, flanked on every side by mounted riders.

As it drew closer, Frances saw that the windows were draped with heavy black cloth. She had been surprised that the King had granted Raleigh's request to travel to his hearing by carriage, rather than barge, knowing that this would attract more attention. If James hoped to limit his prisoner's exposure to the adoring crowds, though, he would be disappointed. Raleigh had pulled back the drapes and was graciously waving his thanks to the people who lined his route back to the Tower. From this distance, Frances could not see the expression on his face, but she judged from the cheers and shouts of 'God save you!' that he was smiling.

'Perhaps the outcome was not as we feared.' But even as she spoke the words, she knew them to be false.

'Sir Walter will go to his death with as merry a countenance as he showed the old Queen,' Anne replied sadly. 'Let us offer up our prayers that he enjoys greater fortune in the next world than he has in this.'

CHAPTER 27

29 October

Old Palace Yard was deserted when Frances arrived. The scaffold had been erected the previous night, just hours after Raleigh's sentence had been pronounced. Thomas told her that Sir Walter had offered a spirited defence at his trial, despite being so weak with sickness that he had barely been able to stand. His courage had only faltered as the verdict had been delivered, and he had sunk to his knees, begging the King to show mercy. His pleas had fallen on deaf ears. The only clemency James had shown was to commute his sentence to beheading.

Frances had not slept that night and had risen before dawn. Raleigh would be brought here in a little under two hours' time, as the bell of St Stephen's tolled eight. Glancing towards the gatehouse, she saw a faint glimmer in one of the windows. The King had ordered that he spend the night there. Frances did not know if it was to save time or lessen the risk of escape. For a moment, she thought of running to the window and calling to him. But the idea faded as quickly as it had sparked. What could she say that Raleigh would be content for his gaolers to hear? *Pray God he will find it in his heart to forgive me.*

Thomas had begged her not to come, but she had been resolute. She had failed to save her old friend from the terror and humiliation of this death, but would be here to pray for him as the life was struck from his body. It had always been a source of shame and regret that she had lacked the strength to do the same for Tom. Looking around the courtyard now, she imagined her lover being dragged there on the wooden hurdle that had conveyed him from the Tower, his emaciated limbs jolting painfully on the cobbles. Thomas had told her that he had met his death with calm acceptance, apparently impervious to the horrors that the King's executioner had visited upon his body. Tears pricked her eyes as she raised them to the heavens, imploring God to give Raleigh the same peace.

A few more people were filtering into the courtyard now, eager to secure a good vantage point. London was still crowded with revellers from the Lord Mayor's Day celebration. They must consider it a boon to be witnessing this spectacle too, Frances reflected. She walked slowly to the opposite side of the scaffold, knowing that Raleigh would pass this way on the short walk from the gatehouse. Drawing up her hood against the cold, damp air, she closed her eyes in prayer.

By the time daylight broke, the courtyard was crowded with spectators, jostling and chattering excitedly. Frances judged that it could only be a few more minutes before eight o' clock. It had seemed an age since the bell had struck seven.

'Make way there!'

The shout rang out across the courtyard, prompting a chorus of murmurs as everyone looked towards the thickset guard who was pushing his way through the crowds. Behind him, Frances could see a procession of finely dressed dignitaries. She recognised Thomas Clinton, the new Earl of Lincoln, and Raleigh's old patron Robert de Vere, Earl of Oxford, who had tried to stir up resistance to the Scottish King in the last days of Elizabeth's reign. Frances craned her neck, hoping to see Bacon, but he was not among them. He had confided to her that he had no stomach for such things and that he would be spending the day in prayer for his old friend. Neither was Buckingham present, much to her surprise. She had expected him to take pride of place at the gruesome spectacle. Perhaps he meant to show, by his absence, how little Raleigh's death mattered.

She was reflecting on this bitter thought when she saw Thomas at the end of the procession. Her heart leaped. He was staring at the ground, grim-faced, but looked up just as he drew level with her. Their eyes met for a moment before the crowds closed in behind him.

A loud cheer rose and all heads turned back towards the gateway where the lords had just entered. Frances stood on tiptoe but for several moments she could see nothing except the waving arms and hats being thrown into the air. Then at last Raleigh came into view. He was dressed all in black, and as he drew closer Frances was shocked to see that he was wearing his nightgown. A matching black velvet cap covered his scalp and he doffed it now and again, acknowledging the adoration of the crowds. It was as if they had come to see him crowned, not have his head smitten off.

He was so close to her now that she could have reached out and clasped his gown, as many others were doing.

'God save you, Sir Walter!' a bald man cried, tears streaming down his face.

Raleigh flashed him a smile, then took off his cap once more.

'Thou hast more need of it than I,' he replied, holding it out to the man, who gazed at it in wonder, as if it had been given to him by Christ Himself.

As the crowds surged behind her, Frances found herself being pushed forward. At that moment, Sir Walter turned towards her.

'Forgive me,' Frances mouthed, her eyes imploring.

He stared back at her for a long moment, then the lines at the corners of his eyes wrinkled with accustomed good humour. Reaching out, he took her hand and quickly pressed something into it. The gesture was so discreet that nobody seemed to have noticed. She looked up at him and he gave the slightest of nods before moving on into the throng. Frances glanced down and saw a tiny, exquisite prayer book. Her eyes filled with tears and she pressed her lips to it, then placed it carefully in her pocket and followed with the rest to the scaffold.

Sir Walter had already mounted the steps by the time she came within view of it. A guard stepped forward and took the black velvet gown from his back. As he stood to survey the crowds, dressed only in his linen nightshirt and breeches, his head uncovered, he looked like the frail old man she had seen on her last visit to the Tower.

'Good people.' Raleigh's voice rang out across the now silent courtyard. 'If I appear to tremble, I beg that you do not put it down to cowardice on my part, but rather to a strong and violent fever that is hindering me in what I intend to say.'

A murmur of dissent ran through the crowds. Frances heard several people around her mutter, 'Shame,' and 'God save him.' It gladdened her heart. The King might have denied Raleigh a public trial, but her friend was going to make the most of this opportunity. He had always known how to play to the crowds.

'I thank God that I came out of the darkness of my imprisonment in the Tower to die in the light,' he continued. 'As for the matter that caused the King to take so great offence against me, I must confess that there was probably some cause, yet it is far from the whole truth.'

Very far, Frances mused, knowing that few of those present would guess at the extent of Raleigh's crimes against the King. He went on to plead God's forgiveness for the manifest sins he had committed throughout his life, then provided a fulsome account of his voyage to Guiana. Frances saw the guard behind him grow restless. He made as if to hurry the prisoner along but, sensing the mood of the crowd, kept his counsel. The tolling of the bell signalled that half an hour had passed since Raleigh's arrival. He seemed not to heed it, but went on: 'I confess myself to be a most wicked, sinful and wretched man, a poor worm of the earth, one who has delighted and trod in all ways of vanity. For I have been a courtier, a captain and soldier – professions in which vices have their best nourishment.'

A chill wind whipped about the courtyard. Frances noticed Sir Walter clench his fists at his sides to stop the trembling. Seizing his chance, the guard stepped forward and muttered something in Raleigh's ear, then gestured towards the small fire that had been lit in a brazier at the back of the scaffold.

Raleigh shook his head and gave a sad smile. 'I thank you, sir, but I have little need of its warmth any more.' He then sank to his knees in prayer, remaining there for so long that the guard grew uneasy again. When at last he opened his eyes and tried to stand, he was shaking so violently that he was obliged to take the hand of the chaplain, who stepped forward to help him. Recovering his composure, he strolled nonchalantly to the executioner, who had been standing by the block throughout the spectacle, and asked him to raise his axe so that he might examine it. The man seemed to hesitate behind his mask and turned towards the guard, who nodded briefly. Sir Walter gazed down at the blade for a few moments, as if in wonder, then slowly ran his finger along it. There was an intake of breath from the crowds as a drop of blood fell from his fingertip onto the straw beneath. 'This will cure all of my sorrows,' he said, with a smile, before bending to kiss it.

The guard stepped forward to guide the prisoner to the block, but Raleigh was there before him. Frances watched as he lowered his neck onto it, turning his head this way and that as if to test for the most comfortable position. His lips were bleeding where they had touched the axe.

'You should face towards the east, sir.' Though he spoke quietly, the executioner's words could clearly be heard. The hundreds of onlookers seemed to be holding their breath as their eyes were fixed upon the scaffold, waiting for the final act in this macabre spectacle.

'It matters not how the head lies, so long as the heart be right,' Sir Walter replied, with a smile, turning to face the opposite way.

The masked man knelt for his forgiveness, which the prisoner, raising himself, bestowed with a warm embrace. He then held out a blindfold, but Raleigh shook his head.

'I pray you, wait for my signal before dispatching me,' he said, then lowered his neck onto the block once more.

Frances's eyes darted across to her husband, desperate for reassurance, but he was staring resolutely at Raleigh, his gaze unflinching. *What comfort could he offer anyway?* she reasoned, trying to push down the feeling that he had abandoned her somehow.

'Into God's hands I commit my body and my soul.'

Raleigh's words echoed across Old Palace Yard, bringing her attention back to him. She watched, as if in a trance, as he slowly raised his right hand, then brought it swiftly down to his side. But the executioner made no move. Frances could see the axe tremble in his hand. An agonising few moments passed and still he hesitated.

'What do you fear?' Raleigh called in a loud voice, as if reprimanding a lazy servant. 'Strike, man!'

With that, the executioner raised his axe. Suddenly unable to bear the sight for which she had spent the past few hours trying to prepare herself, Frances closed her eyes. A moment later she heard a sickening thud. There was an anguished cry from the crowd and she felt the man next to her begin to sway in a faint. She took a deep breath and opened her eyes. It took her a moment to realise that Raleigh's head had not yet been smitten off. Blood was spurting from a deep gash in his neck, and his head was bent forward at a sharp angle. Horror-struck, she stared as the executioner raised his axe again, bringing it down with such force that the blade embedded itself into the block after slicing through what remained of Raleigh's neck.

The guard stepped forward and plucked the head from the straw, holding it aloft by the thick silvery hair at its base.

'So perish all traitors!' he cried. After the words had echoed into silence, the only sound was of the blood dripping steadily onto the wooden boards below.

Frances stooped and cupped another handful of water, splashing it over her face and neck. She shivered as it ran between her shoulder blades, but welcomed its cleansing coolness, wishing she could submerge herself completely in the dark depths of the river.

She knew that Thomas would be waiting for her in their apartment, but could not bear to return to the palace just yet. Accounts of Raleigh's execution would be on everyone's lips, his courage twisted into cowardice, his final words into treason. She knew that the horror of what she had witnessed would never diminish, but prayed that in time whenever she heard his name it would be his handsome face and smiling eyes that she saw, not the ragged, blood-smeared head that had been thrust in front of the silent crowd.

The tears flowed freely now, unchecked by her determination to turn steadfast eyes towards her friend if he saw her from the scaffold. She wept at the thought of everything he had been – might yet have been, if God had only smiled upon his endeavours. She wept, too, at the thought of his grieving widow Bess – of how she had bent to kiss the red velvet bag in which they had placed her husband's head. And she wept for herself, for the loss of a friend with whom she had shared so many confidences and hopes.

Reaching into her pocket for a kerchief, her fingers closed instead over the prayer book Raleigh had given her. She wondered that she could have forgotten it. Taking care to dry her hands and face so that she would not spoil the gilded binding or the delicate pages within, she slowly opened it.

Carefully, she leafed through the first few pages, stopping now and again to read the prayers or gaze at the beautiful illuminations between each one. Then, as she turned another page, she stared. At the end of the chapter was a verse written in an elegant script. Her eyes flicked to the bottom and she saw that it was inscribed: 'By me, Sr Walter Raleigh, this 28th Day of October 1618'. She felt the tears well again but took a deep breath and began to read.

> *Even such is time that takes in trust*
> *Our youth, our joys, and all we have*
> *And pays us but with age and dust*
> *Who in the dark and silent grave*
> *When we have wandered all our ways*
> *Shuts up the story of our days.*
> *And from which earth and grave and dust*
> *The Lord shall raise me up I trust.*

CHAPTER 28

31 October

Frances's shoulders sagged and she surrendered herself to her husband's embrace. She had shed so many tears since Raleigh's death. The shock of his bloody end filled her mind whenever she tried to sleep. But she missed him too. Theirs had been a friendship born in treason but strengthened by mutual affection.

'All will be well,' Thomas murmured into her hair, smoothing some loose tendrils away from her face. She closed her eyes and pressed herself against his chest, wishing she could stay cocooned like this for ever, safe from the dangers that swirled about the court.

'I want to go home, Thomas,' she whispered, lifting her face to his.

He smiled sadly, then bent to kiss her. 'As do I,' he replied. 'I have wanted nothing else for months now. But the King will not allow it. He would not even agree to my taking leave so that we might visit our sons. I did not trouble you with it,' he added, 'for I knew it would grieve you. I would suggest that you returned to Tyringham alone, but leaving court at such a time might raise suspicions against you. Buckingham would be sure to make the most of it.' He grimaced. 'But perhaps when the controversy of Raleigh's death has died down I might petition His Grace again.

There has been talk of another visit to Scotland at the end of the year. If that comes to pass, he can surely offer no objection.'

'Assuming he does not command you to accompany him,' Frances said, dejected.

Thomas was silent for a while. Eventually he brightened. 'I have some happier tidings.' He walked briskly to the bureau and pulled a letter from one of the drawers. 'My agent writes that the lands surrounding Tyringham have finally been leased – and for a higher price than I dared hope. It will not settle our debts, but it is a start, at least.'

He handed the note to Frances. 'That is good news,' she replied flatly.

The ground crunched underfoot as Frances picked her way through the copse that lay on the south side of Hyde Park. She had woken to discover a thick covering of frost over the palace gardens. They looked breathtakingly beautiful in the early-morning sunshine, the hedges and branches fringed with glimmering white as if suspended by some enchantment. The disappointment that she and Kate would not be able to go out riding as planned was tempered by the sheer beauty of the scene. She had been glad when her young friend had agreed to a walk instead.

'Here, let me help you,' she said, holding out her hand.

Kate took it gratefully as she stumbled over another tree root. 'I am so clumsy,' she mumbled apologetically.

'This woodland is hardly made for walking,' Frances replied. She wished her companion would not berate herself so often, as if fulfilling the role that her stepmother would usually inhabit. It was more than two years since the Earl of Rutland had brought his daughter to court – long enough for her to have grown in confidence, Frances reflected. But the die had already been cast and she feared that the young woman would always feel inferior to those around her, even though she exceeded them in goodness and virtue.

They had emerged onto the open grassland now, which was intersected with numerous pathways. Frances chose the one that followed the southern edge of the park. She glanced at her friend. 'You are very quiet today, Kate. I hope it is not too cold for you. I was perhaps foolish to suggest we venture so far.'

'No, not at all,' Kate replied emphatically. 'I longed to be free of the palace – that is, to enjoy some fresh air,' she added. 'There will be few such opportunities now that winter is approaching.'

'Is there any other reason why you wish to escape Whitehall at present?' Frances ventured.

Kate's face reddened. 'It would churlish of me to complain. Many young ladies long for a place at court and I am fortunate enough to be there by virtue of my father's position, without any duties to perform.'

'And yet?' Frances prompted.

She sighed. 'It is not much of a burden to bear, really, and you will think me the most ungrateful wretch for even mentioning it. It is just that the countess has required my presence a great deal lately. I should be honoured, of course, but I confess that I find her company more a trial than a pleasure.'

'I can well imagine it,' Frances replied, with feeling. 'Lady Mary is an overbearing woman, and very fond of her own opinions.'

'Yes!' Kate exclaimed. 'It is such a relief that you share my view. I have tried to remain patient, but her behaviour seems to have grown worse in recent weeks. If ever I decline her invitation to dine, she takes it as a personal affront and complains to my father.'

'He is sympathetic, though, I'm sure.'

'To an extent, yes,' Kate said, 'but he is preoccupied with other cares at present and I do not like to vex him.'

Frances slowed her pace. 'I am sorry to hear it. I confess that I have been a neglectful friend to him of late. Do you know what troubles him?'

'He has received many letters from Belvoir lately. Although he assures me all is well, I fear that my brother still sickens.'

'That must worry him greatly,' Frances said. 'It has been a long time now since Lord Ros first fell ill.'

Kate nodded. 'My father and stepmother have tried everything to bring him back to health. I pray daily that he might show some sign of improvement. Lady Mary has even offered to send her own apothecary to Belvoir.'

'How kind,' Frances observed. Like her son, the countess was not the sort of woman to do anyone a service unless it was in her own interests. 'I will add my prayers to yours, Kate,' she concluded.

Frances tried to focus on the beauty of the scene around them, but her thoughts were too distracted by concern for Kate and her young brother. They had almost reached the path that led southwards out of the park, towards Chelsea, when the clatter of hoofs brought them to an abrupt halt. They stepped aside to let the riders past, but as they drew closer Frances recognised the young man at the centre of the entourage. She swept a deep curtsy, pulling gently on her companion's arm so that she might do the same.

'Your Grace.'

'Please.' The prince gestured for them to stand. Seated on his stallion, Charles appeared more at ease and of greater stature than when Frances had seen him at the various court gatherings he had attended. He was soon to celebrate his eighteenth birthday, she calculated, as she stole a glance at him, and had grown into a fine, if still rather delicate young man. He had the same high forehead and piercing eyes as his mother, and above his top lip she saw a few carefully manicured wisps of a fledgling moustache.

'It is a pleasure to see you, Lady Frances, Lady Katherine.' His voice was much softer than his father's, and higher in tone. 'I had not thought to encounter anyone else from court here on such a cold day.'

'The walk from Whitehall has warmed our bones,' Frances replied, with a smile.

It was the first time the prince had spoken to her and she was a little surprised that he knew her name. But, then, he had been groomed as a future king, so his attendants would make sure he was familiar with his father's court and everyone within it.

He turned to Kate. 'I trust you are well, Lady Katherine?'

The young woman flushed a deep shade of crimson. 'Very well, Your Grace, I thank you.'

'Will you ride far today, Your Grace?' Frances asked, breaking the awkward silence.

'To Greenwich,' he replied. 'I wish to visit Her Grace the Queen. I fear I have been a neglectful son of late.'

Frances resisted the temptation to ask whether his father the King knew of his excursion. He could hardly bear to hear Anne mentioned these days. 'I trust she is well?' she enquired instead, remembering the Queen's pallor when she had seen her on the night of Gondomar's reception.

Charles did not reply for several moments. Then: 'These late events trouble her, I think.'

'As they do all faithful subjects.' She saw that her words had hit their mark.

The prince's gaze intensified. 'We must pray for patience and forbearance.'

Beside her, Frances heard Kate's sharp intake of breath. The King's son had as good as acknowledged that he regretted Raleigh's death, that he shared the faith that united them. Or perhaps she was reading too much into his words.

After an interval, the prince touched the brim of his hat to both women, then nodded to his entourage and rode out of the park, straight-backed and chin held high. Frances watched his slender form fade from view. For the first time in many months, she experienced a flicker of hope for the future.

CHAPTER 29

22 December

The sconces had long since been extinguished, but the room was lit by the soft glow of the fire that still flickered in the grate. Frances stretched out on the rug in front of it, revelling in the warmth that caressed her skin.

'Do you think anyone noted our absence?' she murmured, twisting to look at Thomas.

He bent to kiss her neck. 'With the marquess leading a masque? We could have paraded naked through the banqueting hall and still all eyes would have been on him.'

Frances smiled at the thought. 'I wish we could spend every evening like this. The Christmas revels were so splendid in the old Queen's day but they have long since lost their lustre.'

Her husband groaned. 'And they have not yet begun in earnest. Buckingham has taken it upon himself to arrange an endless series of feasting and revelry. With Gondomar still in residence, he is determined to ensure they are the most dazzling ever staged.'

Frances pressed her back against Thomas's chest. 'He still pushes for a Spanish alliance, then?'

'Relentlessly. Even the King is tiring of his unceasing arguments and persuasions in council.'

She watched the flames gutter and flare. 'He must stand to gain by it somehow.'

'I have no doubt of it,' Thomas agreed. 'King Philip may have failed to find El Dorado, but he has more gold than His Grace could even dream of.' She felt his breath on her neck as he slowly exhaled. 'Let us talk no more of him now, my love. He plagues me during my hours of service, and I would not have him do so when we are at leisure.'

Frances turned over and snaked her hand around her husband's neck, lacing her fingers through his hair and gently pulling him towards her. As their kiss deepened, she felt the warmth of desire uncoil inside her once more.

'My lords!' Buckingham's voice rang out across the hall, bringing the chatter to an end. He had climbed onto a small platform that had been erected on the dais, directly in front of where the King and his family were feasting. Frances saw James's eyes linger on the young man's back and thighs as he swallowed deeply from his cup.

'On this, the eve of the feast of the Holy Innocents, that piteous day when King Herod slew all those babes-in-arms' – he raised his arms, whipping up a chorus of boos and jeers – 'we are required to make merry in preparation for the day of fasting ahead. And so . . .' a dramatic pause '. . . to lead us in our revels and delights, I give you the master of merry disports, the Lord of Misrule!' he shouted, stepping down to make way for the garishly dressed man who had just climbed onto the dais. There was a deafening roar of approval from the assembled crowds as the marquess swept an elaborate bow towards him.

Buckingham had outdone himself, Frances had to admit. This was the latest in a series of outlandish costumes he had displayed before the courtiers during the seemingly endless festive entertainments. The Lord of Misrule was a tall, stout man, made even more imposing by an enormous headdress fashioned from holly, red satin and painted fruits. His green velvet cloak was bedecked with bright scarves and ribbons, gold rings and precious jewels that sparkled in the light from the sconces. Around his legs were tied numerous tiny silver bells with strips of green silk. The man's face was painted brown to resemble the bark of a tree, and he wore a long curling wig of the same colour.

'Where is your king?' he bellowed, the bells jingling as he turned this way and that.

There were loud cries and shouts from the diners as they pointed and gestured towards James, whose lips curled in amusement. But the Lord of Misrule pretended not to hear, and it was only when the King himself called out that he turned. Drawing himself up to his full height, he held out a hand imperiously so that James might kiss it, as tradition dictated. The King flashed a smile at his favourite, then rose to his feet and walked slowly over to the platform.

'I surrender to your greater power, my lord,' he said. A loud cheer went up as he bent to kiss his hand.

The costumed man's eyes flitted across the long table and rested upon the Queen, who was seated next to her husband's empty throne. Following his gaze, James addressed him again.

'As king of this court today, you may have whatever your heart desires – even my wife!' His grin widened at the answering whoops and cheers. Frances saw that Anne was looking on, impervious as ever. How she must long for the peace of Denmark House.

The Lord of Misrule cast a mischievous glance towards the assembled courtiers, then looked back at James.

'Ah, but which wife, Your Grace?' he asked slyly.

The few titters were quickly suppressed and an ominous silence descended. All eyes were trained upon the King, whose face was deathly pale. Behind him, Frances could see Buckingham, eyes alight with fury. A faint tinkle of bells could be heard as the Lord of Misrule shifted uncomfortably on the platform, his gaze darting from his patron to the King. But suddenly James's face brightened and he gave a loud, mirthless laugh. The marquess took up the theme, laughing uproariously and clapping the Count de Gondomar on the back. The ambassador looked at him uncertainly, then joined in. Soon the whole room was in uproar, though Frances judged that they were laughing more with relief than amusement.

Buckingham gave the signal for the minstrels to begin playing. The Lord of Misrule stepped hurriedly down from the platform and half ran from the dais. Frances caught the look his patron shot him as he passed. Any hopes he might have had of further advancement after this night's revels had been dashed. He would be lucky to escape with his life.

'The man only said what we were all thinking.' Bacon took a delicate sip of wine. Frances smiled at him, gratified that he had chosen to sit with her and Thomas, rather than taking a place on the dais, to which his status entitled him.

'That may be so, my lord,' Thomas replied, with a grin, 'but some thoughts are safer in our heads than upon our lips.'

'You are in danger of becoming as seasoned a courtier as the smiling marquess over there,' Bacon retorted. 'Little wonder you have survived in this place for so long.'

Frances placed a hand over her husband's and gave it a squeeze. She rejoiced that he had seemed so much more himself in recent weeks. The burden of their debts had begun to ease, thanks to the rents they received from Thomas's newly leased lands, and Lord Rutland had offered his support, having heard of their troubles from his daughter. Even the constant menace from Buckingham seemed to have abated, now that he was preoccupied with securing a Spanish alliance. He had spent so much time courting Gondomar that he had neglected the royal stables and Thomas had been able to perform his duties unimpeded, for the most part.

'Tell me,' Bacon continued, 'when will I meet your fine boys, of whom I have heard such praise?'

Frances's heart gave a familiar lurch.

'We hoped to visit them two weeks ago, but the King decided to make the most of the fine weather and go hunting before the Christmas revels began,' her husband explained.

'Can you not bring them to court?'

'No,' Frances said, a little too quickly. 'That is, William is too young to travel far, and John and Robert will hardly be parted from him.'

Their housekeeper Mrs Garston had often written of how the two boys doted on their little brother. Although Frances loved to think of the bond between her sons, it pained her that she was a stranger to the youngest. Perhaps John and Robert were beginning to forget her, too.

'How old are they now?' Bacon interrupted her painful reverie.

'John is four and Robert three,' she replied. 'William will be six months old tomorrow.'

'And George?'

Thomas answered this time. 'He is thirteen.'

'A man already,' Bacon remarked. 'I'll wager that beautiful mother of yours dotes upon him.'

Frances smiled but did not trust herself to speak.

'I am sure they are all a credit to you both, my dear,' he said kindly.

The spiced wine warmed her throat as it slipped down, and she felt herself relax. Looking towards the dais, she saw that the King's face had regained its usual high colour and he was guffawing at some jest his favourite had made. On his other side, the Queen seemed to wince, then regained her usual placid expression. Her skin was waxy pale, despite the rising heat of the room.

On the table next to the dais, Frances could see Kate seated opposite her father. The earl was as solemn as she had seen him many times of late, and he spoke little – not that he had much opportunity, given that next to him the Countess of Buckingham was holding court.

At that moment, she caught a movement to the left of her vision and turned to see a liveried servant weaving his way through the tables. He stopped when he drew level with Lord Rutland and bent to whisper something in his ear. Frances saw the alarm on the older man's face, before he recovered himself and forced a bright smile in his daughter's direction. Placing his napkin on the table, he rose and gave a curt bow towards the dais, then hastened from the room, the countess staring haughtily in his wake.

'My dear?'

Frances tore her gaze away from Lord Rutland's retreating figure. 'Forgive me, my lord. The revelry has quite exhausted me. If you will both permit it, I shall retire now,' she said, already rising to her feet. Thomas made to follow, but she laid a hand on his shoulder. 'Please – stay and keep Lord Bacon company,' she said, with a smile. Her husband looked up at her with concern, his eyes searching hers, but eventually gave a nod of acquiescence.

Frances forced herself to walk slowly from the hall, anxious not to draw attention. As soon as she was in the corridor beyond, however, she quickened her pace. The air was much cooler there and the noise of the revellers grew fainter as she made her way through the succession of public rooms towards the earl's apartments. When she reached the courtyard that lay next to them, she saw him standing by the mounting block in the centre. His agitation was clear as he kept glancing towards the archway that lay to the east of the courtyard.

'My lord?

He jumped. Then his shoulders drooped slightly as he saw her approach.

'Forgive me – I did not mean to startle you,' she said. 'Is all well? I saw you leave the feast.'

Lord Rutland turned anxious eyes to her. 'I received a message from Belvoir. Joan Flower and her daughters have been arrested for witchcraft.'

Frances felt suddenly cold.

'The countess has threatened it many times these past months,' he went on. 'Always, I have dissuaded her, tried to make her see how groundless her suspicions are. But while she assented to my requests, I knew that the ill will she conceived against those women persisted – increased, even. She insists that our sons were bewitched and that the only way to lift the spell is to have those who cast it put to death.'

'Your youngest son still lives?' Frances asked tentatively.

The earl pressed his lips together and nodded. 'Though whether the poor boy will still draw breath by the time I reach Belvoir, I do not know. Cecilia writes that he has not woken for days now. That he—' He broke off, his voice faltering.

'I am heartily sorry, my lord,' Frances said softly. 'I wish that there was something I could do to help him. You know I have a little skill in such matters.'

'Thank you,' he whispered. 'But I would not hazard your life by asking. It is enough that poor Joan and her daughters stand accused.' He hesitated. 'There is something you might do, though.'

'Anything,' Frances vowed. 'I would gladly repay your many kindnesses.'

The earl smiled weakly. 'I fear you have little enough to repay. I promised to provide you and your husband with succour but will not be able to arrange it until this business is settled, which may take many months.'

'Please do not trouble yourself. Our affairs can wait – yours are far more pressing.'

'Thank you,' he said again, casting an anxious glance over his shoulder towards the archway. 'Although you can do nothing to help my son, at present, I beg you to look out for my daughter while I am gone. Kate is such a sweet child and so trusting – too much so. I fear she will be preyed upon by those who seek to profit by it.' His jaw twitched as he held her gaze.

'Of course,' Frances replied. 'Lady Katherine is a dear friend to me. I love her as a sister and will protect her as such. You can entrust her care to me entirely.'

The earl bent to kiss her fingers. His lips were as cold as ice.

There was no time to say anything more because the sound of rapid footsteps echoed across the courtyard and a moment later a groom appeared from underneath the archway. 'Your carriage is made ready, sir,' he said breathlessly.

Lord Rutland nodded briskly, bowed to Frances and hastened from the courtyard.

1619

CHAPTER 30

27 February

The chimneys of the palace were coming into view now, the elaborately twisting brickwork silhouetted against the deepening grey sky. Frances looked at her companion, wondering again if she should have brought her there. But the thought of leaving Kate alone at Whitehall, where Buckingham would no doubt be swift to grasp the opportunity, had decided her.

It was two months now since Rutland had left for Belvoir. At first, his letters had been frequent, but neither she nor her charge had heard from him lately. Frances knew that her friend was as troubled by his silence as she was herself. The last news she had received from him had been deeply alarming. Having heard that Joan Flower and her daughters were to appear before the assizes in Lincoln, the sheriff had been instructed to escort them there. It was a journey of some thirty miles, but they had been obliged to make it on foot. Many times since Lord Rutland's letter had arrived, Frances had imagined the three women trudging along the frozen lanes that led northwards to the ancient cathedral city, the icy winds whipping across the flat expanse of fields and pastures that stretched out on either side, as far as the eye could see. Frances remembered the bleak landscape from when she had travelled there to attend her husband as he lay, grievously wounded, in the earl's castle. Poor Joan had not survived the journey – but, then, perhaps that was a mercy, with what surely lay ahead for them in Lincoln.

Kate's young brother Francis still lingered, impervious to the attentions of the earl's physicians. Countess Cecilia's disappointment that her son had not recovered upon Joan's death must have been bitter indeed, Frances reflected.

'We are almost there,' she said now, as Kate turned to her. The young woman looked frozen, though she had made no word of complaint during the long boat ride. She had readily agreed to accompany her to Hampton Court, eager to see the magnificent Tudor palace for the first time.

'Shall we stay for long?' she had asked, when Frances had proposed the visit. She had offered only a vague response. In truth, she did not know if their time there would be brief or prolonged. Lady Ruthven had written only that the Queen, her mistress, had asked for Frances to attend her. Her Grace had spent the past few winters at Hampton Court, enjoying the peace and repose it offered. Frances feared that this latest stay had not been for pleasure but to hide from the prying eyes of the court. Since Buckingham had taken up residence on the Strand, Denmark House had no longer provided the tranquillity the Queen craved. She had retreated to Hampton Court as soon as the Twelfth Night celebrations had ended.

The boatman tethered the barge to the landing stage and helped Frances and her companion to alight. It was a short distance along the covered walkway that led to the royal apartments. As they neared the Queen's presence chamber, Frances summoned one of the pages who were stationed outside.

'Please – show Lady Manners to her chambers.'

'Am I not to attend the Queen with you?'

Frances squeezed her hand. 'Her Grace has asked to see me alone this time,' she replied with greater reassurance than she felt, 'but I am sure she will soon be well enough to receive more visitors, and she cannot but be eager to make your acquaintance. I have told her all about you,' she added quickly, seeing her friend's crestfallen face.

'I hope so,' Kate replied. 'Pray send Her Grace my greetings.'

'The Queen will receive you now,' the groom said, leaving the door ajar.

Frances rose to her feet. On the threshold, she listened for any sound within. All was silence. The shutters were closed against the meagre light that still lingered outside, and only a solitary candle burned beside the Queen's bed. The curtains were drawn around it. There was a rustle of skirts and a sombre lady rose from the seat she had occupied by the fireplace. Frances had not seen her there, but quickly swept a curtsy. She was of about Anne's age, Frances judged, and very finely dressed in a gown of dark grey satin, the bodice and sleeves edged with white lace.

'Thank you for coming so quickly, Lady Tyringham.'

The lilt in her voice made Frances's scalp prickle. She wondered that she had not recognised her. Anne had defied her husband by bringing Lady Beatrice Ruthven with her to England soon after he had inherited the throne. James had always despised her – perversely jealous of the affection his wife cherished towards her – so Anne had kept her hidden. But her secret had been discovered when Lady Ruthven had fallen dangerously ill. The memory of being summoned to treat her upon first arriving at James's court was still vivid in Frances's mind. It had helped to damn her for witchcraft, as well as to expose Lady Ruthven's presence. Frances wondered when her favourite attendant had returned to her service – or whether, indeed, she had ever left it. She said nothing, but inclined her head in acknowledgement.

The older woman led her towards the bedside. Frances saw that the curtains were pulled back a little at the end. Her heart thudded as she drew near. She suppressed a gasp. Anne's face, illuminated by the candle, appeared ghostly. Her cheeks were sunken and her breath rasped between her lips, which were slightly parted. A thin sheen of sweat glowed on her brow.

'Your Grace.' Frances made a deep obeisance, though the Queen seemed to be sleeping.

'Frances?'

Her voice was so faint that Frances wondered if she had imagined it. Anne's eyes fluttered open and flicked quickly from side to side, as if searching for her.

'I am here, Your Grace.' Frances knelt to kiss her hand. The skin felt cold and clammy.

'I am sorry you find me in such a state as this.' Anne croaked, then paused, her mouth open as if she was gasping for air.

'I will do anything I can to ease your suffering,' Frances said. She began to fumble in her pocket for the small pouch of herbs she had hidden there, but the Queen gripped her wrist.

'I fear that I am beyond even your help, my dear.' Her mouth twitched into a smile and her eyelids fluttered down once more. 'Even my eyes have forsaken me – they open only onto darkness now.' Frances was overcome by a wave of pity. 'I asked Bea to summon you here because there is something I must tell you before I die,' Anne continued. 'Please, sit close to me.'

Frances did as she was asked. As she waited for the Queen to continue, she saw that her chest was rising and falling in rapid, jerking movements, as if each breath pained her. A salve of fever-few and spurge would bring her ease, Frances knew. Her fingers itched to prepare some now.

'I know how much you hazarded for his sake,' the Queen murmured, as if in a dream. 'Raleigh,' she said, opening her eyes.

Frances glanced to where Lady Ruthven was seated, her fingers toying with the embroidery on her lap.

'Do not mind Bea,' Anne said, sensing her hesitation. 'She knows all my secrets and can be trusted to keep them. Neither has she forgotten the debt she owes you, my dear.' She fell silent, tears in her eyes. Then: 'I am to blame for his death.'

Frances took care to conceal her shock as she held her unseeing gaze.

'His expedition was my idea,' Anne went on. 'It was I who arranged it with the King of Spain, I who helped to pay for it. I had to do so from my own funds, of course – my husband allows me little enough from the privy purse. Like you, my dear, I staked everything I had upon its success. Ah, I sense that you doubt me,' she said, gesturing weakly. 'I lie here in the splendour of this palace, surrounded by luxury, just as I did at Denmark House. But it is all the king's. I own nothing but the jewels I carried with me when I sailed across the North Sea thirty years ago. Even my dresses are borrowed from the late Queen's wardrobe.'

'I am sorry, Your Grace.' Disappointment was mingled with pity for the Queen. She had allowed herself to hope that Anne might help her and Thomas out of their predicament. It was not a hope she had voiced to her husband – she had been too ashamed even to acknowledge it to herself – but when she had received the summons to Hampton Court, it had flared again. Looking at the Queen now, she felt a wave of remorse for her selfishness. She was little better than the sycophants of court, who flattered and fawned their way to advancement.

'I wish I could make amends – to you as well as Raleigh,' Anne went on, as if reading her thoughts, 'but there is nothing I can do. I must go to my grave knowing I caused the death of a man of truer faith than any in this kingdom, and the ruin of many more besides. I pray—' She broke off, a paroxysm of coughs racking her. Frances raised her on the pillows then poured a cup of water and held it to her lips. She took a small sip, but most of it dribbled down her chin as another fit overtook her. Eventually, the spasms subsided and she sank back onto the pillows.

'You should rest, Your Grace,' Frances murmured.

Anne shook her head slightly. 'I can have no rest – in this world or the next. God will not forgive my sins.'

'He has nothing to forgive, Your Grace,' Frances whispered, clasping the Queen's cold fingers in her own. 'You sought only to honour him, to restore this kingdom to the true faith. There are many sinners at court but you have never been among them. God will reward your righteousness.'

'I should have heeded the signs He sent, Frances,' Anne persisted. 'None of the plots to restore this country to the Catholic faith have succeeded. The Powder Treason, Arbella, Raleigh . . . So many lives blighted – yours more than most, my dear. Can you forgive me, even if God cannot?'

A solitary tear weaved its way down her cheek as she stared towards Frances, her unseeing eyes imploring. Frances tried to answer but her throat constricted, so instead she bent to kiss the Queen's fingers. Anne exhaled deeply and closed her eyes. After a few moments, her breath became slower, more rhythmical. Frances released her hand and rose from the bed. She made to step quietly away, but jumped as the Queen's cold fingers suddenly gripped her own again.

'I beg of you, stay a little longer,' Anne rasped.

Frances held her breath as she gazed down at her.

'I have lost all my children, save one,' the Queen began. 'God saw fit to claim Henry as His own, Mary and Sophia, too. Elizabeth sailed from these shores to marry a heretic, so her soul was lost to me, as well as her body.' Her eyes were wide with grief and she clasped Frances's hand even more tightly. 'I have only my precious little servant now.'

Frances smiled that the Queen still referred to Prince Charles in this way, even though he was now eighteen.

'I know that I should see this as God's will – His punishment of my manifold sins. But I cannot. I *will* not.' Her dark eyes were alight with a fervour that Frances had not seen for many years. 'My husband will soon choke out his breath from lechery and excess. Our son Charles must marry a Catholic princess. Only then will this kingdom be saved.'

Frances stared at the dying Queen in alarm. *Surely she was not asking her to involve herself in a fresh plot, after everything she had just said.*

'Do not be afraid, my dear,' Anne said, her expression softening. 'I know I cannot beg your forgiveness with one breath and ask that you plunge yourself into danger again with another. There are those who have already agreed to do my bidding in this. I ask only that you do nothing to hinder them – no matter how greatly you may wish it.'

Frances looked at her in confusion. She had ceased to involve herself in the plots that swirled endlessly about the throne, but she would always cherish her faith in her heart. How could Anne think that she would defy it altogether?

'I ask more of you than you think, my dear.' The Queen's voice was so faint now that Frances had to lean forward to catch her words. 'Please do not forsake me, after I am gone.'

'I do not understand, Your Grace,' Frances replied, her eyes searching Anne's. 'Why would I betray you – betray our faith?'

But the queen had closed her eyes once more, as if to signal an end to their conference. Frances waited for a few heartbeats, then slowly straightened and padded silently towards the door, her mind racing. Lady Beatrice raised her eyes from her needlework as she approached.

'God go with you, Lady Frances.'

CHAPTER 31

9 March

The cortège was so close now that Frances could see the late Queen's coat of arms picked out in gold thread on the black velvet cloth draped over the coffin. The cart was pulled by four horses, all richly caparisoned, and six of Anne's ladies walked behind. Although their faces were obscured by heavy black veils, Frances recognised Lady Ruthven at the front of the sombre procession. That she had been selected as chief mourner was perhaps a final act of defiance by the late Queen against her husband.

Behind the ladies rode Prince Charles, ashen-faced, eyes fixed firmly ahead. A few cries of 'God save Your Grace' echoed across the Strand, but he did not turn to acknowledge them. Frances felt a surge of pity for him. He had adored his mother but could look for no comfort from his father.

As the coffin passed, Frances bowed her head and discreetly made the sign of the cross over her breast. Raising her head, she watched as the cortège continued its slow progress towards Denmark House, where the Queen's body was to lie in state until arrangements were made for the funeral.

The King had given no indication of when or where this might take place; neither had he made any pronouncement about his wife's passing. Upon hearing the news, he had retreated at once to his privy chamber, giving out that he was too grief-stricken to appear in public. Frances no more believed this than the rest of the court did. She suspected James was using it as an excuse to indulge in several days of uninterrupted privacy with his favourite. The thought sickened her.

As the procession rounded the corner and disappeared from view, Frances uttered a silent prayer that Anne would find the peace in death that had been denied her in life.

'Only a lady so enamoured of nature would be found in these gardens on such a day.' Lord Bacon was dressed as immaculately as ever, in a light blue satin doublet with fine white lace around the collar and cuffs. His exquisitely pointed shoes were made from the same material and Frances noticed that, as usual, the heels were even higher than was the fashion. He was conscious of his diminutive stature.

'Please,' she said, motioning for him to join her on the seat. He shuddered as he lowered himself onto the cold stone. They sat in silence for a while, looking out across the muted greens and browns of the garden. Frances found it hard to believe that in just a few short weeks the barren branches and damp soil would burst forth with life and colour.

'God Almighty first planted a garden,' her companion said. 'And indeed it is the first of human pleasures – even in winter.'

He was right, Frances reflected: there was a melancholy beauty to the garden, as if Nature had lulled it into a deep slumber.

'I am glad to see you,' she told him. 'It is so long since we last met that I had begun to fear you had forsaken me for the marquess.'

Bacon gave a rueful smile. 'Buckingham is as excessively fond of flattery as ever – mine in particular, it seems.' He rolled his eyes. 'But while he might offer riches and preferment to those who serve him, for his intellectual gifts he is as poor as a kitchen boy.'

'Most men would set the first of those prizes at a higher price.' She could hardly blame her friend for courting Buckingham's good graces since the reception for the Count de Gondomar. It disguised his true allegiances. Besides, there was little to be gained by making an enemy of the King's favourite.

He spread his hands in a gesture of submission. 'I have seen little more of the marquess than I have of my dear friend lately,' he said. 'Our Spanish visitor has required his presence a great deal since the Christmas revels. In fact, Buckingham has spent so much time with Gondomar that it has excited the jealousy of his royal master.'

Frances raised an eyebrow. 'I wonder that the count has had time. My husband tells me that he has spent so many hours with the King that he should be assigned lodgings in the privy chamber.'

'Sir Thomas is right,' Bacon concurred. 'They have become known as the two Diegos.'

The King must have been delighted to discover that when translated into Spanish his first name was the same as the ambassador's, Frances thought. 'Perhaps that is why His Majesty has not yet advanced the plans for the late Queen's funeral.'

He caught the edge to her voice. 'The people mutter against it. Her Grace should have been laid to rest long before now. But the King seems more preoccupied with settling her estate. He has appointed me to resolve certain difficulties with her will.'

'Oh?' Frances turned to him. 'I thought the Queen had little to bestow.'

'And so it appeared. The lands that formed part of her marriage settlement have long since been distributed elsewhere and she spent all of her income in the last months of her life – though I am at a loss to find out the beneficiaries. Her Grace was ever generous to those who served her,' he added, casting a meaningful glance at Frances. She suspected he knew well enough that Anne had been among those to venture their fortunes on Raleigh's expedition.

'There were only the jewels she brought with her from Denmark, which she bequeathed to the prince,' he went on.

Frances held his gaze. It was as the Queen had told her. 'Surely the King does not mean to quibble over those?'

Her friend pressed his fingers lightly along his brow, as if to knead away the creases. 'He would not have troubled himself with so trifling a matter, had it not been for Buckingham's suggestion that he should have the jewels valued. I think he did it to vex the prince, who has made his distaste for his father's favourite all too obvious.'

Frances said nothing, though fury surged in her breast. That the marquess should stoop to such pettiness to punish a grieving son was despicable.

'It seems the jewels are worth a great deal more than the King was aware. The prince might build a new palace with them and still have funds left over to furnish it with treasures.'

Frances stared. *Had the Queen known this?* Surely she would not have claimed poverty on her deathbed in order to deceive her. The trust and affection that had grown between them was too great. Frances thought back to the words Anne had uttered. She had told her only that the jewels were all she owned, not that she intended to bequeath them to Charles. Did she hope that the jewels would help to secure the Catholic bride she so desired for him?

'Four hundred thousand pounds.'

It took Frances a moment to heed Bacon's words. 'That is impossible,' she whispered.

'I thought the same,' he replied, with a shrug. 'But the jeweller I consulted was in no doubt. He told me he has seen many treasures in his long life, but never any as rare as this. The pearls alone are worth a king's ransom.'

'Does His Grace know?'

Her friend shook his head. 'No – at least, not yet. But I cannot withhold such information from him for long. The marquess has asked for the valuation every day this week.'

Frances fell silent, considering. 'Can James contest the will?'

'He will try, once he knows what a treasure his wife bequeathed their son,' Bacon said, his voice low. 'But I see no means by which he can prevail, unless it is his intention to wrest the jewels from his son's grasp.'

'Let us hope the prince has them in safekeeping.'

A chill breeze whipped through the garden and Frances felt a few icy drops of rain against her face.

'I must go back to the palace,' she said, rising from the bench. 'My husband will soon return.'

'Then permit me to accompany you,' Bacon replied, holding out his arm, as the clouds darkened overhead.

CHAPTER 32

14 May

'It is no good,' Kate said, turning from the looking glass. 'I look ridiculous.'

Frances smiled kindly. 'Here, let me help you.' She took the ribbon from the young woman's hands and began to weave it deftly between the curled strands of her hair. 'I remember feeling the same about the costume I was obliged to wear for my first masque,' she remarked, tying the vivid green silk into a neat bow at the base of Kate's neck. 'There. That is much better,' she added, standing back to admire her work.

The girl gazed uncertainly at her reflection in the glass. 'Thank you, Frances,' she said, with a small smile. 'You have made me look a little less monstrous.'

'Your father would be proud to see you so gloriously arrayed.' Frances patted her shoulder.

Kate's smile vanished. 'There has been no more news, since . . .?'

Frances shook her head. 'I expect he is preoccupied with arranging matters at Belvoir. I understand that the King hopes to hunt there as soon as the weather turns.'

'I have heard so, too,' Kate agreed. 'Though I pity my poor father for having to turn his mind to such matters when there is so much else to occupy him. I cannot but grieve for Mistress Flower and her daughters, though I know I should think only of the welfare of my little brother. Do you believe them guilty of bewitching him? It is sinful of me to doubt the judgement of the law – and of my mother the countess, I know. But . . .'

'The guilt or innocence of the accused matters little in such cases,' Frances replied quietly. 'Countess Cecilia is not alone in believing that to lift a curse those who cast it must be put to death. I am sure she was not acting out of malice, but a desire to protect her son.'

'Yes of course. I should not have . . .' Kate looked down at her hands.

Frances clasped them. 'I do not believe they inflicted any harm upon your brother,' she said earnestly. 'Fever and sickness are all too common, particularly in childhood, and often take hold suddenly. It is unusual that your younger brother has still not recovered, I admit, but that is more likely due to a natural frailty – or the attention of his physicians.' Her mouth curled with distaste. How she wished she might attend him herself.

'Then I pray God will gather their souls unto him, even though they died without the comfort of absolution.'

Did she mean the last rites of the Catholic faith? Frances wondered. She thought back to the aroma of incense in Kate's chamber, many months before. They had never spoken of it, but the conviction that Lord Rutland's daughter shared his faith had taken root in Frances's mind. A flush was creeping up the young woman's neck now.

'You have spoken no sin,' Frances said softly. Confessing that she, too, was of the old faith was dangerous. Yet she longed for Kate to unburden herself, knowing it would comfort her, strengthen the bonds of their friendship. 'You cherish the same faith as your father, I think?'

Kate's head jerked up in alarm.

'Please, you need have no fear,' Frances urged, stroking the back of her friend's hand with her thumb. 'I believe as you do. It is a secret that I keep hidden in my heart, as all faithful subjects must, but that diminishes neither its strength nor its truth.'

The young woman's shoulders sagged and her eyes glistened with tears. 'I have wanted to speak of it to you for so long, but I promised my father . . .'

'He was right to ask this of you and wants only to protect you while the King still persecutes those of our faith so relentlessly . . . But it is something we might share together, in private.'

Kate's face brightened. 'That would bring me such comfort, Frances!' she exclaimed. 'Sometimes I feel that God does not heed me when I pray alone. I am always so fearful lest someone discovers me that I often forget the words. With you by my side, I know I would have greater courage.'

Frances smiled. 'Perhaps we might pray now for the health of your poor brother and the souls of those who were thought to have bewitched him.'

Kate rose at once and scurried off into the adjoining chamber. Frances heard some rustling, then the click of a key in a lock. A moment later, she returned with a richly embroidered cloth and a rosary. There was something else in her other hand but her fingers were too tightly closed over it for Frances to see. She busied herself with spreading out the cloth for them both to kneel on, then placed the rosary on a small table next to it. Frances came to join her friend and they knelt, heads bowed. Kate made the sign of the cross over her breast, then slowly opened her hand.

'My father gave it to me for my eighteenth birthday.'

Frances looked down at the exquisitely carved marble figure. The Virgin's eyes were downcast, but her mouth was lifted in a beatific smile and her arms were held open, as if for an embrace. Kate raised it to her lips, then set it down on the table and began to pray.

'Hail Mary, full of grace . . .'

A feeling of peace swept over Frances. Here, in this quiet chamber, the troubles of court seemed far distant. The loss of their fortune, Buckingham and his scheming, the heretic King his master, who had shown so little care for his wife's passing that he was staging a magnificent pageant the evening after her funeral: all were as insubstantial as a dream. She closed her eyes and began to repeat the familiar words.

The light was dwindling by the time Frances made her way back to Thomas's apartment. She slowed her steps, savouring the unusual quiet that shrouded the palace. Her hand was on the latch when the door was wrenched open and she almost collided with her husband.

Frances's heart lurched in panic. 'What has happened?'

'It's the King.' Thomas's face was ashen. 'He is dying.'

Frances stared at him, stupefied.

'He has summoned all his councillors to attend him – myself too. I must make haste.'

'But he showed no sign of illness at the pageant,' Frances countered, thinking back to the smirking glances that he and his favourite had exchanged during the ceremony at Westminster.

'He fell into a sudden faint – that is all I know. Please – wait for me here. I will return as soon as I can.'

Frances watched as he walked briskly away and stood there long after he had disappeared from view, her mind racing. *How could this be?* Even the most sudden of fevers usually betrayed some warning signs a day or so before – a pale complexion, a little shortness of breath – but James had appeared in robust health, more so than he had for a long time. Even the gout that had plagued him these past few years seemed to have abated a little. *What could have occasioned such a swift change?* A thought struck her. *Poison?* Raleigh's execution had reignited the fervour of discontented Catholics and every day seemed to bring a fresh rumour of some plot.

A cold wind blew along the cloister. She had hardly noticed it grow so dark since she had been standing there, lost in her thoughts. Quickly, she went inside and bolted the door. To distract herself from her rising agitation, she made a fire and tried to coax the meagre flames to life. The wood must have grown damp these past few weeks, she thought. When at last she was sure that the blaze would not die, she fetched a flagon of wine and poured herself a glass.

The minutes seemed to pass like hours as she waited, her ears straining for the sound of her husband's footsteps. As the wine warmed her, her breathing slowed a little. Wasn't this what she and Thomas – their fellow Catholics too – had wanted ever since James came to the throne? He had been a scourge on this kingdom, blighting his subjects' lives with misery and fear while he lay steeped in sin. She thought of Buckingham, his face as he watched his master's life slip away – his fortunes with it. He should have thought to cultivate the King's successor earlier. She had seen him fawn over the prince at the various entertainments staged for the Count de Gondomar, but Charles had always seemed unmoved. She admired the young man even more for that. God willing, he would make a far more discerning king than his father.

Rapid footsteps jolted her from her thoughts. Frances leaped to her feet and ran to the door, sliding back the bolt with trembling fingers. Thomas stepped quickly inside. She said nothing but led him to the chairs by the fire and poured him some wine. He downed several gulps, then raised his eyes to hers.

'Is he . . .?'

Thomas shook his head. 'Not yet, but I fear it cannot be long. He keeps lapsing into insensibility, and his skin has the pallor of a corpse.'

'Has he a fever?' Frances asked, forcing herself to consider the matter objectively.

'I think not. He seemed rather cold than otherwise and was shivering violently, though every fire in the privy chamber had been lit. He was greatly troubled in mind, too, and kept ranting about the late Queen and the loss he had suffered.'

Frances was scornful. 'How can he mourn one towards whom he showed such little regard in life?'

'Her death did not seem to be the loss he was referring to,' Thomas replied, 'but his words were rambling and his mind so disordered that it was hard to make any sense of them.'

'The marquess must be distraught.'

Thomas lifted the glass to his lips again and swallowed deeply before setting it down on the table. 'He stands to profit by our master's death, even more than by his reign. The King summoned us to witness his decree that upon his death Buckingham will assume the position of lord protector.'

Frances looked at him in confusion. 'But the prince is old enough to rule alone.' As she waited for Thomas to respond, she saw a muscle in his jaw twitch.

'That is of little consequence, it seems. The King has ensured that his son will be in even greater thrall to the marquess than he has been himself. Charles will be king in name only. All of his power will be vested in the lord protector.'

Frances sank back in her chair. 'How can this be?' she whispered. 'Surely the privy council will not allow His Grace to ride roughshod over the laws of this kingdom – to say nothing of the prince himself.'

Her husband shook his head again, as if defeated. 'Buckingham dominates the council, as he does the King. It seems he has been scheming for this since he first entered our royal master's service. The terms of the decree have been set down and all of those present put their names to it.'

'Even Lord Bacon?' Frances asked, incredulous. Arch politician he might be, but she knew that his respect for the law exceeded his ambition.

'He was not there. The King dispatched him on some business in France a few days ago.'

That would explain why she had not seen her friend at Queen Anne's funeral. His absence had perturbed her but she had been too distracted by the events of that day to give it any further thought. The feasting and revelry that had followed the ceremony had made it seem more a cause for celebration than for grief.

'We must prepare to leave this place, Frances,' Thomas said quietly. 'I will send word to my steward at Tyringham. Buckingham will be ruthless towards those he has marked as rivals. He knows that you enjoy some favour with the prince and will not suffer any impediment to the hold he means to exert over him.'

Frances felt cold. Though she longed to escape this place and return to their sons, she knew that for as long as he held power Buckingham would continue to plague them. And what would become of Kate if she abandoned her to his clutches? She could not forsake the promise she had made to Lord Rutland.

'The King may yet recover,' she suggested. 'We should not act precipitately.'

'After what I saw this evening, I cannot believe it likely,' her husband replied grimly. 'We must make ready.'

CHAPTER 33

16 May

Frances held her breath and lay perfectly still. It was not yet light, though Thomas had already left for the stables. Buckingham had become an even more exacting master in the brief time since the King's illness had been announced, as if he already held the title of lord protector. His royal master still clung to life, but the physicians had warned that it could not be long now.

There it was again: a faint knocking. Frances sat bolt upright, her pulse racing. Quickly, she rose and drew on a cloak over her nightgown, then crept to the door. She pressed her ear to it but could hear no sound. Taking a breath, she pulled it open.

A young man stood before her, wearing the prince's livery. 'Lady Frances Tyringham?'

'My husband is not here,' she replied steadily.

'It is you whom I seek, my lady. His Grace requests your presence.'

Frances stared at him in surprise. 'Now? The court has not yet risen.'

The attendant inclined his head. She wanted to ask more, but something in his manner silenced her. With a curt nod, she hastened back into the apartment to dress, then followed the man in the direction of the prince's lodgings.

The presence chamber was dimly lit. Frances glanced around as she waited, distracting her racing thoughts by focusing upon the collection of paintings that hung on the walls. Although the colours were dulled by the gloom, she could make out enough details to tell that they were very fine. She remembered the late Queen proudly telling her that her son had discerning taste in art.

'Thank you for coming, Lady Frances.'

She turned at the prince's soft voice. She had not heard him approach. He stood on the threshold of the chamber, then walked quickly towards her. She swept a deep curtsy. 'Your Grace.'

'Forgive my summoning you here at this time, but I dare not tarry any longer.' His dark blue eyes appraised her closely. 'You know that my father the King lies dangerously ill? Though his councillors have tried to keep it from the court, there are no secrets here. If he dies, this kingdom will be in thrall to that devil Buckingham.'

Frances said nothing.

'My mother told me of your skills in healing, that you could be trusted to assist me if ever the need arose.'

She dared not answer, but inclined her head slightly.

'I beseech you to do so now, Lady Frances. My father's physicians have exhausted every means to cure him of this malady. But I set little store by their potions and tinctures. God knows I suffered by them enough as a child,' he added, with distaste. 'The late Queen had such faith in you, as did my sister, and I always trusted her judgement. Please, will you attend him?'

Frances struggled to hide her consternation. The prince was asking her to save the life of an accursed heretic – one who had almost had her put to death for witchcraft. An image of Robert Cecil flitted before her. It was the late lord privy seal who had brought the case against her, eager to win favour with the new King. Yet she had later tended him as he had lain mortally sick with a tumour, cutting away the growth so that his life might be preserved for a time at least. If she used her skills to treat the King now, and he survived, he might have her arrested as a witch once more. But if she refused and he perished, Buckingham would reign supreme.

'You will suffer no consequences, whether you cure him or not,' Charles continued, anticipating her objection. 'My father has barely woken for two days now, and his thoughts are so disordered that he does not know who attends him. He spoke to one of his grooms as if he were the King of Spain the other night.'

'That may be so, Your Grace, but I will be seen by other eyes than the King's,' Frances reasoned.

'Not if we make haste,' Charles countered. 'The marquess will not rise for two hours at least – his devotion to my father does not run so deep that he will leave his bed earlier than is his custom,' he added, with a sneer. 'I have grown familiar with his habits this past week. There will be few others in attendance at this hour, and those who are can be trusted. They love me more than their master's favourite.' His eyes were imploring. 'I beg you, my lady. You will be rewarded for your pains – in this life or the next.'

Frances thought of Buckingham, his lips curled into a smile as he watched her fall to the ground clutching her stomach, her child bleeding away. 'I will do as you ask, Your Grace.'

The heat in the chamber was so stifling that Frances could hardly breathe. Little wonder the King was so faint. She instructed one of the grooms who stood by his bed to open the windows. The boy's eyes flitted to the prince, who nodded his assent.

Frances breathed in a lungful of the cool dawn air. 'Now douse the fires.'

The groom did as she said – straight away this time. There was a sharp hiss as he poured the contents of a large ewer over the flames, and Frances blinked away the smoke that stung her eyes. James gave a low moan as she approached the bed. Thomas had been right. Even in the dim light of the chamber, she could see that he was as pale as death. She placed her fingers lightly on his neck and waited. After a few moments, she felt a faint, fluttering pulse.

'They are gone – all gone,' he cried out, grasping her wrist.

Frances stepped back in alarm and cast a quick glance at Charles, who gave a slight shake of his head as if warning her not to speak.

'Who has taken my treasure?'

The King's voice made her turn back to the bed. His eyes were still closed but tears were now streaming down his cheeks. Frances waited until his breathing had slowed, then moved to examine him more closely. His skin was burning and his breath had the fusty stench of decay. Now and then, his brow creased and he gave a low groan, as if something pained him. Gently, Frances probed his neck, but there was no trace of swelling. Although his arms were covered with angry red sores, she recognised them as the marks left by the leeches the physicians had applied. Pushing down her scorn, she drew back the thick coverlet and almost gagged at the acrid stench. The King's linen shift had ridden up so that it only just covered his groin. Beneath it, Frances could see that the sheets were stained a brownish-yellow. She motioned for the groom to bring her a candle, then placed a handkerchief to her mouth and leaned closer. There were darker flecks among the stain. Holding the flame as close as she dared, she realised with alarm that it was blood.

Quickly, she set the candle on the table next to the bed. Then, as gently as she could, she slid her hand under the King's back. He gave a loud moan and rolled onto his side. Frances heard the groom's intake of breath as she lifted James's shift above his waist. As she had expected, there was a small swelling on one side of his back.

'When did His Majesty last pass water?' she asked the groom.

'Some two days hence – and then with difficulty,' he replied. 'I did not know that he had . . . that the sheets were soiled. I will order new ones.'

He had almost reached the door when Frances stopped him.

'There is no time for that now. The King needs fresh water. I'll wager he has hardly taken a drop since falling into a delirium.'

The look on his face told her that she was right. 'Bring some vinegar too, some garlic and salt. And a small quantity of saxifrage – the kitchens should have it,' she added quickly, noting his confusion.

'Make haste!' the prince urged, as he hesitated. The boy scurried away. Then, more quietly: 'What ails him?'

'There is a contagion in one of his kidneys,' Frances replied. 'It could have been easily cured, but the ignorance of the physicians has enabled it to take hold. I will do what I can to purge it from his body.'

Charles's eyes darted to his father in alarm. 'Will he live?'

He looked so fragile standing there, pale as death. Frances longed to give him comfort. But she must not offer hope yet. It was too soon.

'I will use what skills I have, Your Grace. God must do the rest.'

The young man took a step forward. 'Will you pray with me, Lady Frances?' He held out his hand and, after a moment's hesitation, she took it and followed him to the end of the bed, where they sank to their knees. The prince closed his eyes and began to whisper a prayer so quietly that Frances could only catch the occasional word. She tried to concentrate on her own offering, but her ears strained to listen.

'Holy Mary, Mother of God . . .'

Frances's eyes flew open. She looked at the prince, who was slowly signing the cross over his chest. Those were not the words of his father's prayer book. *My little servant.* The late Queen's name for her son suddenly took on new meaning. Was it her faith he followed? She had wondered ever since the remark he had made during their meeting in Hyde Park.

Hurrying footsteps interrupted her thoughts. Charles opened his eyes at once. Before she could look away, he turned to her and his expression changed as he realised she had been staring at him. He gazed at her with something like fear, then gave a small, uncertain smile and rose to his feet.

The groom had brought everything she had asked for. Frances set to work at once, glad of the distraction. A pungent aroma rose from the mortar as she ground the garlic and saxifrage into a paste with the salt, adding a few drops of vinegar every now and then. When it was a smooth consistency, she mixed it with several draughts of fresh water and poured some into a glass.

The King moaned as the groom propped him up on the pillows so that Frances could administer the tincture. His nostrils twitched as she brought it close to his lips. James grimaced and looked as if he might spit out the liquid, but Frances clamped his jaws closed, while he writhed and groaned. At length, she saw his throat pulse as the tincture slid down it. She glanced up at the prince, who was watching from the other side of the bed, fearing his shock that she should handle his father so roughly. But he gave a nod of assent. Frances repeated the procedure again several times, the King's resistance becoming weaker with each, until at last the glass was empty.

'That will suffice for now,' she said, glancing at the clock. Despite the prince's reassurances, she knew that Buckingham must not find her there. If his royal master were to die, he would make sure that the full weight of blame fell upon her. 'I will return after the court has retired – if you could send word.'

'Thank you, Lady Frances,' the prince said. 'You have performed a great service. I shall not forget it.'

CHAPTER 34

22 May

'Bravo, my lord!'

Gondomar's cry was echoed by others, and soon the entire tilt-yard was in jubilant uproar. Frances watched as Buckingham took off his helmet and, with a flourish, held it up to the crowds, prompting another chorus of loud cheers.

The joust had been staged to celebrate the King's safe deliverance. His recovery had been swifter than Frances had dared to hope. Even by the evening after her first visit to his chamber, the swelling on his back had significantly reduced and the fever had begun to abate. The prince had been true to his word and had ensured the utmost discretion for her visits. Whether the King knew that she had attended him she could not be certain. He had slept a great deal once her tincture had started to do its work, and she doubted he would remember much about the illness. But even though his delirium had soon passed, he had continued to murmur about the lost treasure. Frances had noticed his son's discomfiture but had said nothing.

'It is as if he brought the King back to health himself,' Thomas muttered beside her.

'I am sure most people here believe him capable of performing miracles,' she responded acidly.

Her husband knew of the service she had performed and had tried to persuade her against it, fearful lest she was discovered and accused of witchcraft once more. But her desire to heal had been greater than her fear.

Another roar rose from the crowd and the Spanish ambassador was making his way down to the arena, flanked by an entourage of attendants all clad in the same black satin, white plumes on their caps. Buckingham dismounted his horse and swept an elaborate bow, then kissed the ring on Gondomar's gloved hand.

'They have dined together twice this week,' Thomas murmured, his gaze fixed upon the two men.

Frances felt a familiar disquiet. She looked down at the marquess, his face wreathed in smiles. He was not courting the ambassador for his royal master's sake alone – of that she was certain. Despite showing Gondomar every courtesy, the King seemed no more inclined to ally with Spain than he had before. Thomas had heard him mutter about King Philip's duplicity shortly before he had fallen sick. But, then, James showed little enthusiasm for anything other than hunting, these days – that, and his favourite, of course.

Unable to bear the sight of Buckingham's preening any longer, she glanced around the stands, which were crowded with spectators, all in their finery. She could see many faces flushed from the heat of the sun, which was now high in the sky. There was not a breath of wind to provide relief from the choking ruffs and heavy gowns. Her back felt damp and she longed to escape to the cool shade of the palace gardens. But she knew the tournament would be followed by a lavish feast and a series of masques lasting long into the night.

With a sinking heart, she looked across at the royal gallery on the opposite side of the arena. Prince Charles was seated under the canopy, his face in shadow. Frances could not imagine he took any more pleasure in the spectacle than she. He had none of his late brother's martial prowess, and was so slight that lifting a sword, let alone wielding it in combat, might be too much for him.

Sitting close by, the Countess of Buckingham was gazing down at her beloved son with an expression of rapture. Frances thought back to the scene she had witnessed at Windsor almost three years before and felt the same revulsion she had experienced then. Any hope that the countess might return to Brooksby Hall had long since been extinguished. The King had even appointed her a suite of lodgings close to those of her son. The only saving grace was that she had never sought out Frances's company, clearly believing her of too little significance to trouble with. If only the same were true of poor Kate. Frances looked across at her friend now and could tell from her fixed smile that she wished herself far away from Buckingham's domineering mother.

At last, Buckingham led Gondomar from the tournament arena and the spectators began to file out from the stands. Frances and her husband remained seated, neither eager to take their places at the feast.

'I wish we could be free of this place,' Thomas said.

'Perhaps the King will grant you leave, once he is fully recovered.' Her longing to return to Tyringham grew stronger with each passing day.

'There is little hope of that, my love. Already His Majesty talks of riding out to Hertfordshire next week, even though he will surely be too weak to sit in the saddle . . . I am anxious to see how our affairs prosper, though. There has been no news from my steward for more than three months now.'

It had pained him to mortgage such a large part of his estate, and for such little return. A succession of poor harvests had caused the price of land to fall sharply. Frances prayed that this year would be better, or Thomas would need to diminish the estate still further.

'We should make haste,' he said at length, breaking the silence that had fallen, like a cold stone, between them.

Frances nodded, and followed him towards the growing cacophony that emanated from the banqueting house beyond.

* * *

A deliciously cool breeze wafted through the privy garden, carrying the heady scent of lavender and rosemary. Frances breathed deeply and closed her eyes, feeling it soothe away the ache at her temples. The evening's revels had seemed endless, the heat in the crowded hall suffocating. Thomas had been obliged to take his place with the other members of the King's household, and she had been seated among tedious company. The saving grace had been the unexpected appearance of Lord Bacon, newly returned from his travels. She had missed him keenly these past few weeks, though his letters had provided some consolation. His descriptions of France – its people, customs and food – had been so vivid that it was as if she, too, had experienced them. She had laughed out loud at his acerbic comments and shrewd observations, imagining him regaling her with them in person.

Although he smiled a warm greeting, he had been too preoccupied by entertaining Gondomar's entourage to spend any time with her. She could hardly feel aggrieved for she knew he had taken little pleasure in the duty, judging from the scowling faces of the Spaniards as they picked at the delicacies laid before them.

Buckingham had held court, like a king, throughout the proceedings, clearly delighting in being the sole focus of attention. Even Gondomar had seemed in thrall to him, though he far exceeded him in status. Such adoration had not made Buckingham more inclined to be gracious towards those who served him, though. Frances had struggled to hide her dismay when, as she and Thomas were leaving the hall, the marquess had ordered her husband to the stables on some needless errand.

She let out a long breath, determined to clear her mind of such irritations, and opened her eyes. Her heart swelled at the beauty of the garden, which was wreathed in the pale light of the moon. She should go back to their apartment soon. Thomas would worry if she wasn't there when he returned.

The snap of a twig made her start. She swung around and saw a figure moving slowly towards her, then relaxed as she recognised Bacon's halting step. The gout must still plague him, she thought.

'It is well that we are unobserved, Lady Tyringham,' he said, with mock-formality, 'or people might suspect that this is our clandestine meeting place.'

Frances grinned. 'Welcome back, my lord. I thought you had altogether forsaken me this time, you have been absent for so long.'

He lowered himself onto the bench next to her and leaned forward to rub his shin. 'My bones are getting too old for such ventures. I have travelled many miles since I saw you last – all in vain.'

'Oh?'

He glanced around them before continuing, his voice lowered. 'The late Queen's jewels have been stolen.'

Frances stared at him, speechless.

'Shortly after the King had had them valued,' he went on. 'His Grace fell into such distress upon being told that I fear it caused his late illness.'

Who has taken my treasure? The King's plaintive cry sounded in Frances's ears as clearly as if he had been sitting next to her, but she said nothing to Bacon. 'He sent you to try to recover them?' she asked instead.

He nodded. 'A few discreet enquiries led me to the port at Dover, where an agent of mine had learned that one of the Queen's former attendants had boarded a ship bound for France. Her fine clothes had excited the curiosity of the boatman, who was affronted by her abrupt manner and therefore unburdened himself without troubling his conscience.'

'Who was she?' Frances asked, already guessing the answer.

'Lady Beatrice Ruthven. The longest-serving of all the Queen's attendants – though, of course, the King did not know it.'

Lady Ruthven had been utterly devoted to her late mistress. Frances could not believe that such a faithful attendant would steal the jewels for personal gain. 'How can you be sure it was her?' she asked. 'Did you find her?'

'Sadly not. But her face is not easily forgotten,' Bacon replied, with a rueful smile. 'She was quite a beauty in her youth.'

'How do you know she had the jewels?' Frances persisted.

Bacon shrugged. 'I cannot be certain, of course, but she fled the kingdom at the precise moment they went missing, and I set little store by coincidence.' He rubbed his fingers over his brow. 'I followed in her wake as far as Saint-Omer, but could find no more trace of her – even with the lure of reward. I stayed on in the town for a few more days, making enquiries here and there, but it was as if she had vanished as suddenly as a dream upon waking.'

Frances's mind was racing. If he was right and Lady Ruthven had taken the jewels, it must have been for some greater purpose than profit. They were worth enough to tempt a ruler as rich as Croesus to do her bidding – enough to raise an army, even. More and more, Frances was convinced that the late Queen had known the true worth of the jewels she had bequeathed her son. She thought back to Anne's words as she had lain dying at Hampton Court. *There are those who have agreed to do my bidding.* Was the prince embroiled in all of this? Frances knew that his physical frailties had led most courtiers to dismiss him as a hapless bystander, entirely subject to his father's will. But his visits to the Queen had grown ever more frequent towards the end of her life, and the prayers he had uttered in his father's chamber made her suspect that he kept much hidden from the world.

'Does the King know?' she asked.

Bacon nodded grimly. 'I thought of concealing it from him until I had better news to report, but I could not risk his hearing it from other lips than mine. His suspicion is so easily ignited, these days.'

Frances knew that well enough. It was one of the many things of which Buckingham had taken advantage. 'What will happen now?'

'The King has dispatched a number of trusted attendants to take up residence in Saint-Omer. He means to smoke the lady out, as he would a fox from its lair. But I fear she has long since fled from that place – the jewels with her.'

Frances found herself hoping he was right.

1620

CHAPTER 35

26 January

Frances rubbed the windowpane, which was misted with her breath. The heavy grey clouds overhead threatened more snow. So much had fallen over the last two days that the roads were barely passable, and the gardens too thickly covered for walking.

'Ouch!'

She turned back to her companion, whose head was bent over her embroidery.

'It is no use,' Kate said, setting it down. 'There are more holes in my fingers than in this cloth.'

Frances smiled. 'The light is very poor in here. Perhaps I should fetch some more candles.'

'Please, do not do so on my behalf. It will make no difference. My thoughts are too distracted today.' She glanced at the clock again. 'They should have been here long before now.'

Frances came to sit next to her. 'Try not to worry. This weather is bound to have slowed their progress. They will be here soon enough, I am sure.' She pushed down her own anxiety. The journey from Belvoir was hazardous at the best of times, with some of the roads little more than narrow, muddy tracks. That Lord Rutland should attempt it at such a time was testament to his desperation. Frances prayed that his young son would survive the ordeal so that she might attend to him, as she had promised.

'If only my father had heeded your counsel and remained at Belvoir until the spring. I cannot but think my poor brother would have fared better there.'

Frances was inclined to agree. 'Shall we read for a while?'

'I fear the words would not come easily today and you would think me a poor student after the care you have lavished on my education.'

'You are a good deal more accomplished than most ladies here at court,' Frances replied firmly. Kate had flourished under her tutelage and Frances had taken great pleasure in seeing her sense of wonder at the worlds that had been opened to her through the numerous books that now lined her shelves. It was one of the many things that had brought them closer since her return to court.

'Tell me, how was the play that I missed two nights ago?' Frances asked. She had pleaded a headache upon hearing that *Doctor Faustus* was to be performed. The King's obsession with the demonic had deepened since the disappearance of his late wife's jewels the previous year. He had become increasingly convinced that the theft was part of some wider conspiracy, and that the sickness with which he had been afflicted had been the result of a bewitchment. Frances prayed that her attendance on him would remain hidden. He would not hesitate to have her arrested, even though he owed his recovery to her.

'I can hardly remember it,' Kate replied.

'What is it?' Frances asked softly.

'It is nothing – truly,' her friend replied, not meeting her gaze. 'I should be grateful, for it was meant as a kindness, I am sure. It is just . . .' She bit her lip and fell silent.

'Kate?' Frances prompted.

The young woman at last raised her eyes. 'I was seated next to the Countess of Buckingham again,' she began. 'She was in an ill humour and I feared that it was because she finds my company irksome – I lack the conversation of her other acquaintance, you see,' she added, as if repeating something that had been said to her.

Frances stopped herself making a retort, lest it discourage her from sharing whatever it was that troubled her.

'In order to divert her, I prattled about how harsh the winter had been, how there had been so few carriages arriving at the palace this past week . . . and then . . . then I said I hoped the furs I had sent to Belvoir had arrived in time for my brother's journey.'

Frances was careful to maintain her composure. The poor girl looked utterly wretched.

'I realised too late what I had said,' she went on. 'I tried to change the subject, but the countess had seized upon my words at once and would not be quietened until I had told her all – though not your part in it, Frances, I swear,' she added. 'I said only that my father had decided to bring my brother to London so that he might benefit from the greater range of medicines that are available here. She insisted that her own apothecary attend him, and though I tried to tell her that my father had already made arrangements, she would not be gainsaid. Already her son has secured the King's support for the idea. Oh, Frances, what have I done? That man is the devil himself.' She began to sob.

Distractedly, Frances stroked her friend's back in an attempt to bring her comfort, but in truth she was as stricken as Kate. Lord Rutland had wisely counselled her and his daughter to say nothing of his plan to bring Lord Ros to London, aware of the danger in which it would place Frances if it became known that she had agreed to treat the boy. Frances had been apprehensive that he had brought Kate into the secret, but had respected his decision, knowing how close the bond was between them. Her friend had not uttered a word of it, even during the time they spent alone together, and Frances had begun to feel more confident in her discretion. But now everything lay in tatters.

Frances knew the 'devil' to whom Kate referred. John Lambe styled himself 'Doctor' but had nothing except the countess's patronage to recommend him. Certainly, he was not part of any guild. It was whispered that he would have been hanged as a witch long before now, if it were not for Buckingham's intercession.

'Calm yourself, Kate,' Frances said. 'It is hard enough to keep a secret, let alone one that concerns your own brother.'

'I do not deserve your kindness, Frances. I should have admitted this sooner, but I was so ashamed of what I had done. Besides,' she added, swiping at her cheeks, 'I told myself that perhaps it was for the best – that this way would keep you safe. I hated to think of the danger in which my father's scheme had placed you. Perhaps . . . perhaps he might reject the countess's offer, find a more trusted physician to attend my brother.'

Frances said nothing. The Countess of Buckingham was not a woman to be contradicted. Her thoughts ran on. There was no longer any hope of concealing Lord Rutland's arrival at court, now that the countess was expecting him. She must intercept him before he arrived, then take him and his son somewhere they could stay without fear of discovery, for a few days at least. The plan had been for Frances to treat the boy in Lord Rutland's apartments at Whitehall, where she was already a regular visitor and so would excite little suspicion. But that was impossible now. The countess would not let the boy out of her sight. His life – or the loss of it – was too valuable to her own son: Kate stood to inherit the entire Rutland fortune if her brother died. Frances shuddered at how easily that fragile life might be snuffed out.

With sudden resolve, she hastened into her bedchamber and pulled on the heavy woollen cloak she usually reserved for long journeys. Her fingers trembled as she fastened the hook and drew up the hood. 'Go back to your father's apartment, Kate,' she told her. The girl was gaping at her with a mixture of confusion and dismay. 'I will come to you later.' She flashed a smile of reassurance that did not reach her eyes.

*

An icy wind whipped around the courtyard. The snow lay so thick that it obscured the cobbles, making it impossible to pick out the paths that lay between them. By the time Frances reached the large archway at the entrance to the courtyard, her soft leather soles were sodden and her toes numb with cold. The exposed cobbles were slippery with ice and she was obliged to clutch at the cold stone wall to stop herself falling.

As she rounded the corner, she saw a slender figure huddled under the Holbein Gate. She stopped, but he had already seen her. Slowing her pace, she proceeded towards him. As she drew closer, she recognised the embroidered swan in chains on his doublet. *Buckingham's livery.* His face was pinched with cold and he kept moving from one foot to the other. No doubt he had been waiting here for some time, Frances thought. He eyed her uncertainly, then gave a short bow and turned back to face the road ahead.

Frances did not think he knew her – certainly she had not noticed him before – but she took the precaution of walking in the opposite direction of her destination, up a small side street. As soon as she was out of view, she turned left into another narrow street and quickly weaved her way along it until she came to the Strand.

Most of the snow had been cleared from the footpath that ran alongside the road, so Frances could quicken her pace. By the time she reached the westernmost end of the street, she had broken into a run. Ahead, the skeletal trees of St James's Park were silhouetted against the grey sky. To her right, the spire of St Martin's rose above the rooftops. Turning towards it, she hastened along the road that snaked northwards. The tolling of the bell sounded as she passed. Three o'clock. *Pray God I am not too late.*

She ran on, panting, her linen shift clinging to her back despite the cold, until she saw the squat tower of St Giles-in-the-Fields up ahead. *Almost there.* Her legs ached and she longed to cast off the woollen cloak that had shrouded her from the cold but now weighed heavily upon her. Lord Rutland's carriage would likely turn down this road after it had reached St Giles's Cross, but she could not be certain so she knew she must reach the crossroads. Keeping her eyes fixed upon the tower, she surged onwards.

A few moments later she was standing, breathless, at the crossroads. She gazed along the wide road that was the main thoroughfare for travellers from the north and west. She had come this way many times before – first from Longford and then Tyringham. Usually the road was crowded with carriages, wagons and stalls, a riot of noise, people and horses. But today just a handful of carriages rumbled slowly along, the horses' hoofs slipping on the compacted snow. Frances prayed that Lord Rutland's would soon be among them.

As her breathing slowed, the cold seeped into her bones and she drew her cloak around her, glad of its warmth once more. Her thoughts returned to the countess: she would not rest until her son had won the glittering prize that they saw as his by right. Buckingham's lavish spending had always outstripped the generous gifts and salaries that the King had bestowed upon him. He would settle for nothing less than the richest estate in the kingdom. That Belvoir lay close to his mother's made it ideal. He would not lack for excuses to visit her, Frances thought, with distaste. She could not help thinking that, for his mother, a large part of Kate's appeal lay not so much in her riches as in her plainness and mild nature. Here was not a woman to rival her own hold over her son.

Frances was so lost in thought that at first she did not notice the sleek black carriage coming into view. Only when a gust of wind sent the white plumes at each corner fluttering did it catch her eye. She ran towards it. The carriage was travelling much faster than the others and before long she could hear the snorts of the horses and see the steam that rose from their flanks.

'Stop! Please!' she called, stepping out into the road.

The coachman muttered a curse and glowered at her, but did not draw in the reins.

'Lord Rutland!' she cried, louder this time.

A moment later, a gloved hand pulled back the heavy curtain and the earl's gaunt face peered out into the gloom. He gave a sharp rap on the roof of the carriage and it came to such an abrupt halt that the coachman lurched forward. He directed another dark look at Frances before climbing down to open the door for his master.

'Lady Frances?'

'Do not be alarmed, my lord. I will explain. But we must make haste – please,' she said, gesturing that she would join him in the carriage. He made room for her at once, but before she climbed in she called up to the coachman: 'Please, wait here for a few moments.' Scowling, he peered over the side of the coach towards his master, who looked briefly at Frances, then nodded.

Frances glanced across at the small form swaddled in furs on the seat opposite. His face was turned towards the back of the carriage and she could just see a few wisps of fair hair beneath his velvet cap. He looked so fragile, so vulnerable that her breath caught in her throat. She turned back to his father.

'The Countess of Buckingham knows you are bringing your son to London,' she said shortly. 'Lady Katherine let it slip – please, don't be angry,' she added quickly. 'The poor girl has berated herself enough already. Buckingham has appointed one of his grooms to look out for you – I saw him on my way here. It is too dangerous to take your son to the palace now. The King has agreed that Dr Lambe should treat him and you can ill afford to cause offence by refusing.'

At this, the fury went out of Lord Rutland's eyes.

'We shall go to my mother's house at Whitefriars,' Frances went on. 'I can attend to your son there and return to Whitehall every evening, in case my absence attracts notice. I will tell Katherine to keep to your chambers as much as possible during the day, so that people will assume I am with her. She can tell the Countess that you have delayed your departure from Belvoir because the roads are impassable.'

Lord Rutland did not reply but eyed her steadily.

'We cannot hope to conceal your presence here in London for long,' she continued, 'but, God willing, I will have time enough to ease your son's suffering.' She looked back at the boy, his frail body jolting as the carriage rumbled along the Strand.

Suddenly Lord Rutland reached across and lowered the window. 'Take us to Whitefriars,' he called to the coachman.

CHAPTER 36

27 January

Frances gazed at the small hand that lay in hers. The skin was so pale as to be almost translucent, and the spidery blue veins showed clearly beneath it. A large fire roared in the grate, but the warmth did not seem to permeate the boy's frail body, which was almost as cold to the touch now as when his father had carried him in from the carriage the evening before.

'You should get some sleep, my dear.'

Frances smiled at Lord Rutland, who was seated on the opposite side of his son's bed. The dark shadows under his eyes told of a restless night for him, too, though Frances had made her mother's lodgings as comfortable as she could.

'I will warm some more broth first,' she said, turning back to the boy. 'He may take a little more, now that he is settled.'

She was careful to keep her tone light, but she knew that Lord Rutland also feared a recurrence of what had happened before. At first his son had seemed to swallow the thin stew easily, but after a few spoonfuls he had begun to splutter and choke, then vomited. Frances had been concerned to see black bile but had said nothing. His father would have noticed it too.

A light tapping on the door made them both jump. Frances waited, straining her ears. Three more knocks, then silence. That was the signal. Exhaling with relief, she padded out of the chamber, taking care to close the door, just in case.

It was all she could do not to throw herself into Thomas's arms when she saw him on the threshold. He smiled down at her with the easy humour she had grown to love so dearly. But as he embraced her she saw his eyes were alight with apprehension.

'I have brought everything you asked for,' he said. Frances took the small casket from him and smiled her thanks. 'How does his young lordship fare?'

'He is very weak,' she whispered, 'and has been unable to stomach anything but water since we arrived. But, God willing, these herbs will do their work.'

'You look tired,' her husband said, stroking her cheek.

She kissed his palm. 'Were you able to speak to Kate, as I asked?'

'I called upon her last night. She was greatly agitated and full of remorse for her mistake. But it was a comfort that you had reached her father and brother in time. She wanted to write to you, but I told her we must not commit anything more to paper. You took a great enough risk in sending that note with Lord Rutland's coachman. He is a surly fellow,' he added, with a rueful grin.

'But a trustworthy one. What of the countess and her son?'

'She was full of scowls at last night's feast and retired early. My *master*' – he placed a sardonic emphasis on the word – 'appeared entirely unconcerned.'

'*One may smile and smile, and be a villain,*' Frances quoted.

Her husband nodded grimly. 'His countenance rarely changes. He may be planning some new revels or plotting treason, for all anyone can tell.'

'Likely both. This delay to his schemes must frustrate him as much as it does his mother, but there is little he can do about it. Even if he were so minded, he could hardly set out to fetch Lord Rutland from Belvoir himself.'

'That is true, my love,' Thomas replied, lowering his voice, 'but you must not tarry here for more than a few days. Should your absence be noted . . .'

'You are right.' She clutched his hands, which were still icy cold. 'I will work as quickly as I can and leave God to perform the rest.'

Frances felt her heart surge with joy. It had been five days since their arrival at Whitefriars, and for the past three she had been able to administer progressively larger doses of the tincture. The boy had kept down more and more of the broth, too, and she had observed that his breathing was steadier.

Lord Rutland turned towards her, his face alight. 'You have restored my son to me, Lady Frances. I can never repay you, no matter . . .' His voice broke and he sobbed into his hands while the boy looked on, bemused.

She beamed at them. 'Your son's recovery is reward enough, my lord. But we must let him rest now,' she added, seeing the boy's eyes grow heavy again. 'Sleep will bring him back to strength, if we have patience.'

'Of course,' the earl said, rising from the bed. He stooped to plant one more kiss on his son's forehead before turning to follow Frances from the room.

'He is not clear of danger yet, my lord,' Frances said, as soon as the bedchamber door was closed. 'The contagion in his lungs will be slow to clear, and he is still very frail. It is no wonder that his skin is cold to the touch when there is so little flesh beneath it.'

The earl nodded gravely. 'But he will recover?'

'In time, yes – God willing,' she assured him. 'You must make sure that he does not exert himself too much. He will be eager to run about and play like other boys his age as his strength begins to return, but you must teach him to be patient.'

'Of course,' he agreed. 'When will we be able to return to Belvoir? There has been no more snow for two days now so the roads will be easier than they were on our journey here.'

Frances knew that the turn in the weather was not the real reason why he was so anxious to leave this place. His nerves were as worn to shreds as hers from the constant, nagging fear of discovery.

'Two days, perhaps – three at most. I will return to court this evening and remain there. I have prepared enough of the tincture to last another week, and you already know how and when to administer it. Make sure your son takes as much broth as he can manage – water too. By the time you return to Belvoir, he will be able to stomach some richer food. Give him whatever he has a fancy for.'

Lord Rutland clasped her hands in his. 'I know you do not ask for my gratitude, but you have it. I shall be for ever in your debt.'

Darkness had fallen by the time Frances passed under the Holbein Gate. As had become her custom, she had taken a circuitous route back to the palace, casting frequent glances over her shoulder to make sure she was not followed. The outer courtyard was a hive of activity as pages, kitchen boys and attendants scurried this way and that in preparation for the evening's revels. For once, Frances was glad of the hustle and bustle as it made her far less conspicuous than when she had first stolen out of the palace almost a week before. As she passed between the liveried servants and carts laden with provisions, her thoughts turned back to the dimly lit bedchamber at Whitefriars. She wished she could have stayed longer, assured herself of the young lord's recovery, but the danger was too great. No, she must have faith – in her own skills, as well as in God. She would offer up her prayers in the chapel tomorrow.

As she neared the archway that led into the next courtyard, Frances glanced up at the ornate clock above it. A little before six. She hesitated then turned her steps in the direction of Lord Rutland's apartment, unable to resist the temptation to tell Kate how her brother fared.

All of the sconces along the corridors had been lit and Frances was glad of their warmth as she walked briskly along. She had just entered the passage when she saw a man walking towards her.

He had a pronounced limp and was hunched over a staff. Frances noticed that it had an ornately carved piece of marble at the top, but the shape was obscured by the man's hand. She kept her eyes firmly fixed on the floor and quickened her pace.

'Beg pardon, my lady.'

His voice echoed along the empty corridor. Frances stopped and turned. His features were in shadow, but she could see that his sharply pointed beard was as white as the snow that covered the courtyard.

'Forgive me – I did not mean to startle you. I have been wandering these passages for an hour or more, looking for the banqueting hall. Whoever thought to build such a maze?'

Frances smiled and felt herself begin to relax. 'Pass through three more courtyards and you will see it ahead of you – and hear the noise from it, too. The feast will begin at seven.'

'Thankee, thankee,' he muttered, shuffling forward a little so that his face was illuminated by the sconce above.

Frances was struck by his eyes, which were so piercing that they appeared to see into her very soul. Looking more closely, she noticed that one was green and the other blue. When he smiled at her, his lips became so thin that they were almost invisible. She glanced down at his garish attire. If she had not known better, she would have taken him to be a jester, but the King's dislike of such entertainment was well known to all. His doublet and breeches were covered with bright blue and red stripes, and slung over one shoulder was a cloak of green satin edged with silver. Most extraordinary of all was the red and gold hat perched on his head. Frances could not decide whether it looked more like a mitre or a crown.

'Will it suffice, do you think?' he said with a grin, giving a slow twirl.

Frances stopped staring and inclined her head, then made to continue on her way.

'Of course, I of all people should not have lost my way.'

'Oh?' she asked, a little impatiently.

'Why, yes!' the old man exclaimed, clearly enjoying the moment. 'We cunning folk can find our way out of the most tangled of labyrinths. We can find hidden treasure too . . . or whatever else may have been lost.'

His words trailed into silence as he fixed Frances with a stare. She felt herself grow cold as realisation dawned. *Dr John Lambe – the Buckinghams' notorious astrologer and physician.*

'The late Queen's jewels are not the only things to have been lost lately,' he went on, emphasising each word with care, as if to measure its impact. Another pause. 'There are lost souls, too. That poor boy. He should have been here long ere now.'

Frances's neck felt warm. 'Forgive me, I do not know—'

He gave a low chuckle. 'It is easier to navigate the corridors of this palace than the words spoken by those within it.' He gave a dramatic sigh, as if defeated. 'Well, well, I must be on my way. The countess does not take kindly to latecomers, and her patience has been even shorter than usual since . . . But enough of such trifles.' He ran his tongue over his upper lip. 'A pretty lady such as yourself does not wish to waste time with a foolish old man when she clearly has more pressing matters to attend to. I hope you will find Lady Katherine in better spirits than I did earlier.'

He let his gaze rest upon her for just a moment too long, then gave another exaggerated sigh and made to leave. As he did so, his fingers slipped briefly from the top of his staff and Frances glimpsed the carving. It was a skull.

CHAPTER 37

28 January

The cawing of a rook made Frances start as she hastened through the deserted streets. She had risen long before dawn, having lain awake since she and Thomas had returned from the previous evening's revels. Dr Lambe had played a prominent part in them, and the King had seemed to delight in his elaborate tricks and conjurations. The gasps and cries of the assembled courtiers sounded in Frances's ears as she recalled the ghostly figure he had whipped up out of smoke, only for it to disappear as soon as he clicked his fingers. *Deceiver's tricks.* The crystal ball he had flourished before the court was as likely to lead him to the 'lost treasure' he talked of as a broken compass.

And yet she had been so unnerved by the old conjurer that she had resolved to warn Lord Rutland to set out for Belvoir without delay. She could see that neither the countess nor her son believed Kate's story that her father had postponed his journey because of the snow. They knew he was too desperate for his son's recovery. It would not be long before their enquiries led them to Whitefriars. The earl's carriage was distinctive enough to have attracted attention as it had passed through the streets of London.

Her heart in her mouth, she mounted the steps to her mother's lodgings and crept silently along the corridor. No light showed from under the door and she could hear nothing as she pressed her ear to it. She took a breath, then knocked lightly, using the same repetition as Thomas.

At length, she heard the creaking of a floorboard and a few moments later the door was opened a crack. She breathed her relief at the sight of the earl's face peering anxiously into the gloom. He ushered her inside at once.

'We must make haste,' she said, without preamble. 'Dr Lambe is at court. He seems to know that you have deceived his patrons – or suspects it, at least. You must leave this place and return to Belvoir. If you hurry, you will be clear of the city's walls before daybreak. I will travel with you as far as St Paul's. Then you and your son can take a carriage northwards. There will be plenty to hire at this time of the morning. I will be back at Whitehall before the court has risen.'

The shadows under Lord Rutland's eyes seemed to deepen as she spoke. 'You have put yourself at great risk in coming here,' he whispered. 'I cannot allow you to increase it by accompanying us. You must go back to Whitehall before the alarm is raised.'

'I am quite safe. I made sure that I was not followed, and there are three hours or more before the court will assemble for breakfast. Please – let us make haste.'

Her friend hesitated, then turned on his heel and strode towards his son's chamber. Frances could hear the boy's quiet moan as his father woke him from his slumber. While she waited for them to emerge, she busied herself with gathering the few belongings that Lord Rutland had brought with him to Whitefriars. She must leave no trace of them here. Her fingers trembled as she fumbled with the lock of one of the coffers, trying to push from her mind the image of Buckingham's men searching these apartments.

'We are ready.'

Lord Rutland was standing on the threshold to the bedchamber, his frail son, wrapped in the fur blanket Kate had given him, in his arms. Frances led them quietly out of the apartment. The streets were as still and silent as a crypt, but every time they passed an alley or doorway Frances slowed her pace lest one of Buckingham's attendants should step from it. She thought of how he had lurked in the shadows of the Bloody Tower that night, shortly before Raleigh had been sent to his death. He hardly needed the services of his mother's seer, Dr Lambe: his spies were everywhere.

Before they turned into the narrow passageway that led to the Thames, Frances saw something move in the doorway of a large house. She stopped abruptly, heart hammering. But then she saw a girl curled up on the steps. She was about George's age, Frances judged. The child's eyes stared up at her from the gloom and she held out her hand in supplication. Frances pressed a coin into it. But they must hurry. Despite her assurances to the earl, there was little time.

The riverside was in darkness, with just a solitary brazier glowing dimly on the landing stage ahead. Their breath misted in the chill air as they stood peering across the dark water. None of the mansions on the southern bank were visible, and Frances envied those who slept peacefully within. As they drew closer to the wooden platform, she smelt the sharp tang of tobacco and soon afterwards heard the low murmur of voices. Two men turned at the sound of their footsteps.

Lord Rutland tried to sound calm as he asked them to take him to St Paul's. Frances saw the boatmen's eyes flick from him to the boy in his arms. She pulled her hood further over her head and kept her eyes downcast. One nodded and led them towards his boat. As they climbed in, Frances took care to keep her face turned away. Neither she nor Lord Rutland spoke, and the only sound was of the steady, rhythmic creak of the oars as they sliced through the dark waters.

The journey seemed to take an age. Frances glanced up at the sky, fearing it was lightening. *Her eyes were growing accustomed to the darkness, that was all*. She glanced at the boy, who was asleep, as peaceful as an angel. It would have been better for him to stay in the warmth of Whitefriars for several more days before the long journey back to Belvoir, but the risk was too great. *We can find hidden treasure*. Though she knew better than to believe in his tricks and illusions, she felt as if Dr Lambe's eyes were following her.

At last, she saw the dark outline of St Paul's tower ahead. She motioned to Lord Rutland, who followed her gaze. A few minutes later, they had drawn level with the landing stage. Frances stepped out, then helped her companion and his son.

'Wait for me here,' she said to the boatman, ignoring his curious stare as she handed him a small purse. Glancing around, she led Lord Rutland and his son towards the crossroads that lay on the northern side of the cathedral. Every step seemed to echo in the silent streets as they hastened along, Frances's eyes darting left and right. But she kept them fixed ahead as they passed St Paul's churchyard, where some of the Powder Treason plotters had met their grisly ends. *She must not think of that now*.

To her relief, as Paternoster Row opened out into a large square, she could see several carriages, each lit by a lantern. A coachman jumped down from the one closest to them and doffed his cap. Frances handed him the coffer she had been carrying and he held open the door so that Lord Rutland could climb in. Frances watched as he laid the sleeping boy on the seat opposite his own. It would be three days at least before they reached Belvoir – more, perhaps, if the snow continued to thaw and the roads turned to mud. But they would be clear of the city's walls by daybreak and, God willing, the danger would recede with each passing mile.

As she made to step down from the carriage, Lord Rutland clasped her hand and pressed it to his lips. 'God go with you,' he whispered, his eyes alight with fear.

'And with you.'

She watched as the coachman climbed onto his seat and, with a sharp tug on the reins, urged the horses forward. The clatter of their hoofs sounded in her ears as she hastened back towards the river.

The boatman was still standing on the landing stage when she arrived – she had smelt his tobacco as she approached. Peering into the shadows to reassure herself that she had not been observed, she climbed into the small vessel and drew her cloak around her as the man began to row back towards Whitehall.

Frances tore off another piece of the warm manchet loaf. The smell of the food that was spread out on the tables in front of the assembled courtiers had made her ravenous. Elation had sharpened her appetite, too. She had stolen quietly back into the palace a little over an hour earlier. The only person to notice her absence had been Thomas. She had expected his anger, but it had soon been supplanted by relief at her safe return. Together, they had prayed for Lord Rutland and his son, who she judged should soon be approaching Waltham Abbey. She did not imagine the earl would stop there to take his ease, as most travellers did.

'They say the King's daughter is likely to lose her crown.'

The mention of her former mistress jolted Frances back to the present.

'Aye, her husband cannot withstand the emperor for long. His army is by far the mightier.'

Two months earlier, news had reached the court that Count Frederick had accepted the throne of Bohemia, in defiance of Emperor Ferdinand, whose territory it was by right. Frances knew Princess Elizabeth would exult in the title of queen and had rejoiced at it herself, little knowing how soon their new kingdom would be under threat. Now she felt cold with terror at the danger her beloved former mistress faced.

A crash at the end of the hall made everyone turn. One of the serving boys was staring, red-faced, at a pile of upturned dishes, their contents splattered over the flagstones. Next to him, Dr Lambe was flapping his arms and mumbling an apology. He made a show of trying to help the boy, a smile playing about his lips. His appearance at last night's revels had been similarly dramatic, but instead of the clatter of plates, there had been the thundering of drums followed by a cloud of smoke. Like his patron, he seemed to thrive on the attention – good and bad.

Frances could see a mixture of interest and apprehension on the faces of her fellow diners as the old man moved between the tables in search of somewhere to sit. She shrank back and fixed her eyes upon the piece of bread in front of her. To her dismay, as Lambe drew closer, the courtier next to her rose to his feet and gestured for the old man to take his place.

'Such trouble, such trouble,' Lambe muttered, as he shuffled along the row.

Frances looked around, as if for some means of escape, but leaving now would draw attention. She could only hope that the people seated around her would engage the physician in conversation. Certainly, they were all eyeing him with undisguised curiosity.

'Ah, my saviour of last night!' he exclaimed, as he saw Frances. 'What happy chance. It seems that God will always place you in my path when I have lost my way.'

'Dr Lambe,' she muttered, aware of the curious stares of the other diners.

'Once more, you have the advantage,' he remarked. Frances breathed the sharp tang of bergamot and violet as he lowered himself onto the bench. 'For you know my name, and no doubt much more besides, yet I know you only by those beautiful eyes and that lustrous hair, which would make the brightest autumn leaves appear dull by comparison.' He reached out as if to touch one of the tresses that lay over her shoulder, but his fingers stopped short of it. Frances kept as still as a statue, though inwardly every fibre of her being cringed from him.

'Lady Frances Tyringham,' she said curtly. Her instinctive fear of him had been replaced by a rising fury at his insolence. Neither did she have any patience for his play-acting. He knew her name well enough – Buckingham and his mother would have made sure of that.

'Tyringham . . .' He stroked his beard thoughtfully. 'I have heard the name somewhere . . .'

'My husband is master of the buckhounds to His Majesty.'

'Then you must spend little time together. The King shows greater passion for the hunt than for *almost* everything else.' He let the emphasis hang in the air, making sure the other diners had noticed it. 'Well now, Lady Tyringham,' he continued, 'how do you fill the many hours of solitude? There is only so much embroidery that even the most accomplished lady can do.'

Frances forced herself to take another mouthful of bread, even though she felt she might choke on it. As soon as she had finished, she would make her excuses and leave. 'King James's court does not lack for diversion, as I'm sure you are aware, Dr Lambe.'

A flicker of a smile. 'Indeed. But most pursuits are more fitted for gentlemen, are they not?'

He was goading her, but she merely inclined her head and took a slow sip of water.

'Hunting, running at the ring . . .' he went on. 'Even the professions here are not suited to the fairer sex. The kitchens are filled with male cooks, the King may only be attended by boys and gentlemen . . . and then there is my own profession, of course . . .' His voice trailed off but his sharp eyes never left her. 'There are women who pretend to such skills, but rarely to any effect. And most are hanged as witches.'

Frances could no longer hear the clatter of dishes or the low hum of conversation that echoed around the hall. She held the old man's gaze. 'It has been a pleasure to see you again, Dr Lambe.' Her words were like shards of ice. 'But you must excuse me, or I shall be late to meet an acquaintance.'

She rose to her feet before he could reply and did not wait for him to make his obeisance. She could feel his eyes upon her as she made her way out of the crowded hall, forcing herself to walk slowly when all she wanted to do was run.

CHAPTER 38

28 January

By the time Frances reached her chamber, her fingers were trembling so much with suppressed rage – fear, too – that she fumbled with the lock. John Lambe's smiling face was before her, his silken words in her ears. The scent of bergamot and violet still clung to her, too. She wished that she could purge herself of it all, as the court physicians would bleed out an evil humour. But it was as if he was at her shoulder now, his thin fingers hovering above her hair.

When at last the latch clicked open, Frances flung open the door and slammed it behind her, with such force that the sound reverberated around the apartment. She started as Thomas stepped out of the bedchamber. He had left for the stables before she had gone to breakfast.

'It is a wonder that old door has not come off its hinges.' He was smiling, but his eyes were filled with concern. 'What has happened, my love?'

Frances's throat tightened but she would not waste tears on that odious man. Besides, he had said nothing to suggest he knew of Lord Rutland's escape. He had made only hints and remarks aimed at drawing her out – a soothsayer's device.

She shook her head, as if to dispel all thoughts of Lambe. 'It is

265

nothing – a conversation with the Countess of Buckingham's astrologer at breakfast. I dislike that man intensely.'

'With good reason,' her husband remarked. 'He said nothing of . . .?'

'No. He was taunting me, that was all.' She looked down at Thomas's boots. 'The King is hunting today?'

'Yes – though God knows what put the thought into his head. The snow has begun to thaw so the roads will be treacherous and the fields will have turned to mud by the time we arrive. Besides, he has business enough to attend to here, given the late tidings from Bohemia.'

'Is there no hope that he will rally troops to support the princess and her husband?'

Thomas squeezed her hand but did not reply. Frances's heart sank as he went back into the bedchamber to continue dressing. 'Where will you go?' she called, drawing off her cloak.

'North-eastwards, towards Waltham Forest.'

The cords fell limp in her fingers.

'Buckingham advised that the ground would be firmer there, with so much woodland to shelter it,' her husband went on. 'He seems to have given little thought to the roads that lie between here and there.'

Frances tried to make herself see reason. *It was a coincidence, nothing more.* Waltham was known for its fine hunting ground, so it was natural that the earl should recommend it. The forest lay some distance to the north of the abbey. God willing, Lord Rutland would have passed it long before the King's hunting party arrived.

'When will you depart?' she asked, as Thomas emerged from the chamber, fiddling with the ties at his wrists. She stepped forward to help him.

'As soon as the King's horse has been saddled. I have prepared the hounds, and my master has ridden ahead to alert the prior.'

Frances's fingers stilled. 'Lord Rutland travelled that way.'

'But that was many hours ago,' he reminded her. 'Buckingham rides like the wind, but he would require the speed of the devil to overtake the earl's carriage.' Frances saw a flicker of uncertainty in his eyes. 'I must make haste,' he said. 'The King will be impatient to set out.'

She nodded, mute, and watched as he strode towards the door.

'God protect you.' The words she always said to him when he set out for the hunt held even greater meaning now. She listened until his rapid footsteps had faded into silence.

'You have bested me again.' Frances laid down her cards.

Kate smiled ruefully. 'You are letting me win today, I am sure of it. I do not usually possess such skill.'

Frances looked out of the window while her friend gathered up the cards and began to shuffle them. The gallery overlooked the northernmost courtyard of the palace, which was why she had suggested they meet there, rather than in either of their chambers as was their custom. It was approaching four o'clock and the light was fading rapidly. Thomas had left several hours before, and with each one that passed Frances's nerves had been pulled tighter.

'The hunting party will soon return, will it not?' Kate asked, echoing her thoughts.

She nodded distractedly.

'You must not fear for Thomas,' Kate went on. 'He is an accomplished rider and you yourself said that he takes greater care since the accident at my father's estate. It is strange to think you were living at Belvoir for so many weeks yet I did not see you.'

Or were prevented from doing so, Frances thought. Kate had been little more than a child at the time, and entirely subject to her stepmother's will. Countess Cecilia would not have wanted her to be introduced to the King, when she had sons of her own to parade before him. She turned away from the window, but her smile faded as she saw the Countess of Buckingham making her stately progress along the gallery, flanked by her usual entourage of attendants. *She has more ladies than the late Queen.*

'What a pleasant surprise to see you here, Lady Katherine!'

Frances saw the girl blanch as she rose to curtsy.

'Lady Tyringham.' The older woman eyed Frances coldly. 'You ladies keep to your chamber so much that I have come to despair of enjoying your company.' Without waiting to be invited, she lowered herself onto an empty chair between them. 'What are you playing there?'

'Primero.' Kate began to shuffle the cards again, but Frances saw that her hands trembled.

The countess tutted. 'Imperial is far better – here, give them to me.' She took the cards from her. 'I will teach you.'

'Lady Katherine and I have played it many times, madam,' Frances said brightly. 'In fact, we have rather tired of it.' She was gratified to see the countess's eyes flash with anger before she regained her superior expression.

'Nonsense.' She flicked the cards into three neat piles as the younger women watched. With a sinking heart, Frances picked up her hand. They played in silence for a few moments.

'You seem distracted, Lady Tyringham. That is the third time you have looked out of the window in as many minutes. I warn you – you need to be on your guard with me. I am a much more accomplished player than Lady Katherine – am I not, my dear?' She patted Kate's hand.

'A prime, I believe?' Frances said, turning over her cards.

The countess pursed her lips. 'Well played,' she replied tightly. 'The best of three?' She did not wait for them to reply before she dealt the cards again, humming as she did so. Frances found her cheerfulness unnerving. It was only the previous evening that John Lambe had remarked upon his mistress's ill humour. She wondered what had changed.

'I hope the King has had good hunting today,' she continued, as they each studied their cards. 'My son too.' Her eyes flicked up to Frances. 'He always catches his prey, in the end.'

Frances looked steadily back at her. *Which prey did she mean – Lord Rutland's son or his daughter? Both, perhaps.* She glanced at her friend, fearful in case she had picked up on the implication. She had decided against telling Kate of her father's flight to Belvoir until she received word that he and her little brother had arrived safely. The poor girl's nerves were worn to shreds as it was. Studying her discreetly now, she could not tell whether her downturned mouth was due to her having picked up on the countess's goading or simply to her natural aversion towards her.

'I wonder that they thought to hunt at all today.' Frances was arranging the cards in her hand. 'It is hardly the weather for it, and there will only have been light enough for a few hours' riding at most.'

'That is all they will have needed,' the countess said, with a smirk.

Frances tried hard to focus on her cards. She must not read meaning into Lady Buckingham's words where none existed.

'Tell me, how are your sons, Lady Tyringham?' she continued. 'Boys are such a comfort to their mother, are they not? Certainly my George is to me.'

More than people realise. 'And Lord Purbeck, of course. You must be looking forward to a first grandchild.' She was pleased to see the countess's lips purse again. That her eldest son was living apart from his new wife was one of the worst kept secrets at court.

'Of course,' Lady Buckingham replied briskly. 'Though I feel sure that George will steal a march on him.' She directed a sly look at Kate, who stared intently at her cards, a flush creeping up her neck. 'I wonder that you do not spend more time at Tyringham Hall,' she persisted, staring at Frances. 'I am sure His Majesty would be only too glad to grant you leave – and my son could arrange it if there is any difficulty.'

'You are most kind, madam,' Frances said, 'but I am not minded to go there at present. When the spring comes, perhaps. I have too much to occupy me here for now.'

'Oh?' The countess arched an eyebrow. 'I cannot think what might entice you to remain here at Whitehall. You have so little company.'

Frances smiled at Kate. 'Ah, but that which I have is worth keeping. I am blessed in my friends – my husband, too.' She was glad to see Kate smile shyly back.

This silenced the countess for a time, and all three women appeared to turn their attention to the game. Frances resisted the temptation to steal another look into the courtyard. It was so dark now that she would not be able to see much anyway. Instead, she allowed her gaze to wander over to the group of young ladies who had accompanied their mistress. Most seemed rather bored and were picking at their dresses or slowly fanning themselves – though the meagre heat from the fire hardly warranted it. Then her eyes alighted upon one who was sitting slightly apart from the rest. She was a good deal younger and appeared ill at ease. When the girl raised her eyes, Frances felt sure she had seen her somewhere before.

The clatter of hoofs in the courtyard distracted her. The countess was first to the window, pushing past Frances in her eagerness. 'My son has returned!' she exclaimed joyfully. 'Excuse me, Lady Katherine, but I must go and greet him. Perhaps you would like to come with me.'

Kate sent Frances a panicked look.

'I promised Lady Katherine that I would help her dress for dinner,' Frances said, with a smile. 'I had not realised it had grown so late.'

'There is plenty of time,' the countess retorted, craning her neck for a better view of the courtyard. 'Besides,' she turned to face them now, with a sly smile, 'I am sure you must be anxious to see your father.'

Frances closed her eyes.

'My father?' Kate whispered, growing pale.

'Why, yes,' Lady Buckingham replied scornfully. 'I wonder that you look so amazed. You have expected him for long enough – as have we all.' She looked from Kate to Frances, as if to make sure that her words had hit their mark, then swept past them and strode along the gallery.

Frances saw her own horror reflected in Kate's eyes as they stared at each other, then hastened in her wake.

CHAPTER 39

2 February

Frances shivered, cowering against the thick yew hedge, as if it might warm as well as conceal her. The chapel bell had long since struck the hour. Her fear that something had happened to prevent Lord Rutland from coming increased with every passing minute.

She knew they were taking a risk in meeting. Buckingham's attendants had kept constant watch on them since Lord Rutland's return to court. The marquess and his mother would not let him escape their clutches a second time – or his precious son. Kate had told her that her little brother was beginning to settle after the fright of his father's arrest at Waltham. Buckingham had been careful not to use that word, of course: he had simply been escorting the earl to court. That Lord Rutland had been heading northwards, away from London, had not been mentioned. As far as the King was concerned, the meeting had been entirely fortuitous. Thomas told her that Buckingham and the earl had been waiting for the royal party at Waltham Abbey when it arrived.

'Forgive me, Lady Tyringham.'

Frances had not heard Lord Rutland approach. A light rain had begun to fall and his hair already hung limply beneath his hat. 'How is your son, my lord?'

He gave a shrug. 'Better, I think – though still very fretful. Kate is with him now. Her presence calms him greatly. She is so gentle, so patient . . .' His voice trailed off and Frances looked away until he had composed himself.

'I have brought some more,' she said quietly, pressing the small glass phial into his hand. 'Use it as before, mixing it into his broth so that he does not taste it.' *Or mention it*, she thought. With Buckingham and his mother paying such regular visits to the boy, she was anxious to ensure that he said nothing that might excite their suspicions.

'Thank you.' He grasped her hand as he took the tincture. His fingers felt warm, despite the chill night air. 'I know what danger you place yourself in by helping my boy. I owe you an even greater debt now.'

'His recovery is the only reward I seek. Has Dr Lambe attended him yet?'

Her friend shook his head. 'No. But I fear it cannot be long. The King sent a message this morning, enquiring after my son and recommending the services of Lady Buckingham's physician.'

'It is a recommendation only. He cannot force you to comply.' Even as she spoke the words, she knew them to be false. A refusal would cause offence at a time when Lord Rutland's favour with the King was already diminishing.

'I would do anything to protect my poor boy,' he said. 'If I cannot ignore His Majesty's recommendation, then I will at least ensure that I am with him when Lambe presents himself.'

'If he attempts to administer any remedies, you must accept them gratefully and promise to give them to Lord Ros yourself. Then bring them to me as soon as you are able, and I will replace them with my own.'

'You truly believe that he means to poison my son?'

Frances knew she must not allow her view of Buckingham and his mother to cloud her judgement. But if Lambe nursed the boy back to health, it would surely destroy their schemes to seize the

Rutland fortune. 'I can see no other reason why they would go to such lengths to have your son brought to Whitehall. You know how much Buckingham stands to gain if he marries Lady Katherine and she becomes your sole heir.'

Lord Rutland nodded grimly. 'He will stop at nothing in his pursuit of riches and power. But I would rather be damned to hell than see poor Kate married to such a devil.'

Frances placed her hands over his. 'We must go back now, but send word as soon as Lambe has visited.'

Frances had examined Dr Lambe's tincture carefully after Kate had slipped it into her hand during a walk in the gardens two days before. She had recognised the smell of rue straight away. It had contained horehound, too, and perhaps a little betony. All as harmless as they were ineffective against the young lord's malady. She had even placed a tiny drop on her tongue, to make sure. The physician had given Lord Rutland just a small amount of the remedy, so Frances knew he would soon return with more. She would examine that just as carefully.

'May I join you, my lady?'

Frances had resigned herself to another interminable evening at court, but now she smiled. 'It is a pleasure to see you, Lord Bacon. I trust you are well?'

'My knee pains me as much as ever,' he grumbled, wincing as he sank onto the seat next to her. 'The poultice I prepared no longer seems to take any effect. But, then, a poor apothecary always blames the herbs with which he works.'

'A little marjoram should help,' she said in a low voice, 'and yarrow, if you can find any at this time of year.'

'Thank you, my dear . . . If only all of my woes could be so easily resolved.'

Frances stole a glance at him. She had heard nothing of the late Queen's jewels since they had last spoken of the matter. The more time that passed, the greater her hope that Lady Ruthven would evade capture. 'The lady has still not been found, then?' she whispered, her eyes upon the groom, who was now smoothing down the heavy scarlet drapes that hung behind the thrones on the dais.

Bacon inclined his head as the Earl of Worcester took his place on the row in front of them. 'She has vanished as if by that conjurer's tricks,' he murmured.

Frances followed his gaze to the far corner of the room, where John Lambe was leaning against a pillar, his eyes roaming over the growing crowd of courtiers assembling for the evening's revels. When he saw her, his mouth lifted and he swept a bow.

'His Majesty means to recall his servants from Saint-Omer,' Bacon continued. 'Though he will not let the matter rest there, I am sure. Well now,' he said, brightening, 'this is quite a gathering. I wonder what has prompted it?'

Frances was about to answer when a loud fanfare of trumpets rang out. Everyone rose to their feet and made a deep obeisance as the King strode onto the dais, closely followed by his son. Behind them came Buckingham. Frances was surprised to see that the Spanish ambassador was not with him.

'My lords.' James addressed the hall from the front of the dais. Frances noticed that his eyes were alight with excitement. By contrast, his favourite appeared unusually subdued. *Surely they had not quarrelled.* 'This evening's revels are staged in honour of a distinguished visitor to my court,' he went on, his voice rising. 'I present to ye' my daughter, the Queen of Bohemia.'

Frances's heart was beating so fast she feared she might faint. She closed her eyes, willing this to be a dream, but when she opened them, Princess Elizabeth was standing before her, resplendent in a gown of silver and white, studded with pearls. A high collar of stiff lace framed her face, which had grown even more beautiful than when Frances had last seen her almost seven years before. Her hair was darker and her figure was a little fuller. It reminded Frances that her former mistress was now the mother of three fine boys – a daughter, too. She had rejoiced at the news of each safe delivery.

Frances realised she had not made her obeisance. Hastily, she dipped into a deep curtsy. When she raised her eyes, she saw the princess flash her a smile before she turned to kneel before her father and kiss his outstretched hand. He motioned for her to stand, then led her to the throne next to his. Frances saw Charles beam at his sister as she sat down. Their father returned to address his court.

'We rejoice at our daughter's return, brief though it will be. It reminds us of the amity that exists between this kingdom and the Palatine – an amity that will soon be proven with men and arms.' He gazed out at his courtiers, as if measuring the impact of his words. Behind him, Frances saw Buckingham scowl at his boots. 'The Emperor Ferdinand has seen fit to challenge my son-in-law's crown and has enlisted the help of Spain in preventing him and my daughter from returning to the Palatine. Such a challenge cannee go unpunished. An English army shall march in my daughter's wake to restore her and King Frederick to their rightful domain.'

Frances peered at her former mistress, who was smiling uncertainly as she surveyed the crowded hall. *So that was why Gondomar was absent – and Buckingham appeared so aggrieved.* His royal master had abandoned the Spanish alliance in favour of his daughter. The marquess had risen so high that he had forgotten how blood always flowed more thickly than water. She felt hope swell inside her for the first time in many weeks.

James concluded his speech and moved to take his seat between his son and daughter. Frances saw Buckingham raise his eyes briefly, but his royal master passed him as if he were invisible.

Bacon whispered, 'It seems the King's angel has fallen from Heaven – for a time at least.'

Frances allowed herself a small smile as she glanced at the favourite. Then her gaze moved to the princess, whose eyes were fixed upon the masque that had begun. Frances hardly noticed the garish costumes or the lively music, though she appeared to delight in both. Inwardly, she praised God for bringing about this unexpected miracle.

When at last the performance was over, the courtiers surged forward to be presented to the princess. It gave Frances such pleasure to see how greatly loved she still was – she had always been the most popular of the Stuart family. *Little wonder that the Powder Treason plotters would have set her on the throne.* Elizabeth received them all with a gracious countenance, betraying no sign of fatigue, though Frances knew she must be exhausted after her long journey.

'Shall we?'

Bacon was gesturing for her to take his arm so that they might progress to the dais. She hesitated, nervous at the prospect of greeting the young woman with whom she had shared so much, but who had been little more than a stranger since her marriage. Though Frances had continued to write to her, she had received only a handful of replies – all hastily written, but full of affection. It was not surprising that Elizabeth had been a poor correspondent, for there had clearly been much to preoccupy her since her husband Frederick had accepted the throne of Bohemia.

'Your Majesty.' She sank into a deep curtsy, then kissed the large sapphire ring that glittered on Elizabeth's right hand. Keeping her gaze lowered, she inhaled the familiar perfume of rose and lavender. Tears filled her eyes. How she had missed her.

'Lady Tyringham – Frances.'

She raised her eyes at last and saw that the princess was smiling down at her with such warmth that the tears spilled onto her cheeks.

'And Lord Bacon.' Elizabeth turned to him. 'It is an honour to make your acquaintance. Frances read so many of your books to me that I feel I know you already.'

Frances saw him flush at the compliment. For once, he seemed at a loss for words.

As they prepared to make way for the courtiers behind them, the princess whispered to her: 'It gladdens my heart to see you. Pray call upon me tomorrow, in my presence chamber. We may talk more freely then.'

With a final curtsy, Frances walked slowly from the dais, heart soaring.

CHAPTER 40

3 February

'Oh, Frances!' Elizabeth exclaimed, embracing her tightly. 'I thought I should never see you again after I left this place. It seems a lifetime ago now.'

'It *is* a lifetime, in some ways, Your Grace,' Frances replied, thinking of the children they had both borne – and lost – since then. 'We had only just received news of Prince Rupert's birth. He is well, I trust?'

Elizabeth gave a sad smile and sank into her chair. 'Quite well. He is a dear little thing – very like my brother Charles. Already he gazes at me with the same solemn expression.' She sighed. 'I hated to leave him so soon – little Elisa too. She clung to my skirts as I climbed into the carriage. I could still hear her howls as we passed the palace gates.' Her shoulders heaved.

'The pain of parting will make the reunion all the sweeter,' Frances said gently, thinking of how William had sobbed when she had last taken her leave of him at Tyringham Hall. His lady mistress had written only last week to say that he was thriving, but it grieved Frances to think of how she had missed his first faltering steps.

'You always knew how to comfort me, Fran.' Elizabeth squeezed her hand. 'I wish I could have you with me again. Frederick has been so kind. He saw how I pined for you, so he arranged for some English ladies to attend me – he would do anything for my ease,' she added, with an affectionate smile. 'But no one could fill your place. And now . . . now everything lies in ruins. Even with my father's help, there is little prospect of reclaiming our lost kingdom.'

'Many here were shocked that the King of Spain should act against your husband, given his alliance with your father.'

'Inconstant wretch!' Elizabeth cried scornfully. 'He changes his coat as often as his breeches.'

They smiled.

'I wonder that my father made peace with him at all,' she continued, 'with Philip as committed a Catholic as ever.'

Frances took a breath. 'The Marquess of Buckingham has been a staunch advocate for the alliance,' she replied, choosing her words carefully. 'He dominates the council.' She did not add that he dominated the King, too.

The princess eyed her closely. 'My brother has spoken of him to me. What is your opinion?'

Although she knew the prince was as distrustful of his father's favourite as she was, loyalties changed with deadly swiftness in this place. 'He enjoys greater favour with His Majesty than any who went before him – even Lord Somerset,' she began. 'Your father has rewarded his . . . service with numerous promotions for himself and his family. Yet still he wants more and is ruthless to any who cross him.'

Elizabeth considered this. 'You have been among them, I think?'

'My husband has suffered most,' Frances replied quietly. 'As master of the horse, Buckingham is his superior.'

'Then I pity him, if what I have heard is true,' she observed. 'I understand that my father named him for St Stephen, yet he has the heart of a devil.'

Frances's silence signalled her assent.

'Well, I have crossed him now too,' Elizabeth went on. 'In

securing my father's support for our war against the emperor, I have ruined the alliance with Spain.'

'And proved the limits of Buckingham's power,' Frances added. 'His pride is so insufferable that he will seek to avenge himself.'

Elizabeth waved her hand dismissively. 'I care little for his threats and sulks. He reminds me of poor Henry when he was in one of his tempers.'

Frances stared at her, surprised. After Prince Henry's death, Elizabeth had been so full of remorse for defying him over her marriage that she had taken Frederick as her husband at once, even though it had been against the wishes of her heart. She had spoken of her late brother with the utmost reverence ever since. But, then, she had hardly mentioned him in her correspondence, Frances realised. The intervening years had evidently brought her to a more measured opinion of him.

'I am glad of it,' she replied, 'though I would urge Your Grace to use caution. The marquess is at his most deadly when he is under threat.' She paused. 'With your permission, I would tell you of a scheme in which I believe he is currently embroiled.'

'Please – go on.'

Frances did not wish to endanger her, but neither could she let this opportunity pass. 'Although Buckingham has received more riches at the King's hand than any servant before him, still he is not satisfied. He means to seize one of the most valuable estates in the kingdom.' She lowered her voice. 'The Earl of Rutland has a daughter, Katherine, of marriageable age. She is his eldest child, but he had two sons by his second wife. A few years ago, they both sickened suddenly – it was said they had been bewitched – and the elder died. His brother survived but his health continued to falter. None of his father's physicians could bring any improvement in him. Lord Rutland became so desperate that he decided to bring the boy here, so that I might attend him.' Elizabeth knew of her former attendant's skills: Frances had nursed her when she had been stricken by smallpox. But she also knew that such things were forbidden in her father's court.

'Please – go on.' Her face was impassive.

Frances told her how their plan had been discovered, how Lord Rutland had fled from Whitefriars with his son, intent upon returning to Belvoir, but had been overtaken by Buckingham and brought back to court.

'Who is Dr Lambe?' Elizabeth asked. 'There has been no mention of him in my father's letters.'

'He is newly arrived at court but has been in the countess's service for some time,' Frances replied, trying to keep her voice even. 'He pretends to be a physician but relies on tricks and conjurations. He claims all manner of powers – from soothsaying to recovering lost treasure.'

'I wonder my father should allow such a man at his court!' the princess exclaimed.

'If Lambe had had a different patron, he would have been hunted down long ago. But he enjoys the countess's protection – and that of her son.'

'And you believe he means to poison Lord Rutland's boy on their behalf?' Elizabeth's gaze did not waver as she waited for Frances to respond.

'If Lord Rutland's son should die, Katherine will inherit the entire Belvoir fortune,' she whispered. 'Buckingham has been courting her for some time. For all her virtues, she has nothing but her riches to tempt a man like him. If he loved her for her own sake, he would have asked for her hand long before now.'

The princess fell silent. Frances knew she had taken a risk: in accusing her father's favourite of plotting murder, she had called the King's own judgement into question.

'I will do what I can to help the poor boy – his sister too,' Elizabeth said eventually. 'I cannot hope to persuade my father to think ill of his favourite. From what you have told me, it is clear that he is utterly in thrall to him. But Dr Lambe . . .'

'Please, Your Grace, have a care. I do not wish to add to your troubles, or to see you risk your father's anger at such a time. You and your husband need the support he has pledged.'

Elizabeth smiled. 'Do not worry, Fran. The King may be blind to his favourite's true nature, but he is still an indulgent father to his daughter.'

The banqueting hall was lit by a thousand sconces and Frances breathed in the warm scent of beeswax mingled with spiced wine. This promised to be the most lavish of the receptions that the King had staged in honour of his daughter. He had not always been such an attentive father, she reflected. Perhaps her long absence had softened his heart.

'Thank you.' She smiled at Thomas as he returned with two glasses.

'It seems that all of London is here.' His eyes roamed the crowded hall.

'Her Grace is as beloved as ever.'

'By you, too, I think? You have seemed a good deal happier since her arrival.'

He was right. The unexpected joy of seeing her former mistress had lifted her spirits beyond measure. Frances had not realised how full of fear and anxiety she had become. For the past two nights, she had slept as peacefully as a child. Although she knew she must not rest all of her hopes upon Elizabeth's ability to help, her very presence in this court was a great comfort. She wished that she might never return to Bohemia.

A sudden hush descended as the King and his daughter processed onto the dais. Elizabeth was resplendent in a gown of emerald satin fringed with tiny pearls that glowed in the candle-light. She smiled graciously as her father's courtiers swept a deep bow, then moved to take her seat next to him. Charles sat on James's right, and Frances saw her own joy mirrored in his eyes as he looked out across the hall. Her smile faded as the Marquess of Buckingham made his entrance. There was no trace of the ill humour that had marked his handsome features when she had last seen him. Instead, the all too familiar grin had returned and he walked with his accustomed air of languor.

As soon as the King and his guests were seated, there was an unseemly scramble for the tables closest to the dais. Thomas and Frances waited until the chaos had subsided before choosing a table halfway down the hall. The servers were already placing an array of steaming dishes in front of their fellow diners by the time they sat down. Frances helped herself to some of the herring in white wine with plump caper berries. Even though it was winter, the King had clearly ordered the palace cooks to raid their depleted supplies for this latest feast. If his daughter stayed for much longer, they would be eating little but salted beef until spring. It would be a small price to pay, Frances reflected.

She was hardly aware of the conversations around her as they ate. Her attention was entirely focused upon the dais, where Elizabeth was talking animatedly to her father. Now and then, he would lean over and kiss her hand, as if to reassure himself she was not some vision that would dissolve as soon as he looked away.

At the far end of the table, Buckingham was toying with the food on his plate, a lazy smile playing about his lips. He did not speak to the companions on either side of him but stared out across the hall, as if appraising every one of its occupants in turn. All of a sudden, his eyes flicked to Frances. She stiffened, but his grin widened and he slowly inclined his head. Seeing this, Thomas placed a protective hand over hers and the spell was broken. Relieved, Frances turned to him. 'The marquess seems in better humour this evening.'

Thomas grunted. 'Whenever that man smiles, I fear the cause.'

The tables were being cleared in preparation for the evening's revels. Frances wished that she might steal away to Lord Rutland's apartment. His son would soon be in need of more of her tinctures. She resolved to prepare some at first light. Finding a way to deliver them to him might prove more difficult.

The King and his guests rose and took their seats at the side of the dais while their table was cleared away. The excited babble subsided. Frances pushed down her rising impatience. *Pray God it is not another masque.*

All of a sudden, the dais was plunged into darkness and a drum roll thundered around the hall, sparking several cries and gasps from the audience. An ominous silence followed. Then a faint tap-tapping echoed across the hall. There was a flash of light and John Lambe's face was briefly illuminated at one end of the dais. A moment later, it appeared again – at the other, which caused a murmur of excitement. Frances stared in dismay. His head seemed to hover in the air as the flame flickered beneath it. Then he slowly parted his lips and raised his eyes to the ceiling in imitation of a death mask. The rising tension in the silent hall was almost palpable. Frances had to fight the urge to get up and run. At length, the old man lowered his eyes and gazed out across the assembled throng.

'Your Majesties, my lords.' His sonorous voice was at odds with his ghostly appearance. 'I will perform such miracles tonight as you will never have seen the like.'

The flame beneath his face was extinguished and there was another loud thunderclap, followed by a blaze of light so dazzling that Frances had to look away. Even from this distance, she could feel the heat of the brazier. The courtiers seated directly in front of the dais shrank away from it, gasping for breath. A slow smile crept across the magician's face as he stared out at them, apparently oblivious to the searing heat. Then with a deft movement, he threw a heavy cloth over the flames and the dais was filled with a thick cloud of smoke.

'God's wounds!' the King spluttered. Next to him, his daughter fell into a paroxysm of coughing. Lambe stepped nimbly forward and held out a large silver goblet. Frances saw her former mistress hesitate. She glanced at her father, who gestured for her to take it. Elizabeth did so, but before she sipped, she rose to her feet and held up the goblet so that everyone in the room could see it. Frances held her breath as she slowly, deliberately, put it to her lips and swallowed. Still standing in full view of the assembled courtiers, she placed her hand on her throat, as if the liquid burned as it slipped down. Suddenly her legs gave way, and with a cry of 'Father!' she sank to the floor.

Everything was in confusion. Frances watched, aghast, as the King rushed to his daughter's side while his attendants flapped helplessly around him. There were cries of dismay from the crowd as everyone surged towards the dais.

'Poison!'

The shout prompted a chorus: 'Treason! Seize him!'

Dr Lambe looked about him in alarm. Buckingham stepped quickly forward, as if to shield him from the baying crowd. Frances sprang to her feet. Before Thomas could stop her, she was pushing her way through the crowds, oblivious to the curses that sounded in her ears. Elizabeth was still lying senseless on the platform, the folds of her skirts fanned out around her. The King was cradling her head on his lap and rocking her to and fro, tears streaming down his cheeks.

'It was nothing – nothing,' Lambe muttered, as two yeomen grasped his arms. 'A simple potion of honey and rosewater – here,' he said, trying to free himself so that he might pick up the goblet, even though most of its contents had spilled onto the floorboards.

'Arrest him!' James cried. 'He has poisoned my daughter.'

Frances climbed onto the dais in time to see the physician being dragged from it.

'Sire, please!'

But James seemed not to notice his favourite as he stared down at his daughter, his chest heaving. Buckingham hovered over them. His face was deathly pale and his eyes blazed – with fear or fury, Frances could not tell. Then he turned on his heel and pushed past her, almost knocking her from the dais.

'Your Majesty, please – let me assist.'

The King looked up at her, his eyes narrowing. 'There has been enough witchcraft for one evening,' he spat.

'I served your daughter faithfully for many years, Your Grace,' she persisted, keeping her voice low. 'When she lay mortally sick,

I alone attended her.' She saw a flicker of remembrance. 'I beseech you, let me do so again.'

James stroked a stray hair from the princess's face.

Frances saw she did not have the pallor of one who lay close to death. 'Please,' she repeated.

The King's shoulders dropped and he gave a nod of assent.

CHAPTER 41

3 February

Frances waited while Elizabeth's attendants fussed around, smoothing the sheets and plumping up the pillows behind their mistress's head. When at last they had finished, she stepped forward and began to examine her as they watched. Clearly, the King would not allow a woman he had once had arrested for witchcraft tend his daughter alone.

Elizabeth's skin felt warm to the touch and, though she still lay unconscious, her heartbeat was strong and regular. Her lips were not parched and there were no blotches on her throat, or any other sign that she had been poisoned. Instead, she appeared in a peaceful slumber. Frances poured a small glass of the fresh water she had asked one of the ladies to bring. Holding it to the young woman's lips, she tilted it and waited for her to swallow. Elizabeth did so without a murmur, her throat pulsing as the water slipped down. Frances gave her a little more, then continued her examinations, working methodically, as the Reverend Samuels had taught her.

Trust only what you observe, not what you assume or fear, he had counselled her. Frances was glad of the lesson now, the words calming her as she repeated them to herself. She motioned for an attendant to lift the princess's shift so that she could look for any spots or rashes on her skin. Here and there, she could see the scars left by smallpox. But elsewhere it was as pure and unblemished as a newly ripened peach.

'Well?'

Frances turned to the lady who had spoken. She was older than the other attendants and had an air of superiority.

'Her Grace does not appear to be in any danger, but I will continue to watch over her. The other ladies may retire now, if they wish.'

The woman pursed her lips. 'We are here at His Majesty's command, Lady Tyringham.' She signalled for her companions to be seated and went to sit on a chair close to the bed. Frances moved to the fireplace and bent to put another log in the grate. Soon, the flames took hold, filling the room with warmth. She moved to the other side of the bed and sat down, keeping her eyes on Elizabeth. After a while, she stole a glance at the other ladies. As she had hoped, their eyelids were growing heavy – the fire was doing its work. Even the older woman was becoming drowsy. Soon her gentle snores could be heard above the crackle of the flames.

Frances took Elizabeth's hand. Her eyes opened at once. Darting a look at the ladies, she turned back to Frances and smiled. Then, slowly, she winked.

'Pray do not worry, Father. I am perfectly recovered.'

The King bent over and kissed his daughter's forehead again. 'I praise God for your safe deliverance,' he replied, his voice cracking.

'Lady Tyringham had a part in it, too,' Elizabeth reminded him, shooting Frances a conspiratorial grin.

The King gave a grunt.

'She is the most faithful servant I have ever had,' Elizabeth continued, 'and should be rewarded as such.'

'Well enough, well enough,' he muttered.

Frances suppressed a smile. The King had not grown any more gracious since his arrival in England seventeen years before, when he had appeared before his new courtiers grumbling that the rain was wetter than it was in Scotland. She did not look for any reward at his hands. It was enough that Lambe had been taken to the Tower and languished there still. The thought of Buckingham's fury gave her a stab of triumph, though she knew he would soon be petitioning the King for the old man's release.

'I hope that sorcerer will receive due punishment for trying to poison me,' Elizabeth said, lifting her chin.

'Hush now, my pet,' the King soothed, patting her hand. 'All is well.'

'You do mean to punish him, Father?' she persisted, her lips quivering as she spoke. Frances could not but admire her artifice.

'Dunnee concern yourself with that wretch,' James replied. 'I will see that he is dealt with.'

'He must not be allowed back in your presence, Father,' Elizabeth protested, her voice rising in panic. 'I cannot return to my husband's kingdom until I am assured that you are out of all peril.'

The King gestured dismissively. 'Ye' have ne' cause to worry. He presents ne' threat to me.'

Frances felt uneasy. It was obvious to her – if not to the princess – that James's fury towards Lambe had abated, that he no longer thirsted for revenge. The marquess had worked even faster than she had predicted. She shuddered to think how he had persuaded his royal master to a different opinion.

Elizabeth sighed. 'I understand that the Countess of Buckingham recommended Lambe to attend Lord Rutland's son.'

The King nodded. Frances waited.

'Well, that is clearly out of the question now, but I cannot abide the thought of that poor boy suffering when something might be done for his ease.' She reached out and clasped her father's hands. 'If Lady Tyringham will assent to it, there is no one in this court better suited to the task.'

Frances gazed at her hands as the King swung around to look at her. She could feel a flush creeping up her neck but prayed that it was not visible above the collar of her dress.

'She isne' a physician, Elizabeth, but a—'

Witch?

'She has some skill in healing, I admit,' he continued, 'but these matters are best left to those who are qualified to deal with them.'

'Such as the physicians and apothecaries who have attended the boy these past six years and more?' the princess countered archly.

The King gave an impatient sigh. 'Very well, my dear. Ye' know I can deny you nothing,' he added, with a rueful grin. 'Lady Tyringham, ye' may attend him, with my blessing.'

Frances felt a searing rush of joy and relief. Not only had she been given the chance to nurse her friend's son back to health, but in sanctioning her to attend him, the King had signalled that any lingering suspicions he harboured against her had lifted. She shot her former mistress a grateful look. Thanks to her, the boy's life might be saved.

'What is the King like?'

Frances stopped grinding the juniper berries and looked at the boy, who was watching her from the bed, eyes wide. 'You will meet him soon enough, I'm sure,' she replied.

'Is he tall?' Lord Ros persisted.

'Not particularly – shorter than your father, certainly. His hair is reddish-brown and he has very dark eyes.'

'Is he a good king?'

Frances added a little oil and a few more pinches of rue to the mortar while she considered how to respond. 'He has shown great kindness in allowing me to nurse you. Tell me, has the pain in your head lessened now?'

The boy nodded and pushed away the hand she placed on his forehead. 'But is he good to everyone?'

'That is quite enough questions for now, young man. You will distract Lady Tyringham from her duties.'

Rutland was standing in the doorway. 'How is my boy today?'

'Better still, my lord.' Frances smiled. 'His appetite grows every day, as does his strength. Apart from a little pain in his head, he seems much more comfortable.'

'I am not comfortable!' the boy protested, wriggling against his pillows. 'This bed is as hard as wood and the covers are too heavy. I long to be out of it.'

Rutland grinned at her. 'My son's impatience is a clearer sign of his recovery than any I have yet seen.'

The boy was watching them with a petulant expression. His skin was no longer pallid and a little more flesh clung to his frail limbs. 'God willing, he will soon be able to return to Belvoir,' Frances remarked quietly. They both knew the boy's health was not the main barrier to that. 'Has there been any more word from the King?'

Rutland glanced towards his son. 'I petitioned him again yesterday, but he was not minded to decide upon the matter. Buckingham was there, of course.' They exchanged a knowing look. 'He made sure to turn His Majesty's mind to other things.'

Frances saw that the boy's eyelids were drooping. He had slept a great deal these past two weeks, but she was glad of it. Sleep would restore his strength even more surely than her remedies.

'What of Lambe?' she whispered.

'Still in the Tower, God be praised, though I hear Buckingham petitions the King daily for his release. Only his daughter's presence prevents it, I fear.'

Frances knew he was right. It was one of the many reasons why she wished her former mistress could stay for longer. But she had been in England for almost three weeks now and her father had already agreed to lend his support to Frederick's war against Spain, so there was no reason to prolong her visit.

'Then I pray the King will assent to your return to Belvoir before Her Grace takes her leave.'

Lord Rutland nodded grimly. 'If need be, I will take my son to the King so that he might see for himself that he is well enough to travel.' He gazed at the boy, who was now sleeping peacefully. 'You have worked a miracle, Lady Frances. I never thought to see his eyes open again, or to hear his voice. It has been so long.' His eyes glistened as he smiled down at her. 'You have brought my boy back to me.'

CHAPTER 42

1 March

The day had dawned bright and clear, and as Frances turned her face to the sun she could feel the faint warmth of its rays for the first time in months. She had grown so used to the cold gloom of winter that she had almost given up hope of spring ever arriving.

A distant chiming of bells was carried on the breeze. *Eight o'clock*. The princess would soon be here. Frances had arrived in Greenwich two hours before, anxious to avoid the crowds that would soon be swarming along the riverside. Thomas had been obliged to stay at Whitehall so that he could join the King's entourage as it made its stately progress along the Thames. She wondered if Lord Rutland would be among it. The King had still not acceded to his request that he might take his son back to Belvoir.

Frances turned at the sound of a light tread on the gravel path behind her. Even though she was dressed in her travelling robes, Elizabeth was still utterly beautiful. Her hair was now almost black, but the sunlight picked out the coppery tresses that had once covered her head, reminding Frances of the eight-year-old girl she had first met at Whitehall fifteen years before.

'Your Grace.'

Elizabeth clasped her hand and they began to stroll slowly along the riverbank.

'Is everything made ready for your journey?'

'Yes, yes – the ladies have been fussing over all the coffers for days,' she replied, with a touch of impatience. 'I'm sure there are more now than when I arrived. But, then, my father has been so generous. Do you like this new gown?'

'It becomes you very well, Your Grace,' Frances replied, with an indulgent smile. Her former mistress had always been easily won by such finery. She was open-handed too, though, and had given Frances and her other attendants many rich gifts as reward for their service. She would not hesitate to come to her and Thomas's aid now, if she knew of their debts. But Frances had always despised those who cultivated royal favour in hope of reward, and in her mind – if not the princess's – it would tarnish their friendship if she asked for help.

'Fran?'

Suddenly aware that Elizabeth was watching her closely, she brightened her expression at once. 'How long will the journey take, Your Grace?'

'Weeks, I expect. It seemed endless on the way here – but, then, I was eager to arrive.'

Frances looked at the young woman, but her eyes were fixed firmly ahead. 'You must be anxious to see your children – and your husband,' she observed carefully.

'Of course,' Elizabeth replied, a little too quickly. 'I have missed my boys dreadfully – Elisa, too. I hope they will not have forgotten me.'

And King Frederick? Frances kept her counsel. She did not wish to vex the princess at such a time.

'But I shall miss you, Fran.' Elizabeth faced her. 'You have been dearer to me than my own mother – God rest her. I came back here as much for your sake as for my husband's. I do not know how I shall bear to be parted from you again.' She blinked away tears as she pressed her lips together.

'Nor I you, Your Grace,' Frances said, when at last she was able to reply. Elizabeth's return had been like a burst of sunlight in a stormy sky, and the clouds would seem all the darker once she had left. Looking at her now, she felt wretched at the thought that they might never meet again. 'I cannot thank you enough for what you have done for me – for Lord Rutland's son, too.'

The princess smiled. 'I was glad to repay your many kindnesses to me, Fran. I just hope it will be enough.' Her face clouded. 'My father will tire of that villain soon, I am sure. His passions burn brightly but are quickly snuffed out. Poor Lord Somerset knows that all too well.'

That much was true, Frances reflected, as she thought of the former favourite and his wife, who still languished in the Tower.

Elizabeth looked over her shoulder towards the palace. 'I should go back now. My father will soon be here.'

Frances nodded but could not speak. She raised the princess's hand to her lips and held it there for a moment, then swept a deep curtsy and walked slowly away.

Frances closed her eyes as she breathed in the heady scent of lavender. The kitchen gardens at Whitehall were enclosed by a high wall, which trapped the fragile warmth of the early-spring sunshine. The weather had continued fine for the three days since Elizabeth's departure and she was grateful for it. She had arranged with Lady Katherine that if the rain stayed away tomorrow, too, they would bring the young lord for a short stroll in the palace gardens. He still tired easily, but the air and exercise would do him good.

Her husband had left for the hunt that morning. The King's mood had darkened after bidding his daughter farewell at Greenwich, so Thomas had suggested they ride out to Esher while the weather held. For once, Buckingham had proved reluctant to join his royal master. His petulance over the Lambe affair still lingered, even though he had at last persuaded the King to release him from the Tower. Frances was glad that the old man had shown enough discretion not to return to court. But she doubted he would stay away for long.

Her breathing slowed as she leaned back against the stone wall behind the bench, taking care to wrap her skirts around the herbs she had gathered, lest they blow away while she slept. She could not help but smile at the thought that the King had not only permitted a woman he had once arrested for witchcraft to treat Lord Rutland's son but that he had placed his own plants at her disposal. *How much had changed in a few short years.*

The scent of rosemary carried on the breeze. It reminded Frances of her mother's garden at Longford. She allowed her mind to wander as she imagined herself there, stretched out on the grass between the flowerbeds, the tiny blades tickling her arms as she dozed. Then the image faded and the familiar sadness returned. It was almost two years since she had last visited, and although her mother had been as faithful a correspondent as ever, her letters had provided only a fleeting consolation for the pain of separation. How George must have grown since she had last seen him. He would be fourteen this July – a man already.

'Frances!'

Her eyes flew open and she looked around her, not certain if she had been dreaming. But then she saw Kate hastening along the path that led from the privy gardens. As her friend drew closer, Frances saw that her eyes were wide with panic.

'You must come quickly – please,' she gasped. 'It's my brother – he has sickened.'

Frances leaped to her feet, the herbs scattering around her. There was no time to gather them up now – Kate was already running back down the path. She hastened after her.

'What has happened?' she asked, breathless, when she had caught up with her. The boy had seemed well when she had left him last night and had settled easily, delighted at the promise of a walk the following day.

'I do not know,' her friend panted, as they passed under the archway of the courtyard. 'He slept well and was cheerful upon waking but complained of a stomach ache soon after he had taken the tincture you prepared last night. The pain grew quickly worse and he started to vomit.'

Frances's blood ran cold. She did not ask more but picked up her pace and sped through the seemingly endless succession of corridors until they reached Lord Rutland's apartment. An acrid smell wafted from it as soon as Kate flung open the door. Frances followed her into the bedchamber, heart pounding.

'My boy. My poor boy.'

Lord Rutland turned stricken eyes to her. His son was cradled in his arms. As Frances stepped forward she saw that the boy's lips were already tinged with blue. His quick, rasping breaths echoed around the chamber. She stared for a moment longer, then, quickly, she ran to the dresser and pulled out her casket of herbs. With trembling fingers, she poured a large handful of mustard seeds into her mortar and began to grind them to a powder, then splashed water into the mixture so that it made a thin paste. She brought the bowl to the child's mouth and tipped the entire contents into it. As she had hoped, he began to retch at once, his small frame racked with convulsions. Then he lurched forward and voided. Frances watched in horror as the dark bile soaked into his already stained linen shift. Exhausted, he sank back into his father's arms, gasping for breath.

'Did he eat or drink anything, other than the tincture?' she asked, as she placed her hand gently on his forehead. He was not feverish and there was no sign of any contagion.

'Nothing,' Kate replied between sobs.

Frances tried to order her thoughts. She had prepared the tincture two days before, in her own apartment, and had brought it last night. It was the same one that she had administered to Lord Rutland's son every day since the King had agreed she might attend him. It could not have caused this reaction unless some-thing else had been added to it.

'Has anyone visited your son or had access to your apartment?' she asked Lord Rutland.

'Only one of the countess's ladies.' He kept his eyes fixed on his son as he spoke. 'She brought some sweetmeats for my son last night, but I didn't give him any in case they would prove too rich for his stomach.'

Frances felt suddenly cold. 'How long did she stay?'

'A few minutes only. She waited in the parlour while I brought the gift in here. But he was sleeping so I did not trouble him for a message of thanks.'

'And my tincture was there also?'

Lord Rutland thought for a moment. 'Yes – yes, I think so. There was still enough in here for his nightly draught, so I saved the new tincture for the morning.' He smoothed his son's hair back from his forehead. 'Is it poison?' he whispered.

She heard a sharp intake of breath from Kate. 'I can see no other cause,' Frances replied. 'Even the sweating sickness would not come on so quickly.'

The boy's chest was rising and falling in quick, jerking move-ments now. She knew he was not strong enough to void again. Besides, it was too late. The poison would already have seeped into his blood by the time she arrived. All of a sudden he gave a deep shudder, then fell still. A long, low rattle sounded in his throat, then all was silence.

Frances watched his chest for any sign of movement, but he lay as limp as a ragdoll. Willing this to be some terrible dream, she reached forward and placed her fingers lightly at the base of his neck and waited. There was no flicker of a pulse. At last, she raised her eyes to Lord Rutland, who looked up from his son's lifeless face as if stupefied.

'I am sorry,' she whispered.

A high-pitched wail sounded across the room as Kate sank to the floor.

CHAPTER 43

7 March

The flames of the torches guttered and hissed as the rain fell more heavily. Frances was impervious to the cold night air as she shuffled slowly along in the procession, her hand resting on Thomas's arm. Ahead, she could see Lord Rutland's tall frame as he followed the pallbearers towards the abbey. She could not bear to look at the small black coffin that was set atop the carriage rumbling along the cobbles between them.

She should have saved him. The thought had run over and over in her mind for the past two days and nights, tormenting her waking hours and depriving her of all but the most fitful sleep. If she had attended the boy earlier that morning, taken the stopper off the tincture herself, she might have smelt the sharp tang of foxgloves before the tainted liquid had reached his lips. The scent had still clung to the small glass phial when she had examined it later that day. That girl must have slipped it into the tincture while Lord Rutland delivered the countess's gift to his son. From the few details that he could remember about her, Frances was sure it was the same girl she had seen begging in the doorway that morning and, later, among the countess's entourage as they played cards; the same girl who had betrayed her and thwarted Lord Rutland's escape.

The slow tolling of the abbey bells sounded along the dark street as they approached. A few people emerged from their houses as the procession passed – more from curiosity than respect, Frances guessed. The death of Lord Rutland's son and heir had excited a great deal of gossip across the city. Rumours of poison had soon spread throughout the court and the King had ordered an investigation. Frances had told his officials about the corrupted tincture, but they had eyed her with scepticism, despite Lord Rutland's insistence that the girl be found and questioned.

Frances knew it would not be long before their suspicions alighted upon her. Already, Buckingham had made a point of having her casket of herbs examined by the King's apothecaries. It did not matter that they had declared nothing amiss: he would soon find another means to have her blamed for the boy's death. Even though his royal master had appointed her to nurse Lord Rutland's son back to health, she knew he would not flinch from having her arrested for witchcraft.

As soon as he had heard of the boy's death, Thomas had urged her to leave for Tyringham. But she felt strangely detached from the matter. Perhaps the weight of grief and remorse with which she was burdened had obscured any feelings of fear for herself. Or perhaps she felt that she deserved to be punished for failing to protect him. As she trudged along, the cold rain seeping into her cloak and making little rivulets down her neck and spine, she realised she hardly cared.

James had ordered that the earl's son should be honoured with the full ceremony of a burial at Westminster, as if royal blood had flowed through his veins. *Was it a penance for appointing a notorious witch to attend his son?* Frances had heard it whispered by two ladies as she had entered the gallery the previous afternoon. Their conversation had stopped when they had seen her approaching. The funeral had been arranged with such haste that it had excited more gossip. Frances herself had wondered at it – particularly given that, as master of the horse, Buckingham had taken charge of the proceedings.

Ahead, the procession was turning left past the ancient church of St Margaret. Frances caught a glimpse of Kate, her head bowed and a heavy black veil obscuring her face. She had been unable to assuage her friend's grief in the two days since her little brother's demise. The poor girl had wept for so many hours that Frances wondered she had any tears left. Kate blamed herself for administering the tincture, insisting that she should have known it was corrupted, despite Frances's assurances that it would have taken a skilled herbalist to notice anything awry. Her wretchedness had been increased by Buckingham's unwanted attentions. The unseemly haste with which he had renewed his courtship had shocked even Frances. She could see him now, walking directly behind Kate, his countenance as cheerful as if he were attending a masque. His mother was at his side, her arm looped over his.

They had reached the west door of the abbey. Frances could hear the haunting voices of the choir echoing through the high stone vaults as she entered the nave. She lowered her gaze to the floor and mouthed a silent prayer.

The King had decreed that the ceremony would take place in the Lady Chapel, among the tombs of his forebears. His own mother lay buried there, close to her cousin Elizabeth, who had ordered her death. James had ensured that Mary's tomb was every bit as magnificent as her rival's. It was a pity he had not shown such respect for her when she had been put to death, Frances thought.

The chaplain stepped forward. As he began to deliver the opening address, Frances's gaze wandered to the stalls opposite those in which she and her husband were seated. Lord Rutland's eyes were fixed upon his son's coffin, which had been laid on an embroidered cloth of gold at the foot of the altar. Kate sat next to him. Frances saw how her hands trembled as she held her prayer book. Glancing along the row, she froze as she noticed Buckingham staring directly towards her. His eyes glittered in the gloom and she saw the flash of his white teeth as he smiled at her. She forced herself not to look away. Thomas tightened his grip on her hand, but when she turned to him, his eyes were full of fear.

The rain had stopped by the time they left the abbey and there was a deep chill in the air. One by one, the mourners paid their respects to Lord Rutland and his daughter, before slowly dispersing. Frances was about to address them when Buckingham stepped in front of her.

'My lord,' he swept an elaborate bow, 'Lady Katherine.'

Frances saw Rutland stiffen.

'Permit me to escort you back to the palace,' Buckingham said, gesturing towards his carriage.

'Thank you, but my daughter and I will walk. It is a fine evening.' He took Kate's hand, placed it on his arm, then made to move away.

'Then I will accompany you. My mother can take the carriage alone – unless of course you wish to join her, Lady Tyringham.'

Frances opened her mouth to reply, but Rutland's voice cut across her. 'I do not need you to accompany us. Nor do I wish it.'

A flicker of a smile. 'Very well. I will bid you good evening, my lord, Lady Katherine.' He bent to kiss her hand but she drew it quickly away.

'God curse that devil,' the earl muttered, under his breath, as they watched Buckingham stroll nonchalantly towards his mother's carriage. 'He murdered my poor boy, I am sure of it.'

'Father—'

'Peace, Katherine. I do not fear him, and I will be avenged for this.'

Thomas took a step forward. 'My lord, your suspicions may be justified, but you would be wise not to voice them – at least, not until you have found something to base them upon.'

Rutland stared at him grimly. 'Then I shall find it.'

'There,' Frances murmured, patting the horse's neck. It dipped its head to drink from the trough in the stable-yard. It was the first time she had ridden out this year and, though the ground was still marshy in places, she had spurred the horse on to a breakneck speed, gasping in lungfuls of the chill morning air as her hair whipped about her. She still felt the rush of exhilaration.

Frances had longed to ride further, beyond the northern reaches of Hyde Park. She would have ridden all the way to Tyringham Hall if she could. The desire to see her sons was so overwhelming that it smote her like a blow. But to return there now would place them in danger. Accusations of witchcraft blighted the lives of families, too.

The horse had finished drinking, so she began to lead him back to the deserted stables. The King had ordered another hunt and Thomas had left before daybreak. The warmth of his embrace had lingered long after he had left their apartment. She knew that he would be anxious to return to her.

Frances had almost reached the stables when she heard brisk footsteps approaching.

'You have returned at last – I have been pacing this yard for an hour or more,' Lord Bacon complained.

Frances was used to him exaggerating but her smile vanished when she saw his grim expression.

'What is it?' Her eyes flicked to the leather pouch that was tucked under his arm.

'Come,' he said, 'we cannot talk here.'

He took the reins from her. Sensing his discomfiture, the horse whinnied as he led it to the stables.

Frances's agitation grew as they walked in silence to Bacon's apartment. As soon as they were inside, her friend poured them both a glass of wine, then sank heavily into a chair opposite Frances. Still saying nothing, he drew a neatly bound set of papers from the pouch and handed them to her. The pages were covered with a small, neat script, and upon one was written a title in larger letters.

The Wonderful Discovery of the Witchcrafts of Margaret and Philippa Flower . . .

Frances froze, her hand suspended over it. 'What is this?'

'My lord Buckingham commissioned it. I wanted to tell you – to warn you – but he ordered me to take it to the printer without delay.' He did not meet her eye.

Frances had seen such pamphlets before. They routinely appeared after a notable witchcraft trial, giving salacious details of the case, the heinous crimes of the accused. Always, there was a pact with the devil, the casting of spells, lives blighted by sorcery and wickedness. The narrative was so similar in each case that Frances had often wondered how her fellow courtiers could seize upon them with such eager anticipation, devouring their contents as if they had never read the like before. She had taken to avoiding the dining hall at such times, knowing it would be filled with animated chatter about the horrors that had been revealed.

'Most of it had been written some time ago, but the rest was left unfinished,' Bacon continued. 'He told me he had set the scribe to work as soon as the young lord breathed his last.'

Frances tasted bile. 'And he has had me named as an accomplice to the women's murderous schemes?'

Her friend placed his hand over her trembling fingers. 'No – you are not mentioned. All of the guilt is placed upon the shoulders of Joan Flower and her daughters – for the murder of both boys.'

'But only one was dead at the time of the trial,' Frances pointed out. 'Surely even Buckingham cannot claim that the poor girls wreaked their vengeance on the surviving son from beyond the grave.'

Bacon shrugged. 'People will believe anything when it comes to witchcraft.'

'Even though the common belief is that to cure the bewitched one must put the perpetrators to death?' Frances persisted. 'That is why the Countess of Rutland ordered the Flower women's arrest, after all.'

'There is no place for reason in such cases,' he replied. 'With this pamphlet, Buckingham has ensured that in the eyes of the world the Flower women are guilty of both murders.'

Frances stared. *What was Buckingham's game?* She had been so certain that he would have her accused of the younger boy's death. God knew he had seemed intent upon her destruction and that of her husband since his arrival at court. Why would he surrender the opportunity? Perhaps he had further torment in mind for them.

'I hope I have done right in showing it to you, my dear.' Bacon interrupted her thoughts. 'I did not do so to cause alarm, but I know how closely you are connected with Lord Rutland and his family.'

Frances nodded absently. 'Thank you, my lord,' she murmured. 'We must wait for the marquess's next move.'

CHAPTER 44

20 March

Kate set down the book and rose to look out of the window. Frances had hoped to distract her troubled thoughts with the poetry, but it was as if she had forgotten her letters entirely.

'It pains me to see my father like this,' she said, peering down into the courtyard. 'Even the smallest matter vexes him since my brother's death.'

The matter was hardly small, Frances thought. Seeing that his flattery and persuasions worked no effect upon Lord Rutland, Buckingham had successfully petitioned the King to intervene in the matter of his proposed marriage. James had summoned the earl to answer for his reluctance to allow his daughter to marry one of the foremost noblemen in the kingdom. But the earl had refused to be bowed, declaring that he would rather see Kate follow her brother to the grave than be wed to such a man. Frances could not help but admire his courage, though she feared for him, too. Buckingham was not a man to be thwarted.

'He wants only to protect you, Kate,' she reminded her. 'There can be few fathers in the kingdom who would sacrifice their favour with the King for their daughter's happiness.' She did not say that Lord Rutland might sacrifice a great deal more besides.

Kate sank onto the window seat. Her shoulders heaved with silent grief. 'Perhaps I should marry him without my father's blessing.' Her fingers worked at the seam of her black silk skirt. 'He would still get my fortune and I would no longer live in fear of what might happen if my father continues to deny him.'

Frances moved to sit by her. 'No, Kate. You would ruin both your lives. Your father would know nothing but grief if you were tied to such a devil, and you, well, I cannot even bear to think of it – and neither must you.'

Her friend nodded miserably. Frances hoped she had convinced her but knew that Kate's love for her father was so strong that she would endure any suffering for his sake.

The silence that followed was broken by a sharp rapping on the door. Kate leaped to her feet. Frances tried to keep her disdain from showing when she opened the door to the Countess of Buckingham.

'How are you, my dear?' the older woman said, fussing over Kate as if she were a lapdog. 'Why, you have become such a recluse that I had begun to wonder if your father had spirited you back to Belvoir! Oh, Lady Tyringham.'

Frances rose to her feet.

'Forgive me, madam,' Kate replied. 'I am still in mourning for my poor brother.'

'*Dear* little boy. Such a shock, of course. But you must give thanks to God that He has ended his suffering at last – and that He has already wreaked His vengeance upon those who sent him to the grave.'

If only God would punish those responsible, the countess might not be standing here now.

'And how are you, Lady Tyringham? I have hardly seen you either, since the young lord's funeral.'

'I have been keeping Lady Katherine company, madam.'

The countess sat down without being invited to do so. 'Well, it is not good for you to be cooped up here, my dear,' she went on, to Kate. 'You look so pale and wan, and that sombre colour becomes you very ill. Nobody can expect you to stay in mourning for ever.'

'It has been two weeks. I do not dress to flatter myself, but out of respect for my late brother.'

At Kate's unusually abrupt tone, Frances was gratified to see the momentary shock on the older woman's face.

'Be that as it may, you must soon enter society once more. The King himself demands it.'

'The King?' Kate echoed in dismay.

'Why, yes. My son heard him remark upon the matter yesterday. George assured him that you do not intend any offence, but you would be advised to prove it by making an appearance.' Kate opened her mouth to respond, but the countess pressed on: 'He does not expect you to attend the feasts and revels, of course – such a thing would be vulgar. But he will take it amiss if you do not soon emerge from your chambers.'

Kate glanced at Frances in alarm.

'His Grace is most kind to trouble himself with such a matter when there must be so many weightier ones to occupy his thoughts,' Frances observed solemnly. 'A ride might do us both good, Kate? We can go tomorrow, if the weather improves.'

'Nonsense,' the Countess interjected. 'All of the parkland will be a mire after this late rain. Besides, I have an altogether better plan. You must dine with me at my house in Chelsea this evening – please, I will brook no objection. It is quite settled. I will arrange for my barge to be at the water gate for six.'

'But, madam—'

The countess was already on her feet. 'The King has sent one of his cooks to help prepare our feast, as well as some grooms to attend us. He would look askance at a refusal after he has been so generous.'

Frances sensed Kate's mounting panic. 'Then permit me to accompany Lady Katherine, madam,' she said firmly. 'She cannot travel alone and I promised Lord Rutland that I would be her constant companion.'

Lady Buckingham gave a sniff. 'As you wish.'

Neither Frances nor Kate spoke as the oarsmen steered the brightly painted barge towards a landing stage that was lit by two large braziers. A groom dressed in the countess's livery was waiting to escort them to the imposing mansion that lay at the top of the rigidly ordered gardens. As they neared the portico, Frances clasped Kate's hand. The fingers were icy cold.

They were ushered into a richly furnished hall. Although she wished herself far from there, Frances was glad of the warmth from the large fire that roared in the grate.

'Lady Katherine!'

The countess was striding towards them, arms outstretched. 'You are most welcome, my dear,' she said, kissing her on both cheeks. Her smile vanished as she flicked a glance at her companion. 'Lady Tyringham.'

She gestured for an attendant to offer them some wine. Frances discreetly sniffed the contents of her glass before taking a small sip.

'I hope the night air has sharpened your appetite. Our feast is almost ready.'

Kate gave a tight smile.

'And I for one am ravenous.' Buckingham flashed Kate a wolfish grin as he sauntered into the room. He bent to kiss her hand, his lips lingering a little too long. A blush crept across her cheeks. The marquess saw it, and his smile widened. *She does not blush from pleasure but shame*, Frances wanted to tell him. But she merely curtsied.

'So the little mouse has been coaxed from her nest,' he remarked, taking a slow sip of wine. 'Tell me, Mother, what bait did you use? A few morsels from your kitchens, perhaps?' He strolled over to the countess and kissed her on the lips as she gazed adoringly at him. 'Or was it the prospect of something more . . . satisfying?'

Frances swallowed her revulsion.

'The feast is ready, ma'am.'

The countess waved away the groom impatiently and snaked her hand around her son's arm so that he might lead her to the dining room. Frances took Kate's hand and they followed at a distance.

The dining table stretched in front of them. The King's cook must have been hard at work for days. The rich aroma of roasted meats, fragrant sauces and spiced wine was intoxicating. Though she had no appetite, Frances could not but admire the countess's lavish hospitality, even if she wondered at its cause.

'Please, my dear.' Lady Buckingham steered Kate towards the chair next to her son. Frances moved to sit on her other side, but the countess was there before her. 'Your seat is over there, Lady Tyringham.'

Frances hid her irritation as she moved to sit down. Kate looked thoroughly miserable as she stared at her plate. She reminded Frances of a lamb that had wandered into a den of wolves.

'May I help you to some oysters, my lady?' Without waiting for a response, Buckingham reached across Kate and spooned a few onto her plate. Frances noticed her cringe as his arm brushed against hers. He helped himself and began to eat, his eyes never leaving Kate as he swallowed each one.

'How do you like Chelsea, my lady?' Frances asked, determined to divert the attention away from her beleaguered friend.

'Well enough,' Lady Buckingham replied airily, 'though it lacks society.'

The conversation turned to banalities. Frances helped herself to some pickled herring as the countess droned on about the forthcoming masque, the King's planned hunting expedition, Count de Gondomar's expected return to court to revive negotiations for Prince Charles's marriage to Infanta Maria . . . Each subject was punctuated by the arrival of more courses. Every time the servers entered the hall, Frances hoped to see them bearing the wafers and hippocras that would signal an end to this interminable feast. She glanced at the clock above the fireplace. It was almost ten. They would soon have to depart or they would miss the tide.

'Tell me, sweet Kate, how does your father fare?'

Frances bit back a reproof at Buckingham's over-familiarity. He was leaning closer to the girl now, his hand resting idly on the back of her chair.

'He is well, thank you, though he grieves for my poor brother – as do I.' She stared down at her black satin skirts. Next to her, the marquess and his mother appeared as brightly painted peacocks.

'Poor Kate.' Buckingham clicked his tongue and gave a sad shake of his head. 'If only there was something I might do to cheer you both. But, alas, your father seems intent upon condemning you to a life of spinstershood.'

'My lord—'

Buckingham waved away Frances's objection and moved so close to Kate that she could see the soft curls surrounding her face stir as he spoke.

'It really is a vexatious business,' he continued. 'The court is filled with ripe peaches that I might pluck, yet this little one,' he trailed his fingers down Kate's neck, 'remains just out of reach.' A pause. 'Or, at least, it has until now.'

Frances rose abruptly to her feet. 'Forgive us, my lady. It is late and we must return to Whitehall before the tide turns.'

Kate made to rise but the marquess gripped her shoulder so tightly that she winced.

'There is no need for such haste – for Lady Katherine, at least,' the countess purred. 'She will be my guest tonight.'

Her smile chilled Frances to the bone. 'That is most kind, but we are expected back at court this evening so I regret that we must decline,' she said firmly.

Lady Buckingham turned to her. 'My invitation does not extend to *you*, Lady Tyringham.' Her words were shards of ice. 'You are free to return to Whitehall, or go wherever you please. It is of no concern to me.'

Kate looked as if she might cry. 'But I have nothing with which to make shift, no nightclothes . . .'

'You will have no need of those,' Buckingham said, releasing his grip. Frances could see the imprints of his fingers on Kate's shoulder. He stroked the base of her neck idly with his fingertips.

Frances could no longer tolerate their games. 'Madam, you know that it is impossible for Lady Katherine to stay here alone. Her reputation would be ruined.'

'Quite so.' Lady Buckingham addressed her as a child who was slow to learn. 'As soon as word gets out that Lord Rutland's daughter has stayed here with my son *unchaperoned* no other suitor will touch her, no matter the riches she might bring. She will be soiled goods, soured milk . . . however you wish to term it. There will be nothing else for it but to marry her to my son.'

'Even your mule of a father will see that, my dear Kate,' Buckingham added. He glanced towards one of the King's grooms, who was standing, impassive, by the fireplace. 'And there are plenty of witnesses to attest to your disgrace.'

'No!' Kate cried, wresting herself from his grasp. She ran towards the door but he was there before her. With a swift move, he had her arms pinioned behind her back and pressed himself against her groin.

'The taking of her will not be such a chore as we imagined, Mother,' he called, over his shoulder. 'A prey tastes all the sweeter if it has tried to evade capture.' Without warning, he thrust his hand up Kate's skirts. She cried out in shock but he silenced her with his mouth. Frances felt as if she had slipped into a nightmare and, for a moment, she was unable to move. Then she launched herself forward, seizing a glass from the table. The countess shouted a warning to her son but Frances had already brought it smashing down on his skull.

Buckingham's hand fell away from Kate's thigh and he stood, panting, as the blood trickled down his neck. Then, slowly, he turned to face Frances. He ran his tongue along his lips, which were almost white. Slowly, he cocked his head and his eyes roamed over her as if he were examining some rare species that the King's sailors had brought back from the New World. Suddenly he dealt her such a blow that she fell sprawling to the floor, her cheek slapping against the flagstones. Her vision clouded as a searing pain ran through her jaw and she tasted blood. The last thing she saw were Kate's skirts as she was bundled into an adjoining room. As she slipped into insensibility, a piercing scream sounded in her ears, as if in a dream.

CHAPTER 45

16 May

The late-afternoon sunlight streamed through the windows, warming the stones of the old chapel, which were bare of paintings or tapestries. The only adornment was a simple gold cross set atop the small altar. The King must approve of such a sparse interior, Frances thought. He was seated next to the altar, so close to his favourite that he might have touched his white satin doublet. She had been surprised to learn that he would be attending the nuptials – even more so that he seemed to take great delight in them. Perhaps he judged that Lady Katherine posed no threat to his own hold over Buckingham. The marquess's passions could hardly be sated by such a plain, timid little creature – or so she had heard someone whisper at dinner the previous night.

Frances glanced at her now and her heart contracted with sorrow. She had seen little of her since that dreadful night – the countess and her son had made sure of that. They had kept Kate a virtual prisoner at Chelsea and even her father had been admitted only once, to sign the marriage contract that he had had little choice but to agree to. Although the court had been scandalised by Lady Katherine's transgression, Frances had made sure that Rutland knew the truth. It still pained her to recall his grief and fury, and she had been hard pressed to stop him seeking out Buckingham and running him through with his sword. The King had denied his request for a duel with his favourite, declaring that whatever their differences, they must be settled without bloodshed. But Frances knew that Kate's father would not rest until he had avenged his daughter's rape. He was standing at her side now, his face a mask of calm, but his eyes blazed as he stared at the man who was about to become his son-in-law.

There were just a handful of guests to witness the marriage at Lumley House, one of Buckingham's more modest residences. That Frances and her husband were among them was the only concession Buckingham had made to his prospective wife. Although she hoped that her presence might bring some small comfort to Kate, Frances railed against her powerlessness to do anything but watch as her friend was bound to that devil.

'. . . for the mutual society, help and comfort that the one ought to have of the other, both in prosperity and adversity . . .'

The Reverend Williams's voice interrupted her thoughts. The young chaplain was clearly revelling in the moment, confident that it would bring him even greater riches from his patron Buckingham. His small eyes darted from the bride to the groom. A few days earlier, he had finally succeeded in persuading Kate to renounce the Roman Catholic faith. Frances had experienced a mixture of admiration and fear for her friend when she had openly declared herself a papist. Such a thing would have spelled death for any but the intended bride of the King's great favourite. Kate's refusal to relinquish her faith had been the only remaining impediment to the marriage, once her father had at last given way. Looking at her friend now, Frances shuddered to think what it had taken to make her submit.

Williams addressed Kate: 'Wilt thou have this man to thy wedded husband, to live together after God's ordinance, in the holy estate of matrimony?'

Frances saw her friend's already pale face grow deathly and her hand trembled as it sought her father's.

'. . . Wilt thou obey him, and serve him, love, honour and keep him . . .'

Rutland grasped his daughter's fingers so tightly that his knuckles showed white.

'. . . And forsaking all other keep thee only to him, so long as you both shall live?'

Silence.

Frances held her breath. Next to her, Thomas edged a fraction closer so that his arm brushed against hers. Her eyes never left Kate. Though her friend's face was turned from her, she could tell from the rapid rise and fall of her shoulders that Kate was struggling to master her emotions. The countess gave a loud cough, prompting. Frances rejoiced at the consternation that this act of defiance must have caused the older woman. Perhaps, after all, the bounties of the Rutland estate would be snatched away from her son at the last gasp.

Even as she thought it, Frances knew it was impossible. Buckingham had bullied, cajoled and schemed his way to this moment and would force the words from his bride's lips if he had to – he had already done far worse.

'Speak up, girl!'

Kate jumped at the King's words, which echoed around the small chapel. Another pause. She turned to her father and gave a small nod. He stared at her for a moment before releasing his grip. His daughter looked back at the clergyman and straightened her shoulders.

'I will.'

PART 3

1622

CHAPTER 46

12 January

'It is a girl.'

Frances watched as her husband set down the note and gazed out over the parkland. His hair had become flecked with grey these past few months, his shoulders more hunched. It was as if their burdens weighed heavily upon his body, as well as his mind.

'Does she have a name?' She kept her voice light, but it pained her that she had not received the news from Kate's own hand. Her friend was hardly at fault, though: Buckingham had kept his new wife a virtual prisoner at Wallingford House, the handsome new mansion close to St James's Park he had purchased from a rival at a good deal less than it was worth. He now owned more than twenty properties in London, by Thomas's reckoning, as well as the numerous country estates that the King had granted him.

Her husband looked back at the letter distractedly. 'Mary.'

Named for the countess. Frances felt a stab of loathing for Buckingham's domineering mother, who now held sway over the ladies at court as if she were queen consort. Even a young woman as biddable as Kate could not help but feel suffocated by her overbearing presence.

'The marquess will be disappointed not to have a son and heir,' she remarked.

Thomas smiled. 'In that respect at least I am a good deal richer than he.'

Frances looked down at the baby sleeping in her arms. *Samuel.* Thomas had suggested the name to honour an uncle who had recently died, but Frances would always think of her beloved old mentor and priest at Longford, the Reverend Samuels. The infant mewed as she stroked the wisps of chestnut hair on his scalp. It had been a troublesome pregnancy. She had been afflicted by sickness from the sixth week and had been forced to retreat to Tyringham well before her confinement was due to begin. *You cannot hope to have an easy time of it when you are so advanced in years for childbirth.* The Countess of Buckingham's remark stung all the more for the truth it carried. As she shifted uncomfortably against the pillows, Frances had to admit that she felt every fraction of her forty-two years. This child would be the last, she was sure. But she could not regret his arrival, even if it had pained her more than the others. He cried more lustily than they had, too, she thought wryly.

Thomas moved to sit next to her and reached out to take their newborn son from her arms. 'A pocket Hercules,' he whispered, gazing down adoringly at the tiny infant, who began to writhe and whimper. 'I fancy you will lead your older brothers a merry dance one day.' He bent to kiss Samuel's forehead.

His expression grew suddenly grave.

'Your steward had no better tidings?' Frances asked.

Thomas shook his head. 'I had little hope of any. There are no more lands left to mortgage, and the interest on our debts has mounted since the last harvest.' He raised his eyes to her. 'I will soon have no choice but to sell this old place.'

Frances could not hide her shock. 'Tyringham Hall has been in your family for generations. It is our home – our sons' inheritance. You cannot relinquish it.'

Her husband drew the sleeping baby closer to his chest. 'I have failed you, Frances – all of you. When we married, I urged you not to embroil yourself in any more Catholic plots, for no good could come of them. I should have heeded my own warning.'

Frances laid her hand on his arm. 'We cannot always deny our hearts, Thomas. I cherished the same hopes for Raleigh's voyage as you did – and many others besides.' She did not add that she would not have ventured so great a sum on such a risky enterprise. Her husband knew his folly all too well. 'How much longer have we?'

Thomas stood abruptly and laid Samuel in his cradle. Their son gave a cry of protest and made fists of his tiny hands. 'Six months – a year at most.' He had moved to the window again and was staring out across the parkland, as if expecting to see their creditors galloping towards them.

'Can you not petition the King? He will surely be generous, after all your years of service. I am sure . . .' The lie died on her lips. She knew as well as he that, even if James was inclined to grant them some funds, Buckingham saw every shilling that left the royal coffers. He would delight in making sure his inferior's request was refused. *Love thy enemy*, the Bible commanded. Such a thing was impossible when that enemy was the devil himself. Her joy in her infant son was momentarily eclipsed by a shard of loathing for the man who had blighted their lives from the moment he had appeared at court.

'We can expect nothing from His Majesty – or any other. Lord Rutland can no longer honour the pledge he made to us now that his fortune rests with his new son-in-law. Buckingham has appointed agents to monitor the earl's coffers. The contract stipulates that the estate he bequeaths to his daughter must be at least equal to the value that it was at the time of her marriage. Besides, our debts are such that they cannot be settled by a gift of money here and there. I can see nothing else for it but to sell Tyringham Hall.'

He leaned his forehead against the glass. Frances longed to comfort him but she had nothing to offer. At the end of her bed, the cradle began to sway as Samuel grew more fretful. She would need to feed him soon. Pray God it would make him sleep a little. She needed rest.

'When will you go?' she asked.

'Tomorrow.'

'But our son was born only three days ago. Surely the King will not expect you to return so soon.'

'Buckingham has sent word that His Grace wishes to hunt on Monday, before Parliament is convened.' He did not look at her as he spoke, his breath misting the windowpane.

'I will come to you as soon as I have found a wet-nurse and am able to travel.'

Her husband turned to her at last. 'Please – tarry here a while. Poor Samuel will already lack his father. I would not wish to deprive him of his mother also.'

Frances swallowed tears. She did not want her husband to see the pain she felt at the thought of leaving their newborn son – his brothers, too.

'I will return to court as soon as I am able,' she repeated, her gaze steady. Thomas had learned not to try to persuade her when her mind was set. 'Now, pray give Samuel to me before he wakes the entire household.'

Frances had not expected to stay on at Tyringham for so long after her husband's departure several months before. She had received only a handful of letters from him since, and although they had conveyed little news, she was under no illusion that this was for any lack of it. Until recently, Lord Bacon had kept her abreast of court affairs – of Buckingham in particular, whose hold over the King had grown ever stronger since his marriage. But even Bacon's letters had become less frequent over the past few weeks. She supposed he was preoccupied with the onset of Parliament.

The thought of what might be happening at court during her absence made her even more anxious to join her husband, but securing a wet-nurse for Samuel had proved difficult. Mistress Penstone had served her well with John, Robert and William, but she was beyond childbearing years now, and none of Frances's enquiries had borne fruit. It seemed that news of their financial difficulties had spread across the county. In the end, Frances had resigned herself to continuing to suckle her baby, until such time as he could be weaned.

Although she had been plagued by misgivings about being away from Thomas for so long, she could not but admit that spending all of this extra time with her sons had been a blessing. They had each grown so much during her prolonged absences at court that it had taken a while to become reacquainted with their new habits and mannerisms, their opinions and pleasures. She pushed away the thought that they would soon become strangers to her once more.

'Mama, look!'

William was peering down at her from the uppermost branches, which swayed perilously as he waved. He had somehow managed to steal a march on his two brothers. A moment later, Robert scrambled up to join him, red-faced and scowling.

'Come down now, boys – it is almost time to dine.'

Only John heeded her. He seemed almost grateful to have an excuse not to climb to the top of the tree. He had inherited his father's caution, as well as his looks. The only time she had known Thomas to act rashly was in his support of Raleigh's expedition. It seemed unfair that they had been punished so severely for it.

'Must you leave, Mother?' John's dark eyes were solemn as he gazed up at her.

Frances stroked his hair, then took his hand in hers. He would never have allowed her to do such a thing if his brothers had been looking on, but he grasped her fingers tightly now. 'Your father needs me with him,' she told him.

'Has Papa written again?'

'The King will be keeping him busy, I'm sure.' That, at least, was the truth. She had heard that James's absences from court had become ever more prolonged. His passion for the hunt made him as oblivious to affairs of state as he was to the weather. The snow had come soon after Thomas's departure for court, but he had still been obliged to prepare the buckhounds for their royal master's sport.

'You must supply your father's place now, John.' Frances saw a mixture of anticipation and fear in his eyes. 'Your younger brothers need a firm hand – even if they seem to be masters of their destiny.'

At that moment, there was a shrill cry as William lost his footing and crashed through several branches, sending a shower of golden leaves cascading down. John was there before his mother and, in a deft move, caught his brother just before he hit the ground.

Frances's relief was soon supplanted by anger. 'You should have heeded my warning, William,' she chided. He cast his eyes to the ground and she could tell from the set of his mouth that he was close to tears. 'Come now,' she said more softly, drawing him to her. 'What will your father say if you have fewer limbs when he next sees you?'

William gave a loud sniff. 'I'm sorry, Mama,' he mumbled. Then: 'Thank you, John.'

The sun was already sinking behind the turrets of the hall by the time they passed under the gatehouse. As she gazed towards it, Frances could not help wondering whether she would ever spend another night under its old roof. Tyringham Hall had become almost as beloved to her as Longford, she realised. Four of her sons had been born there, and the memories of the times they had spent together as a family were as precious as they were brief. *Pray God I will find a way to keep it.*

Mrs Garston came bustling forward as soon as they stepped through the door. 'A visitor arrived for you soon after you and the young masters had left for the woods, ma'am. She is waiting in the parlour.'

Frances looked at the old woman in surprise. Their circle of acquaintance had diminished markedly in the past few years, in line with their shrinking funds. 'Who is she?'

The housekeeper looked a little flustered. 'The lady would not give her name, ma'am, though I asked for it more than once. She insisted that she is an old friend of your ladyship.'

Frances's curiosity was mingled with foreboding. 'Thank you, Mrs Garston. Boys, you may play in your rooms for a while – but make sure you are clean and dressed for dinner,' she called after them, as they scampered upstairs.

The parlour was only dimly lit when Frances entered. The few servants who remained at Tyringham would be preoccupied with turning down the beds, preparing for dinner, and the myriad other tasks that left them exhausted and – Frances thought – more than a little resentful at the end of each day. Her visitor was sitting in a high-backed chair by the window, facing away from her. Frances could see only the top of her head, which was covered with a starched white cap. The woman turned at the sound of her footsteps, but remained seated.

Frances paled. 'Lady Vaux.'

Her guest rose to her feet at last. 'You look astonished, Lady Tyringham. Pray – sit down.' She gestured to the chair opposite her own, as if this was her parlour.

Frances pushed down her irritation. Lady Vaux's arrogance had not diminished during the ten years since she had last seen her.

'This is a pleasant house – though more modest than I would have expected for the King's hunting master. My sister lives but two days' ride from here. If I had known you were so close by, I would have visited you earlier.'

Thank God you did not. 'How is Eleanor?' Frances asked instead. She had always found the elder of the Vaux sisters a good deal more pleasant.

'Oh, well enough,' Lady Vaux replied airily. 'Though, having no children, she fills her time with embroidery and gardening and other such domestic pursuits. Little wonder that she has been so eager for me to visit her.'

Frances gave a polite smile. She doubted poor Eleanor had been given much choice in the matter. She sat down in a different chair from the one her guest had indicated. It was a petty act of rebellion but she had spent too many of her years at court subject to this woman's will. Lady Vaux had schemed relentlessly to finish the work that the Powder Treason plotters had begun and return England to the Catholic fold. Back then, the desire to avenge Tom's death had compelled Frances to do her bidding – as had the unspoken threat that Lady Vaux would reveal he was George's father. But none of her schemes had come to anything, and Frances had learned that the networks of which she had boasted were more imagined than real.

Frances eyed her coldly. 'Why are you here?'

A flicker of a smile. 'That is a fine way to greet an old acquaintance. Well, since you are clearly not inclined to engage in pleasantries, I will oblige you. You and your husband are greatly in debt, I understand – pray, do not deny it,' she said, casting a disapproving glance around the room. 'I can see it for myself. The dust on that fireplace must be an inch thick, and apart from the woman who showed me in, I have seen no servants. Besides, I hear things . . . even in Leicestershire. Such a pity that Raleigh's voyage not only failed to usher in a new dawn but ruined scores of good men in the attempt.'

'What concern is this of yours?' Frances demanded, bristling.

'I am in a position to help you, Lady Tyringham,' she replied. 'My father bequeathed my sister and me a number of estates in and around London. The income I receive from rents alone is enough to purchase Tyringham Hall – and several other houses besides. You have always proved such a friend to our cause – Prince Henry's death proved that. Such endeavours should not go unrewarded.'

'I had nothing to do with that,' Frances remonstrated. 'He died of a sickness.'

The smile returned. 'As you wish, my dear. We shall not quarrel over details.' Her gaze intensified. 'Besides, it is not what you have – or haven't – done, but what you may yet do that matters. I will not toy with your patience any longer, Lady Tyringham – we are too old for such games.'

Frances stopped herself pointing out that Lady Vaux was almost twenty years her senior.

'My proposition is simple. I will help to settle your debts if you agree to embrace our cause once more.'

Frances did not try to hide her disdain. 'What cause, Lady Vaux? The Catholic – or your own?' She saw that her words had hit their mark.

'They have always been one and the same.'

'And they have always come to nothing,' Frances countered. 'You embroiled me in your schemes once before, and I found to my cost that they were as insubstantial as air. I have a good deal more to lose now than I did then.'

Lady Vaux gave a snort of derision. 'I would have thought you had a good deal less. Why, your financial ruin is the talk of the county!'

'I do not speak of material possession, Lady Vaux,' Frances replied, her voice low, 'though, as a spinster, it is perhaps natural that you should misunderstand. My loyalty lies entirely with my husband and sons. I would not hazard their reputation – their lives, even – by involving myself in a cause that was lost many years ago.'

'You are too hasty, Lady Tyringham. You have not asked what our plans are – what role you would play in them.'

'I do not care!' Frances's cry echoed into silence. 'It does not matter,' she continued, once her breathing had calmed. 'How many times has a Spanish invasion been mooted? A huge army of Catholics to oust the King from his throne? It is nothing but words, Lady Vaux – Raleigh and numerous others besides paid the price for believing them. Even if the Powder Treason had succeeded, the King and his government blown to the heavens, what then? Nothing but chaos and division. This kingdom would have been plunged into civil war. No. I will keep my faith in my heart and urge you to do the same.'

'I see that sixteen years of marriage have not diminished your stubborn nature,' the older woman observed. 'But neither has it enhanced your wisdom – or your courage.' She held up her hand to silence Frances's protests. 'Your pride has blinded you, Lady Tyringham. You cannot see that by accepting my offer, you will be protecting that which you hold so dear.'

Frances stood abruptly. 'Our conference is over, Lady Vaux. I will ask that your carriage be brought from the stables.'

Her guest showed no inclination to move, though Frances glared down at her.

'Very well.' Lady Vaux rose to her feet. 'But you are a fool.' With that, she began to walk slowly from the room. When she reached the doorway, she stopped. 'Of course, if you should change your mind . . .'

CHAPTER 47

4 November

'God's wounds, have a care, man!'

Frances watched as Lord Bacon limped after a thickset young man, who was dragging a fine writing desk over the threshold. He took a silk kerchief from his pocket and rubbed at a scratch on the gilding. 'I am no longer so rich that I can replace such treasures . . . unlike your master,' he muttered, under his breath, as the man quickened his pace. As he walked back into the room, a loud bang echoed along the corridor beyond. He winced.

'This will be the death of me, Frances,' he grumbled, sinking down next to her on one of the few pieces of furniture that remained in his once magnificent hall.

It occurred to her that he was not the first owner of York Place to find himself thrown out of office. Almost a hundred years earlier, King Henry VIII's once-powerful cardinal, Thomas Wolsey, had been stripped of all his great titles and forced to hand the keys to his rival, Anne Boleyn. She had not enjoyed her triumph for long. Frances hoped the same would be true of Buckingham, whose residence this now was.

'Perhaps the place is cursed,' Bacon remarked, echoing her thoughts. 'It was always too grand for a poor philosopher like me anyway, so I will not mourn its loss too greatly. It is far more suited to my former patron.'

Frances forced a smile. 'Where shall you go?'

'I have some rooms close to the Temple Church. They will suffice for now – though Alice does not agree. She has gone to stay with relatives in Suffolk. Perhaps it is for the best.'

Frances regarded him sadly. 'Is there no hope of a pardon?'

Bacon gave a bark of laughter. 'His Majesty is more likely to give up hunting than restore me to the privy council – his precious angel has made sure of that.'

Although Frances had lived at court for long enough to expect such sudden twists of Fate, Lord Bacon's had been more sudden than most. His last letter – admittedly written many weeks before – had given no hint of any troubles, but by the time she had arrived at court he had been impeached for corruption. She had heard enough of the charges to know they were groundless. Of all the King's councillors, he was the least likely to accept bribes. But such details mattered little to his royal master when his favourite had persuaded him otherwise.

'Perhaps you might petition His Grace again, once he has had time to reflect,' she ventured.

Bacon shook his head. 'You know as well as I that it would be in vain. I have already assured the King that when hearts are opened mine shall not be found corrupt. I may be frail in body, but in morals I am as Saint Peter himself.'

Frances kissed his cheek. His eyes brimmed with tears.

'Well, it is no matter,' he went on, brushing them away. 'The experience has given me yet another thing in common with my dear friend. Now we are not only fellow herbalists and intellectuals, but victims of His Majesty's summary justice.'

Frances knew that though Bacon was making light of it, his impeachment must have shaken him to the core. He had enjoyed a seemingly inexorable rise since becoming lord keeper. But this had only served to increase his enemies' desire to bring him down – Buckingham in particular. The marquess had been content as his patron until he judged that Bacon was threatening his own pre-eminence in the council.

'I am sorry I was not here when it happened,' Frances said. 'If I had left Buckinghamshire a couple of weeks earlier, I could have attended your trial.'

'I am glad you were spared the experience, my dear. That wretch Coke presided over it,' he added bitterly. 'He could not resist such an opportunity to triumph over me, of course. How he must have delighted in announcing that ridiculous fine. I will never be able to pay it, of course – even after selling the lease to this place and several other properties besides.'

'Then you may console yourself with the knowledge that we have one more thing in common,' Frances observed.

'Forgive me, my dear. I have wallowed in my own misery so much that I have failed to ask how your own affairs prosper. Did the harvest bring no respite?'

'The rains blighted the crops, as they have every year since Raleigh's death. It seems God is punishing us for supporting his voyage.'

'They fall on other lands than yours, my dear,' Bacon reminded her. 'If God is showing His hand, then it is surely against the King, who presides over them all.' He paused. 'I should have helped you when I had the means. Is there no hope of saving Tyringham Hall?'

'Thomas has already instructed his agent to advertise it for sale,' she replied, her voice flat. 'Our sons will go to live with my mother and George at Longford.'

'That at least must be a comfort.'

'It would be more so if I could join them.' Since returning to court, she had seen little of her husband. The King no longer troubled to return there after each hunt, but travelled from one country estate to the next, often staying for weeks at a time. Frances had begun to question the wisdom of her decision to come here. Her time would surely be better served with her sons. Then she thought of Thomas, how wan he had looked when she had arrived here three weeks earlier, and felt ashamed. She would not desert him.

Footsteps echoed along the corridor. Frances and Bacon turned to see two men enter the hall, straining under the weight of an enormous painting. As they set it on its side, the linen cover fell away. Frances stared. The portrait was of a man and a woman in a woodland clearing. They were naked but for two pieces of silk covering their modesty. The man had one hand on his heart and the other around the lady as he gazed adoringly at her. Her expression was uncertain, as if she was ashamed of her nakedness. She did not look at her companion but stared straight ahead. Her breasts were bare and she seemed to cringe away from the man's embrace.

Frances drew in a breath. The resemblance was quite remarkable. She had heard that Buckingham had commissioned a marriage portrait from the celebrated court painter, Van Dyck, but had not expected this.

'*Venus and Adonis,*' Bacon said. 'The Flemish master has excelled himself, has he not? My former patron has never looked so striking.'

Or so predatory, Frances thought. She felt sick with disgust. Had Buckingham not ruined his young wife enough already? Now poor Kate would be forced to suffer the humiliation of a thousand eyes gazing upon her nakedness as their guests supped wine and devoured sweetmeats.

'Should we take a stroll in the gardens?' she asked, turning her back on the monstrous picture. 'The light will soon begin to dim and I would like to see them once more. I doubt I will do so again after this evening.'

'Of course,' her friend agreed. 'But, first, I have something for you.' He went to the fine walnut writing desk by the window. Taking a key from his belt, he unlocked the central drawer and drew out a large book. 'You may think this a poor gift, given how it has been received in certain exalted circles.'

Frances looked down at the beautifully bound volume with pleasure as she traced her fingers over the gilded inscription:

Novum Organum Scientiarum. Carefully, she opened it to reveal the title page, upon which was an engraving of a galleon, its sails billowing as it passed between two enormous pillars.

'The Pillars of Hercules,' he explained. 'I thought it fitting, given the labours I suffered in bringing this to pass.'

Beneath the scene was written: '*Multi pertransibunt & augebitur scientia*'. *Many will travel and knowledge will be increased.*

He had told her of the new system of logic and reasoning that he was beginning to devise some years before, and they had spent many hours discussing it. Frances had predicted it would be his greatest work – certainly it deserved to be. Thomas had been there when Bacon had presented it to the King, who had seemed delighted, declaring that he would rob himself of sleep in order to finish it. He had soon given up, though, and the book had become the butt of ridicule.

'His Grace compared it to the peace of God, for it passeth all understanding.' He was still smiling down at her.

'Then I shall enjoy it all the more,' Frances affirmed, 'for it takes little to surpass the King's understanding.'

'Little Mal! Give her to me, Steenie.'

The infant chuckled as the King bounced her on his lap. 'Why, I think she has grown chubbier still since yesterday. Have you been stuffing her with comfits?'

Frances noticed Buckingham grimace before he recovered his usual simpering expression. 'She takes after her mother.'

Behind him, Kate flushed and lowered her gaze. Frances despised the marquess for the insult and wished that her friend might fling one back at him. But she knew that Kate was as likely to do that as a sparrow might challenge a hawk.

'His Excellency has little time, Your Grace,' Buckingham prompted, casting a glance at Gondomar, who was still kneeling before the throne.

James pretended not to hear him. 'Her teeth are as sharp as a kitten's,' he exclaimed, withdrawing his little finger from her mouth. The child immediately reached out for the gold chain that lay around the King's neck and stuffed it into her mouth. James roared his appreciation, but his favourite stepped forward and wrenched it from his daughter, causing her to wail in pain and disappointment. He then lifted her from his master's lap and thrust her none too gently into her mother's arms.

'Hush, little one,' Kate murmured into Mary's ear, as she rocked her. It warmed Frances's heart to see her tenderness towards her daughter. She hoped that Mary provided her mother with some comfort amid the misery of her marriage.

'Your Grace?' The count's soft voice cut through the silence that followed.

With an exaggerated sigh, the King at last turned to the Spanish ambassador. 'Well?' he demanded, gesturing for him to stand. 'I told you not to attend me again until your master has agreed to help my son-in-law. Is that the case, or does he persist in his stubbornness?'

Gondomar gave a small cough. 'King Philip is most desirous to assist, of course, Your Grace. But the matter is complicated . . .'

James thumped his fist so hard on the arm of his throne that Frances felt the floorboards vibrate.

'The devil take him! Perhaps the matter exceeds his judgement – he is new on the throne, after all. Allow me to explain it again,' he went on, in a sing-song voice. 'King Frederick and my daughter have been deprived of their lands in Bohemia and the Palatine. I have already expended a vast portion of the royal treasury on their behalf, but until your master's forces join with mine we can hope for little success. King Philip is honour-bound to oblige me in this, since it was his father who robbed them of their lands in the first place.'

The ambassador had the grace to look momentarily abashed. 'My master sympathises with King Frederick, Your Grace, but—'

'To hell with his sympathy!' James shouted.

As the ambassador opened his mouth to reply, little Mary began to wail again.

'Take her away,' Buckingham snapped at his wife, who immediately rose to her feet and, bobbing a hasty curtsy, scurried from the room. Seizing her opportunity, Frances slipped away unnoticed and followed in her wake.

Kate was already out of sight by the time Frances passed the yeomen stationed outside the presence chamber. But the aroma of violets trailed behind her. Frances had made the perfume as a gift for her twenty-second birthday. Although Kate had not spoken two words to her since her return to court and had been careful to avoid her gaze, the fact that she still wore it gave Frances hope that their friendship might yet be revived.

As she rounded the next corner, she saw a flash of green silk in one of the archways that led out into a small knot garden close to the royal apartments. Slowing her pace, she walked towards it.

'Kate.'

The young woman leaped at her voice, though she had spoken softly. She cringed away, shielding her child from her, as Frances took a step forward. 'Please, do not be afraid. We are still friends, are we not?'

Kate did not reply but glanced quickly around, as if fearing they were being watched. 'You must not speak to me. My husband forbids it.'

Frances smiled to hide her dismay. 'What harm can there be in two old friends conversing?'

Kate's eyes widened in panic as Frances moved to sit down next to her. Mary peered at her curiously from behind her mother's sleeve and gave a shy smile. Her face reminded Frances of the cherubs that were painted on the ceiling of the royal chapel. *The face of an angel, just like her father*. She pushed away the thought. 'Did my letters reach you?' she asked. 'I wrote to you often, after . . .'

Kate was silent for so long that Frances thought she would not answer. Then: 'I burned them.'

Her words smote Frances. *This was Buckingham's doing*, she told herself. Unless . . . Did Kate blame her for what had happened that night? Did she believe Frances had abandoned her? She felt as if her chest was being squeezed. 'Kate?' she ventured, reaching out to touch her hand. The young woman pulled it quickly away. 'Kate, you must listen to me. I am as true a friend to you now as I ever was. I cannot bear to see you so afraid.'

'Would you not fear the devil?' Kate spat back, rounding on her. Mary gave a little whimper but she seemed not to notice. 'My husband has told me what you are, how you bewitched my poor brother to death and would do the same to me – to our child – if you had the means.'

Frances stared at her in horror. 'Kate, *no*.'

'Lady Buckingham,' she corrected. 'You presume too much upon our former acquaintance.'

Frances fell silent, measuring her words. 'I see that you are not minded to heed me, Lady Buckingham,' she replied, her voice steady. 'I see, too, that your mind has been corrupted. But I speak truth when I say that I have only ever shown you kindness, compassion. And I received the same from you in return. You were the closest friend I have ever had in this place' – although Kate's face was still turned away from her, she saw a muscle twitch in her jaw – 'and I pray God that He will open your heart to me again one day.'

Little Mary made a soft cooing noise and began opening and closing her tiny fists. Frances resisted the temptation to stroke her downy hair, but instead rose slowly to her feet and gave a curtsy of farewell.

CHAPTER 48

19 December

'Frances!'

Someone had gripped her by the shoulders. *The guards must be here already.* She thrashed about, like a fish on a hook, knowing there could be no escape.

'Frances.' Softer, this time – the voice familiar. 'Hush, my love. It was a dream, that is all. You are safe.'

She opened her eyes to see Thomas leaning over her, his eyes filled with concern. She blinked, fearing he was nothing more than a vision she had conjured in her sleep, then flung her arms around his neck and clung to him as if she would never let go.

'I should leave you more often, if this is my greeting,' he murmured into her hair, then planted a kiss on her forehead. 'You feel hot,' he said. 'Is it a fever?'

'No, no, I am quite well,' she assured him, the ghastly image of Buckingham's lifeless face fading now. The dream had been so real: Lady Vaux at her side, urging her on as she dripped the poison into his mouth. 'I should not have laid the extra cover on the bed, only it was so cold in here when I returned from the banqueting hall.'

'Mrs Knyvett should have made up the fire. She has become very neglectful in her duties again lately.'

Frances said nothing. They both knew the reason. Their old servant had been obliged to take on other work to make up for the diminishing wages she received from them.

'I am so glad to see you, Thomas.' Frances ran her fingers through the hair at his nape. 'Did the King have good hunting?'

Her husband rose from the bed and began to undress. 'Good enough,' he replied, as he unlaced his doublet. 'The prince joined us.'

Frances was surprised. The King had long since despaired of his son showing any inclination to share his beloved pastime.

'Buckingham's idea, apparently.' They exchanged a look.

'Perhaps he hoped to humiliate him,' she mused, remembering the last time that the King and his son had ridden out together. James had soon lost patience with the prince's obvious lack of skill in the saddle. Charles had returned to the palace, grim-faced, within the hour.

'So I assumed.' Her husband climbed in next to her and drew her into an embrace. His skin felt cool next to hers as she snuggled against him. 'But he could not have been more solicitous towards him, slowing the pace of his own mount so that they could ride next to each other – even though that meant he hardly saw the King.'

'How gracious.' Her words dripped with sarcasm, but she felt uneasy. 'How was the prince towards him?'

It was only a few short weeks since a furious row had erupted between the King's son and his favourite. Buckingham had been walking with his royal master in Greenwich Park when the prince had turned a jet of water from one of the fountains on him as he passed, soaking him to the skin. James had furiously upbraided his son and Buckingham had stormed off in a rage. Frances wished she had been there to witness it. Although the whole court knew of his dislike of the marquess, for Charles to humiliate him in such a way was quite out of character. Perhaps he would not make such a weak ruler as his father supposed.

'He seemed more astonished than pleased, but thanked Buckingham for his pains. The King berated the marquess for neglecting him, though. Their quarrel could be heard throughout Apethorpe, until Lord Fane ordered the pipers to strike up a tune.'

Frances had not visited the hall since she and Thomas had joined the royal party there eight years before. How different things might have been if Sir Anthony had not permitted the new attendant to serve the King at table. An image flitted before her of the scene she had witnessed in the hunting lodge shortly afterwards.

'Are they reconciled?' she asked.

'Apparently so – at least, they shared a carriage back to London,' he replied, turning to kiss her. 'But let us have no more talk of that now.'

In the bright winter sunshine Frances slowed her pace and looked out across the river. It was the first fine day since the court had arrived in Greenwich, and the ground was still wet underfoot. Her soft leather soles were already sodden, though she had been walking for only a few minutes.

The Christmas celebrations had been more muted this year, James laid low with a heavy cold. He had kept to his chamber throughout most of the twelve days of feasting and revelry. Buckingham had held court in his absence, appearing in an array of magnificent costumes, each designed to draw every eye in the room. He had insisted upon being served on bended knee, choosing from a vast selection of dishes that were laid before him on gilded platters. At the feast of his namesake St Stephen, he had gone further still. There had been a shocked silence as he had lowered himself onto the King's chair. His rival Baron Cranfield, lord high treasurer, had eventually voiced a protest and even Buckingham's supporters had muttered their disapproval. Frances had caught the fleeting look on Prince Charles's face before the marquess had made him smile with some jest. Buckingham should have a care, she thought. Already people were beginning to whisper that he was the *alter rex* – the other King.

With his royal master incapacitated, Thomas had snatched a brief visit to Tyringham to oversee the inventory of their belongings before they were transported to Longford. The boys had arrived there in time to celebrate Christmas with their grandmother and elder half-brother. The thought of how they would be spoiled lessened the pain of knowing they would never see their childhood home again – and of her continued separation from them. Thomas had promised that, as soon as the spring came, they would make the journey west to visit them.

Her eye was drawn to a movement on the river, where a solitary barge was making its way towards the palace. Although it was too far to see clearly, it didn't seem laden with provisions – besides, there were more than enough victuals to sustain the court for the few days they had left here. Neither could she see more than one passenger – a man, sitting at the furthest end from the oarsman. Frances kept her eyes fixed upon him as the vessel drew closer.

At last it reached the landing stage a short distance ahead. The man stepped nimbly onto the platform and pressed a coin into the boatman's hand. He was dressed entirely in black and his face was obscured by a wide-brimmed hat. Frances thought about moving back into the shadows, but she was too intrigued to find out who the newcomer was. He kept his head lowered as he walked towards her.

The cawing of a rook made him look up.

William Cecil.

He saw her and stopped. They stared at each other for a moment. In the ten years since Frances had seen him, he had gained in stature – physically, as well as by dint of his title. He must be in his early thirties now, she judged, and he seemed to have grown taller somehow. Perhaps that was because of the long riding boots he wore, or the high ruff around his neck. Frances remembered him as pale and clean-shaven, but his face now had a more weathered look and he had grown a beard in the fashionable style.

His face relaxed and he raised his hat in greeting, then continued to walk towards her. 'Lady Frances. It is a pleasure to see you again.'

'Lord Salisbury.'

'The years have been kinder to you than to myself, I fear!' He grinned. 'Or perhaps it is being away from court for so long – it certainly dulls the mind. I find that these days my thoughts are filled with crops and militia.'

Frances knew of his appointment as Lord Lieutenant of Hertfordshire. She could not help wondering if it had been the King's way of removing him from court. Although Salisbury's father, her old adversary, had been the most powerful man in government and had groomed his son to succeed him, the younger Cecil had not won favour with the King. Even before Buckingham had risen to prominence, Salisbury had retreated to his father's seat at Hatfield.

'And your growing brood, of course.'

His eyes lit with genuine warmth. 'I have even more children than you, my lady. My father chose wisely. Catherine is the best of wives.'

'Then you are fortunate indeed, my lord. Happiness is a rare blessing in most noble marriages.' She had never met the Earl of Suffolk's daughter but, as a member of the powerful Howard family, Catherine must have brought both political and financial advantage to her husband. 'What brings you here at this time?' she asked. 'The Christmas celebrations are almost over.'

He did not answer but held out his arm so that they might walk on. At a fork in the path, he steered them towards the parkland rather than continuing to the palace as Frances had expected. Only when its walls were out of sight did he begin to speak.

'I came here to find you, Lady Tyringham. It is more than ten years since this kingdom was saved by the death of that heretic prince.'

Frances turned sharply to look at him, but he held up his hand to silence her. 'Have no fear. I do not mean to dwell upon the part you played in it – that must rest with your conscience. What concerns me – concerns all those of our faith – is what will happen when the King dies.'

'Such talk is treason.' Frances glanced around the deserted woodland. 'I want no part of it.'

'Please – hear me, Lady Tyringham,' he urged, grabbing her arm as she made to leave. 'What I have to say is of as much significance to you as to the kingdom.'

Frances wished that she could close her ears to his words, run far from this place. Many times since Lady Vaux's visit she had felt haunted by the ghosts of her past. Now another was standing before her. Was this God's way of punishing her for her sins?

'The King's health is beginning to fail – I hear he has lain sick all through the festivities.'

'Of a cold – nothing more.'

'He is an old man,' Salisbury continued, as if she had not spoken, 'and so steeped in vice and excess that he will hasten his own end, just as the late Queen predicted. All eyes must turn to his successor. Prince Charles has the makings of a fine king, but he cannot restore England to the Catholic faith alone. Heresy has taken such deep root that many would oppose it.'

Frances drew in a breath and waited. All of this felt horribly familiar.

'The King of Spain has pledged to support our cause if the prince marries his daughter, the Infanta Maria.'

'That is hardly a secret,' Frances replied impatiently. 'The Count de Gondomar first proposed the match more than two years ago and has been treating for it ever since.'

He spread his hands. 'What you say is true, my lady, but he is privy to matters that the King is not. As soon as the alliance has been forged and the infanta has been installed as Charles's queen, his master will send an army to bring all England's heretics to heel.'

'This again?' Frances's voice dripped with scorn. 'How many times has a king of Spain promised to rescue those of our faith?

We endured sixteen years of false hopes and empty promises from the old King Philip. Why should you believe his namesake is any different?'

'Because I had the promise from his own lips,' he replied, his eyes bright with fervour. 'I have travelled a good deal further than Hatfield since I saw you last, Lady Frances. Venice, Lyon, Madrid . . .' His voice trailed into silence. Frances was suddenly aware of the soft rustle of branches, the cawing of the rooks as they searched for food in the barren woodland. 'You are right to be distrustful,' he continued. 'It was the same doubts that drove me to visit the Spanish court, to hear the pledge from the dying King – and gain this symbol of fidelity from his successor.'

Frances looked down at the heavy gold ring that was nestled in his palm. She had never seen such a ruby. Even in the gloom of the forest, it seemed to glow like the embers of a fire. 'A pretty jewel,' she said, 'but on its own, it signifies little.'

A small smile. 'I agree. If this were all, I would have nothing but a priceless gift from a foreign prince. But there is a good deal more. Prince Charles is a devout Catholic, though he has concealed it from his father, of course. Younger sons are always raised by their mothers – a tradition that the late Queen was careful to uphold.'

Frances knew this to be true, but scant progress had been made towards achieving Queen Anne's dying wish that her son would marry a Catholic princess. She pushed down her rising irritation.

'The prince is resolved upon this marriage, but his father wavers too much. We must rely upon others to bring it to pass,' Salisbury continued. 'There is only one man in this kingdom with enough power to achieve our ambitions.'

Buckingham. She knew the name before he spoke it. 'You are a fool to believe that he serves anyone but himself, my lord.'

Salisbury moved a step closer. She could feel the warmth of his breath on her face. 'No, Lady Tyringham,' he said. 'Lord Buckingham serves God before all else. He is a truer Catholic than any in this kingdom and would give his life for our cause.'

'I always took you for a shrewd, discerning man, my lord. I can see now that I was wrong. Buckingham is no more a Catholic than the King, whose bed he shares every night.'

'I know the reasons for your low opinion of him,' Salisbury countered. 'He can be ruthless and cruel, but never without purpose. Why do you think he was so intent upon securing the King's favour entirely for himself? Or marrying the richest heiress in the kingdom? It is all for this, not for vain pride or greed.'

'He is a murderer!' Frances exclaimed. There was a loud flutter of wings as a startled rook took off from one of the branches over-head. 'A rapist, too,' she went on, lowering her voice, 'and many more things besides. Yet you expect me to believe that this devil is really an avenging angel, sent by God to do His work here on earth?' She wrenched her arm from his grip and began to stride away.

'Wait!' Salisbury caught up with her. 'I beg you, listen to me. You might pretend to have turned your back on our faith, but I see its light burning in your eyes still. Deny it if you will – it makes no difference,' he went on as she opened her mouth to protest. 'With or without your support, we will restore England to the Catholic fold. Thanks to his marriage, Buckingham has amassed enough funds for a voyage to Spain. He will take the prince with him so that the marriage might be contracted when they reach the Escorial. Everything is in readiness. They will sail as soon as winter has abated.'

Frances stared in disbelief. 'Without the King's knowledge, his sanction?'

He inclined his head. 'We cannot afford to wait for either.'

She fell silent, her mind reeling from what she had heard. The idea that Buckingham was a true Catholic seemed unthinkable. That he had acted out of loyalty to the cause rather than for self-ish motives was preposterous. Even if he did cherish that faith in his heart, it was the lure of power and riches that drove him on. Salisbury was as much under his spell as the King.

But then a thought struck her. The dying Queen had spoken of someone whom she had instructed to bring about her son's

Catholic marriage. *I ask only that you do nothing to hinder them – no matter how greatly you might wish it.* Frances had puzzled over those words ever since. Why would she, whom Anne knew to be of the true faith, obstruct such a marriage? Now it all became startlingly clear. The man whom Anne had appointed to restore England to the Catholic faith was her mortal enemy.

Suddenly aware that Salisbury was staring at her expectantly, she tried to still the thoughts that were racing through her mind. But one word came before all the rest. *No.*

'I cannot forget what you have told me,' she replied at last, her voice quiet and steady. 'Neither will I repeat a word of it to another living soul. But I will have no part in this scheme. You will never speak of it to me again. Good day, Lord Salisbury.'

1623

CHAPTER 49

21 February

A chill wind whipped about the privy garden. Frances leaned closer to her husband. He always felt warm, even on the bitterest of winter days.

'We should go in,' he said, bending to kiss the top of her head.

'In a few minutes, perhaps. It has been so long since we were last able to enjoy these gardens together, and you will be leaving again tomorrow.' She felt the usual sorrow at the prospect but knew that the King would not be gainsaid. Glancing up at the leaden sky, she feared there would be more snow before nightfall. Already the roads were barely passable. Yet the only concession that James had made was to change their destination from Nonsuch to Richmond. Even that short distance would be hazardous in this weather.

'I received word from my steward today.'

Frances grew still.

'Tyringham has been sold.'

It was the news she had dreaded. So much time had passed since their home had been put up for sale that she had begun to hope a buyer would not be found – even though she knew that they desperately needed the funds.

'Why did you not tell me sooner?' she asked, raising herself to face him. The expression on his face was all the answer she needed.

'The estate has been in my family for generations, Frances.' His voice was cracked with sorrow. 'I have brought shame upon us – upon our sons.'

'No, Thomas,' she countered. 'You made this sacrifice for our sakes. I know what it has cost you.' She kissed him. His lips felt dry and still.

'It did not raise as much as I had hoped,' he went on, gazing out across the frozen hedges. 'I wonder if it was even worth it.'

'You had no choice,' Frances reminded him. 'We could not have withstood our creditors any longer.' She drew him to her and they stayed like that for several minutes, her arms encircling him, both lost in their thoughts. She could not help dwelling on that conversation with Salisbury, even though she had recounted it numerous times over the past couple of months. What riches might he have offered her if she had proved a willing accomplice to his plans, rather than rejecting them out of hand? It did not matter, she told herself firmly. There could be no inducement large enough to tempt her back down that perilous path – particularly if Buckingham was involved.

Frances shivered as a snowflake landed on her neck. Several more floated down around them. Soon there would be a flurry, judging by the dark clouds overhead. 'Let's go inside,' she said, rising.

Thomas remained seated on the stone bench, hunched against the cold. 'I think I will stay a while,' he said, touching her hand. 'Make up the fire – I will be with you soon.'

'Peace, Steenie,' the King soothed, as his favourite glowered at his opponent. 'You cannot always be victorious.'

Buckingham stood and swept the cards from the table. 'You are a cheat,' he snapped at his opponent, his voice dangerously low.

Frances saw derision cross Lord Cranfield's face. She had heard rumours that the two men were now bitterly opposed. Even those closest to the King's favourite were tiring of his arrogance, which grew more overbearing by the day.

'Forgive me, my lord,' Cranfield replied, spreading his hands. 'It must have been beginner's luck.'

The marquess's expression showed that he had caught the implied insult. He walked slowly towards his former protégé and brought his face so close to his that Cranfield paled.

'Those who have been made can be unmade,' he muttered. 'You would do well to remember that.'

Frances could see that the lord high treasurer was trying hard to master his emotions. She wondered if fear or fury was the greater.

'Perhaps we should retire, my lords,' Thomas said, rising from the seat next to her. 'We will be leaving early for the hunt and His Grace needs to rest.' Frances caught the gratitude and relief on James's face at his words.

Buckingham turned sharply to him. 'Do you presume to know what the King needs, Tyringham – you, who have command of his *dogs?*'

A heavy silence hung over the chamber. Frances dug her nails into her palms as she waited for her husband to reply. She could not see his face but was unnerved by the stillness with which he held himself. Buckingham cocked his head as he continued to stare at him with curiosity, as if he were examining some exotic beast. Frances was overcome by such intense hatred that it took her breath away. If only she were the witch he had accused her of being, she would ill-wish him, blight his life, as he had blighted theirs.

'And you have command of the King himself, my lord?'

Without warning, Buckingham unsheathed his sword and put the blade to Thomas's throat. Frances watched, horror-struck, as the two yeomen rushed from the King's side and seized the marquess before he could strike. Thomas made no move to defend himself. Drawing a sword in the King's chamber was treason.

'Unhand me, fools!' Buckingham cried, but the guards tightened their grip as he writhed to be free.

All eyes turned to James as he rose slowly from the throne. His expression was unreadable. Frances held her breath, fearing he would reprimand the yeomen. But he merely stood and stared at his favourite.

'You will suffer for this,' Buckingham snarled, then twisted to look at his royal master. 'Tell them to release me.' He ceased to struggle as he caught the look in James's eyes. For the first time ever, Frances saw uncertainty in his own. 'Your Grace?'

The King made no answer, but turned and walked from the room.

News of Buckingham's arrest spread across the court. It had been the subject of conversation at every mealtime, every masque and other gathering held during the five days since. Although she had not joined in the gossip, Frances had taken a much greater interest in it than usual. Each day brought a fresh rumour: a trial would take place two days' hence, the King meant to pardon his favourite, the marquess had escaped from the Tower. She had even heard it whispered that he had already been put to death – privately, as a concession by the King for the affection in which he had once held him. Thomas had tried to find out the truth but James had not spoken of the matter to anyone – even his closest attendants.

Frances slowed her pace as she neared the apartment. She knew it was unwise to come here – Thomas had tried to persuade her against it – but she could not forsake her friend as the rest of the court had. She knocked lightly on the door and waited. There was a high-pitched squeal from the other side, quickly suppressed. When nobody answered, she knocked again, more loudly this time. The door opened a crack.

'Kate – Lady Buckingham, please!' Frances placed her foot in the gap. 'I come in friendship, nothing more.'

Kate's face was hidden, but Frances sensed her hesitate. Then, slowly, she opened the door so that Frances might enter. The room was lavishly furnished and almost as large as the King's presence chamber. The walls were lined with rich tapestries and paintings

– mostly of Buckingham and his family, Frances noticed – and two huge windows at the far end looked out over the palace tilt-yard. Little Mary was sitting on a rug by the fireplace and clutched a handful of brightly coloured ribbons. She beamed when she saw her mother's visitor. Frances drew a lace kerchief from her pocket and gave it to the little girl. Mary's smile widened as she traced the outline of the embroidered peacock with her chubby fingers.

'Why are you here, Lady Tyringham?' Kate's tone was clipped, her eyes cold.

'I was concerned for you, after your husband's arrest. It must have been a shock—'

'So you came to crow.'

'No!' Frances cried in dismay. Then, more softly: 'My regard for you has not changed, Kate, whatever you think of me. I have only ever wanted to be a friend to you.'

The young woman looked down at her hands, but said nothing.

'I have done nothing to harm you or your poor brother,' Frances persisted. She stopped short of saying that the boy had died at other hands than hers. 'For the sake of everything we once were to each other, you must believe me.'

'It is your husband's fault – he provoked him,' Kate retorted, looking up at her in anger now. 'The marquess would never have drawn his sword in the King's presence otherwise. He is the subject of great envy and malice.'

Frances pushed down her anger. 'Thomas sought only to settle a quarrel that had arisen between the marquess and Lord Cranfield,' she replied firmly. 'Your husband's temper has grown ever shorter of late.'

Kate opened her mouth to protest but Frances could see that she knew the truth of her words. No doubt she had suffered the effects of Buckingham's moods herself. 'Have you received any word from him?' Frances asked.

Kate shook her head. All the anger seemed to have left her now and she looked utterly wretched. 'Mary and I will be ruined if—'

She broke off, tears welling in her eyes. 'Our fortune will be forfeit to the King, and my father will hardly receive me – not after my disgrace.'

'Your *disgrace?*' Frances repeated, incredulous. 'You cannot think he blames you for what happened that night? I made sure he knew the truth before you were married.'

'He has not spoken to me of it – in fact, he has barely spoken to me of anything. I have not seen or heard from him since Mary's birth.'

Frances was saddened but not surprised. Lord Rutland had become a stranger to her too. Her letters to Belvoir had gone unanswered. Perhaps he could not bear to be reminded of the court – of all that his family had suffered there. She moved to sit next to her friend. 'Your father loves you deeply, Kate. If he knew what you endure —'

'He must never know!' she cried, so suddenly that Mary dropped the kerchief and stared at her mother, chin quivering. Frances smiled down at her and picked up one of the ribbons. The child watched, mesmerised, as she wound it between her fingers then tied it into a neat bow and held it out to her. Kate shot Frances a grateful look as her daughter took it with a smile and resumed her play. 'No good could come of it,' she continued, more quietly this time. 'He sought to avenge my misfortune once before and might do so again. I could not bear to see him brought low before the marquess – or worse. He is no match for my husband.'

'Once, perhaps. But now?'

Kate's eyes were clouded with apprehension – and, Frances thought, hope. She opened her mouth to speak, but the door burst open and they turned to see Buckingham standing before them. Frances saw her own dismay reflected in her friend's face. Neither moved as the marquess looked from one to the other, his mouth curling into its accustomed smirk.

'Well, this is a fine greeting for a husband whom you had given up for dead.'

Kate rose quickly to her feet and swept a deep curtsy. 'My lord.'

Frances remained seated as he strolled into the room. 'Lady Tyringham,' he drawled, coming to stop in front of her. 'I hope you have not been filling my wife's head with nonsense. She has been so biddable since she broke off your friendship.'

'I should go, my lady,' Frances said, rising briskly.

'So soon?' Buckingham's eyes flashed fire, though his voice was soft as velvet. 'Will you not stay and entertain me a while? I can hope for little conversation from my wife.'

'Good day, my lady,' Frances said, ignoring him.

'Ah, well, at least you may save me the trouble of telling your husband myself.'

She turned to him sharply. Buckingham's grin widened.

'He is to have a new master while I am away. Lord Cranfield has kindly agreed to oversee His Majesty's stables, arrange the hunts,' he continued airily.

'Where are you going?' Kate asked.

Her husband continued to stare at Frances, his eyes boring into hers. 'Spain.'

Frances thought back to her conversation with Salisbury.

'The prince and I are going to treat for his marriage to the infanta,' he continued. 'He proposed the expedition himself, after so graciously persuading the King to order my release. It seems his father will refuse him nothing, these days.'

Frances reeled. *Charles* had secured Buckingham's release? The prince had shown nothing but disdain for his father's favourite, yet now he had not only saved his life but chosen him as a trusted companion for a voyage to Spain. Frances had heard it whispered lately that the marquess practised witchcraft to bend the King to his desires. Perhaps he had also used it on his son. She had all but disregarded the plan of which Salisbury had told her, convinced that the prince would never be persuaded to travel to Spain with a man he so obviously distrusted.

'When will you leave?'

Buckingham turned to his wife. 'I have only just returned to your side, yet you are eager to see me go again?' he purred, pinching her chin between his fingers. 'A week – two at most. Now, Lady Tyringham,' he said, 'if you will excuse us, I must make up for lost time.'

CHAPTER 50

23 May

The King took another grape from the bowl and glared at the young man who nervously plucked at the strings of the lute.

'His Majesty is in an ill humour again this evening,' Frances heard a diner remark.

'Aye, and will be until his *wife* returns,' muttered his companion. There was a murmur of suppressed laughter.

Frances knew they spoke the truth. Any hopes she had cherished that Buckingham's hold over James would be diminished by his spell in the Tower had soon been dashed. Her husband had felt the effects of his royal master's increasingly irascible behaviour. Ever since the departure of his favourite and the prince two months before, he had veered from gloomy introspection to petulant outbursts. Only when a messenger had arrived with news of them – or, better still, a letter from Buckingham – had his spirits lifted. Indeed, he had been so transported with joy when he had first heard from him that he had declared his intention to make him a duke. This was no mere impulse: Thomas had seen the letters patent that had been drawn up the following day.

But the King's dark mood had soon returned. His physical health had suffered, too. With no Steenie to take his mind off the pain of his gout-ridden legs, he had kept to his chambers, and whenever he did venture out into the public court, he leaned heavily upon a staff.

'Will the hunt go ahead tomorrow, do you think?' she asked her husband.

'I doubt it,' Thomas replied. 'Though I have everything in readiness again, of course.'

Frances could not be sorry at the postponement – she had grown used to spending more time with her husband in the last few weeks. But she had hoped that he might use Buckingham's absence to regain some of his former favour.

'Perhaps we might visit Longford, if His Grace will grant you leave.'

'I had the same thought. William turns five next week – we could surprise him.'

Frances smiled and squeezed his hand. If they could not win any advantages at court while the new duke was in Spain, they could secure an arguably greater prize by spending time with their sons. A movement on the dais caught her eye. A slender young man was bowing before the King. His hair was so fair as to be almost white, and his large eyes were of the palest blue. James was watching him with interest.

'Who is that?'

'Arthur Brett – Lord Cranfield's brother-in-law,' Thomas murmured. 'He is newly arrived at court. Cranfield hopes to win him a place in the privy chamber.'

They exchanged a knowing look. It was a clever ploy on Cranfield's part. Although he, too, had failed to gain any greater influence during his rival's absence, he had clearly judged that a younger, more attractive man might.

Gradually, the conversations around them began to die down as people noticed the scene that was unfolding on the dais. The King had invited Arthur Brett to sit by him and was talking animatedly, his cheeks flushed.

'I'll wager His Grace will soon find the separation easier to bear,' murmured the gentleman next to Frances.

'This young buck will be in attendance before the week is out, you mark me,' replied the other. 'The duke has a new rival, it seems.'

Frances took a long sip of wine.

'I will only be gone for two weeks, I promise,' Frances said, clasping her friend's hands. 'The King's passion for hunting has been reignited so Thomas will soon need to return to his duties.' She did not add that other passions had been awakened, too. Master Brett had barely left his new master's side since his appointment as a groom of the bedchamber.

Kate resumed folding Frances's linens into one of the coffers – she had insisted upon helping when she had arrived to find her friend busy packing for the journey. They had met in Thomas's apartment many times over the past month or so. Frances had been overjoyed when the first message had arrived, inviting her for a ride in Hyde Park. There had been more meetings during the weeks that followed, and gradually something of their former closeness had been restored – though Frances had learned not to mention what had happened that night in Chelsea. She had also been careful in her choice of words about the absent duke.

The chimes of the chapel clock sounded through the window as they worked. Kate cast an anxious glance towards it. 'I should go. The countess will soon be calling on Mary and me.'

Buckingham's mother had watched her daughter-in-law like a hawk since his departure for Spain, so Frances and she had been obliged to employ some discretion. 'Have a care, Kate,' Frances said, rising to embrace her.

'God speed your journey. I will look for your return daily.'

Frances breathed in the earthy scent of woodland as the carriage rumbled along the path that led towards the castle and felt the familiar surge of contentment. The journey had seemed endless, such was her impatience to see her sons, her mother and Longford. Glancing at Thomas, she saw the same anticipation in his eyes.

But they were tinged with sadness, she thought. He would never return to his own family home.

Helena and the boys were waiting to greet them at the entrance to the courtyard. Frances scooped a laughing William into her arms and he whooped with delight as she whirled him around. Robert clung to her skirts as soon as she had set his younger brother down and John smiled shyly at her from behind the long brown locks that covered his forehead. Frances experienced a pang as she realised that she no longer had to stoop to kiss his cheek. Behind him stood George. Almost five years had passed since she had seen him, and in that time he had become a man. He was so like Tom that she blinked back tears as he bowed first to her, then to her husband.

'Anyone would think we were at court!' Thomas scoffed, clapping him on the shoulder. Frances was relieved to see her son's accustomed grin as he moved to embrace them both.

'Mama, Papa, I am very glad to see you.' Frances was surprised by how much deeper his voice had become. 'My younger brothers have been running quite wild here in Wiltshire.'

'How you exaggerate, George!' His grandmother shook her head in mock-despair. 'Besides, it is you who has encouraged their more wayward tendencies – all except John, of course.' She planted a kiss on John's head and he flushed with pleasure. 'Now, where is my greeting?'

Frances was in her mother's arms in a moment. 'How I have missed you.'

Helena's eyes sparkled with tears as she examined her daughter. 'You have lost weight,' she declared. 'You look tired, too.'

Frances laughed. 'We have been travelling for three days, Mother.'

'And the King's table is not as fine as yours, my lady marchioness,' Thomas added, as he stepped forward to kiss his mother-in-law on both cheeks. Helena beamed at him. She had always loved him like a son.

'How is Samuel?' Frances asked.

'Sleeping – God be praised,' her mother replied, rolling her eyes. Frances's gaze lingered on her as she turned to address Thomas. Her mother would be seventy-five this year, yet still she had the energy and looks of a woman half her age. There were a few more silvery hairs intertwined with the red, it was true, and her mouth and eyes were more deeply lined than when Frances had last seen her, but her waist had hardly thickened since her youth and she had the same proud bearing that had set her apart from the other ladies of court.

'Come, let us dine,' Helena said now, taking her son-in-law's arm.

The sun was sinking behind the trees that edged the woodland as Frances strolled towards them, following the riverbank. It would take longer this way, but she wanted to commit every detail of her beloved home to memory so that it might sustain her during the long months at court that lay ahead. Although the bells of St Peter's had already struck eight o'clock, there was still warmth in the sun's rays and she longed to unlace her heavy gown. Her stays had grown tighter, too, since eating the succession of delicious dishes that her mother's cooks had prepared.

Longford always calmed her soul and made her troubles seem far distant. That all those she loved most were here made this visit even more special. She allowed her mind to wander, to imagine staying here for ever as she watched her boys grow into men – like George. How proud she was of her firstborn. He would be eighteen next year. Over dinner, they had discussed his plans for Cambridge. Frances had thrilled to hear him talk so animatedly about studying law. He would never know that he was following his father's profession – Thomas was his papa and always would be. To tell him the truth would place his life in mortal danger. The Powder Treason was seen now as an even more shocking crime – against God, as well as the King – than it had been when first discovered. The numerous pamphlets that had been published since had presented it as a satanic conspiracy, aimed at damning

James and all his subjects to Hell. If it was discovered that Tom Wintour's line had not died on the scaffold that cold January day, but that he had a healthy son and heir who had been raised to revere the Catholic faith, the King would not hesitate to have him thrown into the Tower – or worse.

She had reached the edge of the woods now. The scent of bluebells filled her nostrils. The delicate blooms were at their peak, covering the forest floor in a haze of blue-violet. How many hours had she spent as a child lying among them or plucking their delicate stems to make a fragrance for her mother and sisters? She resolved to bring the boys tomorrow. Robert and William would be more interested in climbing the trees, but they would at least gain a good vantage point from there.

As she walked among the tangled roots, her fingers twitched to pluck the tiny white flowers of the wild cherry and the smooth green leaves of devil's spit. Both would make an excellent poultice for gout. If the King had not declared such things witchcraft, she might have eased his suffering. She slowed her pace and closed her eyes so that she could immerse herself in the smells and sounds of the forest. How had she lived without this for so long? The gardens at Whitehall were a poor imitation, where Nature's beauty was clipped and trained into the neatly confined patterns that were pleasing to the King's eye.

Would she and Thomas ever be free of the court? Her heart sank as she thought of how they were more tied to the King's service than ever, now that they had lost their home as well as their fortune. Thomas was too proud to accept the help her mother had offered, but even that would not have been enough to support them for long. She had refused to use the inheritance that Tom had bequeathed her, which she had signed over to George for when he came of age. Their only chance to secure their future and that of their other sons was to win favour with the King and his successor. The royal bounty was the source of fortune and power. Little wonder that men took such risks in its pursuit.

Frances had reached the edge of the woods now. In the distance, she could just see the ancient tower of St Peter's. The light was fading too fast for her to walk there and satisfy her curiosity in meeting the new incumbent. Her mother had written to tell her of Pritchard's death the previous year. Few people in the village would have mourned him – certainly she herself had been glad of his passing, though she knew it was sinful. She had rejoiced, too, upon hearing that his successor was the nephew of her old mentor, the Reverend Samuels. She hoped he would bring the same moderation and kindness that had made his uncle so beloved of those who worshipped there.

The bells began to chime. Instinctively, she reached into her pocket and clasped the smooth beads of her rosary. Had she been right to deny Anne Vaux and Lord Salisbury – and, in so doing, her faith? God had given no sign that any of the plots to bring England back to the Catholic fold were pleasing to Him. The lives of those involved had been blighted, and the heretic King still sat securely on his throne.

She closed her eyes and an image of Buckingham flitted before her. Could he really be the saviour of whom the late Queen had spoken? She thought of everything he had done since he had first come to the King's notice at Apethorpe: the scheming, the ruin of his rivals, the subjugation of an innocent young woman and God knew how many more. She could not – *would* not – believe it had all been to serve anything other than his own interests. This latest expedition was no different. It was the lure of Spanish treasure rather than the prospect of a Catholic princess on the throne that had enticed him.

Her fingers tugged at the beads so sharply that she felt the chain snap. *No.* She would rather be cast out of Heaven than support such a man as Buckingham.

CHAPTER 51

27 August

Frances traced the droplet with her finger as it trickled down the glass. It had rained incessantly for more than three weeks now, ruining the harvests and plunging the kingdom into a deep melancholy from which it seemed destined never to recover. The court had the atmosphere of a prison, nobody having ventured outdoors except to scurry between their lodgings and the state rooms, cowering beneath the downpours. Denied any opportunity to hunt, King James had reverted to the same testy, petulant behaviour that he had displayed when Buckingham and the prince had first embarked for Spain. Even his new favourite had been unable to raise his spirits. The pervading damp had exacerbated the inflammation in his joints, making him more irritable still.

The court's enforced confinement had made the return from Longford even harder to bear. Although she and Thomas had been back at Whitehall for two months now, Frances still missed her old home as keenly as the day they had left. Every time she thought of how she had bade her mother and sons farewell, her throat tightened. It had been a comfort to see Kate again, and her affectionate greeting had warmed her more than the fire that had been made up in their apartment ready for their arrival. But the countess had kept an even closer watch on her daughter-in-law than usual so their opportunities to meet in private had been scarce.

'We should go, my love,' Thomas said, placing a gentle hand on her shoulder. 'Lord Cranfield has commissioned a new masque to distract our royal master from his woes, so dinner will be served even more promptly than usual.'

Frances's heart sank. Another interminable evening to be spent watching garishly clad masquers prance about the stage while the King shouted encouragement and downed glass after glass of Burgundy wine.

'Come now,' her husband said wryly, seeing her expression. 'It is based on the tale of King Arthur so cannot fail to be diverting.'

'How clever of Lord Cranfield to find a way of giving his brother-in-law a starring role,' she replied.

Thomas grinned and kissed her firmly on the mouth. 'We will soon be back here, safe from the world.'

The great hall was already crowded when they arrived. The press of bodies made it stifling, yet all of the windows were closed and shuttered. Frances's temples throbbed as she and Thomas threaded their way between the rows of courtiers in search of somewhere to sit. They were nearing the far end of the hall when she felt a hand on her arm.

'Please – join me.'

It was Lord Rutland.

'My lord.' Thomas bowed.

'I am glad to see you both,' he said, when they had sat on either side of him. 'I have been away for barely three years, yet so many faces are unfamiliar to me.'

Frances tried to hide her shock at how frail he looked. He had always been a slender man, but now his cheekbones jutted out sharply and his fingers were spider-thin. His sombre attire made him seem all the paler, and there was a haunted look in his eyes. 'It is good to see you too, my lord,' she said. 'I trust you are well?'

'A little tired from the journey, but otherwise in good health,' he replied, spooning a small quantity of venison stew onto his plate. Frances noticed that the rest of the food on it was untouched.

'And all is well at Belvoir?' Thomas asked.

The earl sipped some wine. 'We have suffered by this late harvest, as have most other estates in the kingdom. The price of grain will be high this winter.'

'Is the countess managing affairs in your absence, as before?' Frances asked, careful to keep her tone light.

'The countess is dead,' he replied. 'A sudden fever took her last month. I feared it was the Sweat, but none of our household has sickened, praise God. Grief at the loss of our poor boy had weakened her body as well as her mind. She was never the same after that.'

'I am sorry to hear of your sad loss,' Frances said. The news must have been delayed by the weather, which had turned most of the roads beyond the city into a deluge of mud. Though her heart went out to her beleaguered friend, she could not regret Countess Cecilia's passing. The shrewish woman had been as mean-spirited and conniving as her husband was open-handed and benevolent.

'And I am sorry for yours,' Rutland said, turning to face Thomas. 'I heard about Tyringham Hall.'

Her husband nodded his thanks. The animated chatter around them grew steadily louder as their fellow diners enjoyed more of the wine that was served in great quantities at every feast.

'What has brought you here, my lord?' Frances asked.

'The King desired my presence. He has a task for me to perform, but the letter said he would explain it in person. I must admit that I had thought myself quite forgotten.'

Hoped too, no doubt, Frances thought. She glanced around the room but could see neither Kate nor her mother-in-law. The Countess of Buckingham had attended fewer court gatherings during her son's absence, and her daughter-in-law had been obliged to keep her company most evenings. Frances wondered if

Kate knew that her father had returned. 'Have you seen Lady Katherine yet?'

The earl's face clouded. 'I arrived just an hour ago,' he said abruptly.

'You must be anxious to meet your granddaughter,' she persisted, ignoring Thomas's warning look.

'I do not intend to tarry,' he replied. 'As soon as I have performed whatever service the King intends for me, I shall return to Belvoir.'

Frances felt angry on Kate's behalf. It was unjust that her father had rejected her for marrying a man who had forced himself upon her in the most brutal way. But she knew that nothing could be gained by pressing the matter now.

The tables were being cleared, and there was a flurry of activity on the stage as it was made ready for the performance. Frances watched as an enormous painted castle was lifted onto the dais by four red-faced pages. They lowered it into place as Lord Cranfield barked directions at them. James had moved to the left, where he was seated next to Arthur Brett, who had changed into his costume, complete with an oversized crown that glittered with fake jewels. Now and then, his royal master whispered into the young man's ear.

When at last all of the tables had been moved and the guests had taken their places, the masque began. Frances hardly noticed the succession of different actors and props as the tedious narrative played on. She kept her eyes on the King, who sat forward every time Arthur stepped into a scene. His eyes also lingered on the young man who played Guinevere. Only when there was a loud clap of thunder followed by a huge plume of smoke did she focus on the centre of the dais. As the vapour began to clear, a figure dressed as Merlin came slowly into view. Frances stared.

John Lambe.

She had not seen the conjurer for more than three years. He had left court after the death of Rutland's son and there had been no word of him since. Frances watched, horror-struck, as he made circles with his arms, the long sleeves that covered them whirling around him. She was only vaguely aware that he was speaking his lines as her mind ran over why he might have returned when his patron was far away. Was it a sign that Buckingham would soon return?

As the scene wore on, Frances stole a glance at Rutland. His mouth was pressed into a thin line as he stared, unblinking, at the old man before them. Did he believe, like Frances, that he was looking at his son's murderer? At last the masque reached its conclusion, the dancers twirling about, their arms stretched out towards the three central figures of Arthur, Guinevere and Merlin. With a final strike of the drum, the dais was plunged into darkness. Frances heard the rustle of satin as a figure swept past the row of benches where she was sitting, and a moment later she caught the pungent, heavily spiced scent that she remembered from her first encounter with Lambe. When the sconces were relit, she was hardly surprised to see that he was not among the actors who were bowing before the King and his court. He had disappeared into the night, like some phantom.

As soon as the applause had died away, there was a crush of bodies and eager courtiers surged forward to make their obeisance before the King. Frances felt a welcome draught of cool night air as the doors to a nearby balcony were opened.

'I will fetch us some wine,' Thomas said, as they rose to their feet and moved towards it.

The rain was still falling on the dark streets below, but the balcony was sheltered by a large stone canopy. Neither Frances nor Lord Rutland spoke as they took deep breaths of the cleansing air.

'I did not expect to see Dr Lambe here again,' she began, 'at least, not without his patron. He has not appeared at court since . . .'

The earl did not answer but stared out over the deserted street, clutching the edge of the carved stone balustrade.

'Was it him?' he muttered, still gazing straight ahead. 'Did he poison my son?'

'I believe so, my lord,' she whispered. 'Or he supplied the means, at least,' she added, thinking of the large-eyed girl who had served the countess. She, too, had disappeared from court after Lord Ros's death.

This was the first time they had spoken of it. In the days and weeks that had followed his son's demise, Rutland had kept to his apartments, too grief-stricken to take part in the usual court routines, while Frances had lived under threat of exposure as a witch. She had come to fear that the earl had given credence to the rumours that Buckingham had put about at the time.

'That devil had my poor boy murdered so that he could seize my daughter and her fortune. I have long suspected it, but pushed it from my thoughts these past three years, lest it drove me to madness. Cecilia was adamant that our sons had been bewitched to death and would hear nothing to contradict it.' He turned to Frances at last. 'I will avenge my son – Katherine too. He has blighted both their lives.'

'I will help you, my lord.'

Thomas was standing at the doors to the balcony. He walked slowly over and gave them each a glass. 'That villain has ruined our lives too,' he said, his voice low, 'and so many more besides. He will not rest until he has the Crown of England in his hands.'

'This kingdom can have no peace while he draws breath,' the earl agreed. 'It is surely God's will that we send this devil back to the Hell that spawned him.'

Frances looked from one to the other, her heart thudding. She had not told Thomas about her encounter with Salisbury, reasoning that there was nothing to be gained from it. But the concealment had felt like a betrayal. She took a breath.

'What if he is not a devil but an angel, sent by God to restore this kingdom to the true faith?'

Both men stared at her. *She could not go back now.*

'There are those who believe that Buckingham is doing the Lord's work, not his own, that he is plotting to secure this Spanish marriage so that King Philip will send an army to oust James from his throne and set Charles and the infanta upon it.'

Rutland gave a snort of derision. 'Preposterous! The man serves himself alone. God is as nothing to him. Besides, he forced my daughter to relinquish the Catholic faith in order to marry him. It is not possible!'

'Who told you this?' Thomas asked.

Frances saw the hurt in his eyes, as well as the shock. She swallowed hard. 'William Cecil, Earl of Salisbury.'

'*Cecil?* When did you see him? He has been absent from court for years.'

'He came to Greenwich during the Christmas festivities,' she replied, forcing herself not to flinch from her husband's gaze. 'We met by chance, but it seems he meant to seek me out. I told him I would have no part in his schemes.'

The colour had drained from Thomas's face. 'Why did you not tell me of this before?' he demanded.

Frances could no longer bear to look at him. 'Forgive me,' she said. 'You carried so many burdens already that I did not wish to add to them.'

'The word of one man is hardly enough to convince me, when everything else points to his being a self-seeking villain,' Rutland interjected.

'But that is not all,' Frances said. 'As she lay dying, the late Queen told me she had enlisted the help of someone to ensure that her son married a Catholic princess. She made me promise to do nothing to impede it, hinting that the person she had chosen for the task had been an enemy to me.'

This silenced them.

Eventually, Rutland said, 'If what you say is true, then we are faced with a choice. Either we satisfy our honour and that of our families, or we allow Buckingham to do God's work unhindered.'

'*If,*' Thomas emphasised. 'Time will tell whether he serves God or the devil.'

'He serves whichever master will fulfil his own ambitions,' Frances retorted impatiently. 'It is foolish to presume that everyone who acts for the Catholic cause is motivated by the same faith that we cherish.'

'My lords.'

They swung around to see a groom of the King's privy chamber standing by the doors. *How long had he been there?*

'His Majesty requires your presence.'

The men exchanged a quick look before following the attendant into the crowded hall. Frances hesitated, then rushed after them.

'Ah, my lord Rutland!' the King shouted, as they approached the dais. 'You are here at last. Why did you stay away for so long?'

'Your Grace.' The earl swept a deep bow.

'And Tom. The sight of you always does me good.'

Frances smiled at the compliment to her husband. Before the rains had come, the King had spent a good deal of time hunting with him and, freed from Buckingham's overbearing presence, he had come to appreciate Thomas's quiet, steady nature once more. If only the duke would stay away for longer, James's renewed affection for his master of the buckhounds might take firmer root. Already he had hinted at a grant of some lands.

The King was turning back to Rutland now. Frances strained to hear above the excited chatter that echoed around the hall.

'I have summoned you back to Whitehall because I wish you to undertake a great service for me.'

The babble quietened as those standing close to the stage whispered to their neighbours that something of importance was about to be discussed. Before long, the hall had descended into silence.

'My sweet boys have been absent for many weeks now,' James went on. 'Yet I have received word from my ambassador in Madrid that their negotiations with King Philip have foundered. There will be no Spanish marriage.'

This sparked a chorus of gasps and mutters around the room.

'The duke refuses to comply with my wishes and return home. He insists that Philip will be persuaded. But I know better than my dear Steenie. The Spanish King's word is not to be trusted. He has already played my daughter and her husband false, robbed them of their kingdom. I no longer wish to be allied to such a false friend.'

Thomas shot Frances a quick, sideways look. They both knew why Buckingham was proving so stubborn.

'And so, Rutland, I wish you to journey to Madrid and bring back your errant son-in-law – the prince too.'

Frances saw the shock on Rutland's face, but he swept another bow to disguise it.

'I would willingly perform whatever you command, Your Grace,' he vowed, 'but I fear you have greater faith in my abilities than I. The duke is not a man to be easily persuaded.'

'Then drag him back by force, God damn ye!' James cried, with sudden passion, banging his fist so hard on the table that a goblet clattered to the floor. His young favourite, Arthur Brett, cowered in his chair. 'I will not suffer such disobedience, even from one I have raised so high,' the King continued. 'You will remind him where his true loyalties lie.'

They may not lie where you think, Frances mused.

'And you, Tom, will accompany Lord Rutland as far as Plymouth. You will both set out at first light.'

CHAPTER 52

9 October

The whole of London seemed ablaze. As soon as word had arrived that the prince and his entourage had landed safely at Plymouth, bonfires had been lit in celebration. The King had received the news while hunting at Theobalds Palace and had immediately ordered Thomas to make the long ride back to escort them.

A distant cheer could be heard along the Strand. Frances craned her neck to see above the crowds that thronged the streets, waiting to greet the King's son and favourite. Anyone would think they were conquering heroes, she thought scornfully. As it was, their expedition had ended in ignominious failure and relations between England and Spain were worse than they had been before. Frances was eager to see her husband and hoped that Lord Rutland had endured the arduous journey without weakening his already fragile health.

'There they are!'

The shout was soon echoed by a chorus of others. Frances saw a flash of scarlet and gold as Buckingham held his plumed hat aloft in acknowledgement of the cheers. He was riding ahead of the prince, she saw, with dismay. The failure of his expedition had done nothing to curb his overweening pride.

'God save Your Grace!'

Charles, who was dressed more soberly, nodded his thanks. His pale skin was burnished by the Spanish sun, but his eyes were sunken and his shoulders hunched. As he drew closer, he looked to where Frances was standing. She thought she saw the faintest smile of recognition before a shout from the other side of the street drew his attention.

Rutland rode directly behind the prince. He seemed oblivious to the cheers of the crowds but kept his eyes fixed upon the horizon. Frances was shocked by how emaciated he had become. Her heart swelled as she saw her husband at the back of the cavalcade. It was almost a month since he had left for Theobalds and she had received only hurried messages from him since. He did not see her, but she kept her eyes on his retreating form as he gradually disappeared from view.

The people around her surged after the procession, hoping to catch another glimpse of the prince and the duke before they rode into the palace. Frances followed in their wake. She had no desire to see the King greet his favourite, showering him with the gifts he had bought to mark his return. When she reached the end of the wide street that led to Whitehall, a huge crowd was still gathered around Holbein Gate, even though the prince and his entourage had already passed under it and into the first courtyard. She turned instead towards the stables, hoping to see Thomas as he led the horses there while Buckingham basked in the attentions of his adoring royal master.

'God's teeth! What are you about, man?'

The cry rang out from the stable-yard as Frances approached. She stopped as she rounded the corner and saw the duke glowering at her husband, who was helping him untangle his boot from the stirrup. All of the smiles and graciousness with which he had received his hero's welcome were gone. She wondered what could have put him in such a foul temper already.

'Leave it!' he commanded, kicking out at Thomas's fingers. Frances saw her husband's flicker of a smile as he turned to unsaddle the horse. She watched as Buckingham struggled to free his boot then, muttering another curse, took it off altogether and stamped his stockinged foot on the gravel. 'Do not think I am blind to what you have done, Tyringham,' he spat, grabbing Thomas roughly by the shoulders.

Her husband looked calmly at him. 'Your Grace?'

The duke took a step towards him. Frances moved closer, taking care to remain hidden from view. Her eyes flitted to the sword at Buckingham's belt.

'Do not toy with me, churl. You have dripped poison into the King's ear while I have been away, making him doubt my loyalty and question my motives for going to Spain. Why else would he give me such a greeting just now?'

Frances willed her husband to say nothing that might provoke him.

'What other motives could you have had, my lord duke, than to secure a great alliance for this kingdom?' he asked, in mock-innocence.

Buckingham moved so close to Thomas that their foreheads almost touched. Slowly, he reached around to caress the hair at the back of his neck. Nausea rose in her, as Frances watched her husband struggle to stop himself lashing out, knowing that this was exactly what the duke wanted. Suddenly, Buckingham grasped a handful of hair and yanked Thomas's head backwards. 'You may think you enjoy His Majesty's favour now, but it is an illusion. I will see you ruined – you and that pretty wife of yours. I would have rid myself of you both years ago, if it was not so *diverting* to see you suffer. Losing your family seat must have been enough to unman you,' he purred.

Frances saw her husband's hand move to his sword.

'But do not grieve, Thomas, for you and your wife must visit us there, as soon as we have ordered the place to our satisfaction. I wonder that you can have put up with somewhere that lacked so many modern comforts – not to mention fashions. Why, it is quite the relic!'

'*You* purchased it? But . . .'

Buckingham inclined his head. 'Through a second party, of course – I know how touchy men can be about selling to their superiors. Now I have returned, I will have much more leisure to set it to rights. Katherine will manage it for me. It will do her good to spend some time away from court. Goodness knows what company she has been keeping during my absence.'

Frances stared at him. He had released his grip on her husband and was smiling at him.

'Now, please – fetch my boot. I must go and dress for dinner.'

Frances gazed at the long tables lined on each side with courtiers, all looking in her direction. It was strange to see the hall from this vantage point, and although it was a great honour to have been invited to join the King's table, she could not help feeling rather exposed. She was glad that Thomas had been seated next to her, the Earl of Rutland on her other side. She was glad, too, that Buckingham was at the opposite end of the table, several seats away from James and the prince.

'My lords.' The King had risen to his feet. 'We have ordered this feast to celebrate the return of our son and heir, the Prince of Wales.' A cheer rose up around the room. 'And of His Grace the Duke of Buckingham.' Frances was gratified that the cheers petered out. She saw that the duke's smile had become fixed. 'But it is also our pleasure to reward the great service performed by two other gentlemen here this evening. My lord Rutland, Sir Thomas – Tom,' he added, with a grin, 'please accept these small tokens of our gratitude and esteem.'

Frances exulted to see the earl and her husband kneel to receive their gifts. She could not resist flashing Buckingham a smile. Her triumph faded as she saw Kate next to him, staring miserably at her plate. As she reached for her glass, Frances saw an angry red welt at her wrist.

'Congratulations, my love,' she said, as Thomas sat down and showed her the gold medallion studded with rubies with which the King had presented him. She found herself wondering how much it was worth – though she knew they could not risk His Majesty's offence by selling it.

During the feast that followed, Frances drank more than was her custom – partly to celebrate her husband's safe return and his obvious favour with the King, but also to blur the memory of what had happened in the stable-yard. Thomas had refused to speak of it when she had told him she had seen and heard everything. Losing Tyringham Hall had grieved him enough, but the knowledge that it was to Buckingham was too much to bear. Even after several glasses of wine, Frances was aware that the King had drunk much more than she had. His face was flushed and his voice had become progressively louder so that now most of the hall could hear whenever he made a remark.

'Father,' the prince said quietly, as James gulped the contents of his glass, dribbling most of it down his chin.

'Peace, boy!' he retorted. 'I dunnae know what has got into that pretty head of yours. Ye were always so biddable – better disposed than any son in Christendom. But since returning from Spain, ye have been carried away with rash and foolish counsels.'

'Please,' Charles begged, placing a hand on his father's arm in a vain attempt to stop him taking another long draught of claret.

'Silence!' At the King's shout, all eyes turned to the dais. James went on, oblivious: 'Yer head has been turned by our duke there,' he said, wine spilling over the rim of his glass as he gestured towards Buckingham. 'God knows how many devils are within him since that journey.'

The King's favourite took a sip from his own glass, but his knuckles were white as he grasped it.

'Ye have used such cruel words towards your dear dad and sovereign,' he continued, addressing Buckingham directly now. Frances had heard that the duke referred to James in that way but had dismissed it as unfounded gossip. 'I cannae forget nor forgive them.'

Buckingham was gripping his glass so tightly now that Frances feared it would shatter. 'A man might utter any number of foolish words when overcome with excitement to see his king and master,' he replied smoothly.

Arthur Brett, who was seated next to James, suppressed a titter. The duke flashed him a look of such fury that the young man blanched.

'I saw no such excitement,' James slurred, 'only pride and insolence.'

The silence in the crowded hall was absolute, the tension almost palpable, as all eyes were trained on the disgraced favourite. The yeomen standing behind the throne grasped their halberds. For several moments, Buckingham stared back at James, his expression unreadable. Frances found herself willing him to strike out, raise his sword against the King. Such an act could never be pardoned. Instead he set down his glass, rose to his feet and, bowing low before his royal master, walked slowly from the dais.

'Frances.'

The voice was so quiet that for a moment she thought she had imagined it. She stopped and looked around the deserted garden. The sun had not yet risen and she had not expected to see anyone else there. A cold hand gripped her wrist and she swung around. Before she could speak, Kate pulled her towards the entrance to the maze where she had been hiding.

'I could not leave without seeing you,' her friend whispered. There were dark circles under her eyes. 'It grieves me to think what opinion you must have of me – your husband, too. He is an honourable man and does not deserve such treatment.'

'You have done nothing against either of us,' Frances said, clasping her hands.

'Oh, but I have!' Kate whispered, tears in her eyes. 'I am to be mistress of Tyringham Hall, to look on as your husband's beloved home is dismantled, brick by brick, and a new mansion built in its place. And all in my name!' She bent her head and began to sob.

Frances stepped forward to embrace her. 'This is not your doing, Kate – Thomas knows that as well as I. You are as powerless to oppose your husband as we are – more so, perhaps,' she added, looking down at the darkening bruise on the young woman's wrist. 'You must not grieve on our part. God will avenge his sins.'

Kate raised a tear-stained face. 'I wish I could believe that, Frances. I have prayed for it – yes, though I am his wife and should look for nothing but blessings for him. But God seems not to heed my prayers.'

'He will. Such sins as he has committed cannot go unpunished, in this world or the next.' She kissed her friend's cheek. 'Now, go to Tyringham with our blessing – little Mary too. Make sure to take her to the woods that lie just beyond the privy garden. The pansies will be in full bloom by now.'

Kate's face lifted into a smile of such warmth that Frances's heart swelled. 'God go with you, Frances,' she whispered, and hurried back towards the palace.

It was a long time before Frances followed. The day had dawned fine and clear, and the sun's rays carried the promise of warmth. Thomas would have left for the hunt by now, so she was in no hurry to return. She resolved to pay a visit to Lord Bacon at his lodgings near to Temple Church. He always welcomed her warmly, though his circumstances had been pitifully reduced.

She had almost reached the gate in the high brick wall that surrounded the garden when she heard the latch click open.

'Your Grace,' she said, dropping into a deep curtsy.

The prince did not seem surprised to see her. Evidently, Kate was not the only one who knew it was her habit to walk about the gardens early each morning.

'I'm sorry if I startled you, Lady Tyringham. Would you walk with me?'

They made their way in silence along the path that led towards the sequence of small knot gardens. As Frances waited for Charles to speak, she pretended to look at the neatly arranged plants on either side of them, wondering why he had sought her out.

'I have not forgotten the service you performed for my father some years ago, though I have never spoken of it,' he began.

'Neither have I changed my allegiance,' he went on, 'though you would be forgiven for thinking so . . . I promised my late mother I would marry a princess of the faith, so when Buckingham began to promote the Spanish match so vigorously, I decided to fall in with his plans.' His face darkened. 'But I might as well have made a pact with the devil.'

Frances held her breath.

'The duke claims to be of our faith, Lady Tyringham, but I have seen enough to convince me that he uses it to justify a plot that is driven only by greed and ambition. As soon as we reached the Escorial, it was clear that he had struck a private bargain with the King of Spain, whereby my marriage to the infanta would be bought at a terrible price – wresting the throne from my father and placing me on it to rule jointly with my new wife as Catholic sovereigns.'

Still Frances said nothing. *It was all as Salisbury had told her.*

'Buckingham had been promised coffers filled with Spanish gold if he brought all this to pass,' the prince continued. 'But he overreached himself, demanding more power than Philip was prepared to cede to him. He insisted, too, that his daughter Mary be married to the King's brother, Don Carlos. He means to make himself king one day, I am sure of it.'

He turned to face Frances.

'He must be stopped, before he destroys not just my father but the entire kingdom. Our failure in Spain has left him undaunted. He will find another means to seize power.'

Frances's eyes blazed with intensity. 'You are right to fear this, Your Grace. I have heard and seen enough of his plans – his character – to believe him capable of the evil you describe. If he is truly a Catholic, he will do more harm to our cause than those who seek our persecution.'

Charles nodded grimly. 'My father's present anger towards him will soon dissolve – as it always does. Although Lord Cranfield and others have taken advantage of his absence, he will find means to crush them.'

'He is always at his most dangerous when under attack,' Frances agreed. 'I will support Your Grace in whatever way I can – my husband too. You have many allies in this court, if you would use them.'

'Thank you, Lady Frances,' he replied quietly. 'I hope that God will be my ally too.'

1624

CHAPTER 53

2 October

The rhythmic splash of the oars was almost lulling Frances to sleep as the barge made its way slowly along the Thames. They were passing the Bishop's Palace now, its elegant red-brick façade just visible through the trees.

'I have a mind to begin another history. One of the few advantages of my reduced circumstances is having more time to write.'

Frances smiled. Bacon's account of Henry VII's reign had been published to great acclaim two years earlier – even the King had declared himself delighted with it.

'Perhaps you should dedicate it to Lord Somerset, now that he has been restored to favour,' she suggested slyly.

Although news of the King's pardon to his former favourite had been announced several days before, Frances still marvelled at it. Even after their release from the Tower more than a year ago, Somerset and his wife had been living in virtual exile, denied the King's presence as well as his forgiveness. That James had finally shown them his favour had been taken as another sign of Buckingham's diminishing influence. Frances had been as pleased as she was surprised that the duke had failed to worm his way back into his master's good graces as quickly as he had expected.

Although she had had no further conferences with the prince, she suspected that he had played a part in this.

'I was thinking Master Brett might be a better choice,' Bacon replied, raising an eyebrow.

And it was true that the King had grown ever fonder of the young man. With his quiet devotion, Arthur formed a welcome contrast to the overbearing duke, whose temper had been ever more volatile since his return from Spain the previous year. Thomas had borne the brunt of it on many occasions. Frances was glad her husband knew what a powerful adversary his master had in the prince, or he might have been provoked to retaliate, as Buckingham clearly intended.

'Thomas heard the King means to secure him a seat in the next parliament,' she observed.

'Then he will be fortunate enough to enjoy the debate about His Majesty's proposed war with Spain,' Bacon retorted. 'I do hope he will argue against it, as all good men must. It will be so diverting to see the duke in a fury again.'

'A few months ago, he was all for Spain.' Frances did not trouble to disguise her scorn. 'Yet now he would see all Spaniards at the bottom of the ocean. He still smarts from that business with the infanta.'

'King Philip's envoys have made much of his current weakness,' Bacon concurred. 'I hear they are putting about rumours that Buckingham encourages the King to hunt in order to seize the reins of government himself.'

Frances did not remark that there was truth to the rumours. What the duke had failed to grasp was that the more hunts he arranged for his master, the stronger James's attachment to her husband became. Thomas was careful not to boast of it: there was nothing to be gained by antagonising Buckingham further. She only hoped that he would hold on to the King's favour long enough for them to make use of it.

'Tell me, how is the duke's delightful mother?' Bacon asked. 'I no longer enjoy the good fortune of seeing her at court, and I can hardly hope that her delicate footsteps will ever be heard in Temple Church.'

Frances had had to endure several interminable evenings in the countess's apartments at Whitehall. Clearly, the older woman deemed her worthy of interest – or suspicion – even though Kate was far away at Tyringham Hall. 'Still as friendly as a viper. You should have a care, my lord. If she thought you could serve her or her precious son, she would insist you join her for supper too.'

'Then I shall continue to be as insignificant as possible,' he replied cheerfully. Though he was in jest, she knew he still smarted from his loss of favour. He was little suited for a life of quiet retirement, despite the hours it gave him for writing and study.

'How is Lady Alice?' she asked.

'Well enough, I understand,' he replied. 'She has promised to visit, before winter is upon us.'

Frances felt a surge of pity for him. Bacon's wife had been a virtual stranger to her husband since his fall from grace.

'Now, tell me, my dear,' he said, with forced jollity, 'when are you going to give your husband another son? Five is not enough for any man.'

Frances grinned. 'It is impertinent to ask a lady of my years such a question.' She folded her hands over her flat stomach. The truth was that she longed for another child. Much as she loved her boys, a daughter would be such a blessing – one who would grow as close to her as she was to her mother. Now that she was in her forty-fourth year, though, it pained her to admit that she was unlikely to bear another child.

'Nonsense!' Bacon cried. 'You are in your prime, my dear. I see how men look at you, even if you don't. You are your mother's daughter. The marchioness was such a beauty that even my head was turned,' he added, with a playful wink.

They were approaching the landing stage at Whitehall now.

'I hope you are ready to be bested, my lord,' Frances said, as she gathered up her skirts. 'I have yet to be beaten at bowls, though my husband has attempted it many times.'

'Lady Tyringham!'

She had only just alighted from the barge when she saw a groom in the King's livery rushing towards her.

'His Majesty requires your presence at once. Please.' He gestured for her to follow him.

With an anxious glance at her friend, she hastened after him.

'Is it my husband?' she asked, fearing that some accident had befallen him.

'No, my lady, but you must make haste.'

Frances did not question the boy further as they raced through the outer courtyards of the palace but her mind was agitated. *Was it the prince? Had he betrayed her – made a pact with Buckingham and exposed her as a Catholic? Or had the duke at last made good his threat to have her exposed as a witch?* By the time they reached the King's privy chamber, she was struggling to suppress her rising panic.

The groom rushed ahead and announced her arrival. A moment later, the King appeared. Frances hid her shock at his appearance. Tears were streaming down his face and his hair was dishevelled. He was clad only in a shirt and hose, as if he had just been roused from his bed.

'Lady Tyringham, you are come!' he cried, as he limped over and clasped her hands. His own felt cold and clammy, and the bitter aroma of sweat and stale wine filled Frances's nostrils. *Was he sick?* She could think of no other reason why his attendants would have so neglected their master's appearance. 'It is poor Steenie – he is dying.'

It took Frances a moment to understand what he had said. *Buckingham?* Her heart soared. *God had heeded her prayers at last.* Already the King was leading her into the chamber beyond, sobbing as he did so. The windows had been shuttered and the only light came from the dying embers in the grate. At first, Frances could just make out a faint shadow on the bed, but as she edged closer she saw the duke, his naked chest exposed as he thrashed about.

'Fetch me a candle,' she ordered a fearful page standing at the back of the room. He jumped as if she had struck him and hurried off towards the fireplace. Buckingham gave a loud groan as she held the flame close to his face. His hair was damp, but his skin felt cool and dry to the touch and there was no other sign of fever. She set the candle on the table and forced herself to examine him calmly and methodically, as she would anyone else who had fallen sick. His heartbeat was strong and steady as she placed her ear to his chest, and his skin was clear of any rashes or sores.

'Has he vomited?' she asked, peeling back the covers to continue her examinations.

'No, my lady,' one of the attendants replied.

'How long has he been like this?'

'Some three hours or more.' The King spoke this time. 'He had not been here for long when we fell into a quarrel over— It was nothing,' he babbled. 'He turned to leave but fainted away before he had crossed the threshold. He has been senseless ever since, often crying out – from pain or delirium, I cannot tell.'

James was weeping again, his face in his hands. Stripped of his kingly finery, he had the appearance of a frail old man, his sunken chest rising and falling in jerks, his rickety legs ready to give way at any moment. Despite everything she and those she loved had suffered at his hands since he had come to the throne, she could not but feel pity.

A movement from the bed focused her attention back on the duke. She could have sworn that one of his eyes had been open a fraction, but both were clamped shut now. Nothing ailed him that a return to his master's favour would not cure – and he had cleverly secured that. How she wished she could stop his breath with a draught of mandrake root or foxglove. She had both in the small casket she kept locked under the floorboards beneath her bed. It would be a fitting punishment for his deception. But even if the King did not accuse her of bewitching his beloved angel to death, God would never forgive her for such a sin. She must leave any retribution to Him alone.

'You need have no fear, Your Grace,' she said, rising from the bed. 'The duke is in no danger. He fainted, that is all – perhaps it is the unseasonable heat. A little rest will set him to rights.'

The King's face brightened, like that of a hungry child presented with a sweetmeat. 'Thank you, Lady Tyringham,' he croaked, swiping at his eyes. 'I am more indebted to you than I can express.'

Frances bobbed a curtsy. 'Make sure to give him some water when he wakes,' she instructed one of the grooms. 'Oh, and a large draught of woodbine – as much as you can find.' She smiled to herself, though she knew she should be above such petty revenge. It was a small comfort to think that the duke would spend the rest of the day on the close stool.

'How does the duke fare?' Frances asked, as she handed her husband a glass of wine. It was with some satisfaction that she had learned he had been obliged to keep to his bed for the past two days.

'Better for the King's attentions.' Thomas took a long draught. 'But I fancy His Grace's trust is not so blind as it was before Buckingham's expedition to Spain. It seems his prolonged absence worked the opposite effect to the one he intended. The King learned that he could live without his favourite.'

Frances clasped her husband's hands. 'We must take advantage of this, Thomas. His Majesty's esteem for you grows daily. Your modest, steady nature forms a welcome contrast to that of the duke. Little wonder the King seems ever more inclined to hunt.'

Her husband looked grave. 'That may be true, my love, but I have earned His Grace's trust by not involving myself in the intrigues of his court. I would be a fool to forfeit it by changing my stance now.'

Frances pushed down her irritation. She loved Thomas for his constancy, but it made him vulnerable to those with fewer scruples – Buckingham in particular. The duke would not hesitate to act against him as soon as the opportunity arose. But it was futile to try to persuade her husband to take a different course. *If he will not act against the duke, then I must.* For too long, she had watched Buckingham's hold on the King – on the entire court – grow stronger, his lust for power ever more insatiable. He would not rest until he had destroyed everything and everyone in his path, plunging the kingdom into wickedness and sin. Surely the danger of opposing him could not be more deadly than what would follow if he was left unchecked.

CHAPTER 54

9 October

Frances stared in disbelief. *Pray God he may be real*. He took another step towards her, his smile now faltering a little.

'Mother?'

She was in his arms, her tears soaking into his fine wool coat.

'You will squeeze the breath out of me!' he exclaimed, laughing.

Frances drew away from him and reached out to touch his cheek, as if afraid that he would suddenly dissolve before her eyes. She had thought of her eldest son more than ever lately. He had turned eighteen three months ago. It had grieved her not to be with him.

'What are you doing here?' she asked at last, brushing the tears from her cheeks. 'I thought you would be in Cambridge by now.'

'And so I intended. But London lies between there and Longford, and I could not resist the chance to see you – Papa too – though I can stay only a few days.'

'I am so glad you have come, George.' Frances's throat tightened. 'I have missed you so much since we left Longford.' She did not add that she had missed him for many years before that. 'How is your grandmother? And your brothers?'

'They are all well – though Robert and William are still as mad as rabid dogs. I do not know how John will keep order now I am gone.'

Frances grinned. 'I am sure your grandmother will help. Now, shall we go and find your papa? He should have returned from the hunt by now.'

She had barely finished speaking when her son took her arm and led her out of the garden.

'Do you think I might be presented to His Majesty while I am here?' he asked, as they reached the gate.

Frances shivered. The pain she had experienced at being parted from her eldest son all these years had been offset by the knowledge that he was safe from the dangers of court, from the King who had put his father to death. What if James or one of his advisers should see the resemblance between this fine young man and one of the most notorious plotters in the Powder Treason? Although she tried to reason that the King had barely known Tom Wintour, that few of his advisers from that time remained at court, fear still gripped her heart.

'You have already been presented to him.' She kept her voice light.

'But that was years ago, Mother. I was only a boy and hardly remember it. Besides, Papa would surely cause offence if he failed to introduce his eldest son and heir to his royal master. I am eager to see His Grace the prince too. I wonder if he will remember his childhood companion.'

Frances had no answer to this so they walked on in silence. She prayed that James would be exhausted by the hunt and retreat to his privy chamber for several days afterwards, as had become his custom lately. God willing, her son would be on his way to Cambridge by the time he emerged.

'A letter arrived for you, Mother,' George said, as she closed the door behind her. She had left him sleeping when she went to chapel, but had hastened back to their apartment as soon as the service was over, anxious in case her son should decide to explore the palace in her absence.

Frances recognised Kate's careful, looping script. 'May we delay our ride a few minutes longer? It is from a dear friend and I long to know how she fares.'

George gave an exaggerated sigh. then stooped to kiss his mother's cheek. 'I will prepare our things.'

Frances moved to sit on the window seat. Her eyes were not as sharp as they once had been and she needed the light for reading now, as well as needlework. As she broke the seal, she noticed with a pang that the letter was inscribed 'Tyringham Hall'. Kate had been there for almost a year now but had seldom written – whether for fear of exciting her husband's anger or out of the guilt she felt at inheriting Frances and Thomas's former home, she did not know.

> *My dear Frances,*
>
> *I trust you are in good health.*
>
> *I pray that you do not regard me as a faithless friend. I have thought of you often since arriving here. It has been both a pain and a comfort to imagine you in the rooms that I must now call my own. I can see why the house was so beloved of Sir Thomas. The hall reminds me of my father's at Belvoir, and the views are just as fine. But I have taken the greatest joy in the woodlands surrounding the estate. Little Mal delights in them too, as you predicted.*
>
> *The works are progressing more slowly than my husband would desire. I find myself unable to make sense of the plans he gave me before I left court, and therefore cannot direct the improvements as he instructed. It is well that he has not yet visited us here, or he would find the place little altered.*

Frances smiled. Kate had told her how she had once supervised the building of a new lodge at her father's estate while he and the late countess were at court. *She understood those plans well enough*. Frances felt a surge of affection for the young woman – admiration, too, that she was not so easily cowed by the duke as Frances had believed.

The rest of the letter was filled with news of the neighbours whom Frances and her husband had once known, of the imminent harvests, and of how Mal could now recite her Pater Noster. A hurried postscript had been added at the bottom of the page:

> *I pray you will remember me to my father, when he is next at court.*

Frances folded the letter and placed it carefully in the drawer of her husband's writing desk. She had not seen Lord Rutland since his departure from court after the Christmas celebrations at Greenwich. It was a source of frustration that he had failed to take advantage of the King's obvious favour towards him after the Spanish voyage. His desire to rid himself of Buckingham's presence had proved stronger. She wondered if he would ever return.

'Mother?'

George was looking at her expectantly.

'Forgive me. I am ready now,' she said brightly, taking her boots from him. 'Where shall we ride? Hyde Park or Blackheath?'

The walls of the palace were bathed in a deep golden light when they returned several hours later. Frances had delighted to see her son's face flushed with exhilaration as they had raced across the open fields that lay close to Greenwich Palace.

'Will we have missed dinner?' he called over his shoulder, as they passed under the archway into the stable-yard.

'I will have Mrs Knyvett bring us something,' Frances replied. It had been easy to persuade George to ride out further than they had planned. She could not hope to shield him from the court entirely, but she could at least reduce the chances of attracting unwanted attention.

'Papa!'

Thomas was sitting on the mounting block, one of the King's hounds at his feet. At the sound of their horses' hoofs, the animal reared and its baying echoed around the deserted yard.

'Peace, Ezekiel,' Thomas soothed, patting the hound's flank. He stood and helped Frances down from her horse, then kissed her.

'I hope you have not tired your mother out, George,' he called to the young man. 'She does not ride as fast as in her youth.'

Frances gave her husband a playful kick.

'It is I who is tired – hungry too,' George replied, as he dismounted and walked over to embrace his papa.

Thomas led their horses into the stables, the hound trotting at his heels. Frances's heart swelled at George's expression as he watched his retreating form. He had always adored her husband, and would never have any reason to suspect that Thomas was not his real father. Of the many blessings her marriage had given her, this was the greatest.

'Come, let us find something to satisfy that appetite of yours, George,' Thomas said, as he returned. 'It is well that you will soon be leaving for Cambridge, or there would be no meat left for the King's table.'

Frances felt his fingers stiffen. She followed his gaze to a cluster of figures in the distance, close to the entrance to the King's apartments. She froze as she recognised the duke's tall frame. Next to him, the King was leaning heavily on his arm. The prince was supporting his father's other side. Frances's first thought was to lead her son quickly away, but it was too late. Buckingham was looking at them now. She saw him bend to say something in his royal master's ear, then the party began walking slowly in their direction.

'Is that . . .' George's eyes were wide.

'Your Majesty,' Thomas said, as the three men drew close.

Frances tugged her son's arm, prompting him to make his obeisance as she and her husband were doing.

'I hope you are well rested now? Our last hunt left me greatly fatigued too,' Thomas said.

'Aye, well enough,' James replied, a little breathlessly. His gaze moved to George. 'Who is this?'

'Forgive me, Your Grace. This is my eldest son, George. He is here for a brief visit before beginning his studies at Cambridge.'

'Indeed?' James's eyes were alight with an interest that Frances recognised all too well.

'Your Majesty.' George bowed low again.

'Please, please . . .' James gestured for him to stand. 'Master Tyringham, eh? Ye're a handsome young buck.'

'And very unlike your father – in appearance at least,' Buckingham put in smoothly. 'I can see nothing of you in him, Tyringham.'

Frances's fingers itched to slap his smiling face.

'Then he is blessed indeed,' Thomas replied, with an easy grin.

'What will you study at Cambridge?' the prince asked.

'Law, Your Grace.'

'Pah!' the King exclaimed. 'This place is swarming with lawyers already. We have little need of another.'

Frances saw her son smile uncertainly.

'Let us hope you prove a diligent student,' the duke observed, 'so that you might support your father in his dotage.'

'I intend to be, my lord . . .'

'The Duke of Buckingham,' Thomas said shortly, before his master could reply.

Frances was glad that George showed no reaction. Neither she nor Thomas had spoken to him about the duke, judging that it would be to little purpose as they were resolved to steer the young man from a career at court. That decision seemed even more justified now, she thought, as she watched Buckingham appraise her son thoughtfully.

'It is late, Father. We should retire.' Charles's voice broke the silence.

'Dunnae fuss, lad. I am well enough,' the King retorted, his eyes still on George. 'I hope I will see you again before you leave, Master Tyringham.'

Frances saw her son's eyes flash with excitement. 'I would be honoured, Your Grace,' he replied quickly, stepping forward to kiss the hand that James proffered.

Buckingham looked from one to the other, as if measuring his next move. 'Then permit me to arrange it, Your Grace.'

That night Frances could not sleep. Thoughts of the encounter in the courtyard ran endlessly through her mind. Whenever she closed her eyes, Buckingham's smirking face appeared before her. *Why had he been so obliging towards a young man who might one day be a rival?* He had seen the King's interest in George, as had she. It would surely better serve his ambitions if his royal master did not see her son again before he left for Cambridge, so he might be forgotten all the sooner. As the dark hours wore on, the idea that Buckingham meant to embroil George in his own twisted schemes became a creeping certainty.

When at last the fragile wisps of grey appeared between the narrow slats of their shutters, Frances slipped out of bed. Thomas's slow, steady breathing assured her that he was still asleep as she moved silently towards the door, careful to avoid the floorboards that she knew would creak under her tread. In the gloom, she could just see the slender outline of her son stretched out on the pallet bed by the fireplace. How different his reaction to the chance meeting had been. She and Thomas had been hard-pressed to turn his conversation to other subjects. As well as anticipating his next audience with the King, he had begun to talk of how he might serve him after completing his studies. But what chilled her most had been his unstinting praise of the duke. She must hasten his departure for Cambridge before Buckingham could take advantage of it.

Slowly, she lifted the latch and pulled the door closed behind her. As soon as she was out in the corridor, she quickened her pace, desperate to breathe the cool, fragrant air of the gardens, which always calmed her, helping her to order her thoughts. She hastened through the first courtyard, with a glance over her shoulder, though it was still so gloomy that anyone might have been hiding in the shadows.

When she reached the archway on the far side, she hesitated. The corridor to her left would lead her past the kitchens and service quarters; to the right was the succession of courtiers' lodgings that preceded the King's apartments. The latter offered the most direct route to the gardens but Frances usually avoided it for fear of encountering Buckingham or one of his followers. She took it now, reasoning that it was unlikely anyone would be wandering those corridors at such an hour.

She was nearing Buckingham's apartment when the low murmur of voices made her stop. Stepping into an alcove on the opposite side of the cloister, she waited. She heard a latch scrape, then soft footsteps. She strained her ears but caught only the distant trill of birdsong. After a few more breaths, she peered around the wall and thought she saw a flash of grey silk at the end of the corridor before it disappeared from view.

As she continued on her way, she thought of the other encounter she had witnessed upon returning to court several years before. Buckingham must have taken many lovers since then. No doubt the skirts she had seen belonged to the latest. *Poor Kate.* But perhaps it was better that the duke sated his perverted lust on other women – and men – than his wife. *Better still that he was dead.* The thought struck her so forcefully that it took her breath away. She knew it was a sin to wish harm upon any man, even one's enemy, but she could not help it. If only he had been as sick as he had claimed when he had lain in his master's chamber that day. She allowed her mind to wander . . . his lifeless eyes raised to the heavens while his soul was dragged down to Hell. 'God forgive me,' she whispered, as she opened the gate into the gardens.

Frances slowed as she breathed in the heady scent of the myrtle hedges, made more pungent by the dew that clung to the tiny leaves. Already she could feel the tension ease from her shoulders, her racing mind begin to still. The fears that had robbed her of sleep seemed to subside, too. George would leave for Cambridge in two days' time. Although she would miss him keenly, she would be comforted by the knowledge that he was far from this place, from the duke's scheming and the King's lustful gaze. God willing, he would soon forget about them both – as they would him.

As she stooped to pluck a few stems of sage, a movement on the path ahead drew her eye. A woman was hastening towards the gate that led out onto the street, her grey silk skirts billowing around her. Frances watched, transfixed, as she lifted the latch and ducked under the archway, then turned to close the gate. She glimpsed the woman's face through the ornate iron bars.

Anne Vaux.

CHAPTER 55

11 October

'His Excellency, the Marquis de Châteauneuf.'

There was a rustle of silks as James's courtiers greeted the King's new guest. Frances stole a glance at the exquisitely dressed man who was mounting the steps onto the dais. He wore robes of crimson satin edged with silver thread that glittered in the sunlight streaming through the windows of the great hall. On his head was a small cap of the same material, around which curled blond tresses. His flamboyant moustache and long pointed beard only partially hid a mouth that seemed set in a permanent grimace, and his thickly arched eyebrows added to his air of disdain.

'Your Majesty.' His accent was pronounced. He kissed the King's bejewelled hand, then bowed to the prince.

The proposed alliance with King Louis had been announced just a few hours before the arrival of his envoy. Frances had given little credence to the rumours that had been circulating for a few weeks that Prince Charles would soon be betrothed to the French King's sister. She knew that speculation about his marriage was bound to grow more intense as his father's health continued to falter but saw no reason to believe this latest rumour any more than she had the one that preceded it. Even Thomas had been surprised. It troubled Frances to think that the King had chosen not to confide in him, despite the many hours they had spent hunting together.

Judging by the self-satisfied smile on Buckingham's face, the news had not been unexpected to him. Not so long ago he had declared his allegiance to the Spanish King; now it seemed his heart was set on France. He was greeting the envoy now, kissing him warmly on both cheeks. Few people would have believed it was the first time they had met. Beside her, George was craning his neck for a better view. The cold hand of fear clutched her heart as she thought of Lady Vaux. Frances had not seen the woman since, but the thought of what confidences she might have betrayed to Buckingham made her sick with anxiety. She stole another glance at her son. *Had Lady Vaux revealed her secret that George's father was a notorious traitor?* It would surely be their undoing.

Frances watched as Buckingham led the French envoy to a table laid with delicacies. They were soon joined by the King and his son, though Frances noticed that Charles said little during the ensuing conversation.

'I have seen more cheerful faces at a funeral,' Frances heard the man next to her mutter.

'Monsieur le marquis must be confident of success, or he would never have bothered to make the journey,' replied his companion. 'Do you know anything of the lady?'

'Henrietta Maria? A slip of a girl, by all accounts. But at thirteen, she is of marriageable age.'

'I wonder that she has not already been betrothed to some foreign prince. Perhaps there is some impediment.'

'What – apart from her being as stubborn a papist as her brother? I wonder His Majesty entertains the idea at all.'

'He would have the Pope himself to dinner if it pleased his Steenie.'

The two men's sniggers sounded in Frances's ears as she steered her son away from the dais. 'Would you fetch me a glass of wine, George? My throat is quite parched.'

She saw him cast a glance towards the royal party before obeying her request.

'The duke seems very pleased with the new arrival,' she murmured to Thomas, who nodded grimly.

'Whatever fresh scheme this is, we can be sure it will bring him some advantage. French gold is as good as Spanish, after all.'

'And King Louis's sister is as devout a Catholic as the infanta – for that at least we should be grateful. Oh, thank you, George,' she said quickly, hoping her son had not heard any of their conversation. He was looking at the dais now.

'His Majesty is fortunate to have such a servant as the duke, is he not?' George did not seem to notice their silence as he stared at Buckingham in open admiration. 'So full of grace and accomplishments, and nothing escapes his notice – even a lowly subject such as myself.'

Frances turned sharply to him.

'To think that he should invite me to dine with him tomorrow, when he might have kings, princes and ambassadors for company,' her son continued, his eyes alight with joy.

Frances stared at her husband in alarm. She had told him of Lady Vaux's visit. He knew as well as she the danger it might carry.

'It is an honour indeed,' Thomas agreed, 'but you are leaving for Cambridge in the morning.'

'It is worth delaying my departure for, Papa – God knows I would sacrifice a great deal more for such an invitation.'

'But everything has been arranged and there is no time to send word to your master now.'

'He will hardly object, when he knows the reason, Mother.' The excitement faded from his eyes as he looked from one to the other. 'It is as if you are anxious to be rid of me.'

Frances forced a bright smile. 'You know that isn't true, George. I would keep you by my side for ever if I could. But you are a man now and must make your own way in the world. Once in Cambridge . . .'

Her son's face brightened at once. 'I knew you would understand. If I win favour with the duke, he might recommend me for the King's service when my studies are completed.' He bent to kiss his mother's hand, then gave Thomas's arm an affectionate squeeze. 'Who knows where else this meeting might lead?'

Frances shielded her eyes against the sinking sun as she gazed across Hyde Park. Buckingham would have to come this way – there was only one gate on the south side and it led directly to the road he would take back to Whitehall. She had heard of the duke's excursion from Thomas, who had been glad of an afternoon to undertake his duties in the stables unimpeded. He did not know she had left the palace to find Buckingham. He would hardly approve of the idea. The duke had taken great delight in rebuffing his own attempts to persuade him to revoke his invitation to George. Frances could hope for little more success, but she had at least to try.

A distant rumble carried on the wind. Frances peered at the horizon again and saw the outline of a rider. The ground at her feet vibrated as he thundered towards her. He must have seen her by now, but he dug his heels into the horse's sides, urging it on. She forced herself to stand perfectly still, though she might be trampled underfoot. Only at the last did Buckingham pull back sharply on the reins, causing his horse to snort loudly, its front legs rearing so high that Frances was sure the duke would fall.

'Lady Tyringham,' he said, when his horse had lowered its hoofs. 'Do you always happen upon gentlemen in such a fashion?'

She did not reply but waited for him to dismount. He did so slowly, then tethered the beast to a nearby tree and patted its glistening neck.

'How may I serve you, my lady?' His breath felt hot on her hand as he bent to kiss it.

'I wish to speak to you about my son,' she said, knowing it was pointless to dissemble. 'Your invitation for him to dine with you was an honour as great as it was unlooked for. But I regret that he will not be able to attend. He leaves for Cambridge tomorrow.'

The duke's mouth twitched. 'What trouble you have taken to tell me of something so inconsequential. Surely your son could have sent word himself, *if* that was his intention. I wonder he made no mention of his impending journey when I first extended the invitation.' A pause. 'I must say, Lady Tyringham, such a trifling matter seems to have caused you and your husband a great deal of vexation. Tell me, why are you both so determined to prevent it? Fathers are supposed to be ambitious for their sons – the eldest above all. But then . . .'

His eyes blazed into hers as he left the words hanging in the air. Frances could hear her pulse thrumming in her ears. 'But then?' she repeated. *Say it.* Even though it was the thing she feared, she needed to know for certain that Lady Vaux had betrayed her secret.

The duke took a step towards her and cocked his head to one side. As he slowly exhaled, she caught the bitter aroma of stale wine on his breath. There were dark shadows under his eyes and his soft skin appeared pallid and drawn. Even though he had feigned his illness earlier that month, he was not the image of youthful vigour he had once been, Frances reflected, momentarily distracted from the fear that was coursing through her.

He brought his mouth so close to her ear that his lips almost brushed against it. 'George is not his son, is he, my lady?' he whispered.

Frances jumped back as if scalded, her heel jabbing painfully on the bark of a tree. Swift as a cat, Buckingham pinioned her arms and pushed her against the gnarled trunk.

'Who would have believed that such a pious woman would have played the whore?' he drawled. She could feel the heat of his arousal as he pressed his hips against hers. 'And with a notorious traitor. Did the danger of the forbidden excite you, Lady Tyringham?' He trailed his lips along her neck. 'Does it still?'

'No!' she cried, wrenching her arms free and striking him a stinging blow across the face. His eyes bored into hers as he touched the welt with his fingers, then tightened them into a fist. Frances flinched, waiting for him to strike. But he gave a low chuckle and stepped away from her.

'Your virtue is safe, my lady. Such borrowed flesh is hardly enough to tempt me.' He gave a sniff and brushed the remnants of bark from his palms. 'Besides, it is your son who interests me, not you.'

Frances clenched her hands into fists as she stared at him. 'If any harm should befall him— '

'Then it will be entirely of your making. What a torment that must be for you, knowing your treachery has blighted his life. If ever the King should learn that Master George is not his beloved Thomas's son, but the bastard of one of the Powder Treason plotters, he would have your head and the boy's too.'

'He would not believe it,' she spat back. 'What proof could you offer? His Majesty would hardly accept the word of your friend Lady Vaux.'

She caught the momentary shock on his face before he recovered himself.

'I would not need that when there are plenty of men to attest to how greatly your son resembles Tom Wintour.' He moved towards her again. 'The King has long had you marked as a witch and a traitor. Were it not for the love he bears your husband, he would have had that pretty neck snapped long before now. If I should tell him what I have learned, it would merely confirm his suspicions.'

Frances's gaze did not waver, though fury and fear surged through her. 'Then tell him, Your Grace.' Her voice was as sharp as flint. 'But do not think to threaten me. I have no fear of death.'

Buckingham gave a sad smile. 'For yourself, perhaps not. But for your precious boy? Ah, I see that is a different matter. What would a mother not do for her firstborn son?' Another step closer. 'I intend to find out, Lady Tyringham.'

Frances held her breath as he traced his index finger slowly down her neck to the swell of her breasts. 'What would you have me do?' she rasped, swallowing her terror and revulsion.

His eyes flashed with desire as his lips curled into another slow smile. 'I am sure there are many services you might perform for me. My only difficulty will be in deciding which should come first.' His fingers still hovered above the line of her bodice.

Frances could feel the knot in the tree bark press into her back as she shrank away from him. Then she watched as he gave an exaggerated sigh and strolled languidly to his horse, which was grazing contentedly in the lush grass of the park. He climbed into the saddle with practised ease and touched the brim of his hat towards her.

'I do hope we will meet again soon, Lady Tyringham,' he called, over his shoulder, as he ducked under the gateway and out of sight.

CHAPTER 56

12 October

The twelfth chime echoed into silence. Frances pulled her shawl more tightly around her shoulders. There was only a faint glow from the embers now and what little heat they emitted was hardly enough to take the chill from the gloomy parlour.

'Will you not come to bed, my love?'

Her husband was silhouetted against the pale moonlight that showed through the window of their apartment.

'I cannot rest until he has returned.'

'Nor I,' he admitted. 'But you will be warmer under the covers.'

Frances smiled as he held out his hand. She had not told him of what had passed with Buckingham that afternoon. He would be angry with her for taking such a risk – angrier still if he heard what the duke had done. Her arms felt bruised where he had gripped them, and every time she closed her eyes she could feel the warmth of his mouth on her neck. Mingled with her revulsion was a deep unease, as much for what she had felt as for what he had threatened.

'What if he has told him?'

Her words hung heavy in the darkened chamber. Slowly, Thomas lowered his hand. 'I am almost more afraid of that than of anything else,' he said. 'George is as much my son as our other boys.'

'He loves you no less in return, Thomas,' she replied, rising to embrace him. His arms felt stiff as they encircled her.

'I pray God it will be enough, if he should find out the truth.'

Frances pressed her face against his chest. She was just as terrified as he that George would be lost to them if he were to discover that they had concealed the truth all these years.

'Do you think we should warn him about Buckingham, discourage him from spending any more time with him?' she asked. 'He is old enough to form his own judgement of such a man, after all.'

'No,' Thomas replied. 'George may be mature in years, but he knows little of the world. Even men of greater experience have fallen under the duke's spell.'

'He is hardly an innocent,' Frances countered. 'He spent much of his childhood at court and has been managing the Longford estate for three years and more.'

Her husband held her apart from him then, his eyes blazing with sincerity. 'That may be true, my love, but George can have encountered no one as duplicitous as the duke. Besides, if we try to deter him from seeing Buckingham again, he will hardly agree to it without an explanation – and that is something we cannot provide.'

The click of the latch made them both start. George stumbled into the apartment, uttering a curse as he tripped over one of the flagstones. 'You scared me half to death!' he exclaimed, as Thomas moved to help. 'Mama? Why are you not in bed too?'

'We are not so old and dull as you suppose, my boy,' her husband said, before she could reply. 'How was the duke?' Although he kept his tone light, Frances heard its edge.

'The very best of men!' her son exclaimed.

She exhaled as the soft light illuminated his face, which was flushed with excitement. *He did not know.* But her relief soon turned to disquiet as George proceeded to regale them with every detail of his evening – the delights of Buckingham's table, the sumptuousness of his chambers and, above all, the many and varied virtues of his new acquaintance.

'I am pleased it was worth delaying your journey for,' Thomas said, when at last George had paused to draw breath.

'Oh, yes!' he exclaimed. 'The memory of it will stay with me always – though I hope it will soon be superseded by others.'

Frances bristled. 'Others?'

'Many others, I hope,' her son replied. 'The duke made me promise to return to court whenever I have leisure to do so – which will be often, I'm sure. He even talked of visiting me in Cambridge. He has estates close by, apparently.'

'He has estates in every part of the kingdom,' Thomas muttered.

'I can well believe it,' George continued, oblivious to the scorn in Thomas's voice. 'There are no limits to his authority, or to his favour with the King. If I can only remain in his good graces while I am away . . . God's wounds!' he cried, with sudden passion. 'I wish that I was not bound for Cambridge. I would flourish far more by staying here and serving the duke.'

'No, George,' Frances said. 'You are committed to study law, and that will stand you in far better stead than the uncertain promise of favour here. Your grandmother must have told you many times how fickle the court can be.'

In the candlelight, she saw her son's frown crease into a scowl. 'Of course I shall go to Cambridge, Mother,' he replied petulantly. 'But you should be glad that I have ambitions beyond resolving petty disputes over land or inheritance. Here at court is where the greatest prizes are to be had.'

And the greatest dangers. She opened her mouth to reply, but Thomas was there before her.

'They are indeed, and we are proud that they seem already to be within your grasp, George,' he said, giving him a placatory pat on the shoulder. 'Now, get some rest. You have a long journey tomorrow.'

Frances saw that her son's eyes were already heavy. Judging from his breath, he had drunk enough wine to sleep like the dead.

She rose and kissed his cheek, then folded down the coverlet on his pallet bed and watched as Thomas led him towards it.

'God give you good rest, my boy,' her husband said softly, bending to stroke his hair.

'And God keep you from evil,' she whispered, as her son's deep, rhythmic breathing echoed in the darkness.

1625

CHAPTER 57

18 February

Frances watched as her husband helped the King into his saddle. James's face was flushed even from this small exertion, and he shifted uncomfortably, wincing with every movement. Above the line of his boots, she could see that his legs were swollen. The gout had become so acute in recent weeks that he had been obliged to cancel several hunts, which had made his temper all the more uncertain. Little wonder that a crowd had gathered in the stables to watch what would happen this time.

A hound gave a high-pitched yelp as another sank its teeth into its flank. Thomas tapped the troublesome beast on its snout and it skulked away, whimpering. They were growing as restless as the courtiers – Frances included. She had been anxious since George's departure, even though it was now more than four months ago. He had soon written of his safe arrival in Cambridge, but the memory of their conversation that night had turned over and over in her mind. She imagined her son boasting to his new companions of his powerful patron and knew that he would be itching to return to Whitehall so that he could renew their acquaintance. She was just as eager that he stayed away, though she missed him keenly.

She looked across at Buckingham, who was regaling his royal master with some amusing tale. Now and again, James's laughter echoed across the crowded courtyard, his breath misting in the cold morning air. Frances had been careful to avoid the duke since their encounter in Hyde Park and had kept to her apartments as much as she could. But while they had not been alone together, the sly looks he sent her at court gatherings served as a constant reminder.

His threat seemed to hang ever more heavily over her – Thomas, too. The thought of how he might use his knowledge of her son's father against them had continued to plague her. She and her husband had spent so much of the past ten years in his power. Now that he knew about Tom Wintour, there seemed no prospect of their enslavement ending.

At least Buckingham had not made good his threat to visit her son at Cambridge. George had written to her and Thomas several times, begging to know when he might come to Whitehall again. They had always found an excuse – the threat of plague, Thomas being away on the hunt, his royal master laid low with sickness. The latter was true more often than not, Frances consoled herself – she hated lying to her son. She was relieved that his letters had grown less frequent of late, as his studies and companions drew his attention away from the court . . . and the duke.

'Make way!'

Frances turned to see Arthur Brett pushing through the crowds, clutching something. A flash of silver caught the light as he held it aloft.

'I have found the new stirrup, Your Grace,' he announced breathlessly, sweeping a deep bow.

James scowled down at the young man who had been his most intimate attendant until Buckingham's return to favour. 'Give it to Steenie.'

Buckingham held out his hand, but his rival pretended not to notice him and began to fasten the stirrup into place.

His royal master glanced down, his face suffused with fury. 'How dare you defy me, boy?' he cried, kicking at the fumbling fingers. The stirrup fell clattering to the ground and Arthur stared at it, mumbling an apology. Pity for the young man mingled with loathing as Frances saw Buckingham's eyes flash with triumph. Thomas was right: Master Brett's allure had been extinguished.

'Go well, my sow.'

The duke's words rang out across the stable-yard, prompting audible gasps. This latest nickname was the most outrageous yet. Frances had hardly believed it when Thomas had told her. Yet looking at James now, she could see how he delighted in his favourite's over-familiarity.

'Ye're sure ye will not accompany me, Steenie?'

Buckingham shook his head regretfully. 'Please – do not ask again. It grieves me sorely that I am not yet strong enough, after my recent malady. The hours will be long until you return,' he added, kissing his master's hand, then raising it to his cheek.

Frances's lips curled. If he'd suffered from anything, it was an excess of wine the night before. She watched as James brought his fingers to his lips and raised them to his favourite, then pulled on the reins and gave another grimace of pain as his horse broke into a trot. Thomas smiled briefly at her before following in his wake.

The courtiers were quick to disperse, and Frances heard mutterings against the duke as they passed. He would care little for their disapproval. The only thing that would pain him was if they ceased to talk of him at all. She had no desire to engage in idle gossip and waited until the yard was deserted. As the sun emerged briefly from behind the heavy clouds, Frances saw something shining on the cobbles. Realising it was the discarded stirrup, she stooped to pick it up. *Poor Brett.* He had learned all too quickly of how fickle the King's favour could be. Well, he might have some small reward for his pains, she resolved, as she put the beautifully wrought silver into her pocket and made her way towards the palace. She would find an opportunity to give it back to him later.

As she reached the gateway to the outer courtyard, she hesitated. The thought of whiling away the hours in her husband's apartment was hardly appealing, but it was too cold to meander around the privy gardens. Then an idea struck her. It had been many weeks since she had visited Lord Bacon and he avoided Whitehall, these days. A brisk walk to the Temple would revive her, and she could take him the thistle and feverfew tincture she had prepared against the ague that often afflicted him in winter.

A little over half an hour later, she was standing at the door of his humble lodgings. Her cheeks were flushed and her skin prickled as it cooled in the dank air of the dimly lit corridor. After a few moments, she heard the light tread of footsteps on the other side of the door – too rapid for her friend's. She had just begun to wonder if he had at last found the means to employ a servant when a weasel-faced man emerged from the chamber beyond. He darted a furtive look at Frances before scurrying down the passage and out of sight. With mounting apprehension, she pushed open the door, which had been left ajar.

Bacon looked up from his writing desk, his quill suspended over the paper. 'You must truly be a witch, for barely had I written your name than you appear before me.' Although there was humour in his voice, Frances noted his pallor. She closed the door behind her.

'Who was that man?'

He gestured for her to sit down. 'When the King first ordered me to find the late Queen's jewels, I employed a number of associates to help me in the task. That gentleman was one of them. I had not thought to see him again, but it seems he was more steadfast than I gave him credit for. He has just returned from France.'

Frances's breathing quickened. 'He has found the jewels?' she whispered.

'Not quite,' Bacon replied, setting down the quill. 'But he has discovered the whereabouts of Lady Ruthven.' He glanced at the door, as if fearing they were overheard. 'I have had various reports over the years,' he continued, 'that the lady has been sighted in Paris, Fontainebleau . . . even Rome. But it seems that all the while she has been living a day's ride from where she began, in Guînes at the Abbaye du Saint-Benoit.'

Frances was silent, taking this in.

'If this were all, I would be content to let the lady live out her days in peace,' he went on, 'but my agent is not the only one to have discovered her whereabouts. He became aware that someone else was watching the comings and goings of the Abbaye. A few discreet enquiries suggested that the other gentleman was in the pay of the Marquis de Châteauneuf.'

The French envoy. Frances thought back to the various receptions at which she had seen him, always with the Duke of Buckingham in close attendance.

'There is more.' Bacon's words interrupted her racing thoughts. 'A third gentleman arrived in Guînes, before my agent's departure. He visited Châteauneuf's agent at his lodgings and they were in conference for almost an hour. When he departed, my associate followed him to the port at Calais, where he boarded a small vessel bound for England. The crew were dressed in Buckingham's livery.'

Frances stared. It was as she had suspected. Having been abandoned by the King of Spain, the duke had changed his allegiance to France.

'What does he stand to gain from this?' she asked.

Bacon spread his hands. 'What he has always striven for. Riches and power. You can be sure that if Châteauneuf's agent seizes the jewels, the duke will demand his share.'

'In recompense for arranging the prince's marriage to the French King's sister?'

Bacon inclined his head. 'An excellent bargain.'

So that was why Buckingham had declined to join the hunt. He and Châteauneuf had taken the opportunity to conspire in private, now that the jewels were almost within their grasp.

'But what if His Majesty proves unwilling? Châteauneuf has been at court for almost five months now, yet still negotiations have not begun for an alliance.'

Her friend's expression darkened. 'Even before I left his service, I could see that the King was growing frail – in body as well as mind. Buckingham would not flinch from hastening his end, as he has others before him.'

Frances thought of Lord Rutland's son lying lifeless in his father's arms. Although she had not seen Dr Lambe since his appearance in the masque, she had little doubt that Buckingham might summon him at a moment's notice. Or perhaps the duke had learned enough to prepare the poison himself this time.

'There is still the prince . . .' Frances began.

'He is of noble heart but is no match for Buckingham,' Bacon countered. 'The duke would find the means to dominate him as he has his father.'

For several minutes, the only sound in the gloomy chamber was the hiss and gutter of the tallow candles in their sconces.

Frances's voice cut across the silence. 'Then I must find a way to warn Lady Ruthven before it is too late.'

CHAPTER 58

18 February

The prince sat back in the chair, his face ashen. For several moments, he said nothing. Frances began to fear that she had made the wrong choice in coming to him. Thomas would not return for hours yet and, desperate though she was to confide in her husband, she had not wanted to risk delaying. With mounting apprehension, she studied Charles's expression. Had she miscalculated? Was the cordiality that seemed to exist between him and Buckingham more than the pretence she had assumed it was – on the prince's part at least? If so, he might take her words as slander.

'You are quite sure that the duke plans to murder my father, if this alliance does not come to pass?' he asked.

Frances nodded. 'I fear so, Your Grace. He will surely stop at nothing to seize what he considers his share of your mother's jewels.'

His mouth twisted with distaste. 'I'll wager Châteauneuf's master will not share in the spoils. The marquis is as grasping as my father's favourite.'

Frances's silence signalled her agreement.

'The irony is that I am in accord with this alliance,' the prince continued. 'Before she died, I promised my mother that I would marry a princess of the faith. She had in mind the infanta, but the duke destroyed that with his greed and scheming. Young though she is, the French King's sister is praised for her piety. I have no doubt that my mother would have approved of the match. By God, I will not let that man destroy this marriage too.' He banged his fist on the table next to him. 'I should have acted against him before now – the Lord knows I have not lacked the opportunity. But always I have been drawn to caution – to watch and wait for him to damn himself and save me the trouble. I have been a fool. I—' He broke off, his face flushed with fury.

'You must not chastise yourself, Your Grace,' Frances said. 'Other men have shown less restraint – less wisdom, too – and all have fallen at his hands. I shared your hope that he would have destroyed himself by now. But the King is as much in his power as ever. Little wonder it is whispered the duke has bewitched him.'

'Or that devil Lambe,' Charles muttered. 'You are too forgiving, Lady Tyringham. What you describe as restraint and wisdom would be deemed by most as indecision and cowardice. The people of this realm look to me as their future king. I must learn to act with greater resolve, as my late brother would have done.'

And plunged us into disaster. Frances tried to hide her disdain at the mention of Prince Henry. The younger brother whom he had teased so mercilessly had already shown more kingly qualities than James's late heir ever had.

'Buckingham will only act against my father if he believes the jewels are within his grasp,' Charles continued. 'I must find them before Châteauneuf's agent does. I will send a trusted servant to Lady Ruthven. She knows they are mine by right, that my mother bequeathed them to me. I have never believed she stole the jewels but that she has been protecting them until such time as she judges it safe to return them to me.'

Frances considered this. 'How can you be sure that your servant will gain admission to the Abbaye?'

'I will send my mother's ring as assurance.' Charles spoke with conviction, but Frances saw the uncertainty in his eyes.

'Lady Ruthven has evaded capture for more than five years now and has probably spent most of those at the Abbaye – nowhere else could offer her such sanctuary. Even if your mother's ring is passed to her, it may not provide enough reassurance. Such a thing might easily have fallen into the wrong hands in such treacherous times.'

'Then what am I to do? I can hardly go there myself. A prince attracts great notice wherever he is.'

Frances took a breath. 'But I do not.' Her eyes blazed into Charles's. 'Lady Ruthven knows and trusts me. The late Queen summoned me to attend her upon my first arriving at your father's court many years ago. I helped her through a sickness that might have claimed her life. She was there when I visited Her Grace for the last time at Hampton Court. She knows that I am of the true faith.'

Although the prince's brow was furrowed, his eyes were alight with hope. 'You would be putting yourself at great risk, Lady Tyringham. Why would you do so to save the life of a king who has blighted your own?'

'I would do this to honour the late Queen and Your Grace.' *And to destroy the Duke of Buckingham.* The unspoken motive was the strongest, and she prayed that God would forgive her.

The prince clasped her hand. 'Be assured that such a service will have its reward. I know that you and your husband have suffered ill fortune these past years, with the loss of Sir Thomas's estates and no doubt more besides. It has pained me that I have been powerless to assist you. I persuaded my father to restore Tyringham Hall to your husband as a mark of his loyal service, but the duke discovered it and altered his mind – as he always does,' he added bitterly. 'Thereafter the King would hear no further word on the matter.'

Frances's desire for revenge against Buckingham was sharpened by this revelation. He had all the petulance of an indulged child who would not rest until he had robbed his companions of their playthings, even though they were of little worth to him.

'Everything I have is at my father's hands, and for as long as Buckingham has him in thrall I could not grant Sir Thomas so much as a shilling. But the late Queen bequeathed those jewels to me alone. If you recover them, I will restore your fortune – your husband's too – and more besides.'

Frances curtsied and kissed the prince's hand. 'Thank you, Your Grace. But you must know that I am not undertaking this enterprise for material reward.'

Charles inclined his head. 'When I am king – which, pray God, may not be for many years yet – I will surround myself with those who have proven their loyalty . . . and their faith.'

Frances's eyes shone. It was as if God had shown his hand at last. Tom had not died in vain. Neither had everything that she and her husband had suffered been for nothing. This prince, whose heart was as pure as his father's was corrupted, would restore the kingdom to the Catholic fold.

'It is imperative that the King is kept safe from Buckingham until you return, lest the duke should grow impatient and put his plan into place before he has the jewels. My father has talked of going to Theobalds when the winter has abated. I will persuade him to make the journey earlier – already he grows restless for fresh hunting ground so it will be easy enough. I will go with him, as will Sir Thomas, of course. Buckingham will be content to remain at Whitehall if he is promised full authority during my father's absence.'

Frances knew the truth of this. The duke had missed the last few hunting expeditions for the same reason.

'You will not go to France alone, Lady Tyringham. The man I had in mind for the enterprise will accompany you. He has served in the King's army for many years. I would trust him with my life – as I trust him with yours.' He hesitated. 'This scheme must be known to the three of us alone. The more people who hear of it, the greater the risk that Buckingham or the marquis will discover it. I must ask that you keep it even from your own husband.'

428

Frances felt uneasy. She longed to tell Thomas of what she had overheard, seek his blessing for the hazardous venture in which she was now embroiled. She had learned to her cost how destructive secrets were between them. But she knew, too, that if she told him of their plan, he would not let her go. After a pause, she nodded.

'Anyone would think you had never bade me farewell before.' Thomas grinned as she clung to him again.

Frances did not reply, but pressed her cheek against his chest, breathing in the familiar scent.

'We will return within a fortnight – three weeks, at most. His Majesty will not want to be parted from the duke for longer.' Frances caught the bitterness in his last words.

'I wish I could come with you.' That at least was true. She had felt her resolve crumble since her meeting with the prince. The enormity of what she was undertaking had tormented her as she had lain awake that night, the prospect of returning to England with the jewels – and her life – intact seeming more distant with every passing hour. She had hardly slept for the two nights since then, and her nerves had been worn to shreds by the long hours of waiting for the King and his entourage to depart for Hertfordshire.

Buckingham had seemed more reluctant to stay behind than the prince had calculated, and his sullenness had wrought tears from his royal master, who was loath to do anything that grieved his favourite. But Frances was convinced that it had all been for show. For as long as the Marquis de Châteauneuf remained at Whitehall, the duke would not wish to be far away.

'The court will be depleted, it is true, but you rarely seek company here these days,' her husband reasoned, interrupting her thoughts. 'I am sure Lord Bacon would be delighted to receive you. It is many weeks since you have seen him.'

Frances said nothing. She did not wish to entangle herself in more lies.

'You are sure all is well, my love?' Thomas said, holding her at arm's-length so that he could study her face. 'You have been very quiet for the past couple of days. Is it George? His last letter can have given you no cause for anxiety. He seems to have forgotten all about the court . . . the duke too.'

'No, it is not that – it is not anything,' she said brightly. 'I am tired, that is all. Perhaps you will persuade the King to grant you a leave of absence so that we may visit our boys, once . . .' *Once all this is over.* '. . . once the spring has come.' she finished.

'I should like that very much,' her husband replied, with a smile. 'Let us pray that this visit sates his appetite for hunting – for a time at least. Now, I must go and make ready, or there will be no hunting at all.' He kissed her warmly on the lips.

'Thomas,' she said quickly, reaching for his hand as he made for the door. He turned to her, his smile faltering as he saw her expression. 'I love you.'

'And I you – more than ever,' he replied, kissing her once more.

As the door closed behind him, Frances wondered if she would ever set eyes upon her husband again.

CHAPTER 59

25 February

'Draw on the sail,' the boatman commanded. 'The sluice gates are hard by.'

It seemed an age until they had passed through the gates and into the calmer waters of Calais harbour. Frances sucked in a deep breath and felt the nausea recede at last. She stole a glance at the prince's servant. John Felton was a sullen, taciturn man, and had barely spoken two words to her since their first meeting at Rochester. They had ridden from there to Dover in silence. It was as well, Frances mused. The less he knew of her, the better. But she would have liked to know more about him – to find out how he had earned Charles's trust. Admirable qualities must lie hidden behind his surly manner, she supposed. He was certainly physically impressive – broad-shouldered and taller than any man she had met. In that respect, at least, she felt reassured by his presence.

They had reached the landing stage now and Frances waited impatiently while the boatman secured the vessel. She was so glad to step onto the solid wooden platform that she almost forgot the heavy apprehension at what lay ahead. Drawing her hood over her face, she took the arm that Felton proffered, wondering vaguely if anyone would question that they were man and wife, and kept her eyes fixed on the ground as he led her away from the harbour.

It was only a short ride to Guînes, but the familiar motion of the horse and the chill air of the early morning left Frances feeling more refreshed. Felton slowed his mount to a trot as a large stone tower came into view ahead. Drawing closer, Frances could hear the slow tolling of the abbey bell. Her heart skipped a beat. *Was Lady Ruthven even now making her way to matins? Or had Châteauneuf's agent already taken her – the jewels too?* She tried to quieten her thoughts as they rode towards the ancient stone gatehouse of the abbey, which lay just in front of the city walls. She glanced over her shoulder, trying to shake off the creeping sensation that they were being watched, even though the only sign of life was the faint glow of a fire through the window of the gatehouse. Felton said something in French to the aged custodian, who gazed quizzically at them before nodding them through.

Once inside the courtyard, while her companion tethered the horses, Frances studied the high stone walls that surrounded them. On the upper floor, there was a series of narrow oblong windows – the dormitories, Frances supposed. She wondered if Queen Anne's old attendant was watching from one. A loud creak drew her attention to the heavy iron gates at the entrance to the main abbey buildings. A solemn lady swathed in long black robes and a large hood stepped silently into the courtyard. Felton removed his hat and gave a stiff bow, then proceeded to address the woman so quietly that Frances only caught the occasional word – '*une femme . . . la Royne . . . Angleterre.*' Now and again, the abbess glanced in her direction, but her expression remained inscrutable. Finally, she nodded and slipped back through the gates, pulling them closed behind her. Frances and her companion were left standing in the courtyard for so many minutes that she began to fear it was a trap. She imagined the marquis's men skulking in the shadows of the cloister, waiting to pounce.

Frances jerked her head towards a small movement in one of the chambers above. She stared as a shutter was closed – so quickly that it made her wonder if she had imagined it. But Felton was looking in the same direction. After several more minutes, the abbess reappeared at the gates. Her gaze rested upon Frances, and she motioned for her to enter. Felton made to follow, but the woman told him to remain in the courtyard. He looked in alarm at Frances, who hesitated, then gave a slight nod.

As she followed the abbess along a dark corridor, she inhaled the smell of damp stone and incense, drawing some small comfort from it, though her nerves were strung as tightly as the ropes of a truckle bed. Every time they passed a doorway or recess, her skin prickled with fear. At the end, the woman led her up a steep flight of spiral stairs. Frances clung tightly to the rope that had been strung along the cold stone wall to her left, her soles slipping now and again on the steps worn smooth by centuries of use.

Another gloomy corridor lay at the top of the stairs. As they walked slowly along it, Frances could see the dark outline of a crucifix on each of the doors. The woman stopped outside the chamber that lay at the furthest end and knocked quietly three times. The door was opened a crack. After a few moments more, the abbess pushed it just wide enough for her to enter. Casting an anxious glance at her, Frances uttered a silent prayer and walked inside.

'You have travelled a long way to see me, Lady Tyringham.'

Frances stared. In her simple grey habit, the late Queen's favourite was barely recognisable. Not even a strand of light red hair showed under her tightly bound wimple, and her face was devoid of the white paste that had marked her out as a lady of status.

'Please.' Lady Ruthven gestured towards a low wooden stool opposite her own.

'I come on behalf of His Grace, the Prince of Wales.' Her voice sounded hoarse.

'So I understand. How did he know where to find me?'

'You are in danger, Lady Ruthven. The Marquis de Châteauneuf knows you reside here.'

'I do not doubt it,' the older woman replied calmly. 'It is exactly as I intended.'

This was so unexpected that Frances was at a loss as to how to respond.

'So long as I am here, His Excellency will believe that my late mistress's jewels are too – or, at least, that I can lead his spies to them.'

'And you cannot?' Frances whispered.

Lady Ruthven gave a low chuckle. 'Well, I could – but it would involve as long a journey as you have just made.'

Frances looked at her in confusion. 'But you fled with them after the Queen's death. You were seen . . .'

'People will convince themselves that their eyes have seen something that their heart believes. I left England at the same time that the jewels disappeared, so of course it was put about that I had taken them. I am sure that the story grew with the telling . . . that the locked casket I was seen carrying became a chest overflowing with rubies as big as apples and pearls that drooped on their chains. In fact, it contained nothing more than bread and cheese . . . a little malmsey too, God forgive me,' she added, crossing herself.

'So where are the jewels?' Frances's surprise made her blunt.

'Her Grace was a lady of great wisdom and foresight. She knew that the King would attempt to take the treasure she had bequeathed to their son and fritter it away on vanities and favourites. She knew, too, that if the prince managed to keep hold of his inheritance, it could prove deadly – there were riches enough to tempt even the most loyal of her son's attendants to turn traitor. So she determined to safeguard the jewels until such time as the prince had the power to use them for the good of our faith – in short, until he inherits the throne.'

Frances experienced a rush of affection for the late Queen, tinged with renewed grief at her passing. She had been a queen of secrets, outwitting those who sought to disempower her – her own husband above all. 'And they are safe still?' she asked quietly.

Lady Ruthven nodded. 'My late mistress and I resolved upon a plan as she lay dying at Hampton Court. When the time came for her possessions to be moved from the palace after her death, her servants would discover that the jewels were missing and the hue and cry would be raised. I would flee the kingdom – making sure that I was seen boarding a ship bound for Calais – and let people come to the natural conclusion that I had stolen them. The Queen personally arranged my protection in France – she had many friends here,' she added, her voice laced with pride. 'I trusted her with my life – just as she trusted you with it many years before, Lady Tyringham.'

Frances nodded her acknowledgement.

'Her Grace knew that her husband would send men to hunt me down, but that he would eventually relinquish the search. He has none of her steadfastness.' Her lips pursed with disapproval. 'I pledged to remain here until her son becomes king. Only then will I return and restore the jewels to him. Neither the Queen nor I had reckoned on his trying to recover them sooner.'

'It is with good reason,' Frances said, choosing her words carefully. 'The King's life depends upon it, Lady Ruthven.' She saw the fleeting shock in the older woman's eyes and pressed home her advantage. 'There are those about His Majesty who are intent upon forging an alliance with France through a marriage between the prince and King Louis's sister. They pretend to be acting to restore England to the Catholic faith, but their ambitions do not extend beyond their own aggrandisement, however it is attained.'

'You mean the Duke of Buckingham, I presume. I am not as ignorant of worldly affairs as my sisters here.'

'Yes, and he will stop at nothing to get what he desires. It seems the Marquis de Châteauneuf has promised him a share of the Queen's jewels if he brings about this alliance. Only the King stands in his way – he is reluctant to see his son married to a Roman Catholic. But the duke has proven many times in the past that he will not suffer any impediment to his ambition.'

Lady Ruthven grew pale. 'If what you say is true, Lady Tyringham, I cannot but think it is as the late Queen would have wished: her heretic husband removed from power and his kingdom restored to the true faith.'

'But at what cost? England would be subject to the will of a greater tyrant than King James. Buckingham does the devil's work, not God's. It would not be long before he coveted the throne itself. And if the late Queen's jewels fall into his hands, he will have the power to take it.'

'There is no reason to suppose they will,' Lady Ruthven persisted. 'I have lived here unmolested by the marquis or his spies for five years. I am safe in God's house.'

'Not for much longer,' Frances countered. 'A trusted friend has received intelligence that the marquis's agent will soon take you. Even if the jewels are not in your keeping, as you claim, he will wrest their whereabouts from you by whatever means.'

'I will never tell,' the older woman insisted, raising her chin in defiance, though her eyes betrayed her fear.

'A person might confess to anything under torture – I have learned that to my cost,' Frances said quietly, thinking back to that dark chamber in the Tower. 'Can you take the risk?' she added, holding her gaze. When the older woman made no reply, Frances decided to change tack. 'Lady Ruthven, by restoring the jewels to Prince Charles now, you will still be honouring your promise to the late Queen. Even if the King is saved from Buckingham's murderous schemes, he cannot draw breath for much longer. He is an old man and riddled with sickness. What difference will a few months make – less, perhaps?'

At length, the woman's expression changed. 'Very well,' she said. 'But I will recover the jewels myself, as I pledged.'

'Are they far from here?' Frances asked, remembering Lady Ruthven's earlier remark and fearing that by the time she had them and returned to England it would be too late.

Her companion gave a slow smile. 'They never left Hampton Court.'

Darkness had fallen by the time Frances stole out of the Abbaye du Saint-Benoit with Lady Ruthven, both shrouded in heavy cloaks. Felton was waiting with the horses close to the gatehouse, but hidden from view, as arranged. Frances had urged that they set out as soon as her conference with Lady Ruthven was at an end, but he had insisted upon waiting until nightfall.

They picked their way across the fields at a slow canter, guided only by the pale light of the moon. Frances held her breath as they passed each dark copse, certain that one of Châteauneuf's men lurked there. The sudden cawing of a rook made her cling more tightly to Felton's waist. He spurred the horse to a gallop, Lady Ruthven following close behind. It was less than an hour's ride to Calais, but every minute passed agonisingly slowly, the vast expanse of grassland that lay before them seeming to lengthen with every mile.

At last, the dark mass of the fortress came into view, its turreted keep gradually taking shape against the night sky. Frances drew heart from the glimmer of braziers that had been lit around the harbour. God willing, they would soon be aboard a boat that would carry them across the waters. She would gladly suffer any manner of seasickness to reach England's shores again.

As they came within half a league of the city walls, Felton slowed his horse to a trot. 'We must not draw undue attention,' he muttered.

Frances knew the wisdom of this, but it wore her patience even more. They had travelled only a short distance further when a distant rumble carried on the breeze. She felt her companion stiffen.

'Make haste!' he called to Lady Ruthven, as he dug his heels into the horse's sides. Frances saw her own panic reflected in the older woman's eyes before she was distracted by the dark outline of a rider in pursuit. He was gaining on them. They were tantalisingly close to Calais but the thunder of hoofs was now deafening, and a few seconds later the rider drew up alongside them.

'*Arrêtez-vous!*' he called, steering his horse dangerously close to theirs. Her terror intensified as she recognised the marquis's livery on the rider's saddle. Felton did not seem to heed him as he spurred their horse on. But, burdened by two riders, its head was beginning to droop. A few seconds more and their assailant would overtake them.

As he drew level with them again, the man reached over and grasped the reins from Felton. What happened next was so fast that Frances only realised once it was over. The rider stared, open-mouthed, then clutched his hand to his side. Frances watched in horror as blood seeped between his fingers. With a deft move, Felton took back the reins and slid the blade into its scabbard. The man looked down at his wound, his eyes rolled in their sockets and he slumped forward. As the reins went slack in his hand, his horse reared, jolting its rider off the saddle before bolting away. The man's foot had become entangled in the stirrup so he was pulled along behind the horse, his lifeless body jerking up and down with each stride. Only when the animal leaped over a low hedge near woodland was the rider thrown free.

They had reached the city walls now, but Frances could not wrest her eyes from those dark woods. Felton drew in the reins as he followed her gaze. 'He must make his peace with God now.'

CHAPTER 60

1 March

The chimneys of Hampton Court Palace were coming into view, the elaborately twisting brickwork silhouetted against the deep red sky. The sight made Frances spur on her horse once more. Her body was heavy with fatigue and every thud of its hoofs on the frozen turf made her bones ache anew.

They had ridden for three long days, pausing only to take their ease and bolt the simple food Felton procured from isolated farmsteads along the way. They had slept in the shelter of woodland – and, once, in the hayloft of a barn. Frances would never have believed how luxurious it would feel to bed down in the warmth of the hay, lulled to sleep by the snuffles and grunts of the animals below. Exhausted, she had slept as soundly as a child. It had only been during waking hours that the terror of what had happened outside Calais's walls returned to her. The image of the marquis's man lolling forward in his saddle, the trail of his blood, returned to her time and again. How long had it been before his battered, lifeless body had been discovered? As their tiny vessel had bobbed across the mercifully calm seas, every seagull's cry had sounded like the call of an official sent to arrest them. She had uttered a prayer of thanks when they had arrived at Dover, but she knew that the danger was far from over.

Felton had directed that they should ride across the South Downs, keeping to small, often treacherous, woodland tracks rather than following the main road that led from Dover to London. It would take longer but Frances knew he was right. She thought of Buckingham and the marquis at Whitehall, waiting for word of the jewels. Pray God they would not discover Lady Ruthven's flight until Frances and her companions had delivered them into the prince's hands.

She had reached the wide avenue that led towards the western entrance to the palace. Slowing her horse to a trot, she looked behind for her companions. Lady Ruthven was some distance away. The ride had been harder upon her than anyone. Living in seclusion for more than five years had sapped her strength, and many times Frances had seen her slumped against the horse's neck, Felton holding the reins of both horses so that they could keep going.

The letter of recommendation that the prince had given his servant was enough to secure their entry to the palace. Frances avoided the gatekeeper's curious stare as they passed. She saw Lady Ruthven pull her hood further across her face. The clatter of their horses' hoofs echoed across the huge, deserted courtyard beyond.

They mounted the stairs to the great hall. Stripped of the sumptuous Flemish tapestries that usually lined the walls, the close-packed tables and the dozens of braziers all aflame, the vast chamber seemed even more imposing. The rooms beyond were just as eerie, as if trapped in some enchantment. Lady Ruthven was leading the way now, and Frances quickened her pace to keep up. Veering left, they entered the gallery overlooking the chapel and descended the stairs that lay just beyond the Queen's privy closet.

The scraping of a latch broke the heavy silence. Frances saw Felton's hand fly to his scabbard. *Pray God he would not have cause to spill blood in this place.* A man dressed in priest's robes walked slowly from a chamber next to the altar. Following Lady

Ruthven's lead, Frances moved to the altar rail and sank to her knees in prayer. Felton hesitated, then did the same.

The chaplain showed little surprise at their coming, but uttered a quiet prayer of blessing, resting his hand upon each of their bowed heads in turn as he did so.

'Amen,' Lady Ruthven whispered, then slowly raised hers to look at him. Frances saw recognition in his eyes. 'Father Goodman.'

Queen Anne's private chaplain. Frances wondered that she had not realised before. She had seen him only once, fleetingly, as he had attended his dying mistress. It was no secret that the King despised the 'papist preacher', and Frances had assumed that after Anne's death he had either lived in obscurity or fled to the Continent, along with many other disaffected Catholics.

'I had thought the tread of footsteps belonged to more travellers. They call here now and again, in search of nourishment – spiritual or otherwise.' There was a smile in his voice. 'These are your friends, Lady Ruthven?'

Frances looked up at him now. Although he was still smiling, she saw that he was scrutinising her.

'They are *trusted* friends, Father.'

He slowly inclined his head. 'So the time has come. The King is . . .?'

'No – at least, we pray not yet,' Lady Ruthven replied. 'But his life is in grave danger from those who would claim the late Queen's treasure for their wicked ends. I must deliver it into the hands of the prince before it is too late.'

The chaplain glanced at her companions. 'May we speak alone, Lady Ruthven?'

The older woman nodded to them both. Frances rose to her feet at once, but Felton made no move. 'Please.' Lady Ruthven laid her hand on his arm. 'A few moments only.' He stood and followed Frances out of the chapel, staring resentfully over his shoulder at Father Goodman.

Neither of them spoke as they waited in the gathering gloom. Frances shivered as a chill breeze whipped along the passage. It would be another cold night, but she knew they would not be able to rest on their way to Theobalds if the jewels were in their possession.

If.

Even though they had reached Hampton Court without discovery, the prospect of leaving with the prize they had risked so much to gain seemed somehow more distant than ever. *Had Lady Ruthven tricked them? Or Father Goodman? Perhaps he had sold the jewels years ago, as soon as the Queen's beloved servant had left Hampton Court.*

Felton gave an impatient sigh and began to pace up and down. 'What the devil is taking so long?'

At last, the door to the chapel opened and Lady Ruthven was on the threshold. 'Come,' she said quietly, beckoning them back in.

'Do you have them?' Felton demanded.

But Lady Ruthven had swept out of sight. Frances and her companion swiftly followed. She led them back to the altar, where the chaplain was waiting. Frances's eyes darted to a casket that had been placed in the centre of the altar cloth.

'He wishes to bless us, to ask for God's protection.'

Felton grunted but knelt by the rail once more. When the chaplain had finished, Frances made the sign of the cross over her breast. 'Amen.' She watched as he handed Lady Ruthven the casket.

'Unlock it,' Felton barked. 'It might be filled with stones, for all I know.'

Lady Ruthven looked at him sharply but did so. The jewels glittered in the light from the candles. The casket was full to the brim with precious gems – rubies, emeralds and diamonds, as well as strings of creamy pearls and brooches studded with sapphires. Frances blinked back tears as she recognised several and prayed this was not a dream, that she would not open her eyes to realise she had slipped into an exhausted sleep while riding towards the palace. *No.* Everything they had risked had been worth it. Buckingham's schemes would be thwarted at last.

'May these jewels perform God's work, as Her Grace willed it,' Father Goodman said softly.

The journey to Hertfordshire seemed to last an eternity. Guided only by the fragile light of the stars, they were obliged to ride at a slow plod as their horses picked their way through the thickets of woodland and along the edge of fields. For the first few miles, they stayed close to the curving path by the river, passing the old palace of Richmond. Frances swallowed her grief as she thought of the night, almost exactly fifteen years before, when her father had gasped out his breath, imploring her to stay true to their faith. It warmed her heart to think that he would have been proud of what she had done – what she must yet do.

The pale light of dawn was gathering as they reached the edge of the woods that surrounded the vast estate. Following the line of the red-brick wall that marked its outer reaches, they spurred their horses to a canter. Every now and then, Frances glimpsed the turrets of Theobalds Palace through the trees. Built by Queen Elizabeth's most trusted adviser, Lord Burghley, it had been bequeathed to his son – Frances's old adversary, Robert Cecil. He had entertained the King there upon James's arrival in England and numerous times after that. The King had become so fond of the place that Cecil had eventually been obliged to give it to him, in exchange for Hatfield House. It had hardly been a fair bargain, Frances thought, as she looked across the beautifully manicured lawns and neatly kept beds laden with all manner of plants and herbs. The heady scent of marjoram and feverfew carried on the breeze. Frances felt her fingers twitch as she imagined plucking the treasures of the garden, which had been laid out by John Gerard. She still had his *Great Herbal* in her mother's library at Longford, its pages worn with age and use.

The gatehouse was as big as a castle, the house beyond it grander than any Frances had seen. Little wonder the King had coveted it. At the far end, a high turret rose up towards the clouds and a soft light glowed from the large windows on the upper floor. Frances guessed that this was the King's chamber – certainly it must command the finest views of any in the palace. The prince's apartments would be close to it.

Felton drew on the reins as they reached the gatehouse and nodded at the two yeomen, who were dressed in the King's bright livery. Dismounting, he muttered something to them, gesturing towards Frances and Lady Ruthven. Frances climbed down from her saddle, wincing at the stiffness in her joints, then helped the older woman. She took care to obscure the guards' view of Lady Ruthven as she concealed the jewels behind the fur muffler she carried. They summoned a young servant, who scurried into the hall with word of their arrival.

At length, the page returned and nodded to the yeomen, who lifted their halberds so that Felton and the two ladies could progress through the gatehouse. The crunch of the gravel underfoot seemed deafening in the silence of the long courtyard that led up to the main house. As they approached the heavy oak door, it was opened by a groom Frances recognised from Whitehall.

'Will you take some refreshment? The prince has not yet risen.'

'No,' Felton replied gruffly. 'My orders were to attend him as soon as we arrived.'

The man sniffed, then motioned for the page to escort them. Frances hardly noticed the exquisitely woven tapestries or gilded carvings that adorned the walls as they walked briskly through a series of vast rooms, each more richly decorated than the last. They must be near the turret now, Frances calculated, as she glanced out across the gardens.

Sure enough, the page slowed his steps and paused outside a door towards the end of the corridor. He knocked softly on it, then slipped inside. Frances stole a glance at Lady Ruthven as they heard the boy whisper something inaudible. He reappeared and nodded for them to enter, then ran off back down the corridor.

The chamber was so dimly lit that at first Frances could not see anyone within. Then a figure rose slowly from a chair in the corner. Frances heard a bolt slide shut behind them as he turned, a smile of welcome on his face.

Buckingham.

CHAPTER 61

2 March

'Ladies.' Frances watched, horror-struck, as the duke swept an elaborate bow. 'Lucky you brought this . . . *gentleman* with you or your reputations would have been quite ruined by visiting my chambers at this hour. Why, I am barely dressed,' he added, brushing at the folds of his richly embroidered nightgown. He strolled to the dresser and poured a large glass of wine. 'Forgive me – would you care for some? I do so hate to drink alone, especially when there is such cause for celebration.'

Frances bit the inside of her cheeks as she glared at him.

'No? As you wish.' He swallowed a long draught. 'You are looking at me in amazement, Lady Tyringham! Anyone would think you did not expect to find me here, yet where else would I be but by my master's side?'

'The King left you to manage his affairs at Whitehall.' Her voice was as hard as flint.

'You are quite right, as always, my lady, but I knew that His Majesty could never bear to be parted from his angel for long, so I saved him the trouble of summoning me. It is as well I came – he has sickened for want of me.'

Frances felt a shudder of apprehension. *Had he poisoned the King already?*

'Oh, there is no need to fear – he is much improved now. My presence helped, of course, and I had my wife bring our physician from Tyringham, just in case. Dr Lambe was full of the wonders of your old herb garden, Lady Tyringham.' He smiled. 'He has been able to prepare all manner of potions and salves.'

Frances felt as if she might vomit. The idea that the plants she had so carefully cultivated should be put to such evil use was too much to bear. 'You are sure His Grace is out of danger?' she demanded.

'Yes – for now, at least,' the duke purred. 'But stubbornness can stir such foul humours, so my physician is on hand to administer his cures if it persists.'

It was just as she and Bacon had predicted. Buckingham meant to poison the King if he did not agree to the French alliance.

'Well now, God has clearly smiled upon my endeavours in coming here, for He has made sure that I was able to greet you when you arrived. Tell me, how was the journey from Calais, Lady Ruthven?'

'The devil take you!' Felton growled, stepping forward. He made to draw his sword but the duke was there before him. Quick as a snake, he pulled a dagger from the pocket of his gown and held it to the man's throat 'Be still, *dog*,' he sneered. A droplet of blood trickled down Felton's throat as Buckingham pressed the blade into his skin. 'Now, should we dispense with these niceties?'

As Felton struggled to free himself, Frances saw his eyes alight upon something at the back of the room. She turned to see the Marquis de Châteauneuf flanked by two thickset men. They must have been hiding in the shadows. The envoy's smile flashed white in the gloom. Following her gaze, Lady Ruthven's hands tightened on the casket.

'I must say, it is very good of you to save me the journey, Lady Ruthven. When His Excellency told me that his man had been foully murdered, I had a mind to come and find you myself. How surprised the King will be to learn of your presence. He will scarce believe that the woman who flouted his banishment years ago, then fled with his wife's jewels has now been found . . . but without the treasure. He can only conclude that you sated your greed by selling it all.' Lady Ruthven flinched as one of the marquis's men took a step closer. 'I wonder which punishment he will choose? The gallows will be far too good for you.'

'And what of you, Lady Tyringham? You have been unusually silent on the matter. Did you hope to win a share of the jewels and restore your husband's pathetic fortune? One of the small trinkets would have been more than enough for that. Tyringham Hall could fit inside the stables here,' he scoffed. 'Though it is quaint enough, I suppose, and Kate has developed a fondness for the place. Well, she can return there for as long as she wishes now.'

'You should not judge others by your morals, Your *Grace*.' She took a step towards him. 'The only reward I sought was to rid this kingdom of evil . . . to rid it of you.'

Buckingham affected a wounded expression. 'Come now, my lady. Your passions were as stirred as mine by our little encounter in Hyde Park. I have thought of it often since. No wonder your husband looks as sullen as the King's dogs whenever he is apart from you.'

Frances's hand itched to slap him but his blade was still pressed to Felton's neck.

'Neither have I forgotten the matter we spoke of,' he went on. 'That should be enough to buy your silence about the jewels, once the marquis and I have reclaimed them.'

Frances imagined seizing the dagger and plunging it deep into his heart. The desire to see the blood spurt from his chest was overwhelming, visceral.

The marquis gave a small cough, prompting.

'Forgive these petty squabbles, Monseigneur,' the duke said. 'Now, Lady Ruthven, it is time to relinquish the burden you have carried all these years.' He nodded to one of the marquis's men, who seized the woman's shoulders. As she tried to struggle from his grasp, the casket fell to the floor, its contents spilling out. A shard of light glimmered through the shutters, illuminating the glittering haul.

The corners of the duke's mouth curled into a lazy smile. He gazed down at the treasure for a long moment, then motioned for the other man to gather it back into the casket.

A movement over Buckingham's shoulder drew Frances's gaze. The marquis had seen it too. His face paled as he stared.

'How dare you lay hands upon my jewels?'

The prince was standing on the threshold of Kate's chamber, which adjoined the duke's. Buckingham's eyes narrowed as he saw his wife step from behind Charles, her gaze lowered. *She had gone to warn the prince*, Frances realised, her heart surging with admiration for her friend.

Seizing his chance, Felton whipped the knife from Buckingham's grasp and held it to his neck. Frances heard Kate make a small cry when she saw this swift reversal. The prince gave her a brief smile of reassurance and they stepped into the room, followed by four yeomen.

'Give them to me,' he commanded.

The marquis's man looked towards his master, who gave the smallest of nods. Charles took the casket from him and looked down at it for a moment, then closed his eyes and mouthed a silent prayer of thanks.

'My mother bequeathed these to me so that I could use them to do God's will,' he began, looking from Buckingham to the marquis. 'You would have used them to do the devil's work. I thank God that He put an end to your wicked schemes.'

'No, Your Grace,' Buckingham urged. 'It was in God's name that I acted. Through this alliance, England will be saved from heresy. When you are king and married to the French King's sister – a princess of the true faith – you will restore us to the Catholic fold. This treasure will give you the means to crush all resistance.'

The prince faced him. 'You speak treason, sir,' he said quietly. 'My father is king, yet you anticipate his death. What makes you

so certain it is imminent?' He let the question hang in the air.
'You speak heresy, too. His Majesty established the reformed faith
as the one true religion. Anyone who veers from that, or seeks to
make this kingdom a vassal of Rome, is a traitor to the state.'

'But I thought . . .' the duke began, staring at the prince in
consternation. 'Your enthusiasm for this match – and that with
the infanta – led me to believe—'

'That I was a papist too?' The prince glanced at Frances, who
smiled her acquiescence. Charles was right not to trust Buckingham
with the knowledge of his private faith.

'I was doing God's will,' the duke repeated, in rising agitation.

'No, my lord duke. You descended to Hell years ago. You were
damned from the moment you began to seek power, riches,' he
said, holding up his mother's casket.

'She is the sinner, not me,' Buckingham cried, pointing a trembling finger at Frances. 'Her allegiance to the old faith was once
so strong that she involved herself in the plot to blow your father
and Parliament to the heavens.'

His words echoed into silence. Frances saw the prince grow
pale as he stared at Buckingham before turning his eyes to her.
Next to him, Kate looked as if she might faint.

'Does he speak truth, Lady Frances?'

She thought of protesting a denial, of railing against the duke
for voicing such slander. But instead, she remained silent.

'If she will not confess, then I will do it for her.' Buckingham's
voice rose in triumph. 'She even birthed the bastard of Tom
Wintour. George Tyringham is not Sir Thomas's boy, but the son
of a traitor.'

Frances closed her eyes. She could not bear to see the shock in
the prince's eyes, Kate's too, the revulsion that would soon follow.
Neither could she stomach the triumph in Buckingham's. An
image of George came before her, his eyes filled with love as he
bade her and Thomas farewell. Then he was a boy again, in the
saddle as his beloved papa led his horse around the stable-yard.
And now he was a baby cradled in her arms as she rocked him to

sleep in her bed at Tyringham Hall. Now that the duke had betrayed her secret, George's life would be blighted for ever.

Tears streamed down her cheeks as she faced the prince at last. He returned her gaze, not with disgust but pity. 'Leave this place,' he said. Frances lowered her eyes to the floor, then made to walk away but Charles rested his hand upon her arm. 'My lord duke,' he said, more firmly this time. 'Leave this place at once. Go far from here, before I change my mind.'

'Your Grace!' Felton objected, but his master raised a hand to silence him.

'My father's health is too fragile to suffer the shock of your arrest – for now, at least. I will tell him your mother has taken ill and begs your presence. You will not return here – and neither will you, Monseigneur,' he said, turning to Châteauneuf. 'The King is already tired of your presence and shows no greater inclination towards this alliance than he did when you first arrived. Tell your master he may send a different emissary, in time.'

'This is *all*? You have accused me of all manner of crimes. Surely you would see me damned to Hell.' Buckingham sneered. 'And what of *her*? She is the real traitor in our midst. Are you going to set her free too?'

Frances forced herself to hold the prince's steady gaze as he turned to her. 'I have heard nothing but calumny and lies from you, Buckingham,' he said, still looking at Frances. 'Lady Tyringham has been more greatly wronged by you than I or anyone else – your poor wife excepted, perhaps.' Kate flushed and lowered her eyes to the floor again. 'They may choose to forgive you, but God never will. You have spoken with the tongue of the devil. George Tyringham was my childhood companion, appointed to serve me by the late Queen. If you slander him as the son of a traitor, you slander my mother's memory – and call my father's judgement into question too. That is not something he will easily overlook – even from you.'

Frances heard the bolt slide back as the marquis and his men slipped away. Felton pressed the blade against Buckingham's flesh as his master took a step closer. 'Now, go,' the prince whispered. His servant reluctantly lowered the knife.

'May I at least dress first?' the duke drawled, with a lazy smile.

'Your mother will have clothes enough for you,' Charles retorted. 'Do not wear my patience too thin. My guards will escort you from the estate. I do not wish to look upon you a moment longer.'

Buckingham's smile broadened as he swept a deep bow, then strutted from the room, the four yeomen following close behind.

'Forgive me, Your Grace, but was that wise? That villain would have murdered the King, stolen the late Queen's jewels. He is as deadly as a serpent – more so, now that he is out of your grasp.'

Charles smiled and patted Felton's arm. 'You have ever been a loyal servant, John. I will make sure you are rewarded richly for your pains – yes, even though you protest,' he added. 'But you must trust me in this. I am not so foolish – or so forgiving – as you suppose. I spoke truth when I said that I do not wish to see my father vexed at such a time. He is dying.' The prince turned anguished eyes to Frances. 'The very thing that we tried to prevent by staying an earthly hand has been inflicted by a heavenly one. My father will not leave this place alive.' He struggled to master himself.

'I am sorry, Your Grace,' she replied, with genuine feeling. Despite everything she had suffered at the King's hands, she could not but share his son's sorrow.

'You must rest assured – all of you – that when I am king, I will suck the lifeblood from Buckingham, just as he meant to suck my father's from him. Not by violent means,' he insisted, catching Felton's expression, 'but by gradually depriving him of his power. That is what drives him, even more than riches. I will see him suffer the torment of knowing he will never claw back what he has lost.'

Frances knew the prince was right and admired his perception. Being stripped of his influence would be a greater torture than anything that the Tower gaolers could inflict upon the duke. Yet still she felt that gnawing, almost primeval desire for revenge. She would pray that God might forgive her – that, in time, He might lead her down a more righteous path.

'I must go to my father now,' Charles said, interrupting her thoughts.

Frances and Kate dropped a deep curtsy as he walked from the room. Left alone with her old friend, Frances felt suddenly afraid. *Had she believed her husband's words?* She had imagined the horror in Kate's eyes as he had spoken them. If so, she could surely never forgive her.

Frances was startled by the warmth of Kate's hand in hers. She looked up and saw that her friend was smiling. 'I have missed you, Frances,' she whispered.

CHAPTER 62

27 March

'Is your wife here, Tom?'

'She is, Your Grace,' Thomas replied. He led Frances to his master's bedside and she lowered herself onto the chair. Her husband had been shocked at hearing of her voyage to France, of everything that had passed since then. But his anger at the risk she had taken had soon been replaced by admiration for her courage – then joy and gratitude for the outcome. Any hurt he had felt at her concealing it from him had dissipated when the prince had told him how he had ordered her to say nothing of it, even to him.

At first, the King had bemoaned his favourite's absence, but the constant steady presence of his son had soothed him, as had that of his master of the buckhounds. Frances had thrilled to see how, freed from the duke's corrupting influence, James's esteem for her husband had flourished once more. He had asked for him constantly these past three weeks.

He had asked for Frances, too. When she had first been summoned to attend the dying King, she had refused, fearing it was a trick. But the prince had convinced her that his father's request was genuine – that he knew of no one else who might ease his suffering. The irony was not lost on her that a king who had spent so much of his life hunting down witches had summoned one to attend him in his final days.

'I have brought more of the tincture, Your Grace,' she said now, pouring a little of the mixture into a glass and diluting it with water. 'The gardens here have kept me supplied with all manner of precious herbs.'

'Thankee, Lady Tyringham,' James said, as he swallowed a little of the medicine. His chest jerked as he gave a short, sputtering cough that left him gasping for breath. 'But I fear I am beyond your skills now.'

Frances did not reply as she busied herself with preparing a salve to rub onto the King's chest. It had eased his ragged breathing during the past few nights and enabled him to sleep, albeit fitfully. Stealing a glance at his face – the pallid, yellowish skin that clung to his cheekbones – she knew it could not be long.

'I think I will take a little sleep now,' he rasped. 'But first I must ask something of thee.' He clutched her hand so suddenly that it startled her. 'Forgive me, Lady Tyringham.'

She gazed down at him in disbelief.

'Forgive me,' he repeated.

She looked up at Thomas, whose expression was unreadable. *He wants it to be my choice.* After another moment's hesitation, she pressed her lips to the King's cold fingers.

'Thankee,' he whispered, then closed his eyes.

Frances took Thomas's hand and rose from the chair. They both made their obeisance to the prince, who had barely left his father's side since the confrontation with Buckingham. When they reached the door, she looked back at the sleeping King, her eyes brimming with tears.

'How my bones ache,' Frances remarked, as she climbed down from the carriage.

'I will have Mrs Knyvett draw a bath for you,' Thomas said, with a smile.

Frances savoured the warmth of his kiss, then looped her arm through his as they made their way across the courtyard. Looking at the windows of the great hall, she saw they had already been swathed in black cloth. Theobalds lay only half a day's ride from Whitehall – less for an accomplished rider – so news of the King's death would have been quick to arrive.

He had breathed his last barely an hour after she and Thomas had left his chamber that day. The prince – King Charles, as she must get used to calling him – had told them that his father had not spoken again after begging Frances's forgiveness. She felt genuinely grieved at his death – at peace, too, now that the hatred and anger that had gnawed away at her for so many years had crumbled into dust. Perhaps she might soon find it in her heart to forgive Buckingham, too. *No, she was not ready for that yet.*

'We will stay here only until the funeral, won't we?' Frances asked.

'I would not have expected you to be so eager to sit in a carriage again so soon,' her husband teased. 'But, yes, His Grace has granted us leave to enjoy our newly restored estate.'

The new King had been quick to honour his word. At his insistence, Buckingham had been obliged to sell Tyringham Hall back to its original owner at a vastly reduced price. Thomas and Frances could have afforded a dozen such estates with the money Charles had granted them. Kate had already started to make arrangements for the removal of her furnishings. Frances smiled to think that their sons would soon be making their way there from Longford, her mother with them. She had written to George, asking that he might relinquish his studies for a week or so to join them.

As they passed under the archway that led through to the next courtyard, Frances felt her husband's arm stiffen. Following his gaze, she saw the duke strolling nonchalantly in their direction.

'Welcome back to court, Sir Thomas – Lady Tyringham,' he said, then waited for them to make their obeisance. Neither did. After a short, stony silence, Thomas swept past him, Frances following close behind. She knew that he was watching them as they hastened towards their apartment.

'I did not think to see him back here so soon,' Frances muttered, once they were out of earshot.

'Nor I,' Thomas agreed, his words clipped. 'He can hope for little at the King's hands.'

Frances nodded. Charles's dealings with Buckingham over the Tyringham estate had made clear that he would not enjoy the same favour he had in his father's time. She hoped that the new King would soon make good his threat to strip the duke of his offices and titles.

She tried to shake away thoughts of him as they neared the door to their apartment, anticipating the familiar peace and repose that the cosy chambers offered.

'Mother.'

She stared, astonished, at the sight of her eldest son sitting by the fireplace.

'George!' Her smile faltered as she saw his grim expression. He rose to his feet as Thomas went to greet him.

'Sir Thomas.' George waited for them to feel the impact of his words. 'I cannot call you Papa – in truth, I never should have, should I?'

'George, I—' Thomas began, but the young man raised a hand to silence him.

'I will hear no more of your lies – or yours, madam,' he snapped. 'I wish that I no longer had to call you Mother either.'

'You will not speak to your mother like that,' Thomas reprimanded him. 'Whatever has caused this ill humour, we will overlook it as being out of character – the result, perhaps, of too much waywardness in Cambridge.'

'On the contrary, Sir Thomas,' George said, 'I have been a most diligent student and my thoughts have never been so ordered . . . thanks to the duke.'

Buckingham. Frances had known it as soon as she had laid eyes upon her son.

'I received his letter yesterday,' her son continued. 'He was most insistent that I visit him here. My master objected, of course, but I could hardly refuse the duke after his many kindnesses to me. Besides, I was eager to renew our acquaintance. How glad I am that I did, else I would have lived the rest of my life in ignorance.'

'George, listen—'

'No, Mother, *you* listen!' Frances was taken aback by the hatred that flashed in his eyes. 'My father is not this *fine* gentleman here, but a notorious traitor. Were you ever going to tell me that my name should be Wintour, not Tyringham?'

Frances opened her mouth to speak, but her throat tightened over the words.

'You pretend to such virtue, yet you are no better than a whore of Satan.'

Thomas stepped forward then and slapped him across the face before Frances could stop him. Her son put his hand to his reddening cheek, his eyes blazing with fury.

'You have ruined my life,' George spat, his voice rising. 'How will I ever thrive, knowing what I am? If you had not succumbed to your wicked, selfish lust, I would never have come into existence – I pray God that I had not!'

He turned from them then, and Frances could see his shoulders heave. She reached out a tentative hand to comfort him, but he shook her off.

'Goodbye, Mother – Sir Thomas,' he said, still staring at the door. 'You will not lay eyes upon me again.'

Frances stood frozen in horror and watched as her son swept from the apartment. As his rapid footsteps echoed into silence, her legs buckled underneath her and she fell to the floor.

23 August 1628

Frances pressed her forehead to the glass, relishing the momentary coolness. The sultry heat from the late-afternoon sun hung over Whitehall like a shroud, sapping her of energy. In the courtyard below, she could see one of the palace dogs slumped in the shade of a wall. It seemed many hours since she and Kate had been obliged to retreat to Buckingham's apartment, abandoning their walk in the privy garden.

'Perhaps we might play a round of Primero,' Kate suggested, her voice flat and listless.

Frances looked at her. Her face was flushed and a fan lay discarded on her lap. With a smile, Frances set down the book she had been holding. *A History of Life and Death* had been Bacon's last gift to her. It was not his finest work, but she treasured it nonetheless. More than two years had passed since his death, but she still missed him sorely.

'I wonder if the fleet is assembled yet,' Kate murmured, as she pretended to focus on the cards she had been dealt.

Frances kept her expression neutral. The duke had travelled to Portsmouth three weeks earlier on the premise of planning another expedition against the French – as if the voyage to Île de Ré had not been disastrous enough. His vainglorious enterprise had brought him and his wife to the brink of bankruptcy and left England at war with the Queen's native land. Charles had banished him from court, and had petitioned his brother-in-law for forgiveness. But King Louis had not been minded to accede, despite his sister's pleading.

'I do not imagine many men will rally to his cause,' she replied.

Kate nodded. Although she rarely spoke of her husband, Frances knew that she was not in ignorance of how deeply he was despised throughout the kingdom for his overweening arrogance and lust for power, which had become ever more frenzied as he had felt it slipping from his grasp. Rumours that he had had the old King poisoned by Dr Lambe had been fanned by Charles's refusal to comment upon the matter. Soon the physician had become as reviled as his patron.

Lambe had courted further scandal the previous year when there had been reports that he had raped a young girl in the Countess of Buckingham's household. Furious that he had yet again escaped justice, an angry mob had set upon him when he next appeared in London, stoning him to death. The King had pardoned all those who had taken part.

'I am glad Sir Thomas was not obliged to accompany him,' Kate remarked.

'As am I,' Frances replied. Daily, she rejoiced that her husband had risen so high in the King's favour. Charles was not as fond of hunting as his late father had been, so instead he had appointed Thomas to serve in his bedchamber, alongside others who had proven their faith. Among them was Lord Rutland, and it gladdened Frances to see how close he had grown to his daughter once more – though he took care to avoid her husband.

Frances, too, had thrived in the new reign. Her invitation to serve the Queen had been quick to arrive. She had been glad to accept, particularly as Kate had been offered a position too. Henrietta Maria was a pleasant, rather shy young woman, who had soon won favour with her new courtiers – Frances included. She had none of Queen Anne's political guile or shrewdness, but perhaps that was as well, Frances thought. She had shown enough discernment to resist the Countess of Buckingham's persistent flattery and deny her a position in her household. The countess had left for her Brooksby estate in high dudgeon.

Frances and Kate had enjoyed many hours sewing and conversing with their young mistress. When none of the other ladies were present, they would even hear mass in the Queen's privy closet. Frances smiled to think of how this would have warmed Anne's heart if she had known. Her dying wish had been fulfilled beyond anything she could have expected.

Thomas's new duties were hardly onerous – certainly not enough to justify the salary, which was one of the most lucrative in the entire household. He had talked of buying a new estate, but his joy at reclaiming Tyringham Hall was still as fresh as it had been three years before, and there was nowhere else that he and Frances wished to spend their time when they were granted leave from court. Such occasions were frequent now. Secure in the King and Queen's esteem, she and her husband spent more than half the year in Buckinghamshire. She delighted in seeing their sons grow. John was fifteen now, Robert only two years behind. Both had matured into fine young men, full of promise. At ten, William had lost his wilder tendencies, but his younger brother Samuel more than compensated for him in mischief.

A snuffling sound drew the women's attention to the ornate cradle at the far end of the room. Frances watched as Kate padded across the room to gaze at her infant son with a rapt expression.

'Hush, Georgie.' She stroked his downy hair.

The boy was almost seven months old now. He had been conceived in violence, but slipped from his mother's womb as mildly as a lamb. Frances had witnessed the profound change that his arrival had wrought in her friend. Kate now bore herself with greater confidence and seemed more resilient to her husband's taunts and cruelty, which had hardly abated since she had given him a son and heir. Although she still doted upon her daughter, the pride she took in her firstborn son was obvious for all to see.

Frances's smile faded as she thought of her own son George. He had returned to Cambridge straight after that terrible encounter in their apartment at Whitehall. It still made her heart contract with pain, though the wounds had begun to heal. She had not seen him for many months afterwards, and her letters had gone unanswered. She had resolved to visit him in Cambridge, but Thomas had advised against it, saying that he would go there first.

It had been the first step on the long road to reconciliation. George's relationship with her husband had healed more quickly than with her. Still he could not bring himself to call Thomas 'Papa', but she hoped that would soon come. When at last she had seen him, there had been no recriminations, only pain, deep and visceral. He had hugged her fiercely when they had parted, but the next time they met he had been cold and distant. She prayed constantly that God would turn his pain into love, his anger into forgiveness.

'I thank God poor Mal will no longer be burdened with our estates,' Kate said, still gazing at the baby. 'Such a thing is a curse for a woman – as I found. Sons are such a blessing, are they not?'

Frances began to reply but her throat closed over the words. Kate flushed a deeper red. 'Forgive me, Fran. I . . .' She moved to embrace her. 'He will soon be restored to you,' she whispered.

The King had promised to appoint George to his service as soon as his studies were at an end. She was more grateful for this than the many other bounties they had received at his hands. It signalled his complete disregard for what Buckingham had told him of her son's father. Several times, she had heard Charles speak favourably of his former childhood companion. She knew this was for the benefit of the courtiers who might otherwise be inclined to listen to the duke's slanders.

A soft knock on the door interrupted her thoughts. Kate went to answer it.

'Your Grace.' She curtsied as the King entered the room, closely followed by Thomas.

Frances exchanged a glance with her husband before she made her obeisance. He was grim-faced but his eyes seemed to exude something like triumph.

'Please.' The King gestured for the two women to be seated.

'My lady duchess, I bring grave news,' he began quietly. 'A messenger has just arrived from Portsmouth. You must prepare yourself,' he said, taking her hand in his. 'The duke your husband has been murdered.'

Frances held herself perfectly still. She was vaguely aware that Thomas had come to stand behind her and felt the warmth of his hands on her shoulders. Kate was looking steadily up at the King, her fingers resting lightly on his outstretched hand.

'*Murdered?*' Her voice was barely a whisper.

Slowly, Charles released her hand and drew up a chair close to hers. 'Forgive me . . . Katherine. This is a terrible shock for you. Perhaps Lady Frances could bring something for your ease.'

'No,' Kate said firmly, before her friend could respond. Beneath her composure, Frances knew that, like herself, she was shaken to the core. *Buckingham dead?* It could not be true. He had blighted their lives for so many years that she had come to believe they would always be enslaved to him, that his was an evil even God could not vanquish. His declining fortunes in the new reign had only made him seem more deadly: Frances had known he would stop at nothing to regain his former dominance.

'Tell me what happened, Your Grace.'

Kate's words interrupted her racing thoughts.

The King took a breath. 'The duke's late expedition against France excited widespread opposition in this kingdom and left us with a war that we neither want nor can afford. It also made some dangerous enemies for your husband among my militia. It seems that one officer decided to act upon his grievance.'

Frances tried to swallow but it was as if she was being choked.

'He was lying in wait for the duke when he left his lodgings this morning,' he went on, his voice quiet but steady. 'Your husband was stabbed in the heart before he could defend himself. He died a few moments later.'

Frances pictured Buckingham's lifeless body slumped on the ground, his fine linen shirt steeped in blood. But it was soon replaced by an image of the duke as she had last seen him, mocking her and his wife with an ostentatious bow of farewell.

Kate ran her tongue along her lips, which were as pale and dry as stone. 'Who was it?'

Frances saw the King dart a look at Thomas before replying.

'John Felton.'

She had known the name before he spoke it. Kate's brow creased for a moment, then recognition dawned.

'The gentleman who was in attendance at Theobalds when . . .' Her words trailed off. Frances knew that she, too, was replaying that scene in her mind, Buckingham's dagger pressed to Felton's throat, the look of disbelief on the officer's face when his royal master let the duke walk free.

You must trust me in this.

Charles's words came to her now.

I am not so foolish – or so forgiving – as you suppose.

All at once Frances understood. The King had sanctioned this – ordered it, even. He had bided his time these past three years, waiting until the duke was so universally despised that nobody would think it amiss if an officer in his army decided to avenge Buckingham's many sins in an act of summary justice.

'What will become of him?' Frances asked, hoping that even now Felton was aboard a ship bound for the Continent, where he could live out his days in safe obscurity.

'He has already been arrested and brought to London.' Charles's face was ashen, his voice faltering. 'He did not attempt to flee. There was such confusion that he might easily have made his escape, as . . .'

As we had planned.

'But he remained there, steadfast, and was seized by one of the duke's men,' the King finished.

Her husband tightened his grip on her shoulders, as if willing her not to react. She stared at Charles in disbelief. Surely he would not see his faithful servant hanged for carrying out his wishes. The look on his face made her blood run cold, despite the stifling heat of the chamber. At that moment, she knew. Felton had knowingly surrendered his own life to end Buckingham's. Frances understood that, as a man of conscience, he could not have hidden from his crime as the King had no doubt urged him. Tears sprang to her eyes and she saw that Kate, too, was struggling to master her emotions.

'I will leave you to your grief,' the King said softly, resting his hand lightly on Kate's arm as he rose. 'But, please, draw comfort from the knowledge that I will always protect and support you – your children too,' he added, glancing at the cradle.

As if prompted, the baby gave a small, fretful cry. Kate was on her feet at once. She swept a deep curtsy as the King and Thomas made to depart. Frances's eyes met her husband's briefly before he bent to kiss her hand, then followed his royal master from the room.

The sound of the door closing echoed into silence. Frances watched as Kate rearranged her son's coverlet, then walked slowly back to her. Tears were streaming down their faces as they gazed at each other. *It was over.*

'Felton cannot be pardoned, can he?' Kate murmured. 'Even though he was carrying out the King's wishes – the nation's too.'

Frances stroked a stray tendril of hair that was clinging to her friend's cheek. 'May God preserve him – in the next life, if not in this,' she said, then moved to embrace her.

'Let us pray for him – and for my husband's soul,' Kate said, when at last her sobs had subsided.

Frances stared at her friend, humbled by her goodness and mercy. Then they sank to their knees and closed their eyes. As Kate began to murmur the words of the prayer, imploring God to forgive her husband's manifold sins, Frances was filled with a profound sense of peace, such as she had not experienced since coming to court. She closed her eyes and mouthed her thanks, for she knew, with a searing certainty, that the old King's angel had fallen into Hell.

Acknowledgements

With each of the novels in this trilogy, my debt of gratitude to my wonderful editor, Nick Sayers, increases. He has been a gentle, steady source of guidance and inspiration throughout and has been a joy to work with. I am also deeply thankful to my amazing agent, Julian Alexander, for all of his insights and wisdom, both in shaping the book and helping me keep a sense of perspective. My US editor, George Gibson, has provided another steady hand on the tiller, and I am so grateful for his sage judgement and experience.

The supporting team at Hodder have, as ever, been fantastic. Hazel Orme has done another wonderful job with the copyedit, and Will Speed has designed a stunning cover. Huge thanks are again due to Becca Mundy and Caitriona Horne, as well as Amy Batley, and to John Mark Boling at Grove Atlantic. I have also been lucky enough to have the support of the Soho Agency, in particular the ever-efficient Ben Clark and Isabelle Wilson.

In researching the novel, I was able to draw upon the work of numerous scholars. These include Deborah Roil and Melita Thomas of *Tudor Times*, whose excellent *Tudor Book of the Garden* provided invaluable material on contemporary herbs and medicine. Benjamin Woolley vividly evokes Buckingham's character in *The King's Assassin* and also provides intriguing evidence that he may indeed have poisoned his royal master to death. Ronald Hutton is the author of several seminal works on the period in general and witchcraft in particular. His latest book, *The Witch*, is one of the finest. I am also deeply indebted to my fellow historians Alison Weir, Sarah Gristwood, Nicola Tallis and Kate Williams for their continued support and encouragement.

My research took me to a range of archives, libraries and historic sites, and I would like to extend particular thanks to the staff of The National Archives, The British Library, Calke Abbey and Historic Royal Palaces. I am also thankful to colleagues and members of Historic Royal Palaces who have been kind enough to read and give feedback on the other novels in this trilogy. I do hope they will enjoy this one too. I would particularly like to mention the Hampton Court legend that is Ian Franklin, whose knowledge of the palace and its residents is both encyclopaedic and inspirational. Also James Peacock, who alongside his duties at the palace finds time to run the wonderful Anne Boleyn Society. I value their support and friendship greatly.

As with all of my previous books, fiction and non-fiction, my friends and family have been fantastic throughout. Stephen Kuhrt was again the first person to read this novel (in weekly instalments, as before) and his wonderfully positive and timely feedback gave me the confidence to keep going – even on the days when sorting out my paperclips seemed a more alluring prospect. On the other side of the Atlantic, the enthusiastic feedback and encouragement of my friend and colleague Susan Mathieson has meant a great deal. I was chuffed to bits that my lovely friend and fellow Hull alumni Alice Burton chose *The King's Witch* as one of her all-time favourite novels and do hope she'll approve of this latest one.

Heartfelt thanks go to my parents for their steadfast support, which has extended beyond just childcare and now covers pet management. I am also deeply grateful to my sister Jayne for being such a cheerleader for my books and other work. Finally, huge thanks to my wonderful husband for all of his help and encouragement, and to my daughter for asking questions to which I rarely know the answer.

Author's note

As with the first two books of this trilogy, my narrative is based upon real events and characters. I have stayed as close to the known facts as possible, weaving in quotes from original sources where appropriate.

The last ten years of James I's reign were just as turbulent as those that had gone before. Although there was no repeat of the Gunpowder Plot or anything on that scale, the Catholic threat remained very real. The legislation introduced after 1605 had driven most Catholics underground but their networks were still strong. The prospect that Arbella Stuart might make fresh trouble, even from the Tower, remained potent until it was finally extinguished by her death in September 1615. She and her husband, William Seymour, had never seen each other again after he had fled to exile in Flanders four years earlier. He eventually returned to England and became a prominent opponent to James's son and successor, Charles.

International relations became increasingly fraught after 1619, when James's daughter Elizabeth and her husband Frederick, the Elector Palatine, rashly accepted the offer of the Bohemian crown. A league of Catholic forces, including those supplied by the King of Spain, was soon ranged against them. This put James in the difficult position of deciding between family loyalty and maintaining his fragile alliance with one of the most powerful monarchs in Europe.

Burdened by the cares of state and suffering from increasingly frequent bouts of ill health, James spent ever more time away from court on hunting expeditions or in the company of his favourites. Foremost among these was George Villiers, later Duke of Buckingham. My characterisation of him is inspired by contemporary descriptions. One of the most charismatic, sexually promiscuous and ruthless men of the age, his villainy was more real than imagined.

The second son of a sheep farmer and his beautiful but penniless wife Mary (with whom Buckingham had a close but stormy relationship), Buckingham enjoyed a meteoric rise to fortune thanks to the patronage of Sir John Graham, a gentleman of the King's privy chamber. Upon being introduced to the King at Apethorpe in August 1614, he made an immediate impression. Soon after their first meeting, James appointed Buckingham his cupbearer, which gave the new favourite frequent access to the royal presence. In April 1615, he was made gentleman of the bedchamber, knighted and given an annual pension of £1,000 (equivalent to around £135,000 today).

The flirtation between the King and Buckingham almost certainly developed into a sexual relationship – one that would dominate the rest of the reign. During the 1615 summer progress, they caused a scandal by sharing a bed. Although this did not necessarily imply physical intimacy, it was obvious to everyone that their relationship had entered a new phase and that Robert Carr had been supplanted as royal favourite.

In 1616, Carr and his wife Frances were arrested upon suspicion of having Carr's former servant, Sir Thomas Overbury poisoned. They were swiftly convicted and imprisoned in the Tower for the next six years. Although Buckingham appeared to play no part in it, he took full advantage of his rival's absence. He was always quick to capitalise upon the misfortune of others, even erstwhile allies such as Sir Francis Bacon.

Despite being passionately attached to Buckingham, the King expected him to take a wife, as all his high-ranking courtiers did. He had little cause for jealousy in his favourite's choice: Katherine Manners, a rather plain young woman whose attraction lay solely in the fact that she was heiress to the Earl of Rutland. Far from creating a rift between James and 'Steenie', the marriage made them even closer and the King doted upon the couple's four children.

Katherine gave every appearance of an adoring wife, and Buckingham seemed to love her, in his way. But, as I describe in the novel, his father-in-law, Lord Rutland, strongly opposed the match, and there is evidence that his youngest son died by Buckingham hand – or at least at his orders. Certainly, Buckingham had most to gain by the boy's death, given that the Rutland fortune subsequently passed to his wife Katherine. Joan Flower and her two daughters (known as the 'Belvoir witches') were convicted for bewitching both of Lord Rutland's sons to death. Joan died on her way to captivity in Lincoln, and Margaret and Philippa were hanged there in 1619.

Buckingham's protégé, the notorious astrologer-physician, John Lambe, was said to have used sorcery to further his patron's ambitions. Buckingham's favour with the King helped protect Lambe from conviction for witchcraft. He had narrowly escaped such a conviction in 1608, when he had been arrested for bewitching a Worcestershire gentleman. Within two weeks of his trial, forty people who had been present in the courtroom were dead. The true cause was probably gaol fever, but such was Lambe's reputation that he was transferred to London's King's Bench prison. It was during his time there that he met and became a protégé of Buckingham. Thereafter he was commonly known as 'the Duke's devil'. Lambe was also consulted by Buckingham's mother about her son's fate. He was said to have shown Mary in a glass the figure of a large man with a dagger who would murder her son.

In June 1623, Lambe was indicted for the rape of an eleven year old girl, but was pardoned and released a year later. Further charges of sorcery were raised against him in 1627, and in the same year he was examined by the College of Physicians and found to be ignorant of the practice of medicine. On 13 June 1628, Lambe was ambushed by an angry mob of Londoners, who stoned and clubbed him into unconsciousness. He died the following day.

Amidst all this villainy, there was a need for more sympathetic characters. Foremost among them is Sir Francis Bacon, the greatest philosopher and statesman of the age. He rose to prominence during the later years of Elizabeth I's reign but did not receive the hoped-for promotions until James came to the throne. He was immediately knighted and later made Lord Keeper, Attorney General and Lord High Chancellor. But Bacon's literary and philosophical genius was largely lost on the King, who made no attempt to defend him when he was charged with corruption in 1621 and thrown out of office. I have woven in as many details of Bacon's life and works into the narrative as possible, although the latter were so prolific that it was impossible to do justice to them all. As I have hinted, he may have been gay. He and his much younger wife Alice had no children and it was rumoured that she was unfaithful to him.

The other dominant character of both the Elizabethan and Jacobean age was Sir Walter Raleigh. A prisoner in the Tower since the early days of James's reign, he was released in 1616 to embark upon an expedition to Venezuela in search of the fabled El Dorado, City of Gold. His fleet finally set sail in June 1617 and after an arduous voyage it reached Guiana in November. During the expedition, a detachment of Raleigh's men attacked the Spanish outpost of St Thomé. This was against Raleigh's explicit orders and those of King James, who had made it a condition of Raleigh's release that he should avoid any hostilities against Spanish colonies or shipping. The notion that Raleigh plotted to ally with Spain and force James from the throne is fiction.

Upon Raleigh's return to England, the Spanish ambassador, Count Gondomar, demanded that Raleigh's death sentence be reinstated. James, who had never liked the famous adventurer, had no qualms about agreeing. Raleigh was arrested a few weeks earlier than I have it in the narrative, but his date of entry to the Tower was 10 August, as given. The scene of his execution is drawn from eyewitness accounts.

The period covered by this novel witnessed another notable death: that of Queen Anne. James and his wife had lived as virtual strangers after the birth of their short-lived last child, Sophia, in 1607. Anne spent most of her time at Greenwich Palace and Somerset House, which she renamed Denmark House after her native country. Her health deteriorated steadily and in late 1618, she fell seriously ill with consumption and dropsy while staying at Hampton Court Palace. Her devoted son Charles had his bed moved to an adjoining room and was by her side when she died on 2 March the following year. Anne was buried in Westminster Abbey, but her husband chose not to erect a tomb in her memory. Her jewels, which she bequeathed to Charles, were indeed worth a fortune, and it was rumoured that some of them were stolen by one of her ladies after her death.

Anne's son Charles continued to honour his mother's memory. As the sole surviving male heir, he was closely guarded and his activities strictly controlled. On 3 November 1616 he was created Prince of Wales in a lavish ceremony at Whitehall Palace. Naturally shy and physically weak since childhood, he nevertheless showed greater discernment than he is often given credit for. He seemed to be as in thrall to Buckingham as the King and signed his letters 'your constant, loving friend'. But there is evidence that he was not quite so beguiled as he appeared. The incident I refer to when the prince played a trick on Buckingham by soaking him with a jet of water from a fountain in Greenwich Park actually happened, much to the fury of both James and his favourite.

In 1623, Charles and Buckingham went on a covert expedition to Spain at the King's behest to negotiate the prince's marriage to the Catholic Infanta Maria, sister of King Philip IV. There is no hint that Buckingham was a closet Catholic, although his elder brother John made little secret that he was attached to the 'old faith'. They reached an agreement, but Charles was averse to the match and quickly repudiated it once he and Buckingham were back in England. The expedition had given the prince a taste of independence, which made his relations with the King increasingly strained. James also quarrelled with Buckingham and the scene in which they have a public spat upon his return is based upon original sources.

Only occasionally, in the interests of advancing the plot, have I strayed from the known chronology of events. The masque organised by Prince Charles took place on Twelfth Night 1618 rather than 28 March 1619, and the Marquis de Châteauneuf did not arrive as ambassador to England until 1629. In the narrative, Frances's eldest son George begins university at the age of eighteen, although it was more common for boys to attend when they were as young as fifteen or sixteen.

The character around whom I have woven the most fiction is my heroine, Frances. The contemporary records shed precious little light upon her life, but I have included the few details that have survived – notably her marriage to Sir Thomas Tyringham, the fact that they had a large family (as many as five sons and five daughters, according to one account) and that they settled at Sir Thomas's Buckinghamshire estate. Her husband retained the post of Master of the King's Buckhounds until the end of James's reign. Although little is known of his career, given how much of James's later years were spent hunting it is a reasonable assumption that he spent a great deal of time with his royal master and thereby wielded significant influence.

In September 1624, the King's health declined sharply. He had suffered from kidney problems and arthritis for years, and the latter now worsened. In his weakened state, by March the following year he had fallen prey to a fever, stroke and severe dysentery. There is no small irony in the fact that, having hunted witches for years, James called for the services of a wise woman on his deathbed. Her identity is not known, so I hope I can be forgiven the dramatic licence of having my heroine supply the role. I also borrowed some of Henry VIII's last words for James, whose final utterances are less well attested.

Buckingham had raced to Theobalds to be by his master's side. He insisted on ministering to the King himself, brushing aside the royal physicians. James's condition rapidly worsened and within a few days he was dead. By now, Buckingham was widely despised, so it is not surprising that rumours of poison quickly spread across the court. But the new king's apparent favour towards his late father's lover protected him, and for a while it seemed that Buckingham would come to dominate Charles as much as he had James. The ranks of his enemies continued to swell during the years that followed, however, and after leading a series of disastrous military expeditions, the King began to lose faith in him.

On 23 August 1628, Buckingham was stabbed to death by John Felton at the Greyhound pub in Portsmouth, where he had travelled to prepare for another ill-advised campaign. Felton was an army officer who had been wounded during one of the duke's previous expeditions and was said to be aggrieved at having been passed over for promotion. Such was Buckingham's unpopularity by the time of his death that Felton was lauded as a national hero. This was not enough to spare him the gallows, though, and he went to his own death three months later.

Buckingham was buried in a lavish tomb in Westminster Abbey, which bears a Latin inscription meaning 'The Enigma of the World'.